"Get re~~al~~ ... moun~~tain~~ ... ~~an~~d the ~~ni~~ght, the whole town will be talking when you come back down. The Traub bad boy and the kindergarten teacher. I can hear them all now."

She laughed. As if it was funny. "I'm sure they're already talking. We've practically been joined at the hip since the flood. And in case you've forgotten, we spent a whole night together in my dad's barn and the world didn't come to an end."

In case he'd forgotten? He would never forget. Especially not what had happened in the morning. "We had no choice then. It was the barn or drowning. This—you and me, up the mountain together? That's a clear choice."

"What is going on with you? Suddenly you're acting like it's 1955 or something. Like you're worried about my reputation, which is excellent and unimpeachable, thank you very much."

Unimpeachable? She really did talk like a schoolteacher sometimes.

Which got him hot. Real hot. But he wasn't going to think about that.

MAROONED WITH THE MAVERICK

BY
CHRISTINE RIMMER

First published in Great Britain 2013
by Mills & Boon, an imprint of Harlequin (UK) Limited,
Eton House, 18-24 Paradise Road, Richmond, Surrey TW9 1SR

© Harlequin Books S.A. 2013

Special thanks and acknowledgment to Christine Rimmer for her contribution to the Montana Mavericks: Rust Creek Cowboys continuity.

ISBN: 978 0 263 90125 2
ebook ISBN: 978 1 472 00503 8

23-0713

Harlequin (UK) policy is to use papers that are natural, renewable and recyclable products and made from wood grown in sustainable forests. The logging and manufacturing processes conform to the legal environmental regulations of the country of origin.

Printed and bound in Spain
by Blackprint CPI, Barcelona

Christine Rimmer came to her profession the long way around. Before settling down to write about the magic of romance, she'd been everything from an actress to a salesclerk to a waitress. Now that she's finally found work that suits her perfectly, she insists she never had a problem keeping a job—she was merely gaining "life experience" for her future as a novelist. Christine is grateful not only for the joy she finds in writing, but for what waits when the day's work is through: a man she loves who loves her right back, and the privilege of watching their children grow and change day to day. She lives with her family in Oregon. Visit Christine at www.christinerimmer.com.

For my dad.
I love you, Dad.
And miss you so much!

Chapter One

At 2:10 in the afternoon on the Fourth of July, Collin Traub glanced out the great room window of his house on Falls Mountain and could not believe what he saw in the town down below.

He stopped stock-still and swore under his breath. How could the situation have gotten so bad so fast? He probably should have been keeping an eye on it.

But he'd been busy, his mind on work. And it was later than usual when he stopped for lunch and came upstairs.

To *this*.

He could kick his own ass for not paying more attention. It had to be about the wettest day on record in Rust Creek Falls, Montana. The rain had been coming down in buckets since yesterday morning. And Rust Creek, which ran northeast to southwest through the center of town, had been steadily rising.

Collin had told himself it was no big deal. The creek

had good, high levees on either side, levees that had held without a break for more than a hundred years. He'd never doubted that they would hold for another hundred.

And yet somehow, impossibly, sections of the levee on the south bank were crumbling. Through the thick, steady veil of rain that streamed down the windows, he watched it happen.

The levee just…dissolved, sending foaming, silvery swaths of water pouring through more than one breach. It was a lot of water and it was flowing fast and furious onto the lower-elevation south side of town.

People were going to lose their homes. Or worse.

And the water wouldn't be stopping on the edge of town, either. South of town lay Rust Creek Falls Valley, a fertile, rolling landscape of small farms and ranches—and any number of smaller creeks and streams that would no doubt also be overflowing their banks.

The Triple T, his family's ranch, was down there in the path of all that water.

He grabbed the phone off the table.

Deader than a hammer.

He dug his cell from his pocket. No signal.

The useless cell still clutched in his hand, Collin grabbed his hat and his keys and headed out into the downpour.

It was a hell of a ride down the mountain.

One-third of the way down, the road skirted close to the falls for which the mountain was named. The roar was deafening, and the pounding silver width of the falling water was twice what he was used to seeing. He made it past without incident. But if the rain kept on like this, the road could easily be washed out. He'd have himself a real adventure getting back home.

But now was not the time to worry over coming back.

He needed to get down there and do what he could to help. He focused his mind on that, keeping his boot light on the brake, giving the steering wheel a workout, as he dodged his 4x4 F-150 around mudslides and uprooted trees, with the rain coming down so thick and fast he could hardly see through the windshield. Now and then, lightning lit up the gray sky and thunder boomed out, the sound echoing off in the distance, over the valley below.

Lightning could be damned dangerous on a mountain thick with tall trees. But with the rain coming down like the end of the world and everything drenched and dripping, a lightning strike causing a forest fire was probably the last thing he needed to get anxious over today.

Water. Rivers of it. That was the problem.

There were way too many spots where the streams and overflowing ditches had shed their contents across the narrow, twisty mountain road. He was lucky to make it through a few of those spots. But he did it.

Fifteen endless minutes after sliding in behind the wheel, he reached Sawmill Street on the north edge of town. He debated: go right to North Main and see what he could do in town, or go left over the Sawmill Street Bridge, skirt the east side of town and make tracks for the Triple T.

The rest of his family was three hundred miles away for the holiday, down in Thunder Canyon attending a wedding and a reunion. That made him the only Traub around.

His obligation to the family holdings won out. He swung left and crossed the Sawmill Street Bridge, which was still several feet above the raging water. With a little luck and the Almighty in a generous mood, that bridge might hold.

The Triple T was southeast of town, so he turned south at Falls Street until he caught sight of the miniature lake that had formed at Commercial and Falls. He saw a couple of swamped vehicles, but they were empty. He swung left again. Having been raised in the valley, he knew every rutted dirt road like he knew the face he saw when he looked in the mirror to shave. Collin used that knowledge now, taking the higher roads, the ones less likely to be flooded in the troughs and dips, working his way steadily toward the ranch.

About a mile from the long driveway that led to the barns and houses on the Triple T, he crested a rise and, through the heavy curtain of pouring rain, saw another vehicle on the road ahead of him: a red Subaru Forester moving at a dead crawl.

He knew that Subaru. And he knew who was behind the wheel: Willa Christensen, the kindergarten teacher.

In spite of everything, the pounding, relentless rain and the flooded road and the pretty-damned-imminent danger, Collin grinned. Since a certain evening a little more than four years before, Willa had been running away from him—and no, he hadn't been chasing her.

Yeah, he had something of a reputation. People called him a skirt chaser, a player, the Traub family bad boy. But come on. He had better things to do with his time than sniff around after a woman who wanted nothing to do with him. And since that night four years ago, Willa took off like a shot whenever she saw him coming. Collin found her frantic efforts to get away from him pretty comical, if the truth were known.

His grin faded. She shouldn't be out in this mess. The way she drove—so cautious, like some nervous old lady—she was way too likely to misjudge a flooded spot, to get all flustered and stomp the brake and end up trapped in the waters that swamped the low sections of the road.

He knew where she was headed. The turnoff to the Christensen Ranch wasn't far past the one to the Triple T.

But the way she was handling her vehicle, he didn't like her odds for getting there in one piece.

Collin readjusted his priorities, skipping the turn to the Triple T, staying on her tail.

The rain came down harder—if that was possible. He had the wipers on high, beating fast and hard across the windshield. *Thwack thwack thwack thwack.* Even on high, they could hardly keep up with the sheer volume of water falling out of the gunmetal-gray sky.

Lightning flashed, a jagged spear of it striking a twisted oak on a rise up ahead. The red Subaru in front of him lurched to a stop as the old oak crashed to the ground, smoke trailing up in a shower of sparks. Thunder boomed across the valley as the Subaru inched forward once again.

Every dip in the road held a churning miniflood. Each time Willa drove that little red station wagon down into a trough, Collin held his breath, sure she wouldn't make it through the swirling waters streaming across the road. But each time, she surprised him. She drove steadily forward at a safe, even crawl. And each time, the swirling water had to surrender her to higher ground. He went through in her wake, gritting his teeth, letting out a long breath of relief when he made it clear, too.

The sick ball of dread in his gut tightened to a knot when she suddenly hit the gas—no doubt because she'd finally realized that he was the guy in the pickup behind her. Instead of taking it slow and steady as she had been, watching the bad spots on the streaming, rutted road in front of her, suddenly she was all about getting the hell away from him.

"Damn it, Willa," he muttered under his breath, as if she might actually hear him. "Slow the hell down...." He leaned on the horn to get her to ease off the accelerator and watch the next dip. It looked pretty deep down there.

But the honking only seemed to freak her out all the more. She must have lead-footed it right to the floorboards. The Forester shot forward—and then took a nosedive into the water rushing across the low spot in the road.

It was bad. Deeper than he'd realized. As the vehicle leveled out, she was up to her side windows in churning brown floodwater.

And going nowhere. She'd swamped it.

Collin hit the brakes. The pickup came to a stop several feet above the flood. He shoved it into Park, turned off the engine, kicked down the parking brake and jumped out, hitting the rain-slick road at a run. Instantly drenched to the skin, with the rain beating down like it wanted to flatten him, he reached the churning water and waded in.

The Subaru was already drifting, picked up by the current and, half-floating, pushed toward the lower side of the road. The water was too high to see the danger there, but Collin knew that the bank at that spot dropped off into a ditch. A deep ditch. If the Subaru went over the edge, he'd have a hell of a time getting Willa out before she drowned.

She'd been raised in the valley, too. She knew what waited at the edge of the road. Inside the station wagon, she was working the door latch, trying to get it to open. She shouted something at him and beat on the window.

He kept slogging toward her, though the water seemed to grab at him, to drag him back. It was like those dreams you have where you have to get somewhere fast and suddenly your legs are made of lead. It seemed to be getting deeper, the pull of the swirling current more powerful, second by second.

Half stumbling, half swimming, while the Subaru slowly rotated away from him as it drifted ever closer to the shoulder and the ditch beyond, Collin bent at the knees and launched himself at the driver's door.

He made it. His fingers closed around the door handle. He used it to pull his feet under him again.

"You push, I'll pull!" he yelled good and loud.

She just kept pounding on the window, her brown eyes wide with fright.

He hollered even louder than before, "Push, Willa! Count of three."

She must have heard him, must have finally understood. Because she pressed her lips together and nodded, her dark, pulled-back hair coming loose, the soft curls bouncing around her fear-white cheeks. She put her shoulder into the door.

"One, two, three!" He pulled. She pushed. The door didn't budge.

"Again! One, two, three!"

The miracle happened. The Subaru rotated just enough that the current caught the door as he yanked the handle and she threw her shoulder against it. The damn thing came open with such force it knocked him over.

He went under. The door hit him in the side of the head. Not all that hard. But still.

Trying to be a hero? Not the most fun he'd ever had.

Somehow, he managed to get his waterlogged boots under him and pushed himself upright, breaking the surface in time to see his hat spinning away on the current and Willa flailing, still inside the Subaru as the water poured in on her through the now-open driver's door.

Wonderful.

He went for her, diving through the open door, grabbing for her and catching her arm. He heard her scream—or she tried to. The water cut off most of the high-pitched sound. It kept pouring in, beating at them as it filled the cab.

They had to get out and get out now.

He pulled on her arm until he'd turned her, faceup, and

then he caught her in a headlock. Okay, it wasn't delicate. It wasn't nice and it sure wasn't gentle. But with his arm around her neck, at least he could turn and throw himself out the door. She grabbed his arm in both her hands, but by then, she seemed to have caught on to what he was trying to do. She wasn't fighting him anymore. She was only holding on as tight as he was.

He squirmed around to face the open door. The water shoved him back, but at least the rotation of the vehicle kept the door from swinging shut and trapping them inside. He got his free hand on the door frame, knees bent, boots braced on the side of the seat. Another hard push and they were out just as the Subaru went over the bank into the ditch.

The weight of the vehicle going under sucked at them, but Willa slipped free of his hold and started swimming. Since she seemed to be making it on her own steam, he concentrated on doing the same.

Side by side, they swam for the place where the road rose up out of the ditch. His boots touched ground. Beside him, she found her footing, too—for an instant. Then she staggered and went under.

He grabbed her again, hauling her up, getting one arm around her waist. Lightning tore another hole in the sky and thunder boomed as he half carried, half dragged her up and out of the racing water.

She coughed and sputtered, but she kept her feet moving. The woman had grit. He had to give her that. He kept hold of her, half-supporting her, urging her to the high side of the road and up the hill far enough that they were well above the water and reasonably safe.

They collapsed side by side onto the streaming ground as the rain continued to beat down on them, hard and heavy, never ending. She turned over, got up on her hands and knees and started hacking and coughing, spitting up water. He dragged in one long, hungry breath after another and pounded her back for her, helping her clear her airways so she could breathe. When she was finally doing more breathing than hacking, he fell back on the ground and concentrated on catching his own breath.

Lucky for him, he just happened to turn his head and glance in the direction of his truck about then. The water *had* risen. Considerably. It was maybe two feet from his front wheels now.

He turned to the waterlogged woman gasping beside him. "Stay here. Do not move. I'll be right back."

Swearing low and with feeling, he lurched upright and beat feet on a parallel track with the road. When he got even with his truck, he half ran, half slid down the hill, raced around the rear of the pickup and hauled himself up into the cab. The key was still in the ignition—and the water was lapping around his front wheel wells by then.

He turned it over, released the brake, put it in Reverse and backed to the top of the last rise. Once there, he slammed it in Park again and jumped out to see how things looked behind him.

Not good. The road was flooded in the previous trough. Water in front of him, water behind. The truck was going nowhere until the water receded.

Fair enough. He got back in and parked on the shoulder. Taking his keys with him that time, he left the truck and locked it up.

Then he looked for Willa.

She was gone.

Chapter Two

A moment later, Collin spotted her.

She was on her feet and slogging up the long slope of the hill. He knew then where she was headed. There was a big, weathered, rambling structure way at the top—the Christensen barn.

"Willa, what the hell?" he yelled good and loud. "Hold on a minute!"

She didn't pause, she didn't turn. Her hair plastered to her head, and her little white T-shirt and snug jeans covered with mud and debris, she just kept on putting one boot in front of the other, heading up that hill.

He was powerfully tempted to let her go.

But who knew what trouble she'd get herself into next? If something happened to her, he'd end up with a guilty conscience for leaving her all by her lonesome. Plus, well, he didn't have a lot of options himself, at the moment. The floodwaters were all around.

And it might be July, but the rain was a cold rain and the

wind was up, too. He needed shelter to wait out the storm and the barn had walls and a roof. It was better than nothing. Willa was going to have to get over her aversion to him, at least until there was somewhere else he could go.

With a grunt of resignation, he climbed the hill after her, tucking his head down, putting one foot in front of the other, as the water streamed over him and his boots made sucking sounds with each step he took.

He caught up to her maybe twenty yards from the barn. She must have heard the sloshing of his boots at last.

She stopped, her arms wrapped around herself to control the shivers that racked her, and whirled to confront him. "Collin." She tipped her head up and drew her slim shoulders back. Water ran down her cheeks, into her wide mouth and over her chin.

He could see her nipples, hard as rocks, right through her T-shirt and her bra. "What, Willa?"

"Thank you for saving my life."

"Hey." He swiped water off his nose. Not that it did any good. "No problem. Can we move it along? It's pretty damn wet out here. I'd like to get in that barn."

She gripped her arms tighter around herself. "I would like for you to go away and leave me alone."

"Oh, you would, would you?"

"Yes. Please."

He raised his arms out wide, indicating all of it—the never-ending storm, the floodwaters surrounding them, the cold wind and the flash of bright lightning that lit up the sky again right at that moment. The thunder rumbled. He waited for the sound to die away. "Exactly where do you suggest I go, Willa?"

She flung out a hand. "What about your truck?"

He folded his arms across his chest and simply looked at her.

Her shoulders sagged and she let out a low cry. "Oh,

fine. All right. You can come in the barn. Just…fine. Okay." And she turned around again and continued walking.

He fell in behind her.

The barn loomed ahead. When they reached it, she undid the latch and slipped in. He went in after her, pulling the door to, latching it from within.

The barn had another door on the far wall. Someone must have left the latch undone, because that door stood wide-open. It was probably not a bad thing in this situation. The Christensen livestock needed more than a run-in shed on a day like today and the animals had found what they needed through that wide-open door.

The rambling space was wall-to-wall critters. There were cattle, goats, some chickens and several cooing pigeons. Carping blackbirds perched in the rafters. A couple of pigs snorted beneath one of the two windows and somewhere nearby a barn cat hissed and then yowled.

A dog barked. Collin spotted a muddy white Labrador retriever. The dog was headed for Willa.

She let out a happy little cry. "Buster! There you are!" She dropped to a crouch and opened her arms. The dog reared up and put his front paws on her shoulders. Whining with excitement, he licked her face with his sloppy pink tongue. "You are such a bad, bad dog," she crooned in a tone that communicated no criticism whatsoever. "Hey, now. Eww." She turned her head away from Buster's slobbery attentions and saw Collin watching her.

"Nice dog." He'd had a great dog named Libby who'd died the winter before. She'd been sixteen, with him since he was eleven and she was an ugly pup, the runt of the litter wanted by no one—but him.

"Down, Buster." She rose again and tried to brush the mud and water off her soaking wet shirt and muddy jeans.

It did zero good. "Technically, he's my dog," she explained, "but he's always loved it here on the ranch, so he lives here more than with me. He was supposed to be staying with me in town, though, while my parents and Gage are in Livingston for the big rodeo." Gage Christensen, her brother, was the town sheriff. "That dog just will not stay put. He keeps running off to get back here." A shiver went through her. She wrapped her arms around herself again.

"You're freezing," he said. It came out sounding like an accusation, though he didn't mean it that way.

"I am fine." She shivered some more. Her hair was plastered on her cheeks and down her neck. She swiped at a soggy hunk of it, shoving it back behind her ear. "Just fine." She scowled at him.

Whoa. For a minute there, she'd almost seemed friendly—but then she must have remembered that she hated his ass. She turned her back on him and started weaving her way through the crush of horses and cattle. The Lab followed her, panting happily, wagging his muddy tail.

It should have been warmer in there, with all the steaming, milling livestock. But it really wasn't. How could it be, with that far door wide-open and both of them soaking wet? He slapped the bony butt of a little red heifer who'd backed in too close. She let out a cranky "moo," and ambled away—not far, though. There wasn't really anywhere to go.

He found a hay bale against the wall and sat on it as he pondered what he ought to do to make things a little more comfortable. He hesitated to go over and shut the other door. The smell of wet livestock and manure would get pretty strong if he did that.

As he considered what to do next, he watched the dripping brown-haired woman who had spent the past four years avoiding him and now happened to be stuck with him until the rain ended and the floodwaters receded.

Willa was keeping busy shivering and ignoring him, wandering from steer to goat to barn cat to bay mare, petting them all and talking to them low and soft, as though she had a personal relationship with each and every four-legged creature on her family's place. And maybe she did.

She'd always been a fanciful type, even way back when they were kids. He knew this from actual observation.

Collin had run wild as a kid. He was the youngest, sixth of six boys, and his mom was worn-out by the time he came along. She didn't have the energy to keep after him. He went where he wanted and came home when he felt like it. He wandered far and wide. Often, he found himself on Christensen land. Now and then, he'd run into Willa. She would be singing little songs to herself, or making crowns out of wildflowers, or reading fairy-tale books.

She'd never seemed to like him much, even then. Once she'd yelled at him to stop spying on her.

He hadn't been spying. A kid wasn't spying just because he stretched out in the tall grass and watched a neighbor girl talking to herself as she walked her big-haired brunette Barbie doll around in a circle.

Collin tried to get more comfortable on the hay bale. He scooted to the wall, leaned his head back against the rough boards, closed his eyes and tried not to think how cold he was, tried not to wish he'd grabbed a snack to take with him when he'd run out of the house. His stomach grumbled. He ignored it.

It would have been nice if he could drop off to sleep for a little and forget everything. But no such luck. He would just start to doze when a fit of shivering would snap him awake and he would realize anew that they were smack-dab in the middle of one hell of a disaster. He hoped that no one in town had drowned, that the hands and the animals on the Triple T were safe. He couldn't help wondering how much of both the town or his family's ranch would be left standing when the floodwaters receded.

And how much of the state was affected? What about Thunder Canyon, where his family had gone? Were they underwater, too?

Eventually, he gave up trying to sleep and opened his eyes. Willa stood at the window that faced southwest, the one not far from where two spotted pigs were snorting over an upturned bucket of feed. With the white Lab at her feet, she stared out through the endless curtain of the rain. He rubbed his arms to try and warm up a little and knew she must be staring at her parents' place. The Christensen house was about level with the barn, on high ground, atop the next hill over.

He knew he was asking for more rejection to try and talk to her, but he was just tired and dejected enough to do it anyway. "The house should be safe," he said. He didn't mention her brother Gage's house, which was down the slope of the hill behind her parents' place. It wouldn't be visible from Willa's vantage point, which was just as well. As Collin remembered, it was a ways down the hill and probably already below the rising waterline.

She surprised him by replying. "Yes. I can see it. It's okay, for now...." She sounded strange, he thought. Kind of dreamy and far away. She had a few scratches on her arms. And a bruise on her cheekbone. But like him, no serious injuries. They'd been very fortunate. So far. She added, "It's all so unbelievable, don't you think? Like maybe this isn't even actually happening. Maybe I'm just dreaming it."

"Sorry, Willa." He meant that. He *was* sorry. "I think it's really happening."

She sent him a glance. For once, her mouth didn't pinch

up at the sight of him. "I lost my phone." A shiver went through her and her teeth chattered together. "Do you happen to have yours with you?"

"It's in my truck, I think. But there must be towers down. I was getting no signal when I tried using it at a little after two."

Willa sighed and turned back to the window. "Life is so…fragile, really, isn't it? I mean, you go along, doing what you need to do, thinking you're taking care of business, that you're in control. But you're not in control, not really." Outside, lightning flared. Thunder rolled out. "Anything could happen," she said. "It could rain and rain and never stop…." Her lips looked kind of blue, he thought.

He really needed to come up with a way to warm her up a little. Rising, he began to work his way around the barn, looking for a blanket or a tarp or something.

Willa kept talking. "Oh, Collin. I keep thinking of the children in my class last year. And the ones in our summer school program. I can just close my eyes and see each one of their sweet, smiling faces. I hope they're all safe and dry. Our school, the elementary school? It's on the south side of town. That's not good news. And my house is on the south side, too…."

He pushed a goat out of the way as he came to a spot where the wall jogged at a ninety-degree angle. Around that corner was a door. He opened it. "Willa, there's a tack room here."

She sighed again. "Yes. That's right. And a feed room over there." She put out a hand in the general direction of the other shut door farther down the wall. And then she started in again, about life and the flood and the safety of her friends, her neighbors and her students.

Collin took a look around the tack room. There were the usual rows of hooks holding ropes and bridles and bits. He was a saddle maker by trade and he grinned at the sight of one of his own saddles racked nice and neat, lined up with several others on the wall. There was a window. And another door, allowing outside access.

The floor in there was wood, not mixed clay and sand as it was out in the main part of the barn. And the walls were paneled in pine.

And then he saw the stack of saddle blankets atop a big cedar storage trunk. He went over and grabbed one. Shooing out the goat that had followed him in there, he shut the door and made his way through the milling animals to Willa.

She didn't even flinch when he wrapped the blanket around her. "Thank you."

He took her by the shoulders. "Come on. Let's go...." She went where he guided her, back through the cattle and horses and goats, with the dog right behind them. He let the dog in the tack room with them, and then shut the door to keep the rest of the animals out. There were a few hay bales. He sat her down on one and knelt in front of her.

She frowned down at him. "What are you doing?"

He held her gaze. "Don't get freaky on me, okay?"

She looked at him in that pinched, suspicious way again. "Why not?"

"You need to get out of those wet clothes. There are plenty of blankets. You can wrap yourself up in them and get dry."

"But...my clothes won't dry."

"It doesn't matter. Right now, *you* need to get dry."

She considered that idea—and shook her head. "I'll take off my boots and socks. I'll be all right."

He decided not to argue with her. "Fine. You need help?"

"No, thank you." All prim and proper and so polite. "I'll manage."

"Are you thirsty?"

She gaped at him. "Thirsty?" And then she let out a wild little laugh. "In this?" She stuck out a hand toward the water streaming down the lone window.

"Are you?"

And she frowned again. "Well, yes. Now that you mention it, I suppose I am."

He rose. "I'll see if I can find some clean containers in the barn. We can catch some of the rainwater, so we won't get dehydrated."

She blinked up at him. "Yes. That makes sense. I'll help." She started to rise.

He took her shoulders again and gently pushed her back down. "Get out of your boots and shoes—and wrap this around your feet." He held out another blanket.

She took it, her gaze colliding with his. Holding. "What about you?"

"Let me see about setting out containers for water. Then I'll grab a few blankets and try and warm up a little, too."

Half an hour later, he had his boots and socks off. They'd pushed four hay bales together and spread a blanket over them. Side by side, wrapped in more blankets, they passed a bucket of water back and forth.

When they'd both drunk their fill, there was still plenty left in the bucket. He set it on the floor, where Buster promptly stuck his nose in it and started lapping. "You don't happen to have a nice T-bone handy, do you, Willa?"

She chuckled. There wasn't a lot of humor in the sound, but he took heart that at least she wasn't staring blindly into space anymore. "Plenty on the hoof right outside that door." She pointed her thumb over her shoulder at the door that led into the barn.

He scooted back to the wall for something to lean against. "Not that hungry yet."

"I didn't think so." She scooted back, too, settling alongside him, and then spent a moment readjusting the blanket she'd wrapped around her feet. "There." She leaned back and let out a long breath. "I believe I am actually beginning to thaw out."

"That was the plan." Outside, the rain kept falling. The sky remained that same dim gray it had been all day. "Got any idea what time it is?"

"I don't know. Six, maybe? Seven?" She sounded... softer. A little sleepy. That was good. Rest wouldn't hurt either of them. "Won't be dark for hours yet...."

He was feeling kind of drowsy, too, now that he wasn't chilled to the bone anymore and most of the adrenaline rush from the various near-death events of the day had faded a little. He let his eyelids droop shut.

But then she spoke again. "It's really very strange, Collin, being here with you like this."

He grunted. "This whole day has been pretty strange."

"Yes, it has. And scary. And awful. But, well, that's not what I meant."

He knew exactly what she meant. And why was it women always had to dig up stuff that was better left alone? He kept nice and quiet and hoped she wasn't going there.

But she was. "Maybe this is a good chance to clear the air a little between us."

"The air is plenty clear from where I'm sitting."

"Well, Collin, for me, it's just not."

"Willa, I—"

"No. Wait. I would like a chance to say what's on my mind."

He didn't let out a groan of protest, but he wanted to.

And she kept right on. "It was very…humiliating for me, that night at the Ace in the Hole." The Ace was on Sawmill Street. It was the only bar in town. People went there to forget their troubles and usually only ended up creating a whole new set of them. "It was my first time there, did you know? My twenty-first birthday." She sounded all sad and wistful.

He'd known. "I think you mentioned that at the time, yeah."

"Derek had just dumped me for a Delta Gamma." Straight-arrow Derek Andrews was her high school sweetheart. They'd graduated the same year and headed off to the University of Idaho together. "Collin, did you *hear* me?"

"Every word," he muttered.

"Did you *know* it was over between me and Derek?"

"Well, Willa, I kinda had a feeling something might have gone wrong with your love life, yeah."

"You led me on," she accused. "You know that you did." He'd seen her coming a mile away. Good-girl Willa Christensen, out to find a bad boy just for the night. "And then you…" Her voice got all wobbly. "You turned me down flat."

"Come on, Willa. It wasn't a good idea. You know that as well as I do."

"Then why did you dance with me all those times? Why did you flirt with me and buy me two beers? You acted like you were interested. More than interested. And then, when I tried to kiss you, you laughed at me. You said I wasn't your type. You said I should go home and behave myself."

He'd had some crazy idea at the time that he was doing her a favor, keeping her from doing something she wouldn't be happy about later. But with Willa, no good deed of his ever went unpunished. And was she going to start crying? He hated it when a woman started crying.

She sniffled in her blankets, a small, lost little sound. "I still can't believe I did that—made a pass at *you*. I mean, you never liked me and I never cared much for you and we both know that." That wasn't true—not on his part anyway. Far from it. But he wasn't in the mood to dispute the point at the moment. He only wanted her not to start crying—and he thought maybe he was getting his wish when she squirmed in her blankets and grumbled, "Everyone knows how you are. You'll sleep with anyone—except *me,* apparently."

Mad. Now she was getting mad. As far as he was concerned, mad was good. Mad was great. Anything but weepy worked for him.

She huffed, "I just don't know what got into me that night."

He couldn't resist. "Well, Willa, we both know it wasn't me."

She made another huffing sound. "Oh, you think you're so funny. And you're not. You're very annoying and you always have been."

"Always?" he taunted.

"Always," she humphed.

He scoffed at her. "How would you know a thing about me the last four years? Since that night at the Ace, all I see is the backside of you. I come in a room—and you turn tail and run."

"And why shouldn't I? You are a complete tool and you never cared about anything or anyone in your whole life but yourself."

"Which is girl talk for 'You didn't sleep with me,'" he said in his slowest, laziest, most insolent tone.

"You are not the least bit clever, you know that?"

"You don't think so, huh?"

"No, I do not. And it just so happens that I'm *glad* we never hooked up that night. You're the last person in the world I should ever be sleeping with."

He tried not to grin. "No argument there. Because I'm not having sex with you no matter how hard you beg me."

"Oh, please. I mean just, simply, *please.*" She sat up straight then. Dragging her blankets along with her, she scooted to the edge of the hay bales, as far from him as she could get without swinging her bare feet to the floor. Once there, she snapped, "You do not have worry. I want nothing to do with you."

He freed a hand from his blankets and made a show of wiping his brow—even though she wasn't looking at him. "Whew."

"In case you didn't know, it just so happens that I have a fiancé, thank you very much."

"A fiancé?" That *was* news to Collin. The information bothered him. A lot—and that it bothered him bugged him to no end.

"Yes," she said. "Well. Sort of."

"Willa, get real. You do or you don't."

"His name is Dane Everhart and he's an assistant coach at the University of Colorado. We met at UI. We've been dating on and off for three years. Dane loves me and knows I'm the one for him and wants only to marry me and, er, give me the world."

"Hold on just a minute. Answer the question. You're saying you're engaged?"

She fiddled with her blankets and refused to turn around and look at him. "Well, no. Not exactly. But I *could* be. I promised to give Dane an answer by the end of the summer."

He stared at the back of her head. Her hair was a tangle

of wild, muddy curls from her dip in the floodwaters. It should have looked like crap. But it didn't. It looked like she'd been having crazy good sex with someone—and then fallen asleep all loose and soft and satisfied.

And why the hell was he thinking about sex right now? Was he losing his mind? Probably. A few hours trapped in a barn with Willa Christensen could do that to a man, could drive him clean out of his head.

He sat up, too, then, and sneered, "You're in love with this guy, and you're not going to see him until *September?*"

"So? What's wrong with that?"

"Well, I mean, if you're in *love* with him, how can you *stand* to be apart from him? How can *he* stand to be away from you?"

"You wouldn't understand."

"Are you in love with him, Willa?"

She squared her slim shoulders. "I just *told* you that you wouldn't understand."

"That's right. I wouldn't. If I loved a woman, I'd want her with me. Where I could touch her and be with her and hold her all night long."

Willa gasped. She tried to hide the small, sharp sound, but he heard it. "Oh, please. As if you know anything about being in love, Collin Traub."

"I said if I *was* in love."

"Well. Humph. As it happens, Dane has gone to Australia until the end of the month. He gets only a short summer break before practice begins again. And do you know how he's spending his limited free time? I will tell you how he's spending it. At a special sports camp. He's helping Australian children learn about American football. Because he's a good man, a man who *cares* about other people. That's how he is. That's *who* he is…"

There was more. Lots more.

Collin let her heated words wash over him. The point, as far as he saw it, was that she hadn't answered the main question. She hadn't come out and said, "Yes. I'm in love with Dane Everhart."

He felt absurdly satisfied with what she *hadn't* said. She could rant all night about the wonderfulness of this Dane character while talking trash about *him*. At least she was acting like the Willa he'd always known. At least she was full of fire and vinegar and not shaking with cold, shock and fear anymore.

Collin smiled to himself, settled back against the wall and closed his eyes.

Chapter Three

Willa felt Collin's presence behind her acutely.

But she didn't turn to him. She sat on the edge of the pushed-together hay bales and stared resolutely out the tack room's one window as waves of never-ending rain flowed down the glass.

She finished what she had to say about Dane. "It just so happens that Dane would have liked to have taken me with him. But he was going to be very busy with the Australian children and I had things I could bc doing hcrc at home. We have summer school at Rust Creek Falls Elementary, in case you didn't know and I…" Her voice trailed off.

Collin hadn't said a word for a couple of minutes, maybe more. Had he fallen *asleep,* for heaven's sake?

She wouldn't put it past him. He was such an exasperating, impossible man. Always had been. And no doubt always would be.

So why am I starting to feel ashamed of myself?

Willa's cheeks were flaming. She tucked her chin down into the scratchy saddle blanket he'd wrapped around her. At least he couldn't see her embarrassment at her own behavior—not as long as she didn't turn and face him.

Which she was not going to do right now, thank you very much.

Stretched out on the floor by the hay bales, Buster huffed out a long sigh. Willa bent down and scratched him on the head. His tail bounced happily against the rough plank floor.

She gathered her blankets close again. All right, she probably shouldn't have gone off on Collin like that. No matter how humiliating her history with the guy, he'd been there when she desperately needed him. He'd saved her life a few hours ago, at no small risk to himself.

Plus, well, she hadn't really been honest while she was getting all up in his face just now, had she? She hadn't bothered to mention that she had serious reservations about her and Dane. Dane was the greatest guy in the world and he did want to marry her, very much. But Rust Creek Falls was her home and he wasn't about to give up his wonderful career at CU. And more important than geography, Dane somehow didn't quite *feel* like her guy.

Whatever her guy *should* feel like. She wasn't sure. She just had a certain intuition that Dane wasn't it.

And worse than her doubts about her future with an ideal man like Dane, well, there was that longtime *thing* she'd had for Collin—oh, not anymore. Of course not. That night at the Ace in the Hole had put an end to her ridiculous schoolgirl crush on the town bad boy. But before that night she used to fantasize about him now and then.

Or maybe even more often than now and then.

She used to wonder what it would be like if bad-boy Collin were to kiss her. Or do more than kiss her...

Not that it mattered now. None of her past silliness over Collin mattered to anyone. It had been a fantasy, that was all. *Her* fantasy. He'd never been the least interested in her. He'd made that painfully clear on the night he led her on and then laughed in her face.

And really, after all that had happened today, her four-year grudge against him for not having sex with her was beginning to seem nothing short of petty. She really needed to let the past go. She needed to be...a bigger person than she'd been so far about this. She needed to be a *better* person.

And she needed to start doing that now.

Willa cleared her throat. "Um. Collin?"

He shifted a little, back there against the wall. "What now, Willa?" His voice was scratchy and deep. Lazy. What was it about him? He just always made her think of wrinkled sheets and forbidden passion.

In a purely impersonal, objective way, of course.

"I, um, well..."

"Come on. Spit it out."

She made herself say it. "I'm sorry, okay?" She hauled her blanket-wrapped legs back up on the hay bales and wiggled around until she was facing him again. He lay sprawled under his blankets, his head propped against the wall, his eyes shut, his eyelashes black as coal, thicker than any girl's, his full mouth lax and lazy, just like his voice had been, the shadow of a beard on his cheeks. A curl of that impossibly thick black hair of his hung over his forehead. She clutched her blankets tighter to keep from reaching out and smoothing it back. "I shouldn't have jumped all over you like that. I shouldn't have called you a tool. That was...small-minded and mean-spirited of me, especially after all you've done for me today."

He didn't say anything for a minute. And he didn't open

his eyes. Again, she wondered if he'd dropped off to sleep and she had to resist the urge to reach out and shake him. But then those bad-boy lips curved upward in a slow smile. "So you don't think I'm a tool, then?"

"Um. No. No, of course not. I shouldn't have said that. I'm sorry. I am."

"And you think maybe you could stop racing off like your hair's on fire every time you see me coming?"

A fresh wave of embarrassment had her cheeks flaming all over again. But what did it matter? He couldn't see her blush. His eyes were shut. Also, she truly wanted to make amends. "Ahem. Yes. Fair enough. I will do that. I will stop avoiding you."

"Well, all right then. I accept your apology." He patted the empty space beside him. "Stretch out. Try and get some sleep. I'm thinking we're going to be busy when the rain stops and the water goes down."

His words brought reality crashing back down on her. She hung her head. "Oh, Collin. It seems like it's never going to stop. I know my brother's house is already underwater. And what if it just keeps rising, what if we—?"

"Shh." He reached out and clasped her arm through the thick wool of the blanket. His grip was strong. Sure. It made her so very glad that he was here with her, that she wasn't huddled in the family barn all alone, waiting out the endless storm. "Don't go there." His voice was calm and firm. "There's no point."

She lifted her head. His eyes were open now, steady on hers. Shamelessly, she pleaded, "Tell me that we're going to be okay, that Rust Creek Falls will be okay, that we'll make it through this, come back better and stronger than ever."

He didn't even hesitate. He told her what she needed to hear. "We will. Just watch. Now come here. Come on…" He lifted the blanket that covered him.

She didn't think twice. She went down into the shelter of his offered arm, resting her head on his shoulder. He was so warm and big and solid. He smelled of mud and man, which at that moment she found wonderfully reassuring. He fiddled with the blankets, smoothing them over both of them.

Willa smiled to herself. All those crazy teenage dreams she'd had about him. And here she was, damp and dirty, bruised and scratched up, lying practically on top of him, grateful beyond measure to share a pile of saddle blankets with him. The world seemed to have gone crazy in the space of a day. But right now, in Collin's arms, she felt safe.

Protected.

She closed her eyes. "I didn't realize until now how tired I am.…"

He touched her hair, gently. Lightly. "Rest, then."

She started to answer him, but then she found she didn't have the energy to make a sound. Sleep closed over her. She surrendered to it with a grateful sigh.

When she woke, the light was different.

Sun. It was sun slanting in the window—and the window faced east. That meant it had to be morning, didn't it? Also…

She was lying on a man. Collin. He had both arms wrapped around her and his cheek against her dirty, snarled hair. Her head was on his shoulder, one arm tucked in against her side.

Her other arm rested on Collin, which was perfectly acceptable, given the circumstances. But the hand that was attached to that arm? That hand was exactly where it shouldn't be.

And where it shouldn't be was hard.

Blinking, not quite putting it all together as reality

yet, Willa lifted her head from his shoulder and blearily squinted at the morning light. Outside, faintly, she could hear birds singing.

Without moving her hand away from his very definite, very thick and large hardness, she looked down at him. Because, seriously. Could this actually be happening?

It was.

And he was awake. He gazed up at her with the strangest, laziest, *sexiest* expression. "Mornin'."

She puffed out her cheeks as she blew out a slow breath. And then, with great care, she removed her hand from his private parts and whispered, "The sun's out."

He nodded. "The rain's stopped. It stopped hours ago." He was playing along with her, pretending the contact between her hand and his fly had not occurred. Which was great. Perfect. Wonderful of him.

She backed off him onto her knees, dragging the blankets with her, and shoved her hair out of her eyes. "You, uh, should have woken me."

"Uh-uh." He reached out and clasped her shoulder, a companionable, reassuring sort of gesture that made tears clog her throat. She swallowed them down. And he said, "You needed your sleep and so did I. I woke up in the middle of the night and it was quiet. I knew the rain had finally stopped. I thought about getting up, but then I just closed my eyes and went back to sleep."

Buster was up, making whining noises, scratching at the door that led outside. "I should let him out...." He took his hand from her shoulder. She wished he hadn't, that he would touch her again, hold on tight and never, ever let go. But he didn't. And she pushed the blankets aside, swung her legs over the edge of the hay bales and stood up. Barefoot, she went and pulled the door open. Buster went out and she scolded, "Don't run off, now." And then she lingered in the open doorway, staring up at the sky. Blue as a newborn baby's eyes. She glanced back over her shoulder at Collin.

He was sitting up, bare feet on the floor. He had a case of bed head every bit as bad as hers, and he was kind of hunched over, his elbows on his knees. "Come on," he said gruffly. "Put your boots on," He raked his fingers back through all that thick, every-which-way hair. "We'll see if the water's gone down enough that we can get across the ravine to your folks' house."

They put on their damp socks and boots and pulled open the door that led into the main part of the barn.

"Needs a good mucking out in here," Collin said. Did it ever. Most of the animals had wandered off, out into the morning sunshine, leaving a whole lot of fresh manure behind. "You supposed to be taking care of the place all by your lonesome while your folks and your brother are off at the rodeo?"

She shook her head and named off the neighbors who'd agreed to look after things and feed the stock until the family returned. "But I'm guessing they probably all have their own problems about now." At least it was summer and grazing was good. The animals wouldn't starve if left to their own devices for a few days.

Instead of slogging through the mess on the barn floor to one of the outer doors, they ducked back into the tack room and went out through the exterior door there. Buster was waiting for them, sitting right outside the door, acting as though he'd actually listened when she told him not to wander off.

Willa scratched his head and called him a good dog and tried to tell herself that the jittery feeling in her stomach was because she hadn't eaten since lunch the day before—

not rising dread at the prospect of how bad the damage was behind the barn on the next rise over, and along the roads that crisscrossed the valley. And in town...

"It's a beautiful day," she said, tipping her head up again to the clear sky. "You'd almost think yesterday never even happened."

"Hey."

She lowered her gaze to him. Even with his hair sticking up on one side and a smudge of dirt at his temple, he still looked like every well-behaved girl's naughty, forbidden fantasy. "Hmm?"

His dark eyes searched hers. "You okay?"

And she nodded and forced her mouth to form a smile.

On the other side of the barn, the two pigs from the night before were rooting around near the water trough. A rooster stood on a section of busted-down fence and crowed as Willa stared across the ravine at her parents' house.

The house was untouched by the flood, though the water had gotten halfway up the front walk that was lined with her mother's prized roses. Her dad's minitractor lay on its side at the base of that walk. And a couple of steers had somehow gotten through the fence and were snacking on the vegetable garden in the side yard.

Below, in the ravine, the water had receded, leaving debris strewn down the sides of the hill and up the one on which the house sat. There were tree trunks and lawn chairs down there, boulders and a bicycle, a shade umbrella and any number of other items that looked bizarre, scary and all wrong, soggy and busted up, trailing across the pasture. Willa turned her eyes away, toward the road.

And saw her red Subaru. It had drifted past the ditch and lay on its side in the pasture there. It was covered in mud.

"Guess I'll be needing a new car." She tried to sound philosophical about it, but knew that she didn't exactly succeed.

"Come on," he said. "Let's go check out the house. Watch where you put your feet in that ravine."

Buster and the two pigs followed them down there. They picked their way with care through all the soggy junk and knotted tree roots. It was going to be quite a job, cleaning up. And she knew that all the other ranches in the valley had to be in a similar state, if not worse. Her family still had a barn and the house, at least. And as far as she could see, there were no animals or—God forbid—people lying broken amid the wreckage down there.

When they reached the house, they skirted the downed tractor and went up the front steps. She'd lost her keys. They were probably still stuck in the ignition of her poor Subaru. But her mom had left a house key where she always did, in the mouth of the ceramic frog by the porch swing.

They went inside. The power and phone were both out, but still, it all looked just as it had the last time she'd been there, the white refrigerator covered with those silly smiling-flower magnets her mother liked, some of them holding reminders to pick up this or that at the store. There were also pictures of her and her brother and a few recipes her mom was meaning to try. In the living room, the remote sat on the magazine table by her dad's recliner and her mother's knitting bag waited in its usual place at the end of the fat blue sofa.

Her childhood home. Intact. It seemed a miracle to her right then. And she wanted to cry all over again—with a desperate, hot sort of joy.

Collin turned on the water in the kitchen. It ran clear,

but they both knew that the flood could have caused con-tamination of any wells in its path.

She said, "We have wells for the stock. But for this house and Gage's place, we have a water tank that taps an underground spring higher up on this hill. The floodwa-ters wouldn't have reached that far. So the water here, in the house, is safe."

"That's good. A lot of valley wells are going to need disinfecting. Any source of clean water is great news."

She nodded. "And in town, they get water from above the falls. So they should be all right, too, shouldn't they, at least on the north side of the creek?" He shrugged. She knew what he was thinking. Who could say what they would find in town? And what about his family's place? "I know you probably want to head over to the Triple T…."

"Yeah. But let's check out your brother's house first, and then see about getting something to eat."

Gage's house. She realized she didn't want to go there.

But she did it anyway. And she was glad, again, for Col-lin's presence at her side. The house was locked up. They looked in the windows. It was bad. The waterline went three feet up the walls, but the moisture had wicked higher still in ugly, muddy little spikes. Gage's furniture was be-yond saving, soggy and stained, the stuffing popping out.

"Can we get to the propane tank?" Collin asked. "Bet-ter to be safe than sorry when it comes to a possible gas leak." She showed him the way. They were able to turn it off from outside. Then he said, "Come on. There's noth-ing more we can do here right now."

They went back to her parents' house and found plenty to eat in the pantry. She filled Buster's food bowl and the hungry dog quickly emptied it. After the meal, she took the perishables out of the fridge and put them in a bucket in the front yard. The two pigs went right to work on the treat.

By then it was still early, a little after seven. Collin suggested they make use of the safe water source and take showers before they left. There was just no way to guess the next time they'd have a chance to clean up a little. As at Gage's place, the tank was heated by propane, so they even had hot water.

Willa chose from some of her own old clothes that her mom had stored for her in a box under the stairs. She got clean jeans, a fresh T-shirt and a pair of worn but sturdy lace-up work boots to wear. For Collin, she found an ancient purple Jimi Hendrix Experience shirt that belonged to her dad, a pair of her dad's boots that were a pretty decent fit, and some trusty bib overalls. She also gave him a towel, a toothbrush, shave cream and a disposable razor. He took the guest bathroom. She used the master bath, and she made it quick.

Still, as she stood before the steamy bathroom mirror wrapped in one of her mother's fluffy towels, combing the tangles out of her wet hair, she couldn't help but think that Collin was just down the hall in the other bathroom, possibly naked.

Or if he wasn't by now, he *had* been a few minutes ago.

She caught her lower lip between her teeth and glared at her own reflection. "Get your mind off Collin naked," she told her steamy image in an angry whisper. "Seriously. You should get help, Willa Christensen."

And that struck her as funny, for some reason. The idea that she needed counseling over Collin Traub. She laughed. And then she pulled herself together and pinned her still-wet hair into a knot at the back of her head.

A few minutes later, they were out in the kitchen again, deciding what to take with them when they left.

She didn't tell him so, but he looked sexy even in overalls. He'd used the razor she'd given him and his dark stubble was gone, his hair still wet, but minus the dried mud from the flood.

Before they left, they filled a couple of gallon-size plastic containers with water. She stuffed a backpack with a few personal items. Her mom had a key to Willa's house in town and she took that, since hers was lost somewhere in her mud-filled car. She also grabbed a leash and a plastic container of food for Buster. She would have grabbed her dad's first aid kit, but Collin said he had one in his pickup.

"You want to wade out to your car?" Collin asked her. "See if maybe we can find your purse or your keys?"

It was way out there in the middle of that muddy field. And it didn't look promising to her. "We just got dry boots," she reminded him. "Let it go."

Collin didn't argue. She figured he was probably anxious to get to the Triple T.

They locked up the house again and headed for his truck, which waited at the top of the road where he'd left it. Buster hopped in the back and they climbed in the cab.

His cell was stuck in one of the cup holders. He tried it. "Still no signal."

Willa hooked her seat belt. He started the engine, pulled a U-turn and off they went.

It took them over an hour to get to the Triple T. The roads were washed out in several places and they had to find a way around the trouble spots. There was soggy, broken stuff strewn randomly wherever the water had risen, not to mention swamped, abandoned vehicles. Willa tried to take heart that they were all only *things*.

Collin played the truck's radio for news. Roads and bridges were out everywhere. Any number of small towns on the western side of the state from Butte north had sustained serious damage. A third of the state had been designated a disaster area and there were constant warnings—about staying off the roads as much as possible, about exercising caution in flooded buildings, about the danger of snakes and the hazards of rats. About steering clear of downed power lines.

At the Triple T, all the buildings were above the water-line and undamaged, but there would still be one heck of a cleanup to deal with. The hands who'd been taking care of the place were there and safe. Willa told them how to get into her parents' house to get fresh water for the next day or so, until they could disinfect the wells. They said they would check the stock for her as soon as they'd dealt with the animals on the Triple T.

Once Collin seemed satisfied that the hands had things under control, he said, "We should get going, go on into town."

She caught his arm before they got in the cab.

He stopped and turned to look at her. "Yeah?" His skin was so warm under her hand. Smooth flesh, hard muscles beneath. She felt suddenly shy with him and jerked her hand away. He frowned. "What's the matter?"

"I, well, I was just thinking that I'll bet you really want to go back up the mountain to check on things at your place. You could just drop me off when we get to Falls Street and I can hitch a ride in."

He stuck his fists into the front pockets of her dad's overalls and tipped his head to the side. "What the hell, Willa? I'm not leaving you alone on the street."

His words warmed her. But still. She really did need to stop taking advantage of his kindness to her.

Kindness.

Incredible. She'd been so busy judging him as a heart-less, undisciplined sex maniac for all these years, she'd never had a clue what a softy he really was. She shook her head. "Oh, come on now. It's Rust Creek Falls. We both know I'll be perfectly safe."

"We don't know what's going on since last night. And I don't want you wandering around alone."

"Collin, I would hardly *wander*. And I know everyone in town, so I won't by any stretch of the imagination be alone."

"I'm coming with you. I want to be with you when you check on your house." He said the words in a cautious tone. They both knew where her house was: directly in the path of the water. She was already resigned to the fact that it had to be flooded and was hoping that at least some of her clothing and furniture might be salvageable.

"Honestly, I can handle it. I was pretty shell-shocked yesterday, I know. But I'm over that. I'm ready to face whatever comes. You don't have to worry about me."

He was scowling now. "Why are you trying to get rid of me?"

She fell back a step. "But I'm not. I just thought…"

He caught her arm with his calloused hand. It felt so good, his touch. And his grip was so strong. "What?" he demanded. "You thought what?"

She looked up at him, at his smoldering dark eyes and those lips that seemed like they were made for kissing a woman and she wondered what he would do if *she* kissed *him*. The idea made her feel both embarrassed and giddy. She almost giggled.

"Willa," he demanded. "What is going on with you all of a sudden?"

Now she was thinking about earlier that morning. About waking up with her hand where it shouldn't have been— about how he'd been turned on.

Get real, Willa. Just because he became aroused didn't

mean he was dying to have sex with her in particular. It was simple biology, and she needed to remember that.

And if he wanted to keep on being kind to her, well, maybe she'd just let him. Maybe she'd just go right on taking advantage of Collin Traub and enjoying every minute of it. "Nothing is 'going on' with me. I just wanted to make sure I wasn't taking advantage of you."

"You're not."

"So...you don't mind going into town, then?"

"It's not about minding. It's what I planned to do. People will need help. They'll need every able-bodied man."

"And woman," she reminded him.

"Right." He had the good sense to agree.

She pressed her lips together to keep from grinning up at him like some addled fool and said, "Well, fair enough, then. I was just, um, checking."

He seemed to realize suddenly that he was gripping her arm—and let go. "Checking." Now he looked suspicious.

She put on her most innocent expression. "Uh-huh. Nothing wrong with checking, making sure you're okay with what's going on."

"If I'm not okay, you'll know it."

"Well, then, I'll stop checking."

"Good. Can we go now?"

She had that silly urge to grin again. Must be the stress of all she'd been through since yesterday. Yeah. Right. That must be it.

The trip into Rust Creek Falls was as booby-trapped with obstacles as the ride to the Triple T had been.

There was the smell of smoke in the air. It wasn't just from wood fires in stoves and fireplaces. They heard the sirens, saw the roiling smoke in the distance. On the south side of town, some homes had caught fire. Willa prayed her house wasn't one of them—and then she put her house out of her mind and prayed that no lives were endangered by the fires.

Other travelers were on the road by then, most of whom they recognized. Everyone seemed to have somewhere important to go. People waved and honked, but nobody pulled over to talk about what they'd been through or exchange information about the disaster. Collin had the radio on. All the way there, they listened to advice on how to deal with the aftermath of the Great Independence Day Flood.

When they finally got to Falls Street on the southeastern edge of town, they had to circle around and take other roads farther east and then work their way back in. It was nothing but mud, pools of water, swamped, abandoned vehicles and way too much debris south of the creek. The buildings they saw before they turned east were still standing, but bore the telltale signs of water damage within.

Eventually, they reached Sawmill Street and turned west again. The water level was way down from flood stage and the bridge appeared intact. Collin pulled the pickup to the shoulder before they crossed it. They both got out to have a look, to make sure that crossing would be safe. Buster jumped out to follow them.

But then a couple of pickups came rolling across from the town side. Behind the wheel of the second truck was a rancher they both recognized, Hank Garmond. Hank owned a nice little spread at the southwestern edge of the valley.

He pulled to a stop. "Willa. Collin. I see you're both in one piece and still breathing. Could be worse, eh? I'm headin' back to my place. We still got a house, but we lost the barn and sheds. Haven't started counting cattle yet. I just stopped in at Crawford's to try and get a few supplies to tide us over." Crawford's General Store, on North

Main, was a town landmark. The store sold everything from basic foodstuffs to farm supplies, hardware and clothing. "Shelves are already lookin' pretty bare in there."

Collin asked, "How bad is it?"

"In town? Power's out, and all the phones. North of the creek is okay, from what I heard. No flooding, the water supply unaffected. South is not lookin' good. Commercial Street Bridge is washed out. There's damage to the Main Street Bridge. People are bypassing it. We still got this bridge though." He pointed a thumb back over his shoulder. "Praise the Lord for small favors." *Very small favors,* Willa couldn't help thinking. True, it was pretty much what she and Collin had thought it would be, but somehow, to hear Hank confirm their suspicions made it all the more horribly real. "And then there's what happened to Hunter McGee." Hunter McGee was the mayor.

"What?" Willa demanded.

"Tree fell on that old SUV of his. So happened he was in the SUV at the time."

Willa respected Mayor McGee. He was a born leader, a real booster of education and had planned and promoted several school-related fund-raising events. "My Lord," she cried. "Was he hurt?"

"The tree fell on the hood. Not a scratch on him." Hank resettled his hat on his head and Willa felt relief. But then Hank added, "Must have scared the you-know-what right out of him. He had a heart attack."

Willa put her hand over her mouth. "Oh, no…"

"Oh, yeah. It was over real quick for Mayor McGee."

"Over?" Willa's heart sank. "You—you mean he's…?"

Hank nodded. An SUV and another pickup came across the bridge. The occupants waved as they drove by. Hank said somberly, "They took him to Emmet's house. Emmet pronounced him DOA." Emmet dePaulo, a nurse-practitioner, ran the town clinic. "Clinic's flooded, in case you were wondering."

Willa and Collin exchanged grim glances. They weren't surprised. The clinic was south of Main. "Emmet and a couple of his neighbors waded in there and saved what equipment and supplies they could first thing this morning. Luckily, Emmet had a lot of his medical stuff stored on the second floor and the water didn't make it that high. He's set up an emergency clinic at his house, for now."

"They got the volunteer fire guys out on search and rescue?" Collin asked.

Hank shrugged. "Can't say. I ain't heard of anybody dead, hurt bad or stranded…'ceptin' Mayor McGee, I mean. Rest his soul. But I did hear that some county trucks brought in salvage-and-rescue equipment and sandbags yesterday before the levee broke. This morning, the town council put together an emergency crew to patch up the places where the water got through. So that's taken care of for now. And you can just have a look at the creek. Water level's back to normal range."

Collin gave a humorless chuckle. "Yeah, one good thing about breaks in the levee. They tend to bring the water level way down."

"That they do," Hank concurred. "Plus, there's no rain in the forecast for at least the next week. So we're unlikely to have a repeat of what happened yesterday—oh, and the town council called a meeting at noon in the town hall to talk cleanup and such. Wish I could be there, but I got way too much cleanup of my own out at my place and I need to get after it. Bought the bleach I needed, at least. I can disinfect my well." Hank tipped his hat.

"You stay safe and take it slow on the road, Hank," Collin said.

"Will do. You keep the faith, now." The rancher rolled on by.

Collin put his arm around her. "You're lookin' kind of stricken, Willa."

She leaned into him, because she could. She needed someone to lean on at that moment. And Collin was so solid. So warm. So very much alive. "I'd been letting myself hope that at least no one had died—and I really liked Mayor McGee."

"I hear you. Hunter was a good man and this town could sure use him about now." He pulled her a little closer in the shelter of his arm and turned them both back to the pickup, Buster at their heels. The dog jumped in back again and they got in the cab.

As they drove across the bridge, Willa tried not to dread what might be waiting for them on the other side.

Chapter Four

It didn't look so awfully bad, Willa told herself as they drove along Sawmill Street. In fact, there on the northern edge of town, things seemed almost normal. Willa spotted a couple of downed trees and some flattened fences, but nothing like the devastation they'd witnessed coming in.

When they turned onto Main Street going south, they saw that the Crawford store parking lot was packed, people going in—and coming out mostly empty-handed. She supposed she shouldn't be all that surprised. It wouldn't take long to clear out the shelves of emergency supplies if everyone in town and most of the valley's ranchers showed up all at once and grabbed whatever they could fit in a cart.

The Community Church had its doors wide open. People sat on the steps there or stood out under the trees in front. Most of them looked confused. And lost.

"Shouldn't the Red Cross be showing up any minute?" she asked hopefully. "And what about FEMA and the National Guard?"

Collin grunted. "With a lot of the state in this condition, the phones out and the roads blocked, we'll be real lucky if a few supply trucks get to us in the next day or two." And then he swore low. "Isn't that the mayor's SUV?" The old brown 4x4 was half in, half out of the town hall parking lot. It had definitely come out the loser in the encounter with the downed elm tree. The tree lay square across what was left of the hood. The driver's door gaped open. A couple of boys in their early teens were peering in the windows.

"That's just too sad," Willa said low. "You'd think they'd want it off the street."

"Damn right." Collin muttered. "A sight like that is not encouraging." He hit the brake—and then swung a U-turn in front of the library, pulling in at the curb.

"Collin!" Willa cried, surprised. "What in the...?"

He shouted out the window at the two boys. "Hey, you two. Get over here."

Both boys froze. They wore guilty expressions. But then they put on their best tough-guy scowls and sauntered to Collin's side of the truck. They were the older brothers of a couple of Willa's former students and when they spotted her in the passenger seat, they dropped some of the attitude and mumbled in unison, "'Lo, Ms. Christensen."

She gave them both a slow nod.

One of them raked his shaggy hair off his forehead and met Collin's eyes. "Yeah?"

As he'd already done several times in the past eighteen hours or so, Collin surprised her. He knew their names. "Jesse. Franklin. Show a little respect, huh?"

Jesse, who was fourteen if Willa remembered correctly, cleared his throat. "We are, Mr. Traub." *Mr. Traub*. So strange. To hear anybody call the youngest, wildest Traub *mister*. But then again, well, the Traubs were pillars of the

Rust Creek Falls community. Some of that probably rubbed off, even on the family bad boy—especially to a couple of impressionable teenagers.

Franklin, who was thirteen, added, "We were just, you know, checkin' things out."

Collin leaned out the window and suggested in a just-between-us-men kind of voice, "You two could make yourselves useful, do this town a real big favor…."

The two boys perked up considerably. "Well, yeah. Sure," said Jesse.

"How?" asked Franklin.

"Head on up to the garage. See if Clovis has a tow truck he can spare." Clovis Hart had owned and run the garage and gas station at Sawmill and North Buckskin for as long as Willa could remember. "Tell him the mayor's SUV is still sitting in the middle of Main Street with a tree trunk buried in its hood and lots of folks would appreciate it if Clovis could tow it away."

The boys shared a wide-eyed look. And then Franklin said, "Yeah. We could do that."

"You want me to take you up there?"

"Naw," said Jesse, puffing out his skinny chest. "We can handle it ourselves."

"Good enough, then. Thanks, boys—and tell Clovis he probably ought to bring a chain saw for that tree."

"We will." The two took off up Main at a run.

"That was well done," Willa said, and didn't even bother to try and hide the admiration in her voice.

Collin grunted. "Maybe, but do you think they'll make it happen?"

"You know, I kind of do. They're good kids. And this is a way for them to help. And you know Clovis."

"Yes, I do. Clovis Hart respected Hunter McGee and he won't like it that the car Hunter died in is sitting on

Main with the hood smashed in for everyone to stare and point at."

She glanced toward the dashboard clock. It was 10:45 a.m. "So what do we do now?"

"I was thinking we could go and see how your house made out...."

She glanced over her shoulder, out the back window, past a happily panting Buster, at the Main Street Bridge. Someone had put a row of orange traffic cones in front of it to warn people off trying to use it. And one of her brother's deputies was standing, arms folded, in front of the pedestrian walk that spanned one side. "It doesn't look like they're letting folks cross the bridge."

Connor glanced over his shoulder, too. "We could try heading back to the Sawmill Street Bridge, then going on foot along the top of the levee until we get to your street."

"That could be dangerous...I mean, with the breaks in the levee and all. We would have to go carefully, and we don't know what we'll find if we manage to get to my house. It could take hours and we would miss the noon meeting Hank mentioned. I do think we should go to that."

Collin faced front again, his big shoulders slumping, and stared broodingly out the windshield back the way they had come. "You know who'll be running that meeting now Hunter's gone, don't you?"

She did. "Nathan Crawford." Nathan was in his early thirties, a member of the town council. Everyone expected him to be mayor himself someday. He and Collin had never liked each other. It was as if the two had been born to be enemies. Nathan was as handsome and dynamic as Collin was brooding and magnetic. Collin had always been a rebel and Nathan considered himself a community leader.

Rumor had it that five or six years back, Nathan's girl-friend, Anita, had gone out on him—with Collin. Word was Anita had told Collin that she and Nathan were through. But apparently, she'd failed to inform Nathan of that fact. There'd been a fight, a nasty one, between the two men. Some claimed Collin had won, others insisted Nathan had come out the victor. After that, the two had hated each other more than ever.

Plus, there was the old rivalry between their two families. Nathan was a Crawford to the core. The Crawfords not only owned the general store, they were also as influential in the community as the Traubs. And for as long as anyone could remember, Crawfords and Traubs had been at odds. Willa didn't really know the origin of the feud, but it seemed to be bred in the bone now between the town's two most important families. Traubs didn't think much of Crawfords. And the Crawfords returned the favor.

She spoke gently, but with firmness. "I really think it's important that everyone who can possibly be there attends that meeting."

He put his arm along the back of the seat and touched her shoulder, a gentle brush of a touch. She felt that touch acutely. His dark eyes sought hers—and held them. "So you want to go to the meeting first and then decide what to do about getting to your place?"

She smiled at him. "I do. Yes." Right then, a Rust Creek Garage tow truck came rumbling toward them down the street.

"I've got a chain saw in my toolbox in the back." Collin got out to give Clovis a hand.

At ten past two that afternoon the town hall meeting was still going on.

Collin sat next to Willa and wished he was anywhere but there. He was getting hungry, for one thing. And he figured the rest of the crowd had to be hungry, too.

The big multipurpose meeting room was packed. They had a generator for the lights, but there was no air-conditioning, never had been in the town hall. As a rule, it didn't get that hot in Rust Creek Falls. But with all the bodies packed in that room, it was hot now.

Tired, frightened, stressed-out townsfolk had taken every chair. More people stood at the back or along the side walls. There were children, too. People didn't want to let their kids out of their sight at a time like this. And kids got restless when forced to sit or stand in one place for too long.

Babies were wailing and small voices kept asking, "Daddy, when can we go?" and "Mommy, is this over yet?"

There were a lot of big talkers in town and every one of them was insisting on being heard. Plus, that jerk Nathan sat up there on the hall stage with the other useless members of the council and kept banging the mayor's big hand-carved oak gavel for order.

All right, it was true. A lot of people thought the world of Nathan Crawford. And maybe, if Collin were being fair about it, he'd admit that Nathan had a few good qualities. However, when it came to most Crawfords, and Nathan in particular, Collin just plain didn't feel like being fair.

Nathan had the council in his pocket, naturally. They all looked at him like he was wearing a damn halo or something, like he was the one sent down from heaven to single-handedly fix everything that had gone so completely wrong since the day before.

"Everyone, your attention!" Nathan boomed in that smooth baritone that made people think he knew what he was talking about. "We all have to work together here. As I've said before, though phone, internet and TV are temporarily out of commission, we have the radio system at the sheriff's office and we are in communication with

DES—that is the state office of Disaster and Emergency Services. They are well aware of what is going on in Rust Creek Falls and the valley. And, unfortunately, in far too many other communities in western Montana. The good news, however, is that everything is under control and moving along."

Somebody in the crowd made a rude noise.

Nathan banged the mayor's gavel some more. "If we could all just be patient for a little bit longer, we will get these teams firmed up, so we can all get going on the cleanup right away."

Collin knew he should keep his mouth shut. His plan had been to get through the meeting, help Willa deal with the probable ruin of her home and then pitch in wherever he was needed. But Nathan and the council had their priorities turned around. And while there were plenty of people willing to go on and on about the difficulty of the situation and how much they wanted to help, nobody else seemed ready to tell the council they were putting the cart before the horse.

He got to his feet. Beside him, Willa startled and looked up at him, wide-eyed. She did amuse him, the way she always looked so worried about what he might do next. He sent her a glance that he meant to be reassuring. Her eyes only got wider. So much for soothing her. He faced front and waded in.

"I'm sorry. Nobody's speaking up about the real issue here and so I suppose I'm going to have to be the one. Nathan, cleanup is not the issue yet," he said good and loud. "First, we need to get teams into the flooded areas and see who needs help there. We need search and rescue and we needed it hours ago."

A chorus of agreement rose from the crowd. Apparently,

others thought there should be a rescue effort. It was only that no one had been willing to stand up and say it out loud.

Nathan banged his gavel. He looked at Collin the way he always did: as though he'd just crawled out from under a rock. "Order. Please, everyone. I already explained. We have the volunteer firefighters out searching for trapped or injured survivors."

"One team, you're saying? With how many men on it?"

Nathan didn't answer either question. Instead, he went right on with his argument. "Those men are trained for this and know what they're doing. We don't think it's a big problem. No one has reported anyone missing."

"And how're you going to know if someone's missing?" Collin demanded. "People can't call. The phones are out. There can't be more than a third of the people in the valley here at this meeting or hanging around Main Street. Where are the rest of them? Trying to clean up what's theirs? Off to Livingston for the rodeo, or down in Thunder Canyon with the rest of my family? Or trapped on the upper floors of their houses, wondering why no one's come looking for them?"

"But we *are* looking. And I honestly do not believe—"

Collin didn't even let him get started. "And you didn't answer my first question. How many men are out on search and rescue, Nathan?"

Others spoke up then. "Yeah! How many?" someone demanded.

"Not enough, that's how many!" answered another.

Nathan's face had gone a deep shade of red. "People, please. Order!"

Collin stuck his hands into the pockets of Wayne Christensen's overalls and waited for Nathan to stop pounding that gavel. Once he did, Collin answered the question himself. "I'm guessing about nine. Nine men to cover the whole of this town and the valley. Have I got that right?"

"Nine strong, able men who are trained in effective search and rescue," Nathan insisted, his face even redder than before.

Collin kept after him. "It doesn't matter how good they are. Nine men are not enough. We need to put every able-bodied adult on the search until we've made a circuit of all the homes and ranches in town and in the valley. It shouldn't take more than the rest of today and tomorrow, if we get a move on. After that, we can change our focus to salvage and cleanup."

Down the row from him and Willa, one of the Crawford men called out, "Sit down and shut up, why don't you, Traub? Let them that knows what they're doing make the decisions here."

"Yeah," said another voice. "We don't need the likes of *you* tellin' us what to do first."

And that was when Willa shot to her feet beside him. At first, Collin thought she would grab his arm and beg him to stay out of it.

But it turned out he'd misjudged her. "I feel I must add my voice to Collin's," she said in that prim schoolmarm way of hers that never failed to get him kind of hot. "We have no idea how many people might be trapped in their homes or their barns. There are bound to be collapsed buildings. People could be buried in the rubble, praying they'll be rescued before it's too late. We've already lost Mayor McGee."

"Bless his soul," said a woman's voice.

"Amen," said another.

Willa wasn't finished. "Search and rescue is the first job. And we need to give it everything. We can't afford to lose one more precious life in Rust Creek Falls or the valley."

And Collin added his voice to hers. "We've got to save our *people* before we worry about our property."

The room erupted in whistles and applause. People shouted, "By God, he's right!" and "Search and rescue!" and "Collin's said it!" and "Listen to the schoolteacher!"

By the time the clapping finally stopped, even Nathan had seen the writing on the wall. He did what he had to do and went along. "The council, as always, seeks to understand and take action according to the wishes of our citizens. We will call in the nine trained men and reassign them as team leaders."

Willa leaned close and asked softly, "Call? The phones are out...."

He whispered back, "They'll have handheld radios—walkie-talkies."

"Oh. Right..."

Nathan was still talking. "For today and tomorrow—and as long as is needed—those nine leaders will head the teams in our search-and-rescue efforts. Volunteers, seek out a leader. Marjorie?"

Marjorie Hanke, the council member to Nathan's right, stood, picked up a pointer and smacked it against the map of the county that hung behind the council table. The map had already been divided into sections for the proposed cleanup teams. "Team one, section one—and so on," Marjorie announced. "We've been fortunate in that rubber boots, heavy rubber gloves and necessary tools have already been trucked in and will be provided to each of you. Please wear the boots and gloves at all times when searching in mud or standing water. Be on careful lookout, everyone, for vermin of all persuasions. Floods bring out the rats and displace the snakes. Thank you, Nathan." With a nod, she set down the pointer and took her seat again.

Nathan wrapped it up. At last. "Getting around in the flood areas isn't easy, but we are able to truck in supplies from Kalispell for those in need. The Ladies Auxiliary of the Community Church has set out a meal on the church lawn while we've been busy with our meeting here. If everyone will file outside in an orderly manner, Pastor Alderson will lead us in a prayer, after which we will share a late lunch. By then, your team leaders will have returned—and the search for missing survivors can commence."

Chapter Five

Buster, leashed to a railing outside the town hall, whined and wiggled in greeting when Willa went to collect him. She took a minute to pet him and praise him for being such a good dog.

Collin got her pack from his pickup for her and then he walked across the street to the church at her side. When her friend and fellow teacher, Paige Dalton, waved and called her name, Willa quickly looked away and pretended she didn't hear.

No, it wasn't nice of her to treat a friend that way. But she wanted a few more minutes with Collin. Soon, he would be off with one of the search teams. And then he would probably want to go up the mountain, to check on his house. There would be no reason, once he left with the searchers, for them to be together anymore. The time had come when they would go their separate ways.

She would always be grateful to him—for saving her

life in the flood, for helping her make it through those awful first hours trapped in the barn. But she felt a bit wistful, too. For most of that day, it had almost seemed as though she and Collin were a team, ready and able to do what needed doing, fully capable, between them, of handling whatever challenges might arise. It had been a strangely heady feeling.

She wished she didn't feel so sad suddenly. But already, she was looking back longingly on the afternoon and evening before, and at the morning just passed. In retrospect now, it seemed hard to believe that she'd held a grudge against him for four long years. Her recent ill will toward him seemed something from another lifetime—from someone *else's* lifetime. She simply didn't have it in her to feel bitterness toward him now.

Now, she could almost view the flood and its immediate aftermath as some sort of lovely, exciting adventure story come to life, an adventure starring the two of them— which was way too self-absorbed of her and she knew it. This was no adventure story. This was a bona fide real-life disaster. People she cared about were losing everything.

Including herself, if you came right down to it. She wasn't holding out a lot of hope for the condition of her house. And what about all of her stuff? She had so many treasures—her favorite velvet sofa pillow, the fairy-tale books she'd collected since childhood, that spindly inlaid table she proudly displayed in the front hall...

The list was endless. What would be left of the things that she loved?

She ordered herself not to go there. Her belongings might be precious to her, but they *were* only things and she needed to remember that now.

At least she had flood insurance, as did Gage, thank God. Whatever condition her house might be in, there would eventually be money to repair or rebuild. Many people in town and in the valley couldn't afford flood insurance. They could end up with nothing.

Collin nudged her arm. "You're wrinkling up your forehead. What's the matter?"

She tugged on Buster's leash as he dawdled, sniffing at the curb. "Just worrying, I guess."

"Stop." He gave her one of those sexy bad-boy grins of his. "We're going to get fed. It's something to be happy about."

At the church, the ladies auxiliary had been busy. They'd set up rows of tables out on the lawn. And they'd even thought of people's pets. Thelma, Hunter McGee's mother, gave her a bowl of water for Buster and a couple of dog biscuits. The older woman looked pale, Willa thought, and her eyes were swollen and red-rimmed.

Willa wrapped her in a hug and whispered, "He will be greatly missed."

Thelma sniffed and forced a brave smile. "We must soldier on," she said, and bent to give Buster a pat on the head.

Everyone remained standing while the pastor said a short prayer. He praised the stalwart heart and fine leadership of their lost mayor and asked that the people of Rust Creek Falls might find the strength they needed to endure this difficult time. At the last, he blessed the food.

"Amen," they all said softly, in unison.

It wasn't a fancy meal, but when you're hungry, the simplest food can be so satisfying. They had chicken salad sandwiches, chips, apples, oatmeal cookies and all the water they could drink. Collin sat next to her. They didn't talk. They were too busy filling their empty stomachs.

The volunteer firemen started coming in, muddy and looking tired. They washed up in the church restrooms and grabbed sandwiches, which they ate standing up. People rose from the tables and surrounded them, eager to join their teams.

Collin leaned close to her. He smelled faintly of her dad's shaving cream, which made her smile. He muttered, "I meant what I said before. Finish eating and we'll find a way to get to your house. I can join a team after that."

She set down her cup of water. "Thank you, but no. You said it yourself in the town hall just now. The search for survivors has to come first."

He looked at her, a probing sort of look. That dark lock of hair had fallen over his forehead again the way it tended to do. More than ever, she wanted to smooth it back.

But she didn't. Instead, she took a bite of her cookie and downed her last sip of water.

"You sure?" He looked doubtful.

"I am, yes. First things first."

Willa assumed she would end up watching the little ones while their mothers and fathers went out on the search-and-rescue teams. People knew she was good with their kids and trusted her with them.

While Collin went to join a search team, she asked Mrs. McGee about pitching in with child care. Thelma told her to check in with the church nursery. The older woman also volunteered to look after Buster for the rest of the day.

"He's a nice dog," Thelma said, her tone bright and cheerful, endless sadness in her eyes. "Taking care of him will be no trouble at all."

Willa thanked her, gave her another quick hug and ran up the steps into the church, headed for the nursery in back.

Paige caught up with her in the sanctuary. "Willa. I've been so worried about you. The whole south side is flooded. Your house, is it…?"

"I don't know. I haven't been there since it happened. I left to check on the ranch and track Buster down before the levee broke. On the way, my car got swamped."

"Oh, my Lord. But you got out all right...."

"Thanks to Collin Traub." Willa brought her friend up to speed on how Collin had saved her from the flood. "My car's a total loss. And we ended up waiting out the rest of the storm in the barn."

"I don't know what to say. It's awful. But I'm so glad you're okay."

"Yeah. Still breathing and all in one piece—and the barn and my parents' house are fine."

Paige asked hopefully. "Gage's place?"

Willa bit her lip and shook her head. "Bad."

"Oh, Willa." Paige held out her arms.

Willa went into them and held on tight. "It's all so scary..."

"Oh, I know, I know." Paige pulled back, took Willa by the shoulders and gazed at her through solemn, worried brown eyes. "Collin, huh?" she asked gently.

Willa wasn't surprised at her friend's cryptic question. Paige was one of the few people in town who knew about that awful night at the Ace in the Hole *and* about Willa's longtime crush on the Traub bad boy. Willa had told her friend everything on one of those Friday nights they shared now then—just the two of them, watching a romantic comedy on DVD, a big bowl of popcorn between them. Paige could keep a secret. She would never tell a soul.

Willa realized it was time to admit that she'd let injured pride cloud her judgment in a very big way. "I was all wrong about him." There was no one else nearby, but she kept her voice low just in case. "I mean, so what if he turned me down once? It's not that big of a deal. He's a good guy, someone anyone would want at their back in a crisis."

"Well, I can see that, but still…" Paige let the sentence die unfinished.

Willa reminded her friend, "Paige, seriously. The man saved my life yesterday and he was right there, sticking by me all night and this morning, too, when we had to face all the damage."

Paige put up both hands. "All right. He's a hero. You've convinced me." And then she shrugged. "I'm not surprised, really. I always believed there was a good guy underneath all that swagger." Like Willa, Paige knew the Traub family well. She'd even been in love with a Traub once—Collin's brother Sutter. It hadn't worked out for them. Now Sutter owned a stable in the Seattle area. He didn't come home often, and when he did, he never stayed long. "So…" Paige hesitated.

Willa tried not to roll her eyes. "Go ahead."

"Are you and Collin together now?"

Together. With Collin. The thought made her cheeks grow warm. She hastened to clarify, "No. It's not like that. He helped me out when I needed a hand, that's all. He helped me a lot and I'm grateful to him."

"Right." Paige gave her a knowing look. "And there *is* still Dane to consider."

Willa felt instantly guilty. She hadn't given Dane Everhart a thought since last night, when she'd made a big show of throwing the poor guy in Collin's face. "I told you. I really don't think it's going anywhere with Dane—and yes, when he proposed marriage, I should have said no right then and there. But Dane is so sure that he and I are a good match. And he's so charming and confident and… I don't know. We get along, but it's never been anything romantic."

Her friend said softly, "But Dane would like it to be."

Willa gulped and nodded. "It's so completely...*Dane,* to decide to marry me and refuse to take no for an answer. But in the end, he'll have to face facts. He's just not the guy for me."

Page coaxed, "But Collin is?"

"No. Really. Come on, Paige. I said it was nothing like that with Collin."

"But you *always* liked him—and not in that friends-only way that you seem to feel about Dane."

Willa lowered her voice even more. "It was a crush that I had on Collin, a teenage crush, that's all— and stop looking at me like that."

"Like what?"

"Like you think I'm lying to myself."

"Did I say that?" Now Paige was looking way too innocent.

"You didn't have to. And you've got it all wrong. It's just that Collin and I have patched up our differences and we're on good terms now." Okay, she'd spent the previous night in his arms, but only because it had helped them keep warm. And she wasn't even going to *think* about that moment in the morning when they first woke up. Uh-uh. She was just wiping that moment clean out of her head.

"So you and Collin are friends, then?"

Friends? With Collin? It kind of felt that way, but maybe it was just the flood and all they'd been through since yesterday. She had to be careful not to read too much into it. He was off helping with the rescue effort now. When he returned, there would be no reason for him to seek her out. Their future contact with each other would be casual: saying hi when they passed each other on the street, stopping to chat now and then when they ran into each other at the store or the doughnut shop. "I don't know. We're... friendly, okay? We're getting along."

Paige's soft mouth tipped up in that warm smile that always made Willa so glad to be *her* friend. She chuckled. "Honey, you sound confused."

Why not just admit it? "Okay. Yeah. I am, a little…"

"You come and stay at my house tonight." Paige lived on North Pine, well north of the flooded area. "We'll have a nice glass of wine and I'll set you straight."

Willa laughed, too. "Uh-oh."

"Seriously. I want you staying with me as long as you need to. And don't you dare go out and stay at the ranch alone now. You need to be with a friend."

Willa felt suddenly misty-eyed. "Thanks, Paige."

Paige leaned closer. "And I have to say, I like it that Collin stood up in the meeting and got everyone to see that we need to put all our effort on searching for survivors first."

"Yes—and that reminds me. Are you helping with child care? I was just going to the nursery to see if they need me."

Paige caught her arm again. "I guess you didn't hear. The older ladies are taking care of the kids. Women our age in good shape, they want pitching in with the rescue effort. Come on. We'll get ourselves on a team."

Three people were rescued that day: two disabled shut-ins marooned upstairs in their flooded houses, and a rancher, Barton Derby, who lived alone and whose barn had collapsed on top of him. The team leaders kept in communication on their handheld radios and passed on the news when someone was found.

Barton Derby had compound fractures to both legs and had to be taken to the hospital in Kalispell, a long drive with so many of the roads badly damaged or still flooded. The word was that Derby survived the trip without incident.

The two shut-ins were physically unhurt, just very hungry and frantic over the damage to their homes. Willa and Paige's team leader told them that Thelma McGee, who owned a big house on Cedar Street, had taken them both to stay with her until other arrangements could be made.

For Willa and Paige's team, the triumphs were small. They pulled two foundering heifers from a pond, contacted old Barrett Smith, the local vet, to treat an injured horse and brought a frightened cat down from up a tree. Mostly, though, they made the circuit of the houses and outbuildings in their section of the search map and found the owners in residence doing their best to deal with the thousand and one challenges the flood had dumped in their laps.

The teams began returning to Main Street at dusk. The phones and electricity were still out, but there was food in the church multiuse room for anyone who needed it. Makeshift dormitories had been set up in the town hall and Masonic Hall for those who had nowhere else to go.

Paige came with Willa to the church, where they ate with their team by the light of kerosene and battery-powered lanterns. Once they had food in their stomachs, she nudged Willa. "Come on. Let's go to my place and get some rest..."

Willa hesitated. She would have loved a shower and to settle into that nice, big bed in Paige's guest room. But somehow, she couldn't do it. "I think I'll just get a cot in the town hall."

"Willa. Why? I want you to come and stay with me."

"And I love you for that. But I just can't..." It seemed important right then to stick with the other people who had been dispossessed. She wanted to stay close to the center of things, at least for the first night or two, until the search for survivors was finished and she could be certain that everyone in town and in the valley was safe and whole, with food in their bellies.

"You're sure?" Paige brushed her arm, a companionable touch.

Willa nodded. "Yeah. It just…feels right, to stay with the others for now."

So Paige gave her a hug and promised to be back for breakfast before the search began again in the morning. Then she asked around to see who needed lodging. She took Buck and Bella McAnder and their two little girls home with her. The McAnders lived a few houses down from Willa, on South Broomtail Road. All over the north side of town, people were doing that, taking in families who lived south of the creek.

So far, Collin had yet to appear for dinner. Once Paige was gone, Willa checked out the team sign-up sheets that were posted on the wall right there in the church multiuse room. He'd joined Team Three, headed by Jerry Dobbs. It was the team that had rescued Barton Derby.

Team Three came in a few minutes later. Collin wasn't with them. She knew she ought to leave it alone. If he'd been injured in the search, she would have heard about it. There was nothing to worry over.

But then, well, she just *had* to know for sure that everything was okay with him. She approached Jerry Dobbs and asked if he knew where Collin might be.

"A real asset to our team, that Collin," Jerry said. "Without him, we might not have gotten Bart out from under his barn. People can't help but get scared around piles of unstable materials. Some held back, afraid to pitch in. Or worse, some were *too* brave and not careful enough. Collin reassured the scared ones and kept an eye on the chance-takers. The man's a born leader, levelheaded and calm and encouraging to others in a crisis. Plus, he's in top shape and light on his feet."

Willa didn't especially like the sound of all that. Had Collin put himself in danger to get Barton out? It would be just like him, after all. "Yes," she said, and tried to sound cheerful. "Collin Traub has no fear."

Jerry nodded. "And I think he mentioned something about stopping over at the Triple T to see how they were getting along out there."

She should have known. Of course he would have to go see how the hands at the family ranch were managing. She thanked Jerry, shouldered the pack she'd been dragging around with her all afternoon and walked over to Thelma's to get Buster.

By then, Thelma had a houseful of visitors. She'd made room not only for the two rescued shut-ins, but also for a couple of young families who owned houses on the south side of the creek.

"I'll be over at the church for breakfast tomorrow," Thelma said, as Buster sat on the step, cheerfully panting, cocking one ear and then the other, glancing from Thelma to Willa and back again. "I'll be happy to take Buster then. He's been a comfort, I have to tell you. He likes to stick close to me, but he's not in the way."

"He's a good dog," Willa said fondly. Buster made an eager little whining sound in response. "Just don't let him out unsupervised or you never know where he'll head off to."

"I won't," Thelma promised. "I'll keep him close."

Willa thanked her again and said good-night.

In the town hall, the generator was still going strong. It seemed so bright in there compared to the lantern light at Thelma's and in the church. The chairs in the meeting room had been folded up and stacked against the walls.

Rows of narrow cots waited for her and about fifty other people whose houses were in the still-restricted area south of the creek. She was a little anxious that Buster might not be allowed in. But it wasn't a problem. Marjorie Hanke, the councilwoman assigned to supervise sleeping arrangements in the hall, told her that as long as he behaved himself he could sleep beside Willa's cot.

Collin wasn't there. Disappointment tried to drag her down, which was ridiculous. The man had his own life, after all. He had things he needed to do. He could be staying at the Triple T for the night, or over at the church getting something to eat, or possibly bedding down in the other makeshift dormitory in the Masonic Hall. He might even have headed up the mountain to his house.

She truly hoped he hadn't been foolish enough to do that. Not in the dark. After the storm, there was no telling what condition that road would be in.

It was very annoying. He was so unpredictable. A person hardly knew what he might do next.

And really, she needed to stop thinking about him. She needed to be grateful that he'd saved her life and glad that she'd gotten past her issues with him—and let it go at that.

She leashed Buster to a leg of the cot and took her turn in the bathroom, washing up as best she could in the sink. Marjorie was passing out baggies containing personal grooming supplies to those without, but Willa had her own. She'd raided her mother's medicine cabinet for soap, deodorant and a toothbrush, and she'd also thought to grab an old pair of lightweight pink sweatpants, flip-flops and a clean T-shirt from the box under the stairs.

Back in the meeting room, people were settling in, getting as comfortable as possible for the night. When everyone had finished in the restrooms, Marjorie turned off all the lights, save one. She left it on low, for a night-light.

Willa lay back, stared at the dark ceiling overhead and felt certain she'd be awake half the night, worrying about her parents and Gage, who were probably going nuts, wondering what was happening at home. She knew she would end up lying there, eyes wide-open, obsessing over the extent of the damage of her house. She was positive that she would have to firmly remind herself not to get all worked up over the tragic death of the mayor, and not to think about Collin, who surely would not have been so foolish as to head up the mountain in the dark of night.

But strangely, within minutes of zipping up her borrowed sleeping bag, her eyes had drifted shut. With a sigh, she turned on her side, tucked her hand under her cheek, and let sleep steal all her worries away.

The double doors to the town hall meeting room were shut when Collin arrived. He eased through them soundlessly.

Marjorie Hanke, in a cot by the door, sat up and pointed to an empty one a few feet away. Collin whispered a thankyou and tiptoed to the unoccupied cot. It wasn't that far from the door, which was great. He had a big plastic bag full of stuff for Willa and a pack for himself. Both of those, he stowed under the cot.

A couple of rows over, he heard a low, familiar whine. A tail thumped the floor: Buster. So Willa *was* sleeping here. He considered going over there and making sure she was all right.

But come on. His creeping close and peering down at her wouldn't help her in the least.

Uh-uh. If he went to her, he wouldn't be doing it because she needed him right now. It would be because he wanted to see her, plain and simple. In the space of one night and the morning after, he'd found it all too easy to get used to having her around. All too easy to wish she might *stay* around.

He liked her.

Always had, though he knew she used to think he didn't.

Maybe he liked her too much. He needed to keep a rein on himself because he knew that nothing was going to come of his liking Willa Christensen more than he should. She was a nice girl. She had a college-graduate Mr. Good-Guy boyfriend off in Australia, a boyfriend who'd asked her to marry him.

There was no way Collin fit into that picture.

Someone coughed. A cot squeaked as someone else turned over. At the other end of the room near the stage, somebody was snoring. Collin should shuck off his boots, stretch out on the cot and try to get a little sleep. Morning would come way before he was ready for it.

Too bad he didn't feel all that much like sleeping. He moved silently back to the doors and slipped through again. Swiftly, he crossed the dark front hall and let himself out into the cool of the night.

On the steps, he sat down, drew his legs up and wrapped his arms around his knees. It was a clear night, a sliver of the waning moon hanging above the distant mountains way across the valley. He stared up at that moon and tried not to think about the woman sleeping in the dark hall behind him, tried not to think about that morning, when he'd woken up with her soft, pretty little hand on his fly. A bad, bad idea, to think about that. Thinking about that would only get him all worked up all over again.

He heard a faint sound at his back, the squeak of heavy hinges as the door opened behind him. Buster nuzzled his shoulder. He threw an arm over the dog and scratched him behind the ear as the door squeaked shut. The latch clicked.

Willa. He could feel her, hovering there behind him in

front of the door. He was way too glad she'd come out to find him.

"Go back to bed, Willa," he said lazily, not turning to look at her, keeping his gaze front, on that sliver of moon. "How many times do I have to tell you? I'm not having sex with you."

Willa laughed, a low, slightly husky sound, one that seemed to skim the surface of his skin, raising goose bumps as it went. Raising more than goose bumps if he was going to be honest about it. He drew his knees up a little tighter so she wouldn't see how she affected him.

"You are impossible," she said in a voice as low and husky and full of good humor as her laugh.

He shrugged. "So I've been told."

And then she came and sat on his other side, so he was sandwiched between her and her dog. It wasn't a bad place to be. Not bad at all.

She said, "Buster's happy to see you. He woke me up when you came in."

"Sorry."

She leaned toward him a little, nudging him with her shoulder in a way that felt downright companionable. "Don't be."

He stroked the dog's big white head. "He's a great guy." The dog turned, tongue lolling, and gazed at him adoringly. "And so good lookin'."

Willa chuckled again. "Oh, yes, he is."

He still hadn't looked at her. Mostly because when he did, he knew he wouldn't want to look away. "What about you, Willa? You happy to see me, too?"

"I am," she answered in a near whisper. "Yes." She was quiet. He could feel the warmth of her along his side. She smelled of soap and toothpaste—and something else. Something that was simply Willa. Kind of green and fresh and a little bit lemony. Who knew the smell of soap and lemons could get a man worked up? She spoke again. "I was kind of worried you'd tried to go up the mountain to your place."

"Not in the dark."

"Good."

"I went to the Triple T. They got the wells disinfected and are hoping to be using the water by tomorrow or Sunday. Most of the stock survived. And they're busy with cleanup. I stopped in at Clay's house and borrowed a few things—clean jeans and boots, a couple of shirts." Third-born of his five brothers, Clay had recently married. He lived down in Thunder Canyon now, but he still owned a house on the Triple T. "Then I went over to your family's place, just to see if things were okay there."

"You didn't have to do that."

"Willa. I wanted to."

A silence from her, then, "Thank you."

"I used the guest-room shower again. And I left your dad's clothes in the hamper. Hope you don't mind."

"I don't mind at all. How was it there?"

"Better."

"Really?"

"Yeah. The neighbors and the hands from the Triple T had been there. The pigs are back in their pen and the chickens are in the coop. Looked like they even made a start on the cleanup."

"That's good," she said. "Really good. I'm grateful."

He did look at her then. She was staring out toward the moon, the curve of her cheek so smooth in the dim light, her pretty lips slightly parted. She wore a different T-shirt from the one she'd had on earlier, pink sweatpants with white trim and a worn-down pair of flip-flops.

She kept her gaze on the moon, and that was fine with

him. Gave him more time to look at her. He took in everything about her. Her toenails were painted. In the dark, it was hard to be sure of the exact color. Maybe purple. Like plums. He stared at them for a time. When he looked up, she was watching him. "Did you get something to eat?"

He nodded. "I had some stew at the Triple T."

Those cute dimples of hers tucked themselves in at the sides of her mouth as she smiled. "Jerry Dobbs says you're a natural leader, that they might not have saved Bart Derby if not for you."

"Well. You know Jerry, heavy on the 'go, team, go.'"

"I think you're being modest, Collin." Her big brown eyes gleamed at him.

He felt an odd little pinch, a heated tightness in his chest. Also, in his borrowed jeans. "Modest? Me? Not a chance."

Buster got up and wandered down the steps to lift his leg on a tree trunk. When he started sniffing the ground, moving toward the street, Willa called to him. "Buster. Come." He came right back and plopped down where he'd been before.

Collin said, "I filled a bag with clothes from that box under the stairs at your folks' house, in case you need them. I left it back in the hall, under my cot. I brought jeans and shirts and underwear, too." There had been little lace panties and a bra and several pair of socks. "Not that I noticed the underwear or anything…"

"As I recall, it was pretty frayed, that underwear. But I'm grateful to have it at this point." She groaned, lowered her head and put her hand over her eyes. "I can't believe I'm sitting here discussing my old underwear with you."

"Hey." It was his turn to bump her shoulder with his. "What are friends for?"

She looked up and into his eyes, all earnest and hopeful, suddenly. "We are, aren't we? Friends, I mean."

He wanted to kiss her. But he knew that would be a very bad idea. "You want to be my friend, Willa?" His voice sounded a little rough, a little too hungry.

But she didn't look away. "I do, yes. Very much."

That pinch in his chest got even tighter. It was a good feeling, really. In a scary sort of way. "Well, all right then. Friends." He offered his hand. It seemed the thing to do.

Her lower lip quivered a little as she took it. Her palm was smooth and cool in his. He never wanted to let go. "You better watch it," she warned. "I'll start thinking that you're a really nice guy."

"I'm not." He kept catching himself staring at that mouth of hers. It looked so soft. Wide. Full. He said, "I'm wild and undisciplined. I have an attitude and I'll never settle down. Ask anyone. Ask my own mother. She'll give you an earful."

"Are you trying to scare me, Collin Traub? Because it's not working."

He took his hand back. Safer that way. "Never say I didn't warn you."

She gave him a look from the corner of her eye. "I'm onto you now. You're a good guy."

"See? Now I've got you fooled."

"No, you don't. And I'm glad that we're friends. Just be straight with me and we'll get along fine."

"I am being straight." Well, more or less. He didn't really want to be her friend. Or at least, not *only* her friend. He wanted to be *more* than her friend. But sometimes a man never got what he wanted. He understood that, always had. Sweet Willa Christensen was not for the likes of him. But right now, he just needed to look out for her, take care of her a little. Make sure she got through this hard time all right. He added, "And I've been thinking."

"About what?"

"The things that need doing."

She braced an elbow on her knee and dropped her chin in her hand. "Such as?"

"I'm guessing we'll finish up the search for survivors by around noon tomorrow. Meet me at the church when your team comes in. One way or another, we're going to get to your house tomorrow."

Her smooth brow furrowed. "What if they won't let us into the area?"

"You worry too much. They'll let us in. They pretty much have to."

"Not if they don't think it's safe."

"At some point, people are just going to go in anyway. The whole town has pitched in, put their own problems aside to search for survivors. It's not right to expect them to wait forever to get to their homes. Nathan and the rest of them have to take that into account or they'll have trouble on their hands."

"Collin…"

"Your face is all scrunched up again. Relax."

"It's only that I feel kind of bad, to keep on taking advantage of you like this."

"Don't," he commanded gruffly.

She just couldn't let it go. "But I know you need to get up to *your* place."

"My place is fine."

"But you can't be sure."

"Willa. We're going to your house and we're going to-morrow."

"I'm only saying that you don't have to—"

He put up a hand. "I know I don't have to. And you don't

have to worry. It's pretty much impossible to take advantage of me. If I say I'll do a thing, it's because I *want* to do it." And when it came to the woman beside him, well, what he wanted was to do whatever she needed. He added, just to make himself sound tough and uncompromising, "I don't do anything because I think I *have* to. Life is too damn short for that."

Chapter Six

It all went as Collin had predicted, which only made Willa more aware of how completely she had once underestimated him. He understood so much, really. About people. About the way things worked.

The nine teams searched for four hours the next day, covering the rest of the valley and the flooded area south of the creek in town. They found a couple of stranded pets and more cattle that had to be pulled from muddy ponds, but no people in need of rescue.

Willa's team was out at the far western reaches of the valley. They finished up the search of their section by a little past noon and returned to town, where everyone had gathered at the church for the midday meal. Willa sat with Paige and the rest of their team.

Collin sat at another table, his team around him. He glanced up and saw her and gave her a nod that she took to mean he still intended to take her to her house.

Her heart kind of stuttered in her chest and then re-commenced beating a little too fast. Partly because trading meaningful glances with Collin excited her more than it should. And partly because it was happening at last: she would see her house again. She sent a little prayer to heaven that it wouldn't be too bad.

While they ate, Nathan Crawford got up and gave a speech. He thanked everyone for the great job they were doing. He praised Rust Creek Garage for having plenty of gas to share with the searchers and the foresight to own a generator so that the pumps were still working. He said that state and county workers were on the job around-the-clock, trying to get services back online and roads and bridges repaired.

He advised, "If you have family members who were out of town for the holiday and you're wondering why they haven't returned—please don't be overly concerned. The governor has declared a state of emergency and asked that people try and stay off the roads, many of which are badly damaged. Bridges are out all over the western half of the state. It's just going to take a while to get all our services back up and running and for people to get back home."

Nathan also reminded them that the next phase was cleanup. "I hope many of you will pitch in with the community effort, that you'll donate your time if you can spare some. But we're suspending our teams for the rest of the day and all day Sunday so that everyone can handle personal business. Those who live south of the creek will have a chance to visit their homes." The floodwaters had sufficiently receded, he added, and gas and water mains to the damaged areas had been shut off for the time being. The town council realized that people had to be allowed back in to begin to assess the condition of their property.

"Please use the Sawmill Street Bridge only. Follow the newly posted signs for the safest route to your property."

Next, he got to the hazards, which were many. "Please, please, be extra careful about entering buildings. Proceed with caution. If you see a downed wire or pole, keep clear and remember to report it." He reminded them all to wear boots and gloves and watch out for dangerous animals displaced by the flood. "Also, take note. Any buildings roped off with yellow tape have already been determined to be unsafe for entry. We've done our best to personally warn all of you whose houses are in that condition, but the priority until now has been rescuing the stranded. There are assuredly buildings that should have been roped off but haven't yet. Please. Don't approach any houses that are taped off. Search-and-Rescue Team One reports that our elementary school is badly damaged and possibly structurally unsound. So, also, we ask that you stay away from the school and the school grounds."

Willa's heart sank at that news. Beside her, Paige made a low sound of distress. Were they going to lose the school?

That would hit hard. If they had to rebuild, how long would it take? They only had two months until the start of the next school year.

Nathan ended by saying that dinner would be served at six and thanking the charitable organizations that had come through with donations of food and supplies. Then Pastor Alderson got up and invited them all to a brief Sunday service after breakfast the next morning, a service that would include a final farewell to Mayor McGee.

A funeral. Willa sighed. Lately, life was just packed with sad and difficult events. But then again, it was important to give people a chance to pay their respects and to grieve.

She glanced toward Collin again. But he'd already left

his table. She thought of last night, of sitting out on the front steps of the town hall with him. That had been so nice. Just the two of them and Buster, alone under the sliver of moon.

She almost wished she could go back there now, just run away from reality and all the everyday grimness of surviving the worst flood in the history of Rust Creek Falls. Run away and sit out under the moon with Collin, forever.

Even if they were just friends.

"You ready, Willa?" His voice, behind her. A little thrill pulsed through her.

Beside her, Paige frowned. "Ready for what?"

She pushed back her folding chair and gathered up the remains of her meal to carry to the trash and recycle stations. "Collin's taking me to see my house."

Paige looked at Collin. He gazed coolly back at her. "How are you, Collin?"

"Just fine, Paige. You?"

"Wonderful," Paige said in a tone that could have meant anything. She turned her gaze to Willa. "Shall I come with you?"

Willa shook her head.

"Are you certain?"

"Yes. But thank you. I'll be fine."

"You be careful."

"I will. Don't worry."

They got into Collin's truck and he paused before he started the engine. "Where's Buster?"

"Thelma's keeping an eye on him."

"Good. Safer for him if stays at Thelma's until this is done."

She nodded her agreement and he pulled the truck out into the flow of traffic, most of which was going where they were going. Her neighbors were as eager as she was to see firsthand how their homes had fared.

They followed the signs across the Sawmill Street Bridge, down Falls Street and then west on Commercial. They had to move at a crawl, even though road crews had already been hard at work. Fallen trees, utility poles and flooded vehicles had been cleared from the roadway. But the streets themselves were badly damaged, the pavement erupted and broken apart in places, pools of standing water and puddles of mud everywhere, some as big as ponds. The buildings that lined the street had not fared well. Some were partially collapsed and roped off with yellow tape. Yards were still cluttered with household items and who knew what all.

Fires had taken out a whole row of houses on South Pine. A few of them were burned all the way to the ground.

At Main, they passed the elementary school. It was still standing, at least, though sections of the roof had fallen in. There was no way to tell from the street how bad the damage might be.

For Willa personally, the moment of truth came much too soon. They turned onto South Broomtail and pulled to a stop at what was left of the curb in front of her one-story bungalow.

She had to stifle a gasp of dismay at what she saw. Like all the other yards on the street, hers was a mess, strewn with a bunch of mud-caked stuff she couldn't even identify. The roof on one side of her front porch sagged alarmingly. The porch itself was empty. Her white wicker chairs and cute little spray-painted metal folding tables topped with potted geraniums were nowhere to be seen. And the cosmos and columbines, the boxwood hedge and the rows of mums and Shasta daisies she'd so lovingly planted along

her front walk? If they were still there, she couldn't recognize them under the layer of mud and trash.

Collin reached over and took her hand. She wove her
fingers good and tight with his. It helped—his warm,
strong grip, the calloused flesh of his palm pressed to
hers. The contact centered her down, reminded her again
that she *could* get through this, that she wasn't alone.

He said, "You can wait for the insurance people, let
them tell you what can be saved. I can turn this truck
around and get us the hell outta here. You don't have to
try and go in there."

She gripped his hand tighter. "What was that you said
last night? About not wasting any part of your life doing
what you think you *have* to do?"

"So don't. We'll go." He tried to pull his hand from hers.

She held on. "I mean, I *want* to go in. I...need to go
in, Collin."

"Look at that porch roof. It could be dangerous. Someone on one of the county crews should have roped it off."

"I'm going in."

"Willa, it's not safe."

She hitched up her chin and stared straight in his eyes.
"I have to. I do. I don't agree with what you said last night.
Some things, well, a person does just *have* to do."

Collin tried to think of a way to talk her out of it. But
she had that look—so solemn and determined. When Willa
got that look, there was no changing her mind.

Maybe he could bargain with her a little. "Just let me
go in first, okay? Let me make sure that it's safe."

She still had his hand in a death grip. "Great idea. You
can get killed instead of me."

"Willa. I'm not going to get killed—and if you think

that it's too dangerous, well, why are we even talking about going in?"

"It was a figure of speech, that's all. I'm sure it's all right. We can go in together. But you're not leading the way. I won't have it. Do you understand?"

In spite of the very real danger in the situation, he wanted to smile. "You know you sound like an angry schoolmarm, don't you?"

"Well, I *am* an angry schoolmarm. And you'd better not cross me right now, Collin Traub."

He put on his most solemn expression. "No, ma'am. I wouldn't dare."

She let go of his hand and he wished that she hadn't. "Here." She passed him his heavy black rubber gloves. He put them on and she put on hers. They were both still wearing their waterproof search-and-rescue boots. "All right," she said. "Let's get it over with."

They got out and picked their way through the piles of broken, muddy junk in the yard. The smell was pretty bad—like spoiled food and smelly socks and other things he decided not to concentrate too hard on.

"Look," she said, and pointed. "One of my wicker porch chairs. Right there—and look over there. Isn't that a slow cooker?"

He only shrugged. The things she pointed to were unrecognizable to him.

The mud-caked porch creaked in an ominous way when they went up the steps. But it held. One front window was busted out, the other crisscrossed with cracks.

She reached for the door—and then she dropped her hand and laughed. "The key…"

For a moment, he knew relief. She'd forgotten the key. Good. But then she reached into her pocket and came out with it. She stuck it in the lock and gave it a turn.

The door swung inward.

It wasn't anything he hadn't expected. Mud everywhere and water wicking halfway up the walls. The same rotting, moldy smell as in the yard.

They went through the small entry hall and into the living room, where he doubted that any of the furniture could be saved. The large picture window on the side wall had cracked from corner to corner. The fireplace was full of mud.

"My grandmother's clock," Willa said in a tone of hope and wonder. It was on the mantel, a brass carriage clock, untouched. She went over to it, and gathered it into her arms. "It's an antique. A mercury pendulum clock." She glanced up and met his eyes. Hers were suspiciously misty. "Hey. It's *something*...."

They moved on, first to the kitchen and then down the short hallway to the bedrooms and the single bath. It was bad, all of it, every room full of mud. There wasn't much worth saving.

But there were some pictures on the walls that were good as new, and some stuff in the kitchen, dishes and such in the higher-up cabinets. And the things on the counter, too: a red toaster, cutting boards, some glass figurines on the windowsill. He suggested that they try and see if they could scare up some boxes to put the stuff in.

Willa shook her head. "And put the boxes where?"

He wanted to offer his house, but he hadn't made it up the mountain yet, and he knew she'd only argue that she couldn't impose on him. He thought of Paige. He didn't like what had gone down with Paige and his brother Sutter, but he knew Paige was a good woman at heart and a true friend to Willa. She would store Willa's stuff for her in a heartbeat. But then Willa would only give him some other excuse as to why that wouldn't work. "We'll haul them out to your parents' place. How's that?"

She clutched the brass clock like a lifeline and said primly, "That would take the rest of the day. And they are just *things,* after all."

"They're *your* things. And you need to get them out of here." He asked gently, "And what else are we gonna do with the rest of the day?"

"Other people might need our help and we should—"

He didn't let her get rolling. "Need our help doing what? Saving *their* things? We're doing this. Deal with it."

Her lower lip was trembling and her eyes were more than misty now. "I can't… I don't…" He felt a tightness in his chest at seeing her cry. She sniffed and turned her head away. "Oh, this is ridiculous. I have so much to be grateful for. There is no point in my crying over this. My crying will not change a thing…." A tight little sob escaped her.

"Come on. Come here." He reached out his rubber-gloved hands and pulled her close. "It's all right."

"No. No, it's not. I loved this house. I loved my little red Subaru."

"I know," he soothed. "I understand."

"I…I keep telling myself how it doesn't matter, that what matters is I'm alive and in one piece and so is most everyone else in town. But then I think of my…my treasures. My fairy-tale books, my favorite velvet pillow…I want them back, Collin. I want my *things* back."

"Shh, now. I know you do. There's nothing wrong with that. It's natural. Don't be so hard on yourself…."

"Oh, I am being such a big baby…." Sobs shook her slim frame.

He held her. He stroked her back. She curved into him, fitting against him as though she was made to be in his arms. For that moment, he forgot about everything. It all just...receded: her ruined house, the smell of mud and mildew, her grandmother's clock poking into his belly. There was only the woman in his arms. He held her and rested his cheek on her soft hair and waited.

Eventually, she pulled back enough to gaze up at him. Her nose was red and her eyes were puffy and she was so beautiful that his chest got tight all over again. He wished that...

But no. It was never happening. He wasn't going there. No way.

She sniffed. "Well. This is embarrassing."

He took her lightly by the upper arms. "You okay now?"

She sniffed again. "My nose is red, isn't it?"

"Your nose is beautiful."

"Liar."

It all seemed...strange and scary, suddenly. For a moment there...no. *Uh-uh. Not going there,* he reminded himself for the second time. He put on a big, fake smile and asked, "What do you say we go find those boxes?"

It took the rest of the day to scare up the crates and boxes, pack up what was salvageable and drive it out to the Christensen place. Her dad had a storage area off his work shed. They put it all in there.

By then, it was past time for the community meal back in town. They'd planned ahead and brought clean clothes with them so they could take advantage of the chance for hot showers. As before, he took the hall bath and she took the one off her parents' room.

She came out of her parents' bathroom, her brown hair still wet, smoothed back into a knot at the nape of her neck, smelling like flowers and rain and lemons, better than any woman he'd ever known.

And he'd known a lot of them—well, not in the past

couple of years. After he hit twenty-five or so, all that chasing around had begun to seem kind of pointless. But back when he was younger, he'd lived up to his rep as a player. Then he'd been out to have himself a good time every night of the week.

And not one other woman back in the day had ever smelled as good as Willa did right then.

They raided the pantry. As they ate canned stew, crackers and peaches, Willa said how happy she was with the cleanup around the ranch.

"They've done a lot," she said, "in just a couple of days."

Her car was still out there on its side in the pasture and probably would be until she could call her insurance guy or the FEMA people and have it towed away, but the animals were back in their proper pastures and pens. The neighbors were making sure the stock got fed.

They headed back to town at a little after eight, stopping off at the Triple T for a few minutes on the way, just to check on things. In Rust Creek Falls, they went to Thelma's to get Buster, and then they returned to the town hall for the night. There were several empty cots. Some people had found neighbors to stay with and some had gone to live with out-of-town relatives for a while.

Marjorie Hanke turned out the lights at eleven. Collin still felt wide-awake, so he got up and went outside to sit on the steps under the sliver of moon.

What do you know? He wasn't out there five minutes before Buster was nudging up against him on one side and Willa was dropping to the steps on the other.

He almost teased her about how he wasn't having sex with her. But no. Sex seemed a little dangerous to speak of now, something he couldn't afford to joke about.

And then she kind of leaned against him and said,

"Aren't you going to tell me to keep my hot little hands to myself?"

There was nothing he would like better than her hot little hands all over him. However, that was not going to happen, as he knew damn well and kept constantly reminding himself.

He kept it light, meeting her eyes, teasing, "I know I can count on you to do the right thing."

She didn't reply. There was one of those moments. They looked at each other and neither looked away. He would only have to lean in a few inches to capture that mouth of hers, to feel her lips against his.

Finally.

At last.

But he didn't. Apparently, he had some small amount of self-control left.

He thought of the boyfriend, the one who had asked her to marry him. He reminded himself that it was only an accident of fate that had her sitting next to him on the town hall steps at a quarter of midnight on July 6. And somehow, he managed to turn his head and stare at the moon again.

She said, very softly, "Remember when we were kids? You used to spy on me...."

He chuckled. "I had a lot of free time on my hands. And I never thought of it as spying."

"You would watch me when I had no idea you were there. That's spying, Collin Traub. I would look up—and there you would be, staring at me."

He gave her a grin. "You're getting mad about it all over again."

She frowned—and then her brow smoothed out. "You're right. I am. And that's silly. It was years ago. It's like that night at the Ace in the Hole. Better to just let it go." She tipped her head sideways and studied him. "You were so different from your brothers...."

"Yeah, well. My mom was tired when I came along. She had five boys already. Boys are exhausting. They need discipline and supervision. Mom did a good job of that with the rest of them. But she kind of gave up on me. I ran wild."

"I remember," she said wryly.

He elaborated with some pride, "I broke every rule and climbed every fence and spied on you when I knew it would freak you out. I also used to like to tease the bulls."

"Well, that's just plain asking for it."

"Yeah, it is. I guess I had an angel on my shoulder, though. Because somehow, every time I got in the pasture with one of the bulls and danced around shouting and waving my arms, I managed to jump the fence before I got gored."

She was shaking her head. "What were you thinking?"

"That it was fun! I mean, I liked it, being known as big trouble just waiting to happen. I got blamed for everything, sometimes for things I didn't even do. And it kind of got to be a point of pride for me that not a day went by I didn't get grief for some crazy, dumb-ass behavior or other."

She was looking at him again, her eyes shining brighter than the stars in the clear night sky overhead. "So you became known as the family troublemaker, the one no one could ever depend on."

"Because I *am* the family troublemaker that no one could depend on."

"But you're not," she argued. "Just look at you lately, standing up for what's right in the town meeting, getting a couple of kids to make sure the mayor's car was towed off Main Street the day after he died, saving Barton Derby from under the wreckage of his barn...."

"My *team* saved Bart Derby, the mayor's car was not a big thing—and you stood up in that meeting, too."

"What about rescuing me when I would have drowned, and then looking after me during the storm? And what about afterwards, too? What about today, at my house, when you held me while I cried and promised me it was going to be all right?"

"It was what you needed to hear right then."

"Exactly. Honestly, Collin. I don't know what I would have done without you since the flood." She'd better stop looking at him like that. If she didn't, well, he was going to grab her and plant one on her.

"Don't make a big thing out of it, okay?" he heard himself mutter.

"But it *is* a big thing."

"No, it's not...."

"Yes, it is!" She got that bossy schoolteacher look. "And that does it. I'm not sitting still while you minimize all the good you've done. I'm going to tell you how I see it."

"Uh-oh."

"You listen to me, now...."

He tried not to groan. "What will you do if I don't?"

She put her hand on his arm, apparently to hold him there by force. He felt that touch from the top of his head to the tips of his toes—and everywhere in between. "You are a born leader, Collin. This town is going to need a new mayor and I keep thinking that you could be the right man for that job."

Mayor? She thought he should be *mayor?* He couldn't help it. He threw back his head and laughed out loud. "Willa, okay. We're friends now and everything. But you don't know what you're talking about."

"Oh, yes, I do. I am onto you, in a big way."

He grunted. "No, you're not. You're making something out of nothing."

She pursed up her mouth at him. "When you're finished blowing me off, you just tell me. And then I will share my insights with you."

There were a whole bunch of sarcastic comebacks to that one. But for some unknown reason, he didn't use any of them. Probably because he did kind of want to hear what she had to say. "Okay, fair enough. Hit me with it."

"I will. Ahem. So you grew up a wild child, undependable. And as it so often happens in a small town like ours, people get it in their heads what a person is like and that's it, that's just the way it is. No one ever thinks to look at that person differently, to take a chance on depending on him, to expect more than misbehavior. There's a local perception and no one ever tests it. The perception becomes the reality."

"Took psychology at UI, did you, Willa?"

She gave him her sweetest smile. "And I'm not even at the good part yet.... Where was I? Oh, yes. So in the meantime, you're keeping busy fulfilling everyone's low expectations of you. And, as you said yourself, you find that not having anyone expect much of you is actually kind of fun. Because you can do what you want. You're not stuck like all your brothers, bearing up under the weight of everyone's high estimation of your sterling character. You actually have the freedom to live exactly as you please and you never have to worry about letting anyone down."

He could easily become annoyed with her. "Think you got me all figured out, don't you, Willa?"

She didn't back off. "To a degree, yes. You are adventurous and bold, with no desire to settle down. So naturally, in your teens, you become the town heartbreaker.

You do a lot of experimenting with women. Because, as you said, it's fun."

He'd heard about enough. "Come on. You're getting into dangerous territory here. You know that, right? Next you'll be digging up that night at the Ace again, getting all up in my face for not taking you up on what you were offering."

She put her hand on his arm again. He wanted to jerk away—and also to grab her and kiss her senseless. "No. Honestly. I'm over that." And then she smiled. So sweet and open, that smile. He realized that he definitely wanted to kiss her more than he wanted to get away from her. "Even if I am probably the only woman you ever turned down."

He almost told her that wasn't true, but then she'd just say he was bragging. "Seriously. Where are you going with this?"

She tipped her head to the side, frowning a little the way she did when she was thinking something over. "Hmm. I guess I'm just trying to make you see that being defined by other people's low expectations of you isn't really working for you anymore."

"And you know this, how?"

"I'm not blind, you know. I've been around you a lot the past few days. And what has been a tragedy for Rust Creek Falls has brought out the best in you. After all that's happened and all the good you've done—all the good you *will* do in the coming days, you're not going to be able to go back."

"Go back where?"

"To the way things were before the levee broke."

"Believe it or not, I happen to like the way things were."

"Maybe you did. Before. But it won't be enough for you now."

"You have no idea what's enough for me, Willa." He

ached to reach for her. Reach for her and pull her close and kiss her until her head spun and she let him do whatever he wanted with her, until he finally got a taste of what she'd been tempting him with since before he was even old enough to know what temptation was.

She just wouldn't stop. "You've started to expect more of yourself and that is a wonderful thing. Why can't you admit that?"

It was the tipping point. He couldn't stop himself. He reached out and grabbed her by the shoulders good and tight. And then he growled at her with all the frustrated heat and hunger he was trying so hard to deny. "I don't need you telling me how I feel or where I'm going."

She blinked at him and her big eyes got bigger and her mouth looked so soft and surprised he only wanted to cover it with his and stick his tongue inside. "But, Collin. I was only—"

"*Don't*, all right? Just don't." With great care, he straightened his arms, pushing her away from him. Then he let her go.

"Collin, I…"

He stood up. That was pretty damn stupid. He was as hard as a teenage kid caught thumbing through *Playboy*. All she had to do was look and she would see it.

Too bad. He wasn't hanging around to watch her reaction. He mounted the top step, hauled the door wide and went in, pulling it firmly shut behind him.

Chapter Seven

Willa had trouble getting to sleep that night. She felt awful. She knew that she'd gone too far. Yes, she did honestly believe she'd only told Collin the truth about himself.

And really, not a thing she'd said to him had been bad. Some men wouldn't mind being called a born leader. Some men would be pleased to hear how wonderful they were.

But not Collin, apparently.

And all right, well, maybe she'd laid it on a bit heavy. She'd turned her inner schoolmarm loose on him—and not the good, patient, understanding and gentle schoolmarm.

The other one. The bossy one who knew what was good for you and was bound to tell you all about yourself whether you wanted to hear it or not.

Had she wrecked their new friendship?

Oh, she did hope not. Because she really, really liked being his friend. She liked it more than she should, probably. With a guy like Collin, well, a girl could get really confused as to where she stood with him.

On the floor by her cot, Buster whined in his sleep. She reached her hand down to him, ran her fingers over the smooth, warm crown of his big head. He woke enough to press his wet nose against her palm and then settled back to sleep with a sweet chuffing sound.

She thought of all good things Collin had done for her since the flood, of the way he'd held her that afternoon, so tenderly, so kindly, in the muddy ruin that had once been her home.

No. He was a real friend to her now. Too good a friend for her to lose him just because she'd presumed to lecture him about his life.

In the morning, she would apologize. And everything would be all right.

He wasn't there for the community breakfast in the morning and he didn't come to the church service after the meal.

Willa sat with Paige and wished he was there. She worried that he *wasn't* there because she had pushed his buttons and made it necessary, somehow, for him to prove what a tough, bad guy he was—too bad to show up for Sunday services and give Willa a chance to say she was sorry.

The choir sang of sweet comfort and the pastor quoted inspirational sections of scripture, verses meant to be uplifting in hard times. He gave a sermon on sacrifice and the meaning of community. He talked about how the Lord was with them and that each and every one of them was proving their worth and their goodness by their deeds in this time of trial.

And finally, when the sermon was over, Pastor Alderson led them in a prayer for Mayor McGee and the service became a farewell for Thelma's only son.

People stepped up with vases full of flowers, picked wild or from their own gardens. The choir sang the songs that Hunter had liked best, a couple of country-and-western love songs, "Red River Valley," a Bob Dylan ballad and some other songs Willa hadn't heard before.

It was during one of those other songs that she sensed movement at the end of the pew. She glanced that way.

Collin.

He wore clean jeans and a white shirt and his face was smooth from a recent shave. Had he made it up to his house on the mountain, then? He caught her eye, just for a moment. He didn't smile. But he wasn't scowling, either. She could have stared at him forever.

But she didn't. She forced her eyes front again while he made his way along the pew toward her. He muttered soft apologies as their neighbors slid their legs to the side, giving room for him to pass. Shelby Jenkins, a friend who sometimes worked as a substitute teacher at the elementary school, was sitting on her left.

She heard Collin whisper, "S'cuse me, Shelby..."

Shelby slid over and he took the empty space next to Willa. He smelled of soap and aftershave and her heart just lifted up when he settled in beside her. She couldn't even look at him right then, there were so many strange and powerful emotions chasing themselves around inside her. She had a dopey smile on her face, she just knew it, a totally inappropriate expression for a funeral.

He did that thing—that thing they'd started when they sat out on the town hall steps in the evening—leaning to the side in her direction, nudging her so gently with his shoulder.

She had to press her lips together to keep from letting out a silly squeak of pure joy. Because he wasn't all that mad at her, after all, evidently.

Because now she knew that everything between them would be all right.

The service continued. Pastor Alderson invited folks to stand and a say a word or two, to speak their testimony on the life of Hunter McGee.

In the front pew, Thelma stood first. Her voice only shook a little as she spoke of how proud she was to be Hunter's mom, as she told a little story about his boyhood, about his dreams for Rust Creek Falls, about how his one true love had died too young and he'd never known the joy of fatherhood, but he had loved Rust Creek Falls. It had meant the world to him that the people of his town had elected him their mayor.

When Thelma was finished, others stood, one at a time, taking turns, telling about growing up with Hunter, about the many ways that he'd helped them or made their lives richer, somehow. Each of the town council members took a turn, with Nathan Crawford going first. Willa had thought she might speak, but then it turned out that the things she would have shared were already said. She felt content to let it be.

The testimonies went on for over an hour. Until finally, one of the older Daltons sat back down after speaking of how Hunter had pitched in to help repair the Masonic Hall. There was a silence in the chapel. Willa thought that the sharing was done.

But then Collin shifted at her side. She blinked and looked over at him as he rose to his feet. He looked a little nervous, she thought, and so very handsome and dear.

Everyone turned and watched him expectantly. As a rule, Collin Traub didn't speak out in public, but Willa knew they all had to be remembering his impassioned arguments in the town hall the other day and eager to hear whatever he might contribute now.

Collin cleared his throat. "I just want to say that Hunter McGee was a man we all thought of as a friend. He had a way about him. He was wise and he was patient, too. But he had a killer sense of humor and that gleam in his eye that let you know he didn't judge you and he wanted only the best for you, no matter how big a troublemaker you might happen to be." Collin paused then, and glanced around with an abashed sort of expression.

People grinned and a few even chuckled.

Collin continued, "Somehow, Hunter always managed to get to the heart of an issue without ever choosing sides. He had a rare sort of fairness in him and a willingness to help. Yes, he's gone to a better place now. But at the same time, it seems to me that he's still here with us in spirit, that he's working beside us now, in this tough time when we need men like him the most. We haven't really lost him." Collin fisted his hand and laid it against his heart. "He's right here." He raised his hand and touched his temple. "And he's in here, too, in all of us. We can remember all he showed us about how to live and work together. And we can be grateful that we have his fine example to carry us forward as we work side by side to rebuild this town."

Collin sat back down.

There was a silence. Somebody murmured, "Oh, yeah."

And someone else said, "Tell it, Collin."

Several more "Oh, yeahs" and one or two "Praise Gods" followed.

Collin turned and looked at Willa, which was when she realized she was staring at him. He gave her a scowl, mouthed, *What?*

She only shrugged and faced front again and tried not to feel smug that he had just proved the truth in what she'd said to him the night before.

* * *

Outside after the service, Thelma embraced Collin and laid her hand gently on the side of his face. "Such a fine young man," she told him softly. And then she raised her lacy handkerchief to dab at her wet eyes.

A couple of the Dalton men clasped his shoulder as they filed out of the chapel. Willa observed all this and tried really hard not to feel too self-righteous about the things she'd said the night before. He really was a born leader, but what he did with that talent had to be of his own choosing.

Paige touched her arm. "I'd ask you to come sit with me for lunch, but I have a feeling you've got plans."

Willa gave her a hug and they parted. Buster whined at her, eager to be released from the iron bench where she'd leashed him. She went over and got him, crouching to pet him and make a fuss over him for being so good during the long church service.

"Rumor has it the church ladies are serving pizza for lunch today," Collin said from behind her.

Buster whined and wagged his tail in greeting and Willa's heart seemed to do a sort of forward roll under her breastbone. She asked, without turning, "Does the rumor mention pepperoni?"

"Yeah. Pepperoni and sausage, too." He dropped to a crouch at her side. Buster wiggled closer to him and head-butted his hand. Collin scratched the dog behind both ears and Buster lolled his tongue in doggy bliss.

Willa felt terribly shy suddenly. She stared at his hands as he petted her dog. "I, um, should walk Buster first...."

"Hey."

Her throat had a big lump in it. She gulped it down and made herself meet those low-lidded black eyes. "Hmm?"

"We okay, you and me?"

She remembered that she was going to apologize. "I lectured you. I shouldn't have done that. I'm sorry."

"You got nothing to be sorry for." His voice was low and more than a little rough. The sound of it sent a warm, lovely shiver running underneath her skin. He added, "You got a right to your opinion."

"But, well, you did get mad."

He smiled then, one of those slow smiles of his, the kind that used to make all the girls back in high school sigh and fan themselves. "So then, *I'm* sorry. I had no right at all to jump all over you for telling the truth as you see it." He kept on looking at her, a deep look that made her whole body feel sensitized, excited. Wonderfully alive. "Forgive me?"

That lump was back in her throat again. She gulped a second time to clear it. "I do. And yes. We're okay."

"Whew."

She felt her mouth tremble into a smile that answered his. "Did you go up to your house, then?"

"No. I'm hoping I'll get to that tomorrow. This morning, I went out to the Triple T and had breakfast with the hands. They got the wells in working order, so I had a shower, too." He swept upward and she stood, too. "Let's walk this dog," he said.

"Good idea."

"The park? We can let him run."

"Perfect."

After lunch, the governor dropped in—literally—in a helicopter.

The chopper landed in the middle of Main Street and the governor emerged, waving and smiling, trailed by a guy in a FEMA vest and another, more muscular fellow in dark glasses. Waving as he went, the governor ran up and stood on the town hall steps, where the town council members waited. He shook hands with each of them.

And then he gave a little speech—more of a pep talk, really. He said the same things Nathan was always saying: that road crews and the power and telephone companies were working around-the-clock to get the roads open and services back online. He asked everyone to sit tight until services were restored and, whenever possible, to stay in the Rust Creek Falls Valley until the roads were declared safe for travel.

He praised their spirit of independence, their ability to roll up their sleeves and do for themselves. Since the good people of Rust Creek Falls seemed to be managing better than most in the stricken areas, he could see that the Red Cross and the National Guard wouldn't be needed there— not at that point anyway.

After the governor spoke, the FEMA guy talked about the services FEMA offered and the progress of the cleanup. And then, with more smiling and waving, the three visitors ran back and boarded the helicopter and off they went.

Collin leaned close and said in her ear, "Wasn't that inspiring?" She gave him a look and left it at that. And then he said, "I was thinking we could try and see what we can salvage from Gage's house."

She wanted to grab him and hug him—for being so generous, for thinking of her poor brother, who had to be worried sick about now and was no doubt moving heaven and earth to get back to town. "Yes. Please. Let's do that."

The church ladies had several boxes they could spare. So she and Collin put them in the back of his pickup and headed for the ranch, where they worked until after five packing up things at Gage's and putting them with Willa's boxes in her father's work shed.

They made it back to town in time for dinner at the

church. As they ate beans and rice with ham, Nathan got up and proudly announced that cell phone service was restored. He reminded them of the places that had generators where they might charge their batteries. People applauded the news—and then hurried off to find the phones they'd stopped carrying around with them for the past three days.

In the pickup, Collin called his mother first. Willa had run out with him and ended up sitting in the passenger seat beside him as he nodded and listened, and seemed to be having trouble getting a word in edgewise. He kept trying to tell his mom what had happened there at home, but Ellie Traub had never been the quiet type. As soon as he started talking, she would get going again and he ended up mostly saying, "Yeah. Okay. All right. That's good, Mom. Really…"

When he finally said goodbye, he reported to Willa that his mom, his dad and his brothers were fine. "They got the rain down there in Thunder Canyon," he said, "but flooding was minimal. Mom says they're willing to wait a few more days until the governor gives the go-ahead. But if the okay doesn't come soon, they're heading for home." He added that the people of Thunder Canyon were already talking about ways to help Rust Creek Falls with flood cleanup and the rebuilding that would follow.

And then he handed her the phone. "Go on. Call your folks."

Again, she had a really strong urge to hug him. But instead she started dialing.

Lavinia Christensen cried when Willa said hello. "We've been calling and calling," she sobbed. And then she wanted to know why Willa wasn't calling from her own cell.

Willa explained that she'd lost it in the flood. "This is Collin's cell."

Her mother sniffled. "Collin *Traub?*"

"Yes." She cast Collin a warm glance. "He's been great to me, Mom. Wonderful." Collin sent her one of those *knock-it-off* looks when he heard her praising him. She pretended not to notice.

Her mom was kind of sputtering. "Well, I, ahem. The Traubs are good people."

"They certainly are—and if you need to reach me, just call this number. Collin will make sure I get back to you until I can get a phone of my own."

"I…I will. Yes. Of course."

Willa assured her mom that she was all right and that the ranch house was fine and so was the barn. She said that most of the stock had survived the flood and the neighbors had all pitched in to keep the animals fed and to clean up the mess. Her mom cried some more when she heard the bad news about Willa's house and Gage's place.

It turned out her folks were still in Livingston, waiting for news that the roads were clear. Gage, however, had set out for home.

When Willa called him, she had to explain all over again that he should call her on Collin's phone for the time being. He started quizzing her about Collin.

She cut him short. "What about you? Where are you now?"

He said he'd been held up three times so far with washed-out bridges and roads, but he wasn't giving up and had spent each night since the flood in a different town. Willa got teary eyed then and told him about the condition of his house—and hers. Her brother said he loved her and not to cry and he would be there as soon as he could. He said he'd visited the sheriff's stations in the towns where he'd stayed and used their radio systems to contact his office. So he'd known that she was all right and he'd been told of the death of Hunter McGee.

When he mentioned Mayor McGee, Willa started crying all over again. She'd been dry-eyed at the funeral, but there was something about her brother's voice. She could tell that the mayor's death had hit him hard. Collin hauled a box of tissues from the glove box and passed it to her. She grabbed one and wiped at her streaming eyes.

When she hung up with Gage, she gave the phone back to Collin. He turned on the pickup so he could hook up his car charger and then, with the phone plugged in, he called a couple of his brothers in Thunder Canyon and then his brother Sutter, in Washington State.

When he hung up, he said in a tone that dared her to argue, "I think a lot of Sutter. He's a damn good man."

Willa only nodded. There were people in town who didn't approve of the stand Sutter had taken when their older brother Forrest went off to fight in Iraq. And then there was the way he'd broken Paige's heart. But still. Willa had always liked Sutter and if he and Collin were on good terms, well, that was just fine with her.

Collin narrowed those almost-black eyes at her and his full mouth curved down at the corners. "You got something on your mind, Willa, you ought to just go ahead and say it."

Willa answered sweetly, "You love your brother. There is nothing wrong with that."

That evening, the number of citizens requiring emergency shelter was a third what it had been the first night. FEMA had brought in some trailers that day for people to stay in temporarily. And more people had either left town to stay with relatives or moved in with friends. A lucky few had discovered that the damage to their homes wasn't bad enough to keep them from moving back in.

Willa and Collin stayed in the town hall again that

night. After the lights were out, she took Buster and went to join Collin under the stars.

"Been waiting for you," he said when she dropped down beside him.

A little thrill shivered through her at his words and she had to remind herself not to be an idiot. It wasn't a man-woman kind of thing between them. They were friends. Good friends, amazingly. But that was all. He wasn't interested in her in *that* way and he never had been.

She wrapped her arms around her knees and rested her chin on them. "Are you still planning to go up the mountain tomorrow?"

"Yeah. In the afternoon. It should be fine up there. The generator automatically kicks in when the power goes out, so what's in the fridge and the freezer stays cold. I've got a freezer full of food I'll bring down and donate to the church kitchen."

She stared at him, thinking how smoking hot he was—because, hey, even if they were just friends, there was no law that said a girl couldn't look. She could get lost in those eyes of his. And even in the darkness, his hair had a shine to it. And it was so thick.

That night four years ago, at the Ace in the Hole, before he laughed at her and told her to get lost, they'd danced to a couple of slow numbers together. She remembered so clearly the feel of his hard, hot shoulder beneath her hand. His lips had looked soft and dangerous, both at once. And the scent of him: incomparable, a heady mix of aftershave, man and something temptingly wild. The rush of blood through her veins had been dizzying. And she would never forget her powerful desire to slide her fingers upward, over the hot flesh of his neck and into that thick, crow-black hair of his.

He asked, "Do I have dirt on my nose?"

She chuckled, the sound surprisingly husky to her own ears. "No. Why?"

He held her gaze as though he never planned to look away. "You're staring at me."

Right. She supposed that she was. She went on staring and told him way too dreamily, "Buster and I are going with you."

"Going with me where?"

"Up to your house tomorrow."

Those thick inky brows drew together. "It's not a good idea."

Too bad. He wasn't talking her out of it. But for now, she played along. "Why not?"

"The road up there is bound to be a mess. It could be dangerous."

"All the more reason you shouldn't go alone."

"You're going to protect me, are you?"

She braced her chin on her hand. "I am. Absolutely. You're a big, tough guy and all, I know. But even tough guys sometimes need a little help."

The way he was looking at her now, she could almost imagine that he did think of her *that* way. Which probably meant she was being an idiot again. But so what? There were a lot worse things than being an idiot. A girl could live her whole life without ever getting her fingers into Collin's black hair. That would be sad. Immeasurably so.

Now he was looking stern. "It's not a good idea."

"You already said that."

"I'll probably end up staying up there overnight."

"So? I'll take the sleeping bag from my cot. It will be fine."

He seemed a little insulted. "I have a guest room—and believe it or not, it has a bed in it, complete with sheets and blankets and pillows."

"Wonderful. So it's settled."

He wasn't going for it. "I told you. You need to stay here."

"We'll see...."

"I mean it, Willa. You are not going up the mountain with me."

The next morning, Collin rejoined his team.

Before he left to help with cleanup down in the area around the flooded clinic, Willa told him that she and Paige and some of the other teachers had been asked to reconvene summer school. Since the day would be a clear one, they would hold their classes in Rust Creek Falls Park. On rainy days, classes would be hosted by some of the parents—and a few of the teachers, as well.

When he came in for lunch in the church, he returned a call from his mom, one from his brother Clay and another from Sutter. Then he made calls to a few top CT Saddles customers. He apologized for the fact that he would be filling their orders late. They'd all heard about the flood and told him not to worry, to stay safe and take his time.

Willa wasn't there at the church for lunch. He ignored the little curl of disappointment in his chest when he didn't see her. Every day he was with her, it got easier to let himself think that there was more going on between them than friendship.

There wasn't. Once things got back to normal, her bigshot boyfriend would show up. She would realize what that other guy could offer her and she would end up with his ring on her finger. Which was the way it should be. Willa deserved the best.

Dolly Tabor, one of his teammates on the rescue-turned-cleanup crew, had kids in summer school. She mentioned that the church ladies were delivering the school lunches to the park.

So, great, he thought. Willa was having lunch with the kids in the park.

He asked Dolly, real casual-like, when summer school would be over for the day. Dolly said at three.

Collin made his plans accordingly. He knew Willa and he knew her ways. She thought she was going up the mountain with him. And there was more than one good reason why he couldn't let that happen. For one thing, the trip up there was likely to be hazardous. He wasn't putting Willa in danger. And then, if they ended up stuck at his place for the night, well, that would present a whole other kind of danger.

It was one thing to be alone with her for an hour out on the town hall steps at night, or while they worked side by side hauling stuff out of her brother's flooded house. It was another thing altogether to spend the night with her at his place, just the two of them, alone on Falls Mountain.

Uh-uh. That would be asking for the kind of trouble they weren't going to get into together. He had to face reality here. He'd done what he could to help her through the worst of it after the flood. Her family would be back in town any day now. From what she'd said about Gage working his way north, her brother could be home already.

Collin needed to start getting a little distance from her. He had to stop spending so much time with her, had to give up those nighttime talks out on the town hall steps. He needed to stop kidding himself that it was innocent, that they were just hanging out, joking around a little before turning in.

It wasn't innocent—not for him anyway. Every night it got harder to keep his hands to himself. If he didn't get some distance, he would end up making a move on her.

He knew she really wanted to be his friend and all that. But he wanted more than friendship and where was that going to go? He liked his relationships with women to be simple—and short.

Nothing with Willa was simple. So he would put an end to it, make sure it never even had a chance to get started. She would be hurt and probably angry with him for taking off up the mountain without a word to her. But too bad.

It was for the best.

He got Jerry Dobbs aside and said he was heading up to his place. Jerry clapped him on the back and told him to be careful on the road up there.

Across the street at the town hall, he collected the plastic bag full of clothes and personal items he'd left under his cot. Marjorie Hanke was there, so he told her he wouldn't be needing the cot anymore.

And that was it. He was free to get the hell outta town.

He shouldered the bag and headed for his truck in the parking lot in the back, feeling more down than he should have, wishing things could be different and calling himself ten kinds of fool to want a thing he was never going to have—and wouldn't know what to do with anyway.

He almost tripped over his own boots when he caught sight of Willa. She was leaning against his rear wheel well, Buster on one side, her bag of stuff and backpack on the other.

Chapter Eight

She had her arms folded across her middle and her head tipped to the side. The early-afternoon sun brought out bronze highlights in her coffee-colored hair. She gave him a slow once-over. "I knew it."

He glared at her, trying his best to look pissed off. "You knew what?"

"You were just going to sneak away without even telling me. That's not very nice, Collin."

"I did tell you. I told you last night."

She tightened her arms around herself and pressed her lips together. "And I told you that I was going with you." She pushed off the wheel well and stood up straight. "So here I am."

His bag of clothes rustled as he let it slide to the pavement. He was actively ignoring the rapid beating of his heart, the ridiculous surge of happiness that was blasting all through him.

She really did want to go with him. She wasn't letting him get away without a fight.

But so what? He needed to focus on the goal: to get her to give up this insanity and go back to the park. "No. It's a bad idea. And aren't you supposed to be over at the park teaching summer school?"

"Shelby Jenkins is helping out. She took over for me."

"But you—"

"I'm going, Collin. Don't mess with me on this."

How in hell could he do the right thing if she kept pushing him to screw up? A voice in the back of his mind kept chanting, *She wants to come, she wants to come.* And the bad-acting idiot inside him kept whispering, *Man, if it's what she wants, why not?*

He ground his teeth together. "I wasn't planning to come back until tomorrow."

"That's okay. I've got my stuff. And you've got a guest room. It's all good."

"I thought you had summer school."

"I told you, Shelby's helping out. I explained to her that I was going up the mountain with you and we might not make it back until later tomorrow. She'll take my kids for me. I'm covered."

"Get real, Willa. You go up the mountain with me and spend the night, the whole town will be talking when you come back down. The Traub bad boy and the kindergarten teacher. I can hear them all now."

She laughed. Like it was funny. He watched the dimples flash in her pink cheeks and he thought about licking them. "I'm sure they're already talking. We've practically been joined at the hip since the flood. And in case you've forgotten, we spent a whole night together in my dad's barn and the world didn't come to an end."

In case he'd forgotten? He would never forget. Especially not what had happened in the morning. His fly. Her hand. Sitting there on the edge of that hay bale, willing the humiliating bulge in his pants to go down. He strove for calmness and reasonableness. "We had no choice then. It was the barn or drowning. This—you and me, up the mountain together? That's a clear choice."

Her mouth had pinched up tight. "What is going on with you? Suddenly you're acting like it's 1955 or something. Like you're worried about my reputation, which is excellent and unimpeachable, thank you very much."

Unimpeachable? She really did talk like a schoolteacher sometimes. Which got him hot. Real hot. But he wasn't going to think about that. "It's a very small town, Willa. People here are conservative. You know that as well as I do."

She just wouldn't back down. "You're making way too much of this. Everyone in town knows me and respects me. No one has—or will—judge me for being your friend." In her excitement, she unfolded her arms and waved them around. "In fact, Crawfords aside, this town happens to think the world of *you,* in case you haven't been paying attention."

"That doesn't mean they won't gossip."

"Oh, please. You never cared about people talking before."

"I care now."

"I don't believe you. Here's the way I see it. If you really don't want me along, if you're sick of having me around and you want to get rid of me, that's one thing. If you just *have* to have a little time to yourself, well, okay. I can accept that. But all this other stuff you've been handing me about my reputation and how it's 'a bad idea,' how I should be over at the park instead of with you, well, you can just stop that, Collin Traub. You can just…get a little bit straight with me. Please." And with that, she blew out a hard breath and flopped back against the wheel well again, folding her arms across her chest once more.

"Crap, Willa." He folded his own arms. He told himself that this argument was over and he'd won it. Because she'd just given him the out that he needed. He only had to say he didn't want her with him, that he preferred to be alone. He only had to lie to her.

Which he had no problem doing, under the circumstances. After all, it was for her own good.

Buster whined and stared up at him hopefully. And Willa simply waited.

He opened his mouth and said, "Fine. Get in the truck."

Willa had always loved the drive up Falls Mountain. It was paved only a part of the way up, but when the pavement ran out, the dirt surface was well tended and the ride reasonably smooth—or at least, it always had been until the flood.

The narrow road proceeded in a series of switchbacks under the tall evergreens. Now and then a switchback would lead out onto a rocky point before doubling back. You could park your vehicle and stroll to the edge and gaze out over the whole of the Rust Creek Falls Valley below, a beautiful sight that never failed to steal her breath away.

And then, two-thirds of the way to the summit, you would round a sharp turn—and see the falls up ahead, hear their splendid, endless roar. The air would turn misty and the sun would slip through the spaces between the trees and light up the falling water with a million pinpricks of shining light.

This trip, however, wasn't so much about the scenery. This was about getting safely to Collin's place and deal-

ing with whatever obstacles the big storm might have left
in its wake.

As they set out, you could cut the tension between them
with a knife. He was pretty steamed at her. He seethed
where he sat, strong hands viselike on the wheel, staring
out the windshield with fierce concentration, never once
glancing in her direction.

And frankly, well, she was annoyed with him, too. She
only wanted to help. And he could have gotten rid of her
just by honestly saying he didn't want her around.

But no. It had to be all about protecting her good name.
Please. She wasn't buying that silliness and he should give
her more credit than to imagine she would.

So she spent the first part of the ride until the pavement
ran out keeping very quiet, not pushing her luck with him.
Buster was in the back and they'd taken their bags of stuff
up front with them. She had them both on her side, his on
the floor, hers tucked in next to her with her pack against
the console. She leaned on the door armrest and stared in-
tently out at the trees and the occasional glimpses of blue
Montana sky and told herself that when they got to his
place, they would talk it out.

She was so busy staring out her side window she didn't
see the first downed tree until he stopped the truck.

"This'll take a while," he said sourly. "Hope you brought
a book or maybe a little knitting." He leaned on his door
and got out.

Oh, for crying out loud. As if she hadn't helped her father and brother clear any number of fallen trees off the
ranch in her lifetime. She'd come ready to work. She had
on her old lace-up work boots from the box at her mother's.
Her jeans were sturdy and her sleeves were long. She dug
around in her plastic bag until she found the pair of work
gloves she'd borrowed from Thelma.

Collin's chain saw roared out as she left the truck. Buster was already down from the bed and sniffing around on the side of the road. He would probably take off if she didn't put him on his leash, but he looked so happy and free, she didn't have the heart to tie him up.

So she decided to leave him free, but keep an eye on him. If he started ranging too far, she'd call him back.

She went to join Collin at the fallen tree.

Willa hauled and Collin expertly stripped the branches from the log, then cut the log into sections. When he was done with the saw, he helped her drag off the brush.

As they cleared the brush, he finally started speaking to her again.

"I hate to waste firewood," he said. "But I've got more than enough up at my place."

They left the stove-size logs and the cleanest parts of the branches stacked on the side of the road for anyone in need to collect. It wasn't that big of a tree. In an hour, they had the roadway clear.

She took off her gloves. With her sleeve, she wiped sweat from her brow. And then she remembered to check on the dog. Wouldn't you know? "Buster's run off again."

He put two fingers between his lips and let loose with a whistle so high and piercing, she put her hands over her ears. As soon as he stopped, Buster came bounding out of the trees. He ran straight to Collin and dropped to his haunches in front of him.

"Good dog," Collin said. "Stay."

Willa blinked in admiration. "Wow."

"I used to call Libby that way. Never failed."

She remembered his dog. A sweet-natured brown-spotted white mutt that followed him everywhere. "What happened to Libby?"

"Lost her last winter. She was pretty old."

"I'm sorry. She always seemed so devoted to you."

"Yeah. I guess she was." He made a low, thoughtful sound. "I still miss her. Now and then I think I see her out of the corner of my eye. I forget for a split second that she's gone and I turn to call her to me...."

Willa was nodding, thinking of Mr. Puffy, the barn kitten she'd claimed as her own when she was five. Puffs had become a house cat and lived to be seventeen. "Oh, I know the feeling. It's like they're still with you, somehow, even though you know that they're gone...."

"That's right." He regarded her for a moment that seemed to stretch out into forever. He didn't seem angry anymore and she realized that neither was she.

"Thirsty?" he asked at last.

At her nod, he turned and started walking, pausing only to signal her with a wave of his powerful arm.

"Come on, Buster." She fell in behind him.

A trail took off below the road. They followed it, pine needles crunching under their feet, Buster taking up the rear.

Maybe two hundred yards later, they came to a ditch full of rushing, clear water. They both got down on their bellies to drink. Buster tried to join them, but she shooed him downstream a ways.

It was so good, that water. Fresh and cold and perfect. When they'd both drunk their fill, they scrambled upright and returned to the pickup. They got in, Buster hopped in the back and off they went.

After that, it was stop and go. There were three more downed trees to clear and any number of rutted, rough places scattered with rock, where instant streams had formed during the storm, destroying the road surface, dragging debris. Often they would have to get out and clear away the biggest of the boulders. It was dusty, thirsty work. But there were plenty of ditches to drink from once the road was passable again.

At one of the outlook points, they found that the road had fallen away at the edge of the cliff. It was just wide enough for the pickup to proceed. Twice on that narrow spot, she felt the back wheel on her side slip over the edge.

But Collin had done a lot of driving on narrow, treacherous mountain roads. He knew when to change gears and when to hit the gas. Both times, there was only a split second of falling and then the truck gained purchase again and they went on.

They didn't reach the falls until a little after seven. More than two hours of daylight remained to them, so they stopped the truck. Buster following behind them, they walked close to admire the view.

"It was twice as wide when I came down on the Fourth," he told her, as they stared at the wall of shining water.

"So beautiful." She stood near the edge, looking over, entranced by the plumes of mist that rose from the rocks below. A prayerful kind of feeling came over her. It happened every time she visited the falls.

When they turned for the truck, he said, "It's not that far now." He put down the gate long enough for Buster to hop in the back again. Then he joined her in the cab.

Around the next sharp curve another tree lay, uprooted, across the road. They got out and got to work. By the time that one was out of the way and he was starting up the truck again, it was nine-thirty and the sky was steadily darkening.

He sent her a glance across the console. "We're there in five minutes, barring more crap in the road."

She grinned. "I will pray for an absence of crap."

"Good thinking." He started to shift into gear—and

then stopped. "I would be sleeping in this truck tonight, three fallen trees back, if not for you."

"If more crap happens, you could still end up sleeping in this truck."

He arched a brow. "That was a thank-you."

She felt hugely gratified. "Well, all right. You're welcome."

"And an apology."

"Which is accepted."

They did that thing, the eye-contact thing. The moment stretched out. Finally, he said, "I'm glad you're with me."

"That is so nice to hear." She said it softly, a little bit breathlessly. "Because I'm glad to be with you."

They shared another endless glance. The world seemed a fine place, exciting, a place where anything might happen. A place where a girl's lifelong forbidden fantasies might just come true.

Friends, she reminded herself. *We are friends and that's all.*

But the way he was looking at her, well, a girl could definitely get ideas.

"We should get going," he said.

"Yeah," she whispered, as though there was some kind of secret they were sharing.

He buckled his seat belt and put it in gear.

The headlights were on, the powerful twin beams cutting the thickening shadows. Everything looked clear up ahead. The road was very steep, though, there at the last. Gravel spun out from under the tires as they kept losing traction. But Collin held it in low, with an even pressure on the gas. They climbed steadily upward, almost there.

"One more switchback," he said. The sharp turn loomed ahead. Tires spinning, gravel flying, the truck slipping to one side and then the other, Collin guided them around it.

They'd made it without having to sleep in the cab. Through the tall, thick trees, she could see the shadowed form of his house up ahead. A light shone in the window, one he must have left on when he raced down the mountain four days ago, a light that still burned because he had a generator.

Lights that wouldn't be turned off promptly at 11:00 p.m. How wonderful. She had a couple of bestsellers she'd borrowed from Paige in the bottom of her bag. Why, she might read late into the night if she felt like it. She might blow-dry her hair—well, if only she'd thought to scare up a blow-dryer.

And not only would there be light that was hers to control, she would sleep on a real bed, in a real bedroom, without all those other people nearby snoring or mumbling in their sleep....

The truck slid, snapping her back to reality, and she felt a stomach-turning lurch as the rear wheels lost contact with the road. Collin swore under his breath.

The truck—and the world—hung suspended by two front wheels.

It was bad. She knew it. She tasted copper in her suddenly dry mouth. Her heart boomed, the sound a roar in her ears.

It took her a second or two to realize what had happened. As they came around the turn, the road had collapsed on the cliff side, just dropped off and fallen away under the back wheels.

"Oh, dear Lord," she whispered, and nothing more. Words were lost to her.

The truck was sliding backward, the bed dropping, dragging. They were going to go over the cliff, tail first....

But Collin hit the gas then. The front wheels grabbed

and held. Praise heaven for four-wheel drive. He eased the throttle even higher.

The truck lurched again, jumping forward this time, grabbing at the road. The front wheels had good purchase. Gravel flew every which way, grinding grooves in the dirt, but they did move forward. The truck leveled out as the rear wheels reached the road again.

He had done it. He had all four tires on solid ground again. She heard him suck in a long breath and realized that she was doing the same thing.

"We're okay," she whispered, as though to say it too loudly would somehow send them rolling backward over the cliff once more.

But then she glanced through the rear window. Buster wasn't there.

Chapter Nine

"Collin, Buster's gone!"

Collin hit the brake as Willa's door flew open. "Willa. Wait…" But she didn't wait. She was out the door before the truck came to a full stop. "Be careful at the cliff edge!" he shouted.

Not that she heard him. She was already out and running back to that last almost-deadly turn.

He slammed it in Park, turned off the engine, and shoved in the parking brake, grabbing a flashlight from the glove box before he jumped out and ran after her. "Stay back from the edge, damn it, Willa!"

She was already there, craning to see over, calling the dog. "Buster! Buster, here, boy!"

He went to her, grabbed her arm and hauled her back a few feet. She tried to shake him off, but he held on. "Don't," he warned. "It could be dangerous."

"But Buster…" Frantic tears clogged her voice.

He shone the light on the ground at the edge he'd dragged her back from. Hard to tell, but it looked pretty solid. "Careful, okay?" Reluctantly, he let her go. "Just take it easy... slow."

Together they moved toward the cliff again. He shone the flashlight down into the darkness, spotted the small ledge created by two joined sets of tree roots maybe thirty feet down. Buster was young and agile. All he would have needed was something to break his fall and chances were he would have been okay.

No sign of him on that ledge, though.

"Buster!" Willa called again, more frantic than before. "Buster!"

Not knowing what else to do, Collin put his fingers between his teeth and let out with the whistle that always brought the dogs running. He glanced over at Willa, at the tears already streaming down her soft cheeks.

He was just about to start blaming himself, when he heard the scrabbling sounds over the side, up the road a little, near where he'd stopped the truck.

Willa whipped around toward the noise. "Buster!" Collin turned the light on her, so she wouldn't trip on the uneven road surface as she took off again in the direction of the sounds.

About then, the white dog scrambled up over the bank, apparently unhurt. He got to the road and shook himself.

"Buster!" Willa dropped to a crouch and threw her arms around him. The dog whined and swiped his sloppy tongue all over her face and wagged his tail as though he'd just done something pretty spectacular.

And maybe he had.

Collin went to them. With another happy cry, Willa jumped up and threw her arms around *him*. "He's fine. He's okay. Oh, thank God." She buried her face against his neck.

He held her close and tried not to let himself think about how right she always felt in his arms.

Buster rode the last short stretch inside the cab, sandwiched between Willa's feet.

Collin didn't much care for dogs in the front. But he wasn't complaining. A couple of minutes after they'd piled in the truck again, Collin parked in the flat space not far from the front door to his house.

"We made it," Willa said softly. "I can hardly believe it."

He reached over and grabbed his bag out from under Buster's big feet. "I'm starving. Let's scare up something to eat."

Inside, he got Libby's bowl down from a cupboard and filled it with kibble leftover from last winter. Buster went right to work on the food.

Willa stood holding her black plastic bag, her pack slung on one shoulder, staring out the wall of windows that faced the valley. With the lamps on and the antler chandelier overhead casting its warm glow, there was nothing to see but her reflection in the glass. "This is so beautiful, Collin."

He left the open kitchen area and went to stand beside her. "Pretty dark down there tonight. Usually, even with the great room all lit up, you can see the lights of town."

She turned to him, her eyes so soft and bright. "You'll be seeing them again before you know it."

He took her arm and tried not to feel too happy to have her there, in his house, alone. "Come on. I'll show you the guest room and the spare bath."

Her face lit up. "A shower? You mean it?"

"Right this way."

Willa pushed her empty plate away. "Steak. A baked potato. Even a salad." She sent him a mock glare. "And to think, if I hadn't made you bring me along, it would have been macaroni and canned ham all over again."

He gave her one of those grins that always made her pulse speed up. "Is that what the church ladies are serving tonight?"

"I believe so, yes." She sat back and looked around her. The living area was all one room, with a comfy-looking sofa and chairs grouped around a rustic fireplace. He'd built a small fire that crackled cheerfully. Up on the mountain, even summer nights had a bite to them.

The galley-type kitchen had butcher-block counters, the cabinets painted a woodsy green.

She asked, "This place was your uncle's?"

"That's right." He polished off his beer. "Uncle Casper was an independent old coot—and he was always good to me."

She remembered Casper Traub. He had a handlebar mustache and he always wore a white Resistol hat. "A confirmed bachelor."

"Damn straight. Uncle Casper and I got along. We just seemed to understand each other—but I've made a lot of changes to the house since he passed. This area had a wall down the middle before, the kitchen separate from the living room. I like it open. And I had bigger windows put in to take advantage of the view."

"You did a great job." She stared up at all the lights strung on the antler chandelier. "It's comfortable and homey. Inviting, but not cluttered."

"That's good." He gestured with his empty beer bottle. "It's pretty much what I was going for."

"You got it right."

He was watching her. "But not what you expected." It wasn't a question.

She confessed, "Not really. I was thinking you would have more of a woodsy man-cave, to tell the truth."

Twin creases formed between his brows. "It's not a woodsy man-cave?"

"Collin. You can't have a man-cave with all those windows. With a man-cave, there would be stacks of girlie magazines. And the decor would focus on empty liquor bottles lining the walls."

He pretended to look wounded. "You're serious. You see me saving empty liquor bottles to use for decoration, surrounded by girlie magazines...."

"Oh, come on. You know I'm just kidding."

He shrugged and pointed the beer bottle at the big-screen TV. "Well, I've got the right TV anyway. And I get cable up here now, believe it or not—or I do when the cable service isn't down. Even my cell phone works most of the time." He grinned that wicked grin of his. "Admit it. You're impressed."

"Bowled over." She took a small sip of the beer he'd given her. "You miss your uncle?"

He gave her a slow nod. "Every day. He taught me all I know about the business and he left it to me with the house when we lost him. My shop's in the basement."

"*You* make the saddles now?"

He sent her a wounded glance. "Who would if I didn't? You think I keep a bunch of elves down there?"

"Of course not." But she *was* surprised. She'd known that Casper Traub had left everything to his favorite nephew, but somehow she hadn't really thought about what exactly that would mean—and that made her feel a little ashamed. The past few years, she'd been so busy judging him, she'd never stopped to think about who he was as a person, how he might have changed and grown from the wild, rude boy who used to spy on her out in the back pasture.

He got up, got a second beer from the fridge and twisted the top off. "You want one?"

She still had half of hers. "I'm good."

He came back to her and dropped into his chair again. "What? You're having trouble believing that I work for a living?" He took a drink, his Adam's apple sliding up and down in his strong brown throat. "You have one of my saddles in the tack room of your dad's barn."

Yet another surprise. "My dad's precious CT Saddle? *You* made it?"

"I did."

"But he got that saddle three years ago."

"I've been making saddles since before high school. Uncle Casper had me working with him as soon as I was tall enough to stand at a workbench."

"Oh. I...didn't know."

He grunted and shook his head. And she felt really bad. He seemed to sense her distress, and leaned across the table toward her. "What'd I do? Willa, come on. You look like you're about to cry."

She waved a hand. And then she sighed. "You didn't do anything. Honestly. It's only that I'm disappointed in myself, I guess."

"Why?" He asked it so quietly. Like he didn't want to push her, but he really did want an answer.

She gave him the truth. "We live in a very small town, where everyone knows everything about everyone else. Yet, I didn't know you made the most beautiful saddles in Montana. I didn't know much at all about you. In high school, I never wanted anyone to know that I was..." Her throat clutched. She gulped to loosen it. "Um, attracted to you. So I made real sure that I acted like I couldn't care less whenever anyone mentioned your name. That meant I never learned anything about you—about who you really are. Except that everyone said half the girls had been with you and the other half wished they might."

"Willa…" His voice was husky and his eyes were so soft.

She suddenly felt all warm and quivery inside and she had to force herself to say the rest. "And then, well, after that night at the Ace in the Hole, I was just so…bitter. So angry at you. And that meant I kept on not letting myself know anything about you, kept on judging you without even knowing you. It was all just so narrow-minded and, well, *small* of me, you know? And I like to think of myself as an open-minded and fair person. But maybe I'm not. Maybe I'm already just an old busybody, listening to rumors, believing the worst about people. Never stopping to find out what's really going on."

"You're too young to be an old busybody."

She wanted to smile—but he was letting her off too easy. "Don't be nice to me about this. I don't deserve it."

He set down his beer, got up and came around the table to her, dropping to a crouch beside her chair. "Hey." He took her hand. Heat flowed up her arm, into her heart. And lower down, too. "And I have to tell you, I kind of got a kick out of you avoiding me for four years."

She groaned. "You didn't."

"Oh, yeah. You were so determined. I'd walk in a room—and out you went through the other door."

"But still. Be honest. It did hurt your feelings a little, didn't it?"

"I survived."

She looked down at their joined hands and then back up into those beautiful deep-set eyes of his. "So you forgive me?"

"There's nothing to forgive." He seemed so earnest right then, his face tipped up to her, that lock of hair falling over his forehead the way it always seemed to do.

She couldn't stop herself—she didn't *want* to stop herself. She dared to smooth it back. It was just as she'd always imagined it might be—thick and warm and so very silky, a little bit damp from his recent shower. "I don't know what I would have done in these past few days without you."

"You would have been fine."

She grew bolder. She pressed her palm to his cheek. It was smooth, freshly shaved. "I would have drowned that first day. You know it as well as I do."

"Uh-uh. You're too ornery to drown."

"You think so?"

"Oh, yeah. You would have gotten that door open and made it to safety." His voice was rough and tender, both at once.

Her breath caught in her throat. *A kiss,* she thought.

What could a kiss hurt?

Just one. No harm in that.

His gaze seemed to burn her and his sensual mouth was slightly parted. He smelled so good, clean and fresh and manly.

"Oh, Collin..." She dared to bend closer—and then blinked in surprise when he caught her wrist and gently guided her hand away from his face.

He swept to his feet, grabbed up his empty plate and the salad bowl and carried them to the sink. Without turning back to look at her, he said, "You want to watch a movie or something? I've got a bookcase full of DVDs."

Her face was flaming. Talk about making a fool of herself.

What was her problem anyway? The poor guy couldn't be nice to her without her trying to jump his bones.

She reminded herself, as she'd reminded herself about a hundred times in the past few days, that he liked her and he was her friend. But he was not interested in her in *that* way and she needed get that in her head and keep it there.

His friendship mattered to her. She was not going to lose him because she couldn't stop throwing herself at him.

He still had his back to her as he rinsed out the salad bowl and then scraped off his plate in the garbage and stuck it in the dishwasher.

She picked up her plate and carried it over there.

He took it from her. "So. Movie?"

"As long as I get to choose which one."

He did let her choose. His taste ranged from horror to Western and action/adventure to raunchy guy comedies. Not a tender romance to be found.

She chose a Jason Statham shoot-'em-up. It was fast-paced and entertaining. When it was over, she let Buster out and waited on the step for him to take care of business. Back inside, she told Collin good-night and headed for the guest room, Buster at her heels.

The bed was big and comfortable and she'd worked hard all afternoon. She should have gone right to sleep.

But, no. She kept thinking about what an idiot she'd been at the dinner table, kept wondering if she should have done something other than pretend for the rest of the evening that nothing had happened.

Then again, if not that, what? Certainly they didn't have to discuss the fact that she regretted throwing herself at him and would try really, really hard not to do it again.

Sheesh. How pathetic. That was a conversation she just didn't need to have.

Willa plumped her pillow and turned over. Then she turned over again. Then she sat up and pushed back all the covers but the sheet.

Then she pulled the covers back over herself again.

It was hopeless. Sleep was not in the offing. She turned on the lamp and got her book from the bag and tried to read.

But she couldn't concentrate. The clock by the bed said ten after one.

Maybe she could find some cocoa in the kitchen. Or just some milk to heat up. Or *something*.

She threw back the covers. On the rug by the bed, Buster lifted his head—and then settled back to sleep with a soft doggy sigh. She yanked on a worn plaid shirt over the camisole and knit shorts she'd worn to sleep in and decided to just go barefoot. Flip-flops made too much noise anyway. She didn't want to take the chance of disturbing Collin. At least one of them should be allowed to get a decent night's sleep.

His bedroom was down at the far end of the hall. The door was open, but there was no light on in there.

Not that it mattered. She had no intention of bothering him. Willa went the other way, out to the great room and into the kitchen.

She flicked on the light and was heading for the fridge when Collin said, "Go back to bed, Willa. How many times do I have to tell you? I'm not having sex with you."

With a cry of surprise, she whirled toward the sound of his voice. He stood over in the living area, wearing his jeans and nothing else, his strong legs planted wide apart, hands linked behind him, staring out the wall of windows on the dark town below.

She didn't know whether to laugh or throw something at him…but wait.

On second thought, she did know. The latter. Definitely.

Okay, she'd tried to kiss him and she shouldn't have. But he didn't have to be mean about it. In fact, the more she thought about it, the more she realized how sick and tired she was of hearing him say he wouldn't have sex with her. It had been funny, for a while—but tonight, well, it was downright hurtful.

She zipped around the island counter that separated the living area from the kitchen and marched right for him. "Oh, please. Will you give that up? I couldn't sleep, that's all." She halted a few feet from him and glared at his broad back. "Nobody here is thinking about sex."

"Speak for yourself." Slowly, he turned and faced her. She gasped at the yearning she saw in his eyes.

Chapter Ten

Collin couldn't take it anymore.

The sight of her, in those little purple velour shorts and that skimpy, lacy top…well, it was too much. Even if she did have on an old plaid shirt over the top. That old shirt wasn't hiding anything. She hadn't even bothered to button it up.

He could see her nipples very clearly, poking at him through the thin fabric, could make out the tempting, ripe curves of her breasts. She was driving him crazy, that was what she was doing. He'd held out for years, done the right thing by her, even though she'd ended up hating him for it.

But tonight, well, it was too much.

And hadn't he known that it would be? She shouldn't have kept after him until he brought her up here with him. She shouldn't have tried to kiss him. Shouldn't have come out of her room dressed in those soft purple shorts and that skimpy silky top that didn't hide a damn thing.

He burned. He was on fire—to take her breasts in his two hands. To touch the skin of her thighs, to rub his rough palms along all that smooth softness, to inch his fingers upward, under the hem of those shorts, to touch her at last where he knew she would be hot and wet and waiting for him.

He wanted her, wanted sweet Willa Christensen, probably always had, from way back. From before he even realized what he was wanting. Oh, yeah. He wanted her.

And to hell with what was best for her. She wanted him, too. She'd made that more than clear on more than one occasion.

Tonight, he was going to give her exactly what she wanted.

Reaching out, he took her by the arms and hauled her up close to him, reveling in the feel of her body brushing along the front him, making him ache all the harder for her.

He brought his face good and close to hers, so close he could taste the heat of her breath. "You should have stayed in town tonight like I told you to, you know that, don't you?"

She licked her lips and gulped. "Um. I…" Her eyes were so wide. Wide and soft and wanting.

Those eyes of hers called to him. They always had. Those eyes said she knew him, was waiting for him to finally reach out and take her. Those eyes said she would do anything he wanted.

Truth to tell, those eyes had always scared the crap out of him. They seemed to hint of things a guy like him didn't deserve to know.

Things like forever. Things like a lifetime.

Things he wasn't planning for. He lived his life alone.

Which led back around to the basic issue: he shouldn't be doing this.

But too bad. He *was* doing this.

He was through making jokes about it, through trying to discourage her from wanting a little hot fun with the town troublemaker. If she wanted him so much, who was he to tell her no?

"Oh, Collin…" She said it so softly. So willingly. And then her eyes changed. All at once, they weren't so open and sweet anymore. They'd gone determined. They were sparking fire. "No. Uh-uh. I should *not* have stayed down in town. I'm here with you and I'm *glad* I'm here."

Some final scrap of that protectiveness he'd always felt for her prompted him to give her one last out. He met those eyes of hers. He didn't look away. "What I'm saying is, just tell me no, Willa. Just do it. Do it now."

She let out a strangled sound. It might have been a laugh. Or a sob. "Are you kidding? Don't try and pretend that you don't get it. All I've ever wanted was the chance to tell you yes."

It was the last straw.

"Tell me yes, then. You go ahead. You say it right out loud to me."

She didn't even hesitate. "Yes, oh, yes. Please, please make love to me."

So much for her last out. She'd refused to take it. So be it.

He closed that small distance between her mouth and his. He kissed her.

For the very first time.

He touched her mouth with his and it was…everything. A forbidden dream realized.

A promise so long denied, finally kept.

She kissed him back, sighing so sweetly. She melted into him, all that pride and orneriness and softness. Everything that was Willa.

Right there. In his arms.

Her breasts flattened against his bare chest, the way they'd only done in his dreams up till then. Through the flimsy material of that lacy top, he could feel her nipples, hot. Hard. She opened her mouth to him. He swept his hungry tongue inside and the kiss became something more than a dream. Deeper than a promise.

She moaned as he kissed her, and she ran her slim hands up over his shoulders, into his hair.

He needed…more of her. *All* of her. He had his arms good and tight around her, his aching hardness pressed into her belly. He let his hands roam freely, over the slim, smooth shape of her back, up under that cotton shirt, and then down to the cove at the base of her spine.

Her hair was loose. It brushed his forearms and the backs of his hands. Like feathers. Like a cloud of silk. He speared his fingers up into it, fisted them, pulling her head back so he could scrape his teeth along the slim, pure curve of her white throat.

She cried his name. He covered her mouth again and drank the sound.

He needed…more. More of her.

He had to have the feel of her bare skin under his hands. The plaid shirt was in the way. He fisted it by the sides and peeled it back over her slim shoulders. She moaned a little, as though in protest at having to let go of him, but she let him guide her arms down so he could push the shirt off. He whipped it away and tossed it in the general direction of a chair.

Then he clasped her bare shoulders. So smooth and tender, her skin. White, but with a pink flush on it. Beautiful.

He cupped her shoulders, pressed his palms against her upper chest—and lower, until he had her sweet breasts in his two hands with only the thin fabric of that clingy silky thing to protect her from his hungry touch.

She lifted up to him, sighing, offering him whatever he wanted from her.

And he knew what he wanted. To taste her.

He kissed his way down her slim throat again, scattered more kisses along the ridge of her collarbone, down the sweet-smelling skin of her upper chest and lower, over the tender swell of her breast.

He reached the goal at last and latched onto her nipple, sucking it through the silky fabric, flicking it with his tongue.

She clutched at him, holding him to her, whispering, "Yes. Oh, Collin, yes…"

He couldn't have agreed with her more. She smelled like flowers and lemons and a little bit musky, too. All woman, his Willa.

His? Well, fine, maybe not. Not forever. But at least for tonight.

The lacy thing—what did women call those things?— a cami. Yeah. The cami had to go. He grabbed the hem of it…and then got lost in the feel of her skin again. He eased his fingers up under it, stroking the tender flesh of her back, and then bringing both hands around to the front of her, caressing her flat, smooth belly.

She was breathing so frantically. He lifted his head and kissed her again. She moaned into his mouth.

And he moved his hands higher. He cupped her bare breasts under the cami. They were so perfect, so firm and round—not too big, not small, either. They fit just right in his hands.

He thought about seeing her naked.

He wanted to do that. Right away.

Now.

She made no objections, only moaned eagerly and whispered "yes," and "yes" again, as he pulled off the cami and took down the little shorts.

There.

At last.

He had everything off her. She was silk and fire and magic, all he'd ever wanted. Right there in his arms.

He bent enough to wrap his hands around the twin globes of her bottom. She moaned again and he went on kissing her as he lifted her up, dragging all that softness against him. He moaned, too.

It felt so good. *She* felt so good.

She wrapped those soft, smooth thighs around him and hooked her ankles behind his back.

Now he could feel her, feel the womanly heart of her, right there, pressed tight to his fly. He was so hard it hurt. Hurt in the best, most extreme, most perfect kind of way.

And then, still kissing her, her hair a froth of silk and shadows sliding across his skin, her mouth to his mouth, his breath to hers, he started walking.

Well, reeling was more like it.

He reeled across the great room and down the hall to his room at the end. She held on. She went on kissing him. She wrapped those soft, long arms and slim, strong legs around him like she would never, ever let him go.

In the doorway, he paused. Or more like staggered. He braced his back against the door frame and indulged in just kissing her. She didn't seem to mind that he'd stopped moving toward the bed. She just went on kissing him, went on rocking her hips against him, went on making him want to get out of his jeans and into her softness, pronto.

But then again...

No.

He didn't want to rush it. How many times in his life did

a man hold a dream in his arms? Once, if he was lucky. A man would be a fool to rush something like that.

Yeah, okay, he had a whole boatload of faults. And maybe he was a fool in some ways. But not when it came to holding Willa in his arms. He was taking his time about this.

He was making it last if it killed him.

And he was kind of afraid it just might.

She framed his face in her two slim hands. "Collin…"

He opened his eyes, stared into hers, which were shining so bright, even in the dim light from all the way back in the kitchen. "Willa."

She wrapped her legs tighter around him. He groaned at the perfect friction as all that willowy softness slid along the front of him. "You do have protection?"

He nodded on another groan.

"Oh, good." And she sighed and kissed him again.

Paradise. They went on kissing, there in the darkened doorway. Endlessly.

Until a terrible thought occurred to him. He broke the kiss so suddenly that his head bounced against the door frame.

She cried out, "Oh! I'll bet that hurt." And she clucked her tongue and fussed over him, rubbing the bumped spot in a gentle, soothing way. "Be careful…."

Gruffly, he reassured her. "I'll live—Willa, look at me."

She blinked at him owlishly, adorably. In the faint glow of light from up the hallway, her dark hair was a wild tangle all around her sweet, flushed face. A dream. No doubt. This had to be a dream. "What?" she demanded. "What's the matter now?"

"I need you to tell me. Is this your first time?" He did not have sex with virgins.

She pressed those amazing lips together, nervous. Un-

sure. And then she buried her face against his neck. "No."
She said it softly.

"Good." Relief was coursing through him. That fat-
headed idiot from high school, Derek Andrews, no doubt.
And probably Mr. Wonderful, who wanted to marry her.

Mr. Wonderful, who was another reason Collin shouldn't
be seducing Willa. She deserved a bright future with the
right kind of guy.

But somehow, at that moment, he wasn't feeling all that
guilty about Mr. Wonderful. What guy in his right mind
proposed marriage and then went to Australia? Mr. Wonderful deserved a little competition for leaving her on her
own at the mercy of a guy like him.

She pressed her plump lips to the side of his throat and
he felt her tongue slide along his skin. He groaned and
wrapped his arms tighter around her and was very, very
glad that she wasn't a virgin.

He supposed he should have known she wasn't. She
didn't act like a virgin. She acted like a woman who knew
what she wanted.

"Willa," he whispered, and then again, "Willa…" He'd
always loved the feel of her name in his mouth.

"I'm right here." She lifted her head from his shoulder
and nuzzled his ear as he kissed his way across her cheek
to take her mouth once more.

Then he gathered her tighter, closer, and launched them
from the doorway, making it to the bed in four long strides.
He laid her gently down and turned on the lamp, and then
he just stood there above her, looking down at her, so slim
and pretty, naked to his sight.

At last.

"So beautiful…" The words came out of him on a bare
husk of sound.

She met his eyes—or at least she did at first. But then

she grew shy. She did that thing that women do—an arm across her pink-tipped breasts, a hand to cover the shining brown curls in the cove of her silky thighs.

"Don't…" His voice sounded desperate, ragged to his own ears.

And she reached out. She put a hand against his belly, palm flat. A groan escaped him when she did that. Her touch felt so good, so exactly right. Like the scent of her that seemed to call to him, to beckon him to her.

She said, gently, politely, "Take off your jeans, please."

He couldn't do what she wanted fast enough. Two of the buttons were undone anyway. He undid the rest and shucked them off and away.

"Oh, Collin, you're so…you're beautiful, you are."

"Men aren't beautiful," he argued gruffly.

"Oh, yes. They are." She held out her arms to him. "I'm so happy. After all this time, I never thought…never imagined…" She seemed to run out of words. It was all right. He understood, he knew exactly what she meant. "Come down here. With me…."

He pulled open the bedside drawer and got a condom from the box in there. And then he went down to her. He stretched out beside her, covered her mouth with his and let his hands wander.

Her body moved beneath his touch, so tempting, so soft. He kissed her as he stroked her hair, her throat, the smooth roundness of her shoulder.

So much to explore, all of her. Beautiful and willing and pliant and tender. The slim curve of her waist called to him. He stroked his hand from her rib cage to the swell of her hip and lower, down the long sweep of her thigh.

He palmed her knee and gently guided it open. Then he did what he'd dreamed of doing, sliding his palm up the inside of her thigh as she rolled her hips and tossed her head and moaned his name in hungry encouragement.

The dark curls were already wet with her excitement. He parted them. She cried his name out good and loud then.

He kissed her slow and deep. He whispered against her lips, "Like this, Willa?"

She gasped. "Yes, oh! Yes…"

He slipped a finger in. Two. Wet silk inside, warm and slick, welcoming him. Her hips moved rhythmically now, her thighs open, offering him everything. So much. All she had to give.

"Collin…" She said his name against his mouth. And then she gave him her tongue to suck. He kissed her endlessly as he stroked her.

And by then, touching her in that most intimate place wasn't enough. He had to taste her there.

He kissed his way down the center of her. She clutched his shoulders, murmured his name over and over, like she couldn't get enough of saying it. He just kept kissing her, all of her, as he lifted up and slid over and settled between her open thighs. She shifted, adjusting herself with a long, slow sigh, bracing her heels on his shoulders.

The scent of her was so sweet, lemons and musk. And the taste? Exactly as he'd dreamed it. Only better. Endlessly better…

He used his fingers and his mouth and she moved against him, sighing, her hands in his hair, her head tossing on the pillow. She was rising, reaching for the peak, and he stayed with her, all the way. Until at last she went over, crying his name as the soft explosion of her climax pulsed against his tongue.

The condom had been lost somewhere in the tangle of bedclothes. He felt around for it—and got lucky. His fingers closed around it as she sighed once more and went all loose and lazy.

He didn't stop kissing her. She tasted so good.

She moaned his name. And finally, she pleaded, "Oh, please. Oh, my. I can't…it's too much…"

With a low chuckle, he relented, backing off a little, resting his head on her thigh. She stroked his hair, traced the shape of his ear. He was aching to continue. He'd been hard and getting harder forever, it felt like right then.

But at the same time, he was satisfied just to lie with her that way, naked. Together. Unashamed.

A few minutes later, he sat back on his knees. She followed him, sitting up, brushing her wild hair out of her eyes, laughing. "Here. Let me…"

So he gave her the pouch. She tore the end off with her teeth. Hottest thing he ever saw. A guy didn't need those girlie magazines she'd teased him about having in his man-cave. Not with Willa Christensen naked in his bed.

She peeled away the wrapper and set it neatly on the bedside table. Then she bent close to him. She rolled it down over him.

He shut his eyes and tipped his head back and tried not to lose it just from the feel of her sliding it down over him. "Collin?"

He let a low groan be his answer.

And then the bed shifted as she rose up on her knees and bent close to him, all tart and sweet and womanly. Her hair brushed his shoulder and her mouth touched his, lightly, teasing him.

It was too much. He rose up and took her shoulders and rolled her under him.

She let out a little cry and a soft laugh. And then he was on top of her, his elbows braced on either side of her, framing her sweet face in his hands, her hair all around them. He stared down at her and she looked up at him.

"Willa…"

"Collin."

"Willa, I…" There were no words. And it didn't matter. He was right where he'd never dared dream he would be.

"I'm so glad," she whispered.

He had her arms trapped at her sides. But she could move her legs.

And she did, lifting them, hooking them around the backs of his thighs. He was positioned just right, nudging her where she was so soft and wet and open.

She felt like heaven. Like some lost paradise, found at last, after he'd given up believing he would ever get there.

He entered her slowly, by aching degrees. And he held her gaze the whole time. He needed the sight of her face as he claimed her, so beautifully flushed. Lips softly parted.

Completely willing, with nothing held back from him.

She moaned as he went deeper. He made an answering sound and kept pressing, filling her.

Finally, he couldn't go slowly anymore. With a forceful thrust, he was all the way in.

She gasped. Her eyes widened. Her sweet lips invited.

He lowered his mouth to her and kissed her as he began to move.

After that, time folded in on itself. He lost control and rocked wildly against her. She held him closer, tighter than before.

She made soft, willing sounds that only drove him higher. Deeper. Harder.

His mind was gone, shattered. There was only her body and his body inside her, the feel of her soft, willing mouth pressed to his.

He hit the peak and sailed over, knowing a faint echo

of regret that he couldn't hold out for her—and then, all at once, learning he hadn't left her behind, after all. Her body pulsed around him, drawing him deeper. Pushing him higher.

Hurling him outward through a midnight-blue universe of fast-spinning stars.

Chapter Eleven

Faintly, far away, Willa heard music playing. It was that Joe Nichols song, "Tequila Makes Her Clothes Fall Off."

She smiled. She'd always thought that song was kind of cute.

The song stopped. And the bed shifted. She remembered.

It was Collin's bed....

"My cell," said a groggy, very masculine voice not far from her ear. He nuzzled her hair. "I left it charging in the kitchen...."

"Um." She cuddled closer to his big, hard, naked body. He wrapped a muscular arm around her and drew her closer, tucking her into him, spoon style, settling the covers more snugly around them.

She smiled some more and opened her eyes to morning light.

Amazing. It really had happened with Collin. Just like

in all her forbidden fantasies. It had been incredible and it had lasted all night long.

He smoothed her hair away from her neck and kissed her there. "You smell good...." Down the hallway, the phone beeped.

"Voice mail," she said on a lazy yawn.

His lips brushed her neck again. "It's after eight. I'd better go see if it's anything important."

She grabbed the arm he had wrapped around her and pretended to sulk. "Oh, no..."

But he only kissed her hair and pushed back the covers, pausing to tuck them around her again. "I'll be right back."

She rolled over and watched him get up. He looked so good without his clothes on. He had a cute little happy trail and a real, true six-pack.

And a beautiful tattoo on the hard bulge of his right shoulder, one of those tribal designs. She'd spent a while the night before studying it, tracing its curves and angles with her fingers. It looked a little like a mask, with horns and a pair of eyes that also seemed to resemble sharks, somehow. She'd asked him what it was supposed to represent and in typical Collin fashion, he'd answered, "Whatever you want it to represent."

He put on his jeans and buttoned them partway, which somehow only made him look manlier and more naked. "Keep the bed warm."

"Will do. Let the dog out?" Buster, who'd ended up on the rug by the bed, was already up and wagging his tail.

He nodded. "C'mon, Buster."

She watched him go, Buster close behind. The view of him walking away was every bit as inspiring as the one from the front.

She heard the outside door open and shut as he let Buster out. And then he came back.

He held out the phone to her. "Your brother."

She sat up, pulling the sheet with her to cover her breasts, and took the phone from him. "Um. Thanks." She hit the icon for voice mail.

Gage's voice said, "Collin, this is Gage. I'm in town. And looking for my sister. Could you have her call me?" He didn't sound especially cordial.

Collin was watching her. "Good old Gage. Finally made it into town and he's wondering where the hell his baby sister's gotten off to."

Willa hitched up her chin and put on a smile. "Oh, I doubt he's wondering. I'm sure someone in town has already told him exactly where I am."

His dark gaze ran over her. She thought of the night before and a hot shiver went through her. "Not feelin' quite so *unimpeachable* now, are you, Willa?"

She pursed up her mouth at him and narrowed her eyes. "Don't start. I do not regret a thing. Last night was beautiful. I mean that. Do you understand?"

He gave her a slow, insolent once-over. "Yes, ma'am."

She puffed out her cheeks with a frustrated breath. And then she whispered, "Come here. Please?"

His fine mouth curled. "You should call your brother back."

She reached out her hand.

He looked at it for a count of five. Her heart sank. She was certain he would turn and walk away.

But then he reached out, too. Their hands met, fingers lacing together. Relief, sweet and good as a long drink of cool water, washed through her.

He dropped down onto the bed at her side. "I feel bad, okay? I don't want to cause you problems with your family."

She dropped the phone onto the sheet and wrapped

her other hand around their joined ones. "You're not. You couldn't."

He leaned closer. She tipped her mouth up to him and their lips met. "Call him," he said against her lips. "I'll let Buster back inside and put the coffee on." He lifted their hands and kissed the back of hers.

Reluctantly, she let him go, picked up the phone again and called her brother back. He answered on the first ring.

"Gage, it's me."

"Willa. Where are you?"

She could tell by his tone that he already knew. "I'm up at Collin's. We drove up yesterday. The road's a mess. I helped him clear the way."

A silence on Gage's end, then, "I don't get it. You never even liked Collin Traub, and all of a sudden, you two are—what? What's going on, Willa? What about you and Dane?"

Dane. Oh, Lord. She'd really messed up with Dane. She never should have let him talk her into taking time to think things over. She'd put off the inevitable and now she felt like a two-timer.

"Willa, are you still there?"

"Yes. Right here." And no way was she getting into all this on the phone. "Listen. I'll call you as soon as we get back down into town. We can talk then—or, whenever you can get a minute."

"*When* will you be back in town?"

"I don't know for sure yet. Collin may have things he has to do up here. And we cleared the road as best we could, but there are some rough spots and some places where the cliff side collapsed. It could take a while to get down."

"Buster okay?"

"He's fine. Yes."

"And you?" He sounded worried. "You…okay?"

Love washed through her. Her brother was such a great guy. "I am just fine. I promise you. And I'm glad you're here. So glad." Rust Creek Falls really needed him now. But she didn't say that. She knew him, knew he had to be beating himself up that he hadn't been there when the levee broke. Telling him how much he was needed would only make him feel worse about everything.

"Call me," he said. "As soon as you're back in town."

When she entered the kitchen, Buster was in the corner, his nose buried in Libby's old food bowl. The coffee was brewing. And Collin stood at the stove, laying strips of bacon in a pan.

She leaned a hip against the counter and stuck her hands in the pockets of the flannel robe she'd found on the back of his bathroom door. "I hope you don't mind. I stole your robe." Her purple shorts, cami and plaid shirt were strewn around the living room.

He glanced over. "Looks better on you than on me anyway."

She wanted to go to him, brush his hair back off his forehead, tell him...

What?

She wasn't quite sure. "That bacon smells so good."

He tipped his head toward the open shelves with the dishes on them. "Put the plates on the table?"

She nodded and then got busy setting the table. He cooked the bacon and scrambled some eggs. She made the toast and poured the coffee.

They sat down to eat, the silence between them both sharp-edged and a little too deep.

She made herself break it. "Gage is fine. I said I would call him when we got back down into town."

"You need to get going right away, then?"

She sipped her coffee. "No. There's no hurry."

"You sure about that, Willa?"

The question seemed to hang heavy in the air between them.

Willa pushed back her chair. He watched her, dark eyes wary, as she went around the table to his side and did what she'd wanted to do since she entered the kitchen. She smoothed his hair back off his forehead. "I'm sure. No hurry."

He caught her hand. But he didn't push it away. Instead, he brought her fingers to his lips and kissed the tips of them. "Your food will get cold...."

"Um. Can't have that." She bent and he tipped his head up. They shared a quick kiss and she returned to her chair.

After that, the silence didn't seem so oppressive. But the romantic and sensual mood of the night before, of that morning before the phone rang, was definitely absent.

She wanted to talk—about everything. About how she was never going to marry Dane Everhart and she'd been wrong not to simply say no when Dane proposed, about how her brother would be fine with her and Collin being together, once she had a chance to talk with him. About how beautiful last night had been and how she was looking forward to more nights just like it.

But somehow, she didn't know where to begin. And that had her looking back wistfully at their recent nights on the front steps of the town hall, when talking with Collin had been as simple and easy as breathing.

And now, here they were. Lovers, at last. And it was suddenly neither easy nor simple. She had so much to say—and yet she feared she might mess things up if she started talking. She might end up blurting out something that would turn him off.

Was it true then, what they said about sex ruining a perfectly good friendship? She did hope not.

Collin knew he had to get her back to town as soon as possible. Her brother's call had been like a bucket of icy water in the face. It had snapped him back to reality hard and fast.

He shouldn't have taken her to bed. He knew that. Really, where was it going to go with them?

Nowhere. Things were crazy now, after the flood. Their whole world had been turned pretty much upside down. He knew that was all it was with the two of them: one of those things that happen when a man and a woman were thrown together by necessity in a crisis, with emotions running high.

It could never be anything permanent. She was a nice girl with a certain kind of life ahead of her. And his life suited him fine as it was. He liked his independence, always had. And she was going to marry a big shot from Colorado. She would remember that soon enough.

Probably already had. She'd been pretty damn quiet ever since she'd talked to Gage. Collin figured that just the sound of her brother's voice had gotten her to thinking twice. She'd realized it was a bad idea, what they'd done last night, that it never should have happened and it needed to stop now.

They loaded the contents of his freezer into coolers, strapped them into the pickup bed, and left for town.

The trip down went smoothly, all things considered. Collin knew the places to be extra careful—and they'd cleared away the worst of the storm debris on the way up.

He handed her his cell when they reached the base of the mountain. "Call Gage."

She made the call.

It was, "Hi, it's me...Yes...All right, I will...A few minutes...Okay." She handed him back his phone and asked him to let her off at the sheriff's office.

He pulled up to the curb.

She hooked Buster's leash to his collar and turned a dewy smile his way. "I...well, I can't tell you to call me, since I don't have a phone." She really did sound like she *wanted* him to call her.

But that had to be wishful thinking on his part. His chest was tight and his throat felt like it had a log stuck in it. "I'll see you." It came out way too gruff and low.

She searched his face. Whatever she was looking for, he didn't think she found it. He reminded himself how that was for the best. "Um. Okay, then. Have a good one."

"Yeah. Say hi to Gage."

"Will do." Another blinding, too-wide smile. And then she shouldered her pack, grabbed her big plastic bag of stuff and got out. Buster jumped down after her.

He didn't allow himself to watch her walk away. As soon as she shut the door, he put it in gear and got the hell out of there.

Gage was waiting for Willa in his office. He was on a cell phone arguing with someone about roadblocks or something, but he cut it short when he looked up and saw her in the doorway.

"Willa." He gave her a tired smile and ended the call. Then he got up and came around the desk to her. She ran to him and he hugged her close. He said in a voice rough with emotion, "I'm so glad you're all right." She let her bag and pack drop to the floor and hugged him back, hard. He'd always made her feel safe and protected. And right then, after the way Collin had seemed so eager to get rid of her, well, it felt good to have her big brother's arms around her.

When he let her go, she asked, "Have you been out to the ranch?"

His mouth formed a grim line. "Yeah. What a mess. I'll be staying down the street, in a FEMA trailer for a while."

"Why not stay at Mom and Dad's?"

"It's better if I'm right here in town, where I need to be." There was a tap on the door. He went over and opened it and said to the dispatcher, "I need a few minutes here. Won't be long." Then he shut the door again and turned to her. "Buster?"

"He's good. I tied him out in front."

He came back to her, clasped her shoulder and glanced down at the pile of belongings she'd dropped at her feet. "I heard you've been staying over at the town hall on a cot—until last night anyway."

She nodded, her gaze on his handsome face. He looked so weary, the faint lines around his eyes etched deeper than before. "It worked out."

He took charge, the way he always did. "So, then. You need a car, a phone and a place to stay."

She *had* a place to stay—with Collin. Or at least, she'd thought she did until a couple of hours ago. "A car and a phone would really help." She was going to have a long talk with Collin that evening, whether he liked it or not. And then, if that didn't go well, she'd find somewhere else to stay. "I need to get hold of the insurance people—for the house and for the Subaru."

"Have a seat." Gage gestured at one of the guest chairs and then went back to sit behind his desk, where he pulled open a drawer and took out another cell phone, a charger and the key to his pickup. "I've got cells I can use and the county provides me with a vehicle. For now, you take my cell and the pickup."

"Oh, Gage. I can't take your truck."

"Oh, yes, you can. And you will." He shoved it all across at her. "I programmed the number of the cell I'll be using into this phone. So you know where to reach me whenever you need me. Get a hold of your insurance agent. And call Mom. She's been asking about you."

"I will. Thanks."

"And with the truck, you can get around. Got money?"

She admitted, "I lost my wallet in the Forester."

He passed her some cash and a credit card. "You should get over to Kalispell and replace your license. And you need to call about your credit cards...."

She granted him a patient glance. "Yes, big brother."

He went right on. "There's gas available, too. The garage just got its tanks refilled. With the truck, you'll be able to stay at the ranch."

She wasn't committing to that. At least not until she'd had it out with Collin. "I'll be okay. Please don't worry."

He was looking way too bleak. She knew what was coming next. And she was right. "So...you spent the night at Collin Traub's." He practically winced when he said Collin's name.

She sat up straighter. "Yes, I did—and you can just stop giving me that pained look. Collin's not what I always thought, Gage. I'm ashamed of how completely I misjudged him. He's a great guy."

He had a one-word response to that. "Dane?"

"Dane is not the issue here."

"Willa." He used her name as a rebuke. "The man asked you to marry him. I thought you were considering it."

"I blew it, all right? I never should have told Dane I would think it over when he proposed. There's nothing to think over. Dane is not the man for me."

"You say that now...."

"Yes. And I should have said it from the first. As soon

as Dane's back in the country, I will apologize to him for keeping him hanging."

"Dane's a good man. Are you sure you want to just cut him loose?"

"I am absolutely certain."

"Well, even if that's so, it doesn't make the Traub wild man right for you. Willa, come on. You know about Collin Traub. He's not a man to hang your hopes on. The guy never met a heart he didn't break. And he's spent more than one night cooling his heels in the jail cell out there for being drunk and disorderly and picking a fight."

She refused to waver. "People mature. They change. Collin grew up without a lot of supervision. Yes, he went a little wild."

"A *little?*"

"He's just not like that anymore. I…I care for him and I respect him." Gage started to speak, but she didn't let him get a word in. "Listen. I know you only want to protect me and I love you for it. But I don't want or need protecting. I'm an adult and I know what I'm doing." *I hope.*

"Well, I don't like it."

"Gage…"

He surprised her and admitted, "All right. I know that he's made a go of his uncle's saddle-making business. I give him credit for that." Willa started to relax a little. At least Gage realized that Collin had created a productive life for himself. But then he went on, "However, when it comes to women, Collin Traub is bad news. I want you to stay away from him. Can you just do that, just stay away from him for my sake? Please."

"I'm sorry. No. You're the best brother any girl could have. But being the best doesn't give you the right to tell me how to run my life."

He started to rise. "Now, you listen here—"

"Sit down, Gage," she instructed in her best school-teacher tone. Surprisingly, he sank back to his chair. And she pressed her advantage. "I'm a grown woman. And I am fully capable of making my own decisions about my life—and the men in it. I want you to give Collin a chance."

"A chance to what?" he demanded. "To hurt you and mess you over?"

"No. A chance to make you see that there's more to him than your old ideas about him. All you have to do is ask around town and you'll learn a thing or two about everything he's done for Rust Creek Falls since the flood. He saved my life, Gage. He's been at the front line of the rescue efforts and the cleanup. He's a natural leader and he's right there when he's needed—and no, I can't say if what's happening with Collin and me is going to last forever. But I do know that, however it ends up with us, I will never regret being with him."

Gage gave her a long, dark look. And then he grabbed a pencil, pulled open his pencil drawer and tossed it in. He shut the drawer good and hard. "I'm not happy about this."

"That's your prerogative."

"But what can I say?"

She gazed at him coaxingly. "That you'll give Collin a chance."

He blew out a breath. "Fine. I'll stay out of it. For now. I'll just knock myself out being open-minded about Collin Traub."

She beamed him her fondest smile. "Thank you."

"But if that wild man breaks your heart, you can be damn sure I'll be first in line to break *his* face."

Willa spent the day taking care of personal business.

She used the cell Gage had loaned her to call her insurance agent and the FEMA flood insurance number.

The clerks she talked to took her number and promised she'd get calls back from adjusters within twenty-four hours—for the car and for the house and for her separate government-run flood insurance policy. Next, she made calls about her credit cards. That took a while, since she no longer had the cards, she was calling from someone else's phone and her records had been turned to mush in the flood. But in the end, she gave the ranch as a temporary address and was promised that new cards would arrive there within the week. After that, she decided to go ahead and drive to Kalispell to visit her bank and her cell phone provider, and to get a new driver's license.

As soon as she got her new phone in her hand, she called everyone back and told them she had her own phone now. Then she called her mom in Livingston.

"You got your phone back," her mother said when she answered. "Oh, honey. We miss you...."

"I miss you, too, Mom."

"I talked to Gage just today..."

"Yeah. He finally made it back. He loaned me his truck."

"Good. There are still a lot of problems with the roads, so we thought we'd just stay here in Livingston a little longer."

"That sounds wise, Mom."

"Gage says they're giving him a trailer so he can stay in town."

"Yes. You know him. He needs to be where the action is."

"Honey, I've been meaning to ask. You *are* staying at the ranch, aren't you?"

"Uh, no."

"But why not?"

Willa didn't want to go into her relationship with Collin. Not now. Not on the phone—and not after last night and the awkwardness of that morning. It was all too new and exciting and scary. Not to mention, up in the air. And evidently, Gage had stayed out of it and said nothing to their parents about where she'd slept last night.

Thank you, big brother.

"Willa? Are you there?"

"Right here. And I've been staying in the town hall." It was true. She had been. Until last night. "They have cots set up for people whose homes were flooded."

"But surely you should be out at the ranch. Even with the power out, it seems to me that you would be so much more comfortable there than sleeping on a hard, narrow cot in a public building...."

"Mom. I'm managing. It's working out fine."

"Just think about it, won't you? Consider it."

"I'll manage, Mom."

Her mother muttered something under her breath. "Always so independent."

"I love you, Mom. Give my love to Daddy. I have to go...."

"And we love you. You're eating right, aren't you? Taking care of yourself...?"

"I'm perfectly healthy and I'm getting plenty to eat. And I do have to go."

With a sigh, her mother said goodbye.

Willa and Buster got back to Rust Creek Falls at a little past three in the afternoon. She stopped in at Gage's office and returned his cell phone. Then she visited the town hall and the Community Church in hopes that Collin might be at one or the other.

He wasn't. She tried not to feel too disappointed. The

man could be back up on the mountain working in his shop, or out on flood cleanup—or just about anywhere.

She considered calling him, but decided to wait. Tonight, one way or another, she would track him down.

Summer school was out by then, so she went to Paige's house. Shelby was there with her little girl, Caitlin, who would be in Willa's class next year. Willa got a full report on the day's activities at the park. Shelby said the day had gone well and volunteered to fill in again for Willa whenever she needed a hand.

Willa thanked her. She really liked Shelby, who was a wonderful mother and a talented teacher. Shelby wasn't having an easy time of it raising her little girl alone. A blonde, blue-eyed beauty who had once been the most popular girl at Rust Creek Falls High, now Shelby made ends meet tending bar at the Ace in the Hole. Willa had been encouraging her to apply for a full-time teaching position with the district.

When Shelby and Caitlin left, Willa stayed to brainstorm with Paige on new projects for their summer school kids—projects that would lend themselves to an outdoor classroom setting.

At five-thirty, Willa put Buster on his leash and Paige walked with them to the church for dinner. The gas had never stopped working on the north side of town, but the power was still out. Paige had no generator, which meant she couldn't keep food refrigerated. The church, with the help of donations from a number of sources, would continue to provide meals for the community as long as people needed them. Refrigerated trucks brought in food daily.

Halfway there, Paige asked gingerly, "Are things okay with you and Collin?"

Willa sent her a sideways glance. "Ask me in a day or two."

"I'm here and ready to listen anytime you need me."

Willa hooked an arm around her friend's slim shoulders. "I know. It's just another reason why I'm so glad you're my friend."

At the church, Willa spotted Jerry Dobbs sitting at a table with three other members of Collin's cleanup team. Collin wasn't with them.

Willa told Paige she'd join her in a moment. She got a bowl of dog food from one of the church ladies and took it outside to Buster. As the dog wolfed down his dinner, she gave Collin a call.

He didn't answer.

She left a message. "Hey. It's Willa. Note this number. It's mine. I went to Kalispell and replaced my cell phone today, along with my driver's license. I also dealt with replacing my credit cards, insurance adjusters and with my bank…" And really, did he need a blow-by-blow? She realized she was nervous because he hadn't picked up when she called. She tried again. "Right now, I'm down at the church for dinner. No sign of you. Give me a call…." She couldn't think of anything else to say, so she left it at that.

Back inside, she went through the serving line and sat down with Paige. Throughout the meal, she kept waiting for the phone to ring.

Didn't happen.

She couldn't help but feel a little bit dumped. Which was ridiculous, and she knew it. How could she be dumped? To be dumped implied that you'd shared some sort of at least semi-committed relationship with a guy. She and Collin? They were friends who'd slept together. One time.

So then, did that make her just another of Collin Traub's one-night stands?

Oh, dear Lord. She did hope not. Collin couldn't be that disappointing and hurtful. Could he?

She wished she could stop remembering her argument with Gage that morning.

Was Collin going to go and prove her big brother right? *No.*

She needed to stop this. She was not going to think like this. If she kept on in this vein, she'd be right back where she started before the flood: racing out of rooms just because Collin Traub entered them.

That morning, she'd argued fervently with Gage on Collin's behalf. She'd said how Collin had grown and changed from the no-strings wild boy he used to be. And she had absolutely believed what she'd said.

Collin *had* changed. And if he could do it, so could she.

The friendship they'd found since the flood meant a lot to her. And last night had been beautiful—no matter what happened next. One way or another, she was working this out with him. If he didn't want to be with her in a man-woman way, well, that would hurt.

A lot.

But she would get over it.

Right now, what she needed to do was talk this out with him. And to do that, she had to *find* him.

Jerry Dobbs had finished his meal. He was busy putting his tray away, tossing his trash and separating his dishes from his flatware.

Willa told Paige she'd see her tomorrow, picked up her tray and went to ask Jerry if he might know where Collin had gone.

Collin tried to concentrate on the intricate pattern of leaves and vines, on the good, clean smell of veg tan topgrain leather, on the slow, exacting process of stamping the custom design with his stylus and mallet.

But his mind was not cooperating. His mind was on a

certain brown-eyed woman. On the scent of lemons, on the way it had felt to have her tucked up against him naked all night long.

She had called over an hour ago. He hadn't answered and he hadn't called her back, though he *had* played her message. Three times. So far.

Yeah, he was being a real jerk and he knew it.

Still, he kept thinking it was better this way. Let her be completely disappointed in him, start avoiding him again.

Better for everyone.

Being her friend was one thing. But taking it further...

Bad idea. He'd blown it and he knew it. He shouldn't have given in to that thing he'd always had for her. He'd seriously stepped over the line and he wasn't going to let it happen again.

The sound from upstairs stopped his thoughts in midramble and his mallet in midair.

Someone was knocking on his front door.

He dropped the mallet and stylus and headed for the stairs as fast as his boots would carry him.

"Why do I get the feeling you're avoiding me?" she asked when he pulled open the door. She stood there in old jeans and a frayed T-shirt, her hair loose on her shoulders, Buster at her feet. He'd never in his life seen a sight quite so beautiful. She tapped her booted foot. "Do I get to come in or not?"

Chapter Twelve

Collin glanced past her shoulder, saw her brother's pickup parked next to his. Of course, Gage would have seen to it that she had transportation.

He accused, "The road up here is still dangerous."

"You'll be happy to know that Buster and I made it just fine." She stuck out her chin at him. "Ahem. May I come in?"

It was a bad idea. And he was way too crazy happy to see her.

"Collin. *Hello?*"

He stepped back automatically. She moved forward, the dog right behind her. He edged around her, shut the door and turned to her. "What?"

She squared her shoulders, kind of bracing herself. "Look. If you regret last night, that's fine. I can deal with that. I would rather you *didn't* regret it. I would rather be, um…" She paused, swallowed. He watched the warm color flood upward over her sweet, soft cheeks. "I would rather be your lover. But if you don't want that, well, okay. If you think it was a big mistake, what we did last night, okay. I won't like it and it…hurts me. But I *will* get over it. Because what I really want, most of all, Collin Traub, is to still be your friend."

He drank in the sight of her. It occurred to him that he would never get tired of seeing her pretty, clean-scrubbed, earnest face. "My friend." It came out low and kind of threatening, though he didn't really mean it that way. "You want to be my friend."

She hitched her chin higher. "Yes. I do. I want to *remain* your friend, above all."

"What about that guy you're going to marry?"

"Collin. I'm not marrying Dane. And I will tell him that as soon as I get a chance to talk to him."

He wasn't sure he believed her. "Why keep the guy hanging if you're only going to say no?"

"I'm not keeping him hanging. He asked me to think it over. I said I would. I *have* thought it over and I'm not going to marry him."

Collin still wasn't really buying it, still had that feeling that this thing between them was only temporary, something born out of the chaos caused by the flood. Not the kind of thing that lasted.

Which should have been fine with him. He'd never been a guy who worried about whether or not what he had with a woman was going to last.

Because for him, it never did.

Three steps separated them. He took the first one. Couldn't help himself. Looking at her was like drowning in a whirlpool, the spinning current dizzying, sucking him down.

And then, when he was only two steps away, well, he had to get even closer. He took the second step.

And the scent of her came to him: sweet and tart and way too womanly.

That did it.

To hell with trying to do the right thing here. She wanted him and he wanted her and why shouldn't they both have what they wanted?

He snaked out a hand and caught her wrist.

She gasped. "Collin! What...?"

He pulled her to him, wrapped an arm around her. How could she be so perfect, so slim and soft and way too exciting, bringing the scent of lemons and Ivory soap to drive him wild? She stared up at him, her eyes so wide. Heat flared in his groin. "Right now, Willa, I'm not really thinking about being your friend."

That full mouth formed a round O. "Well." Breathless. Hopeful. "It's all...workable. Don't you think?"

"Thinking," he said roughly. "Who's thinking?"

And then she lifted a hand and cradled the side of his face. "Don't be afraid...."

Another wave of heat blasted through him. He put on a scowl. "I'm not afraid."

"Right." Soft. Indulgent. Way too knowing. Her eyes had that gleam in them now.

He still couldn't really believe she was here, in his house. In his arms. "You shouldn't have come up here."

"Yes. Yes, I should have."

"Your brother warned you about me, right?"

"Gage is willing to be open-minded."

"You mean he warned you and you argued with him."

"And now he's willing to be open-minded."

"I know how you are, Willa. So damn determined."

She smiled then, dimples flashing. "I am, yes. It's one of my most sterling qualities."

He bent his head closer, nuzzled her hair, breathed her in. Nothing. No one. Ever. Not like her. "Willa..." It came out harsh, low. Hungry.

She clung to him. She felt like heaven. She closed her eyes and pressed her lips to his throat. "Yes." She kissed the word into his skin, once. And then again. "Yes."

He put a finger under that stubborn chin of hers. With a sigh, she opened her eyes. He advised, "I should send you back down the mountain right now."

"Oh, but you won't." She clucked her tongue. Softly. "It's much too dangerous, remember?"

He pulled her even closer. "*This* is what's dangerous." There were a thousand reasons they should stop right now. He tried to remember at least a few of them, but it wasn't happening. "I'm not the right guy for you."

"That's for me to decide. All you have to figure out is whether *I'm* the right girl for *you*."

"I don't—"

"Shh." She put two fingers against his mouth. It took all his will not to close his teeth around them and suck them inside. "We don't have to decide anything now," she whispered. "We can just...be together, you and me. Just enjoy every minute we have, for now. Just kind of wing it and see where it takes us."

"It's not a good idea, Willa." He formed the words against the soft pads of her fingers.

"Your mouth says one thing, but the rest of you is sending another message altogether." She pressed herself against him, snugger. Tighter.

He caught her fingers, touched his lips to them. Somehow, he couldn't help it—couldn't help holding her, touching her. Wanting her. "You're getting pretty bold lately...."

She lifted her mouth higher, offering it to him. "Must be the company I'm keeping."

That did it. He dipped his head and settled his lips on hers.

She sighed in welcome.

He wrapped his arms tighter around her and kissed her slowly. With care and attention and longing and heat.

She responded by sliding her hands up his chest to his shoulders, by sifting those soft fingers up into his hair. By sighing her willingness against his parted lips.

And by then, he'd pretty much forgotten all the reasons they shouldn't be doing this.

If she wanted to be with him, he could only put up so much resistance. After all, *he* wanted to be with her.

He burned to be with her.

And now, tonight, again, at last, he *would* be with her.

He started undressing her, right there in the entryway.

She didn't object—on the contrary, she started undressing *him*. He got rid of her T-shirt and she returned the favor. He unhooked her bra. She undid his jeans.

And then he lifted her high and carried her down the hall to his bedroom. He set her on the bed and knelt to unlace her boots. He got one off, and the sock beneath it, and he was starting on the other one when she reached out and laid her palm on his hair.

He looked up.

She gazed down at him, her eyes and her mouth so soft. So tender. "Collin…."

He kind of lost it then. He got her other boot off, ripped away the sock. And then she was clasping his shoulder, pulling him up to her.

It all happened so fast. He got the condom from the drawer as she pulled down her jeans and panties and kicked them away.

Her hands were on him again, pushing his jeans down. He still had his boots on. Neither of them cared.

He rolled the condom on and then went down to her. He tried to take it slow, to make sure she was ready.

But she tugged at him. She was so insistent, making tender sounds of need and encouragement, wrapping her arms and her long legs around him and pressing herself up to him, inviting him.

What could he do, given an invitation like that?

Accept. With enthusiasm.

And he did. He kissed her deeply as she slid her arm down between their bodies. She closed her soft fingers around him and guided him home.

After that, he was lost. Lost in the best, sweetest, hottest way.

She was all around him, all woman and softness and heat.

He surrendered. She moved against him, calling him down.

He was lost in her. As his climax rolled through him, he couldn't help hoping he might never be found.

When he could move again, he took off the rest of his clothes and pulled the covers up over them.

They made love again, more slowly that time.

And then, for a while, they just lay there, arms around each other, watching the shadows lengthen out the window across from his bed. He started talking about his Thunder Canyon relatives, about the wedding of his long-lost cousin that had taken place over the Fourth of July.

She asked, "Why didn't you go to the wedding with the rest of your family?"

He stroked her hair. "I had work that needed doing. And anyway, weddings have never been my kind of good time. They're like family reunions—there was one of those going on down in Thunder Canyon, too, over the Fourth—both are just excuses for the old folks to ask me when I'm getting married and how come I'm such a troublemaker."

She laughed. "Well, when *are* you getting married? And why are you such a troublemaker?"

"I'm not getting married. And troublemaking's fun."

She wrapped her leg across him, ran a soft finger down his arm in a slow, teasing caress and whispered, "I think you've put a big dent in your troublemaker reputation lately."

"Naw."

"Yeah. Jerry Dobbs told me you talked old Mrs. Lathrop into putting her shotgun away and relocating to a FEMA trailer today."

He traced the wings of her eyebrows, one and then the other. "You know Mrs. Lathrop. She's so, so proud. She moved back into her house, even though it's not safe in there since the flood. We had to talk her into leaving."

"Jerry said *you* talked her into leaving—and that she had her shotgun on you while you did it."

"Jerry exaggerates. And is he the one who told you I'd gone on up the mountain?"

"Mmm-hmm."

"Jerry's also got a big mouth."

"Oh, now. You like Jerry. You and Jerry get along."

He pressed his nose against her throat. He loved the texture of her skin almost as much as the way she smelled. He also cupped her breast. Because he could. Because it felt so good. Because it fit his hand just right. "Stop trying to make a hero out of me."

She laughed again, husky and low. "Oh, I'm not trying anything. You're being a hero all by yourself."

* * *

Willa had decided to take the advice she'd given Collin that Tuesday evening.

She was going to take it day by day. Enjoy being with him.

And she wasn't expecting anything. She was letting this beautiful, exciting thing between them unfold in its own way.

She taught summer school both Wednesday and Thursday. In the afternoons, she met with insurance adjusters.

She and Gage, as it turned out, were two of the "lucky" ones. Their houses would have to be taken down to the studs and rebuilt—but at least they had flood insurance. Too many didn't.

In the evenings, Willa and Buster went up the mountain, where Collin was waiting. Those two nights were glorious, perfect. Just Willa and Collin all wrapped up tight in each other's arms.

Friday, Willa got a call from her insurance company. They would provide her a rental car until the replacement check came through. After summer school was done for the day, she gave Gage back his truck and Collin drove her to Kalispell, where she got the keys to a green Forester.

By then it was after six, so they stopped in at a little Italian place Collin liked. It was wonderful, to sit in a restaurant lit by actual electricity and be served crisp salads, fragrant garlic bread and piping-hot lasagna. She was feeling so festive she even had a glass of red wine while Collin enjoyed a cold beer.

"I could sit here forever," she confided when her plate was empty and the waitress had whisked it away. "It's funny how easy it is to take simple things like restaurants and electricity for granted. I keep telling myself that I'll never consider basic services as a given again."

He was looking at her so…intimately. A look that curled her toes and made her think of the night to come. "How 'bout dessert?"

They ordered gelato with yummy waffle biscuits. Willa took her time savoring the cool, creamy treat.

It was almost nine when they started back to Rust Creek Falls. The plan was to skip stopping in town and caravan up the mountain, but when Willa saw that the Sawmill Street Bridge lights were on, she honked at Collin, who was in the lead.

He pulled over and she swung in behind him, jumping out to run to his side window. He rolled it down. "Looks like the power's back on."

She felt like a little kid at Christmas. "I can't believe it. I sat in that restaurant fantasizing about all the lights coming on. And what do you know?"

"Let's go into town. See what's going on." His eyes had a gleam to them, one she completely understood. He had that troublemaker image he sometimes hid behind, but she wasn't fooled, not anymore, not since the flood. He loved Rust Creek Falls as much as she did. Every step toward recovery from the disaster that had wiped out half the town mattered. To both of them.

She glanced across the bridge. It wasn't fully dark yet, but the streetlights were on. "Yes!" She ran back to her rental car and followed him across the bridge.

Main was blocked off between Sawmill and Cedar. They parked in the Masonic Hall parking lot. Willa left the windows down partway for Buster and they went to investigate.

It was a street dance.

They ran into Thelma on the corner. She told them that not only was the power back on, the landline phones were operational again, too. People had decided to celebrate by throwing a party.

At least half the town was there. Several local musicians had grabbed their instruments and formed an impromptu band. They were set up on the sidewalk midway between the two roadblocks. Folks stood around, clapping and laughing. And the street was full of dancers, everyone spinning and whirling under the streetlights. Willa spotted Paige dancing with her dad and Shelby and little Caitlin dancing together. Gage stood over by Nathan Crawford across the street from the musicians. He spotted Willa and gave her a wave.

Collin grabbed her hand. "Come on." He led her out into the crowd and they danced a couple of fast ones. And then came a slow one. He pulled her against him. She went into his arms and closed her eyes and swayed with him beneath the streetlights, thinking how the moment was about the most perfect that ever could be: dancing with Collin in the middle of Main Street on the night the lights came back on.

The next day, Saturday, Collin's parents and brothers returned at last from Thunder Canyon. They all rolled in to the Triple T in the early afternoon.

Collin was in his workshop up on the mountain when his mother called.

Ellie had a lot to tell him. She and his dad and his brothers and Dallas's three kids hadn't come home alone. They'd brought friends from Thunder Canyon, people who wanted to help and who had the kinds of skills that would be needed to begin to rebuild the south side of town. There were several members of the Pritchett family, who owned a carpentry business. And there were also Matt Cates and his dad, Frank, of Cates Construction, among others. Lots of others.

"You come on down to the ranch for dinner tonight," his mom commanded.

He thought of Willa. He'd been indulging himself in a big way with her, spending every spare moment at her side. She'd gone down the mountain to help with a food drive at the church that morning, but she would be back around five. He'd been looking forward to that—to a quiet dinner, just the two of them.

To another whole night with her in his bed.

On the floor by his feet, Buster raised his head from his paws and twitched an ear at him. Collin bent and gave the dog a pat. It had just seemed a natural thing that Buster would stay on the mountain with him while Willa went to help out down in town.

They were getting real…settled in together, him and Willa. He probably needed to dial it back a notch with her.

But somehow, every time he thought about that, about putting a little space between the two of them, he got this ache in the center of his chest. It was the kind of ache a man gets when he's making himself do something he doesn't want to do.

Because he didn't want to dial it back with Willa. He only thought it would be better for her if he did.

But not for him. Uh-uh. He liked it with her.

He liked everything about being with her.

He liked it too much.

"Collin?" His mother's voice sent his dark thoughts scattering. "You're too quiet. What's going on?"

"Not a thing. I'm right here."

"You come home for dinner."

"Tomorrow, okay? Tonight, I have plans."

"I said, tonight. Your family's home and we want to see you. Bring that sweet Willa Christensen. I'm so glad you're seeing her. I always did like that girl."

Swear words scrolled through his mind. His mom already knew about Willa.

Was he surprised?

Not particularly. His mom knew everyone and he had no illusions that he was the only one in town she'd been talking to while she was away.

"Who told you about me and Willa?" He knew he shouldn't ask. But he was kind of curious.

"Are you kidding me? Who didn't? She's a prize, that girl. I never dared to hope. My own Last Straw and the dear little Christensen girl." *The Last Straw.* It was his mom's pet name for him. She always claimed it was only because he was the last of her children. He knew better and so did everyone else. She called him the Last Straw because he'd given her so much grief with his bad behavior and untamed ways. "I'm very pleased," she added. "Very. Don't you blow it with her, now. Hear me?"

"S'cuse me, Mom. But what's going on between Willa and me has got nothing to do with you."

Ellie sighed. Deeply. "Dear Lord in heaven, you are a trial to me. I only asked you to come to dinner tonight and bring Willa. Please. Six o'clock. Don't be late."

"Mom, I…" He let the objection die unfinished. He was talking to dead air anyway.

Willa's cell rang as she carried a case of baked beans into the church's multiuse room.

She passed the beans to Mindy Krebs and took the phone from her pocket. The display read "Collin." Her heart did a happy dance and she was grinning like a lovestruck fool as she answered. "What?"

"My mom, my brothers and about half of Thunder Canyon just arrived in town. Mom knows about you and me. And she wants us both to come to the ranch for dinner."

Willa couldn't help laughing. "Collin. You should hear yourself. You sound like a covert operative passing state secrets."

"She drives me nuts."

Willa had a hard time believing that. "But your mom's so thoughtful and generous and smart and perceptive. I just love her."

He made a low, growling sound. "So does everyone else in town. And she's a good mom, don't get me wrong. She's just way too damn pushy sometimes, that's all. At least when she's dealing with me."

"Because you never did do what she told you to do."

"That's right. It's kind of a point of pride with me never to do what my mother says."

"You know that's childish, right?"

A silence on his end, then, in a surly tone, "Will you come to dinner at the Triple T with me tonight?"

She smiled widely. "Of course. Dinner at the Triple T would be lovely."

Ellic and Bob Traub knew how to throw a barbecue.

Their house was packed with people. Neighbors, friends, ranch hands, Thunder Canyon visitors and a whole lot of family spilled out onto the wide front porch and into the yard, where Bob had two smokers going along with a grill.

Gage was there. Willa spotted him on the front porch when she and Collin arrived. She worked her way through the groups of people to give him a hug.

He offered his hand to Collin. The two men shook.

And Gage said, "Been hearing good things about you lately."

Willa felt a wash of love and appreciation for her brother. He'd done what he'd promised, kept an open mind about Collin and been willing to listen when people told him all Collin had done for their town since the flood.

Collin grunted. "But you know not to believe everything you hear, right?"

Gage chuckled. "Word is you have good ideas, you don't lose your head and you're willing to pitch in." He grew serious. "So I'm asking you for what Rust Creek Falls needs from you. I'm asking for your help with the big job ahead of us."

Willa hid her smile at Collin's wary expression. "Sure," he said at last. "What can I do?"

"Come to the town hall Monday morning at ten? We're putting a group together. We'll start figuring out ways to get funding and volunteers to rebuild south-side homes for folks who had no flood insurance. Also, there's the clinic. We want to get it operational again. And most important, the elementary school. The high school isn't big enough to hold the younger kids, too. We have to do something so the K through eighth graders have a place to go in the fall."

Willa was nodding. "Good. September is just around the corner."

Gage asked, "So what do you say, Collin?"

He didn't hesitate. "I'll be there."

"Willa, dear." Ellie Traub descended on them, all smiles. "I'm so glad to see you!" She grabbed Willa in a bear hug.

Willa laughed in surprise at being clutched so close by Collin's mom. "Good to see you, too, Ellie."

Ellie took her by the shoulders. "I heard you were flooded out—and Gage, too." She sent Willa's brother a sympathetic frown. "It's horrible. Awful.…"

"We'll survive," Willa said. "And we'll rebuild."

"Lavinia and Wayne…?" Ellie asked about Willa and Gage's parents.

"They're fine," Gage assured her. "I talked to them just

an hour or so ago. They should be back at the ranch some-time tomorrow."

Collin said, "They were in Livingston, at the big rodeo, when the storm hit."

"So was I," Gage told Ellie, regret in his voice. "Mom wouldn't leave me alone until I agreed to go with them. She had some idea I was working too hard and needed to take a break and forget everything for the holiday."

"She knows what you need better than you do, huh?" Collin sent his mother a meaningful glance.

"Yes, she does," Gage confirmed, sounding weary. "Just ask her."

Ellie grabbed Collin. "We only do it because we love you. Now, give me a hug," she demanded fondly.

"Aw, Mom…" Collin embraced her with obvious af-fection.

Then Ellie hooked one arm with Collin's and the other with Willa's. "Gage, there's beer in the cooler out on the lawn."

"Thanks, Ellie."

Eyes shining, Ellie commanded, "You two come with me. I want everyone to know how pleased and happy I am that you're both here—together."

"It was embarrassing." Collin grumbled much later that night, when they were alone in his bed. "Dragging us all over the yard, announcing over and over again that you were with *me*."

Willa lay with her head on his broad chest. She could hear his heartbeat, so strong and steady. There was no place in the world she would rather be than right there, held close in Collin's strong arms. "She loves you. She's proud of you."

He made one of those low, growly sounds. "She can't

believe that someone as amazing as you would be hanging around with me."

"That's not so."

"Yeah, it is." He pressed his lips to her hair.

"No."

"Yeah—and what do you want to bet that Nathan Crawford will be at that meeting your brother talked me into going to Monday morning?"

She tipped her head back and kissed his beard-scratchy chin. "Probably. But you can handle him."

He looked down into her eyes and said gruffly, "You realize my mom is right, don't you? You're much too fine a woman to be wasting your time with me."

"I am not wasting my time. And I really get annoyed with you when you put yourself down."

"It's only the truth."

"No, it isn't." She tried to look stern. "Will you stop it? Please?"

He smoothed her hair and answered grudgingly, "Yes, ma'am."

She gave him a slow smile. "Actually, I'm a lot like your mother."

He widened his eyes in a comical way and faked a gasp of shock. "Don't say that. Anything but that."

"Oh, but I *am* like Ellie. I'm pushy. And determined. And very sure of what's good for the people I love...."

Love. She'd said the word so casually.

But then, as soon as it was out, she didn't feel casual at all.

Love. Once the word had escaped her lips, it seemed to hang by a thread inside her mind, slowly swinging. Tempting her to grab it and run with it.

Love.

The big word, the one that mattered. The word that changed everything.

She dared for the first time to admit to herself what was happening to her, how her life had become something new and fresh and beautiful. The world had a glow to it now.

Because of him.

I love you, Collin Traub.

Buoyant light seemed to fill her. All at once, she was weightless, defying gravity through pure joy.

I love you, Collin Traub.

She opened her mouth to say it—and then she shut it without making a sound.

Saying it out loud would be dangerous. Risky.

He was frowning down at her. "Hey."

She kissed his chin again. "Umm?"

"You okay?" Cautious. A little worried. "You seemed a thousand miles away just now."

"I'm right here." She took his arm, wrapped it snugly around her and settled herself more comfortably against his warm, broad chest. "And I'm fine. Better than fine."

He chuckled then. "You certainly are—and never admit you're like my mother, unless you're purposely trying to creep me out."

She laughed and promised, "Never again," as her heart cried, *I love you, Collin. I love you, I do.* The simple phrases seemed to tickle the back of her throat, working themselves closer to being said.

But she didn't say them.

Not yet. It had only been nine days since the flood, and only five since that first night she'd spent in his arms.

Yes, to her, what they had together now wasn't all that surprising. It felt like a simple progression, a natural unfolding of something that had been there all along. She'd known him all her life, wanted him for so long, been waiting, even when she thought that she hated him, for a chance with him.

She was more than ready to talk about that. About their lives, about their future.

About love.

But she was no fool. She knew that *he* wasn't ready.

So, then, she could wait.

She had a feeling it wouldn't be long.

The time wasn't right yet.

But it would be.

Soon....

Chapter Thirteen

Collin had an ever-growing backlog of work he needed to get going on down in his shop. The next morning, as they were finishing breakfast, he told Willa he would have to spend the whole day at it.

She pushed her empty plate away and rose slowly from her chair.

He stared at her, feeling suddenly wary. "I'm not sure I trust that look in your eye."

She gave him one of those sweet, innocent schoolteacher smiles of hers as she came around to his side of the table. He gazed up at her, narrow eyed. He knew she was up to something. She sat on his lap.

He growled her name in warning.

She only brushed his hair back from his forehead with her soft, cool fingers and then kissed his cheek. "Come to church with me."

"Willa…"

"Please. It'll only take a couple of hours, total, including the drive up and down the mountain. After church, I promise I'll leave you alone to work in peace for the rest of the day."

The problem with her sitting on him was that the feel of her only made him want to touch her. To kiss her. And then to kiss her some more.

He caught her earlobe between his teeth and worried it lightly, because he couldn't quite stop himself. She trembled and let out one of those reluctant little moans that always drove him crazy.

"Shame on you, Willa Christensen," he scolded. "Talking about church while you're sitting on my lap. You know very well what happens when you sit on my lap...."

She wiggled her bottom against him and then he was the one trying not to moan. "Church," she whispered way too damn seductively. "It'll be over before you know it and then you can come right back up here and work all day and half the night if you want to...."

"Wiggle like that again and I won't be getting any work done. We won't be going to church, either. We won't be going anywhere but back down the hall to bed."

"Church. You take your truck and I'll take the Forester. That way, as soon as the service is over, you can head right back up the mountain." She kissed him. And then she slid to the floor and stood above him.

He grabbed her hand. "Get back down here...."

She bent close and kissed him again. "I'll be ready in twenty minutes."

They went to church.

It was kind of nice, really, Collin thought. His family was there, his mom all smiles at the sight of him and Willa together. Pastor Alderson gave a sermon about finding joy in simple things.

Collin could relate to that, especially lately. Just being around Willa all the time, that was a pretty damn joyful thing for him.

Yeah, it was partly the sex, which was amazing…and which he probably shouldn't be thinking about in church.

But the thing was, the sex wasn't everything.

It wasn't even the most important thing.

Willa herself. *She* was the important thing. The way she would laugh, kind of husky and happy both at once. The way she cuddled up close to him, her ear against his chest like she only wanted to listen to the sound of his heart beating. The way she listened so close when he talked, but then had no problem speaking up if she didn't like something he'd said.

The way she could be so kind and gentle—and then turn right around and be tough as nails when something mattered to her. The way she could pull on a pair of work gloves and keep up with him clearing storm debris all the way up the mountain. The way she wasn't ashamed to be with him in front of everyone. Even if she *was* a school-teacher with a certain reputation she really ought to be looking out for.

He'd thought he was happy before Willa.

But the past few days, he'd started thinking that before Willa, he hadn't even known what happiness was.

He was living in a dream, and he knew it. This thing with her, well, it couldn't last. He was who he was and he'd always seen himself in an honest light. He'd grown up wild and he hadn't been to college. He could change some, but not completely.

Not enough to be with a woman like Willa in a forever kind of way.

The pastor told them all to rise. They sang an old hymn that Collin had known since childhood.

Out of the corner of his eye, in the pew across the center aisle, he caught sight of Nathan Crawford, standing so tall and proud, singing good and loud. Nathan saw him looking and shot back a narrow-eyed glare. Nathan would probably be ticked off that Gage had asked him to the meeting about flood relief tomorrow.

Well, too bad. Collin was going. He had a few ideas for raising money and getting folks together to rebuild what they'd lost. And he wanted to help in any way he could.

There were other Crawfords in church that day. He got a few scowls from more than one of them. They'd always looked down on him. Not only was he a Traub, he was the no-good, skirt-chasing, *troublemaking* Traub.

Since he and Willa started in together, he'd worried that the Crawfords might come after her for being with him, might smear her good name. So far, that hadn't happened. But it still nagged at him. In a little town like Rust Creek Falls, people had certain standards. They didn't like to think of their schoolteachers living in sin. Especially not with the local bad boy.

Willa nudged him with her elbow. He sent her a glance. She sang even louder, brown eyes full of teasing laughter.

He forgot his worries and let himself enjoy just being with her. It couldn't last forever, but as long as it did, he intended to enjoy himself.

After church, Willa longed to ask Collin to take her to the doughnut shop for a Sunday snack. The shop had reopened the day before and it was a Sunday tradition in town. Folks went to church and then to the Wings to Go or Daisy's Donuts over on North Broomtail Road.

But he did need to work and she'd already made her

deal with him. So she kept her word and sent him back up the mountain.

When he got in his pickup, Buster whined to go with him. Collin shot her a questioning look.

"Go ahead," she said indulgently. "Take him." So Collin got out and let the dog in—ever since the day Buster fell from the pickup bed on the way up the mountain, they'd been letting him ride in front. "I'll be back by five or six," she promised. Thelma was expecting her to help sort donated clothing for flooded-out families.

Collin kissed her, a warm brush of his lips against her cheek—and then he climbed back up behind the wheel and headed for Sawmill Street.

Willa's mother called her from the ranch at a little past two. "We're home," she announced, then, "Where are you? We've missed you."

"I'm at Thelma McGee's, helping out."

"Honey, we would love to see you. Can you come on over?"

"I'll check with Thelma…"

The older woman made a shooing gesture. "Go on, now. Go see your mother. Give her my best."

When Willa arrived, her dad was out in the northeast pasture somewhere, repairing a fence.

Her mom had the coffee ready and a box of bakery sweet rolls she'd picked up in Kalispell. After hugs and greetings, they sat at the table together, each with a steaming mug and a treat from the bakery box.

Willa knew her mother. She could tell by the way her mom sipped her coffee thoughtfully and then said nothing for a moment, her head tipped to the side, that she was working up to broaching an uncomfortable subject.

"Ellie Traub came by," Lavinia said at last.

Willa got the message then. Ellie must have mentioned her and Collin. Willa picked up her fork and ate a bite of cheese Danish. "I'm sure she's happy to have you home safe and sound."

Lavinia took a big sip of coffee and set the mug down a little too firmly. "Ellie's *happy* because she's always liked you so much. She's always hoped that you might end up with one of her boys."

"I like Ellie, too, Mom. But then, you know that."

Her mom gave up on subtlety. She leaned across the table. "Oh, honey. *Collin?*"

Willa drew in a slow, calming breath and reminded herself that she'd gotten through to Gage about Collin and she could get through to her mom, too. "I care for Collin. I care for him a lot. Since the flood, I've gotten to know him—really know him. He's strong and good and brave. And he doesn't give himself enough credit, but I'm working on getting him to see that he's a much better man than he's willing to admit. And I've been staying with him, up at his house, since last Monday night."

Her mother winced and sipped more coffee. "Staying."

"Yes."

"But is that wise?"

"I'm proud to be with him, Mom. He's a wonderful man. He's done a lot to help people, to keep people's spirits up, since the flood. Ask around town. Please. Ask Gage. *He'll* tell you."

Her mother frowned. "Gage hasn't said a word to me about you and Collin Traub."

"I'm sure Gage was waiting for me to talk to you first. I appreciate his staying out of it."

"But you never even seemed to *like* Collin. And what about Dane Everhart?"

"I *always* liked Collin. A lot more than I ever wanted to admit."

"But—"

"And as for Dane, it was never going to work with him and me." Lord, she was tired of explaining about Dane. It was her own fault, though, and she had to remember that. She should have had the courage to say no when she meant no. "Dane's a great guy. He's just not the guy for me."

"But Collin is?"

Willa sat back in her chair and folded her arms across her chest. "I love you, Mom. A lot. I will always be there if you need me. But I'm twenty-five years old and perfectly capable of managing my own life. I can't say what the future will bring, but I am with Collin now and I am proud to be with him."

Her mother tipped her head to the side again. Willa braced herself for another onslaught. But her mom surprised her and slowly smiled. "I always did kind of wonder about you and Collin. I had a feeling there might be a spark or two between you…"

A burst of relieved laughter escaped Willa. Her mom was going to be all right with Collin, after all. She teased, "No way."

Lavinia nodded, looking smug. "Yes." And then she scolded, "But you really must clear things up with Dane as soon as possible."

"You're right. And I plan to. I'll be going to see him as soon as he gets back from Australia."

Her mom got up, brought the coffeepot over and refilled their mugs. "Collin has done well with the saddle-making business. He made your dad's CT Saddle, did you know?"

"I didn't know. Until Collin told me."

"And I hear that he's turned that old cabin of Casper's into something quite beautiful."

"Yes, he has. You and Daddy will have to come up for dinner. Maybe next weekend."

"We would enjoy that, honey. Very much."

* * *

Willa got back to Collin's at five. The main floor was deserted.

She called down the stairs. "I'm here!"

Buster came bounding up. As she scratched his ears in greeting, Collin called from below, "Half an hour?"

"Take your time!"

She fed Buster. There was leftover meat loaf and several servings of browned potatoes in the fridge. She put them in the oven to reheat and cut up a salad. Then she set the table.

By then, fifteen minutes had passed. The oven was on a timer, so she felt safe grabbing a quick shower.

She was rinsing off when the shower door opened and Collin stepped in.

"S'cuse me," he said with that slow smile that seemed to fire all her circuits at once. "Just need to freshen up a little…."

She laughed as he grabbed her close. "Don't get my hair wet!"

Of course, he took that as a challenge, turning her beneath the spray so the water poured down directly over her head. "Oops."

"Collin!" she sputtered, trying to wiggle free.

But she didn't try too hard.

And then he kissed her again. She realized it didn't matter that her hair was soaking wet.

All that mattered was that his mouth was pressed to hers and his arms were nice and tight around her.

The meat loaf was a little dry when they finally sat down to eat.

"Delicious," he said, and poured on the ketchup.

She asked him how the work was going. He said he'd

made progress, but there was still a lot to catch up on. Tomorrow he had that morning meeting in the town hall, but after that, he would come right back up the mountain and work for the rest of the day.

"I've been thinking I'm going to need to hire someone to work with me," he said. "Not right now. But it's coming. I know a couple talented saddle makers in Kalispell. I'm going to contact them, see if they have any interest in joining forces with CT Saddles. They could work in their own shops, but put in some of their time on projects I bring them."

"Growing the business. Excellent. And you can't do everything yourself—especially when you also want to help out with the rebuilding effort."

"There should be more hours in a day."

"No argument there." She ate a bite of potato. "Thelma told me today that she thinks you should run for mayor. She thinks you're the one to carry on, to build on what Hunter started."

He sent her a look from under his thick eyelashes. "Don't."

"Don't what?" She widened her eyes at him.

"Don't start in about me running for mayor. It's not going to happen."

She cut off a bite of meat loaf neatly. "I think it is."

"You don't know what you're talking about."

She set down her fork and put up a hand. "All right. Subject closed." She pressed her lips together to keep from smiling. "For now."

He made a low, grumbling sound, but let it go at that.

She ate the bite of meat loaf. And then she said, "My parents got back today. I went out to the ranch and had a nice visit with my mom."

He studied her for a moment, his grumpy expression

softening. "Sometimes I don't believe you're actually here, in my place, heating up the meat loaf, naked in my shower, harassing me over dinner...."

Tenderness filled her. "I like it, being here with you. I like it a lot." For a moment or two, they simply gazed at each other. They were both smiling by then. She remembered what she'd been about to tell him. "*Your* mother got to *my* mom before I did."

He forked up more meat loaf. "That doesn't sound good."

"Well, it was kind of scary when Mom started in on me, I'll admit."

"Started in on you about being with me?"

"She was surprised, that's all."

"Your mother knows you're too good for me," he said in that voice that seemed to be joking—but really wasn't.

She set down her fork. "No. She doesn't think that. She doesn't think that at all."

"Yeah, right."

"And neither do I, which you really ought to know by now."

He grabbed the big glass of milk he'd poured himself and guzzled about half of it. "This is a dumb thing to argue about."

"I agree. As soon as you admit what a great guy you are, we can *stop* arguing about this."

He actually rolled his eyes. "Okay, okay. I'm great. I'm terrific."

She raised her own glass of milk in a toast. "Yes, you are." She drank. When she set the glass down, she asked, "Would you mind if we had my parents up here for dinner? Maybe Friday or Saturday night? I was thinking we could have your folks, too. And maybe Gage and any of your brothers who wanted to come."

He was silent. A definite hesitation. "I have a lot of work I need to be doing, Willa."

"I understand. But I would do the dinner. You only have to come upstairs when everyone gets here."

"The road is still iffy."

"I go up and down it every day. As long as you know the spots to watch for, it's fine. I'll just tell them all where to be extra careful." She waited. He said nothing. Finally, she said, "If you don't want to have the family here, I think you ought to just say so."

He looked away. "It's not that."

"Then what is it?"

He pushed his plate away. "Come on, Willa. People get…expectations. Especially in this town. You saw how my mom was last night, dragging us all over the yard, making sure everyone got that you and me are together."

She had a sad, sinking feeling—at the same time as she told herself not to be in such a hurry about everything. She needed to let him adjust to what they shared in his own way, in his own time. She reminded herself that it had only been six days since they became more than friends, and that only a few minutes ago, he'd told her how happy he was just to be with her.

"So." She made an effort to keep her voice calm and reasonable. "You don't want to have the family up here for dinner this weekend. Am I right?"

He gave it to her straight, at least. "That's right."

Something shifted within her. Something died just a little. For the first time since they became lovers, she found herself thinking that it was simply not going to work out with them.

And then she told herself to stop. Just stop.

Maybe it was pushing it a little, to have the whole family over for dinner so soon. He did have a lot of work to do. And he was also unaccustomed to being half of a couple.

In fact, from things he'd said in the past, she had a sense that he'd never planned to be part of a couple. She needed to let him deal, give him the time and the space to start to see himself in a new light.

"You're mad," he said softly. Sadly.

She swallowed and shook her head. "No. It's okay. Really. It's fine."

The rest of the evening was lovely, Willa thought.

Collin was tender and attentive. He was passionate in bed. They talked for over an hour before they fell asleep. There was laughter. He held her close.

He honestly did seem happy just to be with her. More than happy.

Still, Willa couldn't shake the feeling that he'd drawn a line between them when he told her he didn't want the family over. An invisible but uncrossable line, a line that cut them off from a future together.

For him, they were lovers. The best of friends.

But no more than that.

Never more than that.

On Monday, Willa told her mother that she would have to put the family dinner on hold for a bit. Her mom didn't push. She said she understood. Everyone was scrambling since the flood, trying to catch up with their lives, to get things back to normal. Of course, Collin needed to focus on his work. They would all get together for an evening soon enough.

Willa smiled and nodded. But she was thinking, *I love him. I love him so much.*

And she was starting to get the feeling that loving him

wasn't enough, that he would never want to hear her say what was in her heart for him.

That she would never wear his ring.

Collin knew that he'd hurt Willa when he'd dug in his heels about having the family over.

He was trying not to think about that, about how he'd hurt her. He was trying to keep her with him, even though he knew that in the end, what she wanted and what he wanted were two different things.

Tuesday afternoon he sat through a second endless meeting with Gage, Nathan, Thelma and the rest of the group of community leaders they'd put together to come up with ways to speed flood recovery. When he finally left the town hall, he spotted Dallas, his oldest brother, coming toward him on the sidewalk, looking bleak.

But then, who wouldn't be bleak in Dallas's position? His wife, Laurel, had left him and their children last year. He was a single dad raising three boys on his own.

The brothers shook hands and clapped each other on the back. Dallas said he'd driven into town to pick the boys up from summer school.

"You got a little time to kill?" Collin asked him. "We could grab a beer at the Ace…." It was one of those invitations made only for form's sake. Collin had work waiting on the mountain and didn't really expect Dallas to say yes.

But his glum-faced brother surprised him. "Sure. I got about a half an hour until they turn the boys loose. Let's go."

They sat at the bar and ordered a couple of longnecks.

Collin asked how things were going and his brother said, "I'm proud of my boys and I'm getting by—and what's going on with you and Willa Christensen?"

Great. Getting grilled about Willa by his gloomy big

brother. That hadn't really been in the plan. Collin sipped his beer and tried to decide how to answer.

Dallas kept after him. "You've made Mom happy for once. I'll say that. But come on. Everyone knows Willa's living up at your place. Yeah, you're the hero of the day and all. You definitely manned up when the flood hit. But do you really think moving Willa in with you was such a great idea?"

By then, Collin just wanted to cut through the crap. "Dallas. What are you getting at?"

"Willa's a great person. And you're not so bad yourself. But she's the marrying kind and we both know it. The big question is, are you?"

Collin wanted to tell his brother to mind his own business. Unfortunately, Dallas had a point. "I'm nuts over her," he said low, so only his brother would hear him. "I've got it bad."

"I kind of noticed that. But let me point out the obvious. You don't move a nice girl like Willa into your place unless you're putting a ring on her finger real soon. Especially not when she's the kindergarten teacher. That's not a thing a man should do—well, maybe in New York City. But not in Rust Creek Falls."

Collin thought about what his brother had said. He thought about it a lot—constantly, as a matter of fact.

He felt bad. Rotten. Low.

He never should have let Willa move in with him. It wasn't good for her. He should have thought of her first, instead of how much he wanted to be with her, instead of indulging himself just because he couldn't shake the hold of needing her so bad.

Wednesday night, she asked him if something was bothering him.

He didn't know how to answer. If he told her that he was feeling like a low-down loser for living with her when he never intended to marry her, well, where would that lead?

To her moving out.

He knew her. There was no way she was going to hang around if he told her to her face that it was going nowhere between them.

And he couldn't let her move out. Everyone would say that he'd dumped her. She would be shamed in front of the whole town. He couldn't ever let that happen to her.

Plus, he didn't *want* her to move out. He just wanted to be with her. And not to have to think about what was going to happen next.

But then, he *did* think. He thought way too much. His mind was like a hamster on a wheel. A hamster on speed, thoughts going nowhere fast, endlessly chasing themselves in a circle.

He thought about that other guy, that guy from Colorado, the one who'd asked her to marry him. The other guy was a stand-up guy, she'd said.

She'd also said she was telling him no.

But *should* she be telling him no?

It made Collin feel sick in the pit of his stomach to think of her with that other guy. But what if the other guy was the *better* guy?

Collin wanted her. A lot. But he also wanted the best for her. And if the best for her was that other guy, well, Collin ought to step aside and give her some space to make the right decision.

He could do that much for her, at least.

But he did nothing.

Every day, every hour, his thoughts got more and more tangled up and confused. He didn't know how to talk to her about all of it. So he didn't talk to her.

He lied and acted oblivious and said there was nothing wrong—and that only made him more disgusted with himself. He started thinking how he really had a problem with seeing ahead to the consequences of his own actions. He had a part missing, emotionwise. He'd always been that way, chasing the thrill, hungry for excitement. Not thinking who would be hurt or damaged by his doing exactly what he wanted to do when he wanted to do it.

All day Thursday and half of Friday, as he worked in his shop to catch up on his orders, he tried to figure out what he was going to do to make things right with Willa. By three in the afternoon on Friday, he finally came to an actual decision. He realized there was only one choice for him now, only one thing to do.

He took a quick shower, put Buster in the pickup and headed for Kalispell.

It was no good lately with Collin, and Willa knew it.

Things had only gotten worse with every day that passed since Sunday, the day he'd told her he didn't want the family over. Every day since then, he'd become more distant, more uncommunicative. And she wasn't sleeping well at night now. She kept waking up and staring at the ceiling and trying to lie very still so that Collin wouldn't notice she wasn't asleep.

Wednesday, she'd asked him about it, about what might be on his mind. He'd looked right in her face and told her there was nothing.

She'd wanted to believe him. But she didn't believe him.

There was a falseness now between them. And it was growing. She needed to break through it.

But how?

It was starting to seem to her that there was only one

way to get through to him. She needed to put herself out there, tell him the hardest thing.

She'd wanted to wait a while, to simply be with him and let the closeness between them grow. But the only way they were growing since Sunday was further apart.

Yes, opening her heart to him was a big risk. She could end up without him. From the way he'd been behaving lately, she probably *would* end up without him as soon as she uttered those three oh-so-dangerous words.

But who was she kidding? In the deep ways, the ways that mattered, she was already without him.

So why keep lying to herself? She might as well go for it, might as well pull out the stops, put her heart on the line and accept the consequences. At least then she would know she'd given it her best shot.

On the way up the mountain Friday afternoon, she decided she would tell him as soon as he came upstairs from his workshop.

But when she got there, the house was empty. He'd left a note on the table: *Quick trip to Kalispell. Took Buster. Back by six.*

All right, she thought. She would tell him when he got back.

She could start dinner....

But no. Dinner could wait. She was much too on edge to think about food right then. She had lesson planning she could do, so she went to the spare room, where she'd set up a desk and computer, and she got to work firming up her choices for activities for the following week, making lists of materials she hadn't pulled together yet.

An hour dragged by. She finished at the computer and went back out to the kitchen to face the prospect of cooking something.

Anything to keep busy until he returned.

She was standing at the refrigerator with the door wide-open, staring blankly inside, when she heard the crunch of tries on gravel outside.

Her heart gave a sick lurch inside her chest and then started beating so fast she felt dizzy. She shut the refrigerator door and turned toward the hall and the short entry area.

The door opened. She heard his boots on the wide planks of the hardwood floor, heard the door close, knew he would be pausing at the coatrack to hang up his hat.

Buster came bounding in ahead of him. She knelt and pressed her face to the warm, sweet scruff of his neck. He wiggled and made happy whining sounds—and then left her to lap water from his bowl.

Slowly, her knees feeling absurdly shaky, she rose.

And there he was. "Willa." He wore clean jeans and a blue chambray shirt rolled to the elbows and her heart just ached at the sight of him. "Come here…." He held out his hands.

She hesitated. She couldn't…read him, had no idea what was going on with him. He seemed to be looking at her so seriously, with such determined intention. "I…" Words simply failed her.

And then he was right there, so close. In front of her. He smelled of mountain air, of pine trees. He took her hand. "Come on…" And he pulled her with him, around the jut of the counter, into the main living area, over to a fat brown chair by the window. "Sit down."

She did what he told her to do.

And then he was kneeling at her feet, looking up at her, his jaw set, his full mouth a determined line. He had something in his hand.

And then he was sliding it on her finger.

A ring. A beautiful diamond solitaire on a platinum

band. Exactly the kind of ring she would have chosen for herself. She stared at it, gaping. "Collin, what…?"

And then he said, "Marry me, Willa. Be my wife."

It was just what she'd hoped to hear him say someday. And for a moment, she knew the purest, most wonderful spiking of absolute joy.

It was all going to work out, after all. She would have her life with him. They would be married, have children. Be happy forever, just as she'd almost stopped dreaming they might be.…

She opened her mouth to tell him how glad she was, to say how much she loved him and how scared she had been that it was all unraveling, all going wrong.

But then, before a single sound got out, she saw that it wasn't right, after all. She realized what he *hadn't* said. It was the part about how he loved her. He'd left that out.

And instead of saying *Yes,* or *Oh, Collin, I do love you,* what came out of her mouth was, "Why?"

He blinked.

He actually blinked.

And that was when she knew that it wasn't going to work.

To his credit, he managed to pull it together. Sort of. "It's the right thing. And I'm nuts for you. That's not going away anytime soon. It's the right thing and…"

She stopped him by reaching out and pressing a finger to his lips. "The right thing, why?"

He swallowed. "Well, we *are* living together. And I want to keep on living with you and I…" He paused, tried again. "Okay. I love you, all right? I love you and I want to marry you and all you have to do is say yes."

She laughed. It wasn't a happy sound. The laugh caught in her throat and ended on something very much like a sob. "Oh, Collin. You're not telling me the truth. I know it. *You* know it. Can't you just say it? Just tell me what's going on with you, whatever it is."

He gazed up at her. He looked absolutely miserable. "You're not going to say yes to me, are you?"

She took off the beautiful ring. "I can't say yes to you. Not like this. I just can't." She reached for his hand. Reluctantly, he gave it to her. She put the ring in his palm and folded his warm, strong fingers over it. "You don't really want to get married, do you?"

He rose then. He gazed down at her, dark eyes so deep, full of turmoil and frustration.

She stared up at him and asked him again, "Do you?"

His mouth curved downward; his big body stiffened. And then he turned from her to the wide windows that overlooked their town. He stared out, showing her his broad, proud back. "What I want is you. What I want is for you to be happy, for you to have what *you* want. I don't want folks in town saying crappy things about you. I want you to have the best of everything. I don't really think I'm it, but you've told me over and over you won't marry that other guy, so it kind of seems to me that you'd better marry me."

"You *want* me to marry Dane?"

"No." On that, he didn't hesitate. "But you deserve the best. Is he the best? The way you talked about him the night of the flood, I guess so."

"I was stupid and small and petty the night of the flood. I wanted to get to you, to hurt you. I'm sorry I did that. It was wrong. Now, how many times do I have to tell you, Dane is not the guy for me?"

He didn't say anything. He only shook his head.

She tried again. "Who said crappy things about me?"

He still wouldn't look at her. "No one. I don't know. I just... I don't want them to, okay? And as long as you're living up here with me without my ring on your finger, well, they could, all right? In a small town like ours, they might. Especially the damn Crawfords. They'd do it just because I'm a Traub—the troublemaking, skirt-chasing Traub—and you're with me."

She got up then. And she went to him. When she stood at his shoulder, she said, "But they haven't."

He faced her at last. "Not that I know of." It was a grudging admission.

She wanted to touch him, to clasp his muscled shoulder, to lay her palm against his cheek. To lift up and press her lips to his, to kiss him until he pulled her close and kissed her back, until she forgot everything but the taste of him, the heat and wonder of him in her arms.

But no. Better not.

She said, "You keep evading the basic question. So I'll tell you what I think. I think you are a wonderful man—a much *better* man than you're willing to give yourself credit for. But I don't think that you want to get married. And you know what? I want *you* to have what *you* want. What you need."

He scowled down at her. "I don't like the sound of this, Willa."

Her throat clutched. The hot tears were pushing at the back of it. She refused to let them fall. "I love you," she got out on a bare husk of sound. "With all of my heart. And that's why I'm going to pack up my things and go."

Chapter Fourteen

It was five minutes to eight when Willa arrived at the ranch that night. Buster leading the way, she came in the door carrying two big boxes full of her things. Her parents, settled into their recliners for a quiet evening at home, glanced over at her with matching expressions of surprise.

Her mom jumped up. "Willa. What in the world…?"

The tears broke free then. They streamed down her cheeks. "Collin asked me to marry him. He bought me the most beautiful ring. The perfect ring. And I said no."

Her dad got up, too, then. He came and put his big, rough, rancher's hand on her hair, pressed a kiss to her forehead. And then he took the boxes from her and carried them down the hall to her old room.

"Oh, honey…" Her mom held out her arms.

Willa went into them, into the kind of a comfort only a mom can give. "Oh, Mom. I love him."

"I know, I know…."

"But it's not... Oh, Mom. It's just...not..."

"Shh. Shh, now. It's okay. It's all right."

She was openly sobbing by then. She couldn't seem to stop herself. "It's not. No, it's just not..."

And her mom held her and stroked her hair and patted her back and kept saying how everything was going to work out. Her dad came back up the hall. Buster followed him out as he went to get the rest of her things.

After Willa left him, Collin went down to his shop and he went to work. He worked straight through Friday night. When the sun came up Saturday morning, he climbed the stairs, plodded down the hall and fell into bed.

He slept for a couple of hours, his dreams full of Willa. It was still morning when he woke up, by himself, in the bed that he'd gotten way too damn used to sharing with her.

In those first few seconds when consciousness found him, he forgot she wasn't there. He reached for her, but there was only emptiness on the other side of the bed.

That was when it all came flooding back. She was gone.

He got up and went back down to work.

Willa woke up early that Saturday. There was no summer school, but she went to town anyway. She wanted to talk to her brother before somebody else told him that she and Collin were through.

Gage was in his office.

She went in, closed the door and said, "I broke up with Collin. It's not what you think, so please don't try any big-brother heroics."

He was already looking thunderous. "What do you mean, it's not what I think?"

"He asked me to marry him. I turned him down. I made the decision to move out, not him. He wanted me to stay—

and do not ask me why I left, because I'm not explaining myself. All I'm saying is that he only wanted to do the right thing."

Gage got up from behind his desk then. He came around and he took her by the shoulders. For several seconds, he simply held her gaze. And then he pulled her close and gave her a hug. When he stepped back, he said, "So what you're saying is, you want me to stay out of it. You don't want me to bust his face in. And you want me to keep him on the Recovery Committee, to treat him like nothing has changed."

"Yes," she answered softly. "That is exactly what I'm saying."

Around five in the afternoon that day, Collin trudged back upstairs. He drank a quart of milk and ate a tuna sandwich standing up at the counter. Then he went down the hall and fell across the bed. When he woke up a few hours later, he returned to the lower floor and worked some more.

That was kind of the tone for the whole weekend. He didn't bother to shower or shave or even use a toothbrush. He worked. When he started to feel like he might fall over or hurt himself with his own tools, he went upstairs, grabbed something to eat, fell across his bed for an hour or two—and then woke up, remembered all over again that Willa was gone and staggered back down to his shop.

On Sunday, his mother called twice. He let the calls go to voice mail.

He might have stayed on the mountain indefinitely, but on Monday morning as he stood at the counter, staring blankly into space, downing a mug of coffee, he heard a scratching noise. And then a whine.

He went to the front door and opened it.

Buster.

The dog whined again and wagged his tail. When Collin only stared down at him, he plunked his butt on the porch boards and whined some more.

"You're not supposed to be here."

Tongue lolling, the dog stared up at him hopefully.

"Fine." Collin stepped back and Buster came in. He went right to his water bowl and lapped up what was left in it. Then he sniffed the food bowl. "Oh, pardon me. I had no clue you were coming." Collin laid on the sarcasm. Unfortunately, it was wasted on Buster. "Okay, okay." He went and got the bag of kibble. Buster sat and waited as he filled the bowl. "Go for it." And Buster did exactly that.

Willa was probably worried about the mutt. He would have to call her....

His heart lurched into overdrive and his throat felt tight, his tongue thick and heavy in his mouth as he autodialed her cell.

She answered on the second ring. "Collin." A small voice, so soft. And then she must have realized why he'd called. "You have Buster?"

"Yeah. He just now showed up at the door."

"Oh. I'm glad. We were worried...."

"I'll bring him down today."

"You don't have to. I can drive up after—"

"I said I'll bring him. I have a meeting anyway." A meeting he hadn't planned to go to, but hey. He couldn't hide in his shop forever. Life went on. Such as it was.

"I have summer school."

"Yeah, I know." He was aching for the smell of lemons, for that soft place in the curve of her throat. He loved to kiss her there.

"I'll call Thelma. She never minds watching him."

"But she's going to the meeting."

"It's okay. I'll ask her to wait for you. He's fine in the house without her. I'll pick him up there after school."

So, then. He wouldn't see her. That was good. Or so he tried to make himself believe. "All right, then."

"Thank you for bringing him...."

He tried to think of what to say next.

But then it didn't matter. She was gone.

Off the phone. Not in his house. Out of his life.

I love you, she'd told him. *With all of my heart.*

The bleak numbness of the weekend was fading. He'd started getting the feeling that he'd messed up bad, that he'd gotten stuck somewhere in his mind, stuck being some guy he really wasn't anymore. He'd thrown away what he wanted most because he didn't have the sense to say the things Willa needed to hear. It was all doubly discouraging because the things she needed to hear really were there, inside him, even though he'd gone and pretended they weren't.

He'd pretty much told her to go marry that other guy. The more he thought about that, the more disgusted he got with himself. It would serve him right if she took his advice.

Thinking about it all made his head spin. A spinning head and a broken heart were a real unpleasant combination.

He told himself that now, to be fair, he had to wait. He had to let her work it out with Dane Everhart one way or another. If she turned down the guy from Colorado, then maybe...

Maybe what? Seriously, what was the matter with him? What he needed to do was leave her alone. If there'd ever been any hope for him with her, he'd pretty much blown that by the way he'd treated her.

He scrambled some eggs and ate them, took a shower,

loaded Buster into his pickup and drove down the mountain. He dropped off the dog and went to the meeting.

Gage was there. Once or twice, Collin caught the other man watching him. But Gage didn't say a word about Willa. They discussed the donations that were coming in—and how to get more. They talked about the volunteers who'd come in from Thunder Canyon and elsewhere and how best to put them all to work rebuilding Rust Creek Falls. The meeting lasted three hours and they were still only two-thirds down the agenda. They agreed to meet Wednesday, same time, and finish up.

Collin drove to Kalispell and stocked up on groceries. He went home and went back to work—and deleted, unheard, all the messages his mom had left him over the weekend and that day.

The next morning, there was Buster, big as life, waiting at his front door. That time he texted Willa instead of calling. It just seemed wiser not to talk to her. Not to put his overworked heart under that kind of pressure, not to give himself any opportunity to make an idiot of himself all over again by begging for another chance. He took the dog to Thelma's and went back up the mountain.

On Wednesday morning, he couldn't help expecting Buster to show up again. But he didn't. They must be keeping a closer eye on him.

Which was good. For the best.

He was standing at the counter drinking his coffee, staring into the middle distance, wondering what Willa might be doing at that moment, when someone knocked at the door.

Willa?

He choked in midsip and his pulse started racing. Hot coffee sloshed across his knuckles as he set the mug down too hard. He wiped the coffee off on his Wranglers and made for the door.

It couldn't be her....

And it wasn't.

It was his mom, wearing tan pants, riding boots and an old plaid shirt, her straw Resistol in her gloved hands. She'd come on horseback, ridden her favorite mare, Sweetie, who was hobbled at the foot of the steps, nipping at the sparse grass.

"You deleted my phone messages, didn't you?" She asked the question softly. Kind of sadly. And that, somehow, was a thousand times worse than if she'd just started lecturing him as usual, if she'd called him her Last Straw and threatened to hit him upside the head to knock some sense into him.

He shrugged. "Yeah. I deleted them."

"Are you all right?"

"No."

"Sometimes you can be your own worst enemy."

"That's a fact."

"Not so much now as when you were younger, though." She almost smiled, but not quite. "I'll call that progress."

"You want to come in?"

She shook her head. "I'm just checkin' on you. I didn't check on you enough when you were little. Too late to make up for all that now, I guess."

"You're doing all right."

She put her hat back on. "You keeping fed?"

"Mostly."

"There's no law says you can't try again, and do a better job than you did before. Messing up is just practice for the next time, when you get it right." She turned and started down the steps.

"I love you, Mom," he said softly to her retreating back.

The words felt strange in his mouth. He knew he hadn't said them to her enough. And this time she probably hadn't even heard him.

Gathering the reins, she mounted. "Love you, too." She clicked her tongue and the horse turned and started back down the road. He stayed in front of the open door, watching her, until she disappeared from sight.

About then, he heard a whine. He glanced over and saw Buster sitting in the scrub grass beside the porch.

For the first time in days, Collin smiled. He slapped his thigh.

The dog barked, jumped to his feet and came running.

That morning, Willa got the call she'd been dreading.

The one from Dane. "Willa. My God. I just came from the airport, just heard how bad the flooding was in Rust Creek Falls. Are you all right?"

"I'm fine. Really." *Except for the little matter of my shattered heart.* "I lost my house and my car, though."

"Oh, sweetheart. I'm so sorry."

"Dane. Listen. I need to see you. I'm coming to Boulder, right away." Shelby could fill in for her. And Buster had taken off again, but it was no mystery where he'd gone. Maybe she would just call Collin and ask him if he could look after the dog until she got back.

"Coming to Boulder?" Dane boomed. "Not on your life."

"But, Dane, I—"

"I'm coming to you."

"No. Really, I'll find a flight and—"

He interrupted her. Again. "Sit tight, honey. I've got a plan."

Lord. She blew out a long breath. "Don't you always?"

He laughed, a bold, booming sound. "I'll be there before noon, you watch me."

"We'll have to arrange to meet somewhere. As I said, my house is a total loss." And she didn't want to meet him at the ranch. Too awkward, with her parents there....

"How about the middle of Main Street? You'll see me coming. I'll be the one in the CU helicopter."

"A helicopter?" How very, very Dane.

"Yeah. I'm getting the use of it courtesy of a generous alumnus. I'm coming, honey. I am as good as on my way...."

Collin, Gage and the rest of the committee were finishing up their endless meeting in one of the town hall conference rooms when they heard a helicopter overhead.

Nathan frowned. "We're not expecting a visit from the governor."

But then the helo loomed outside the window, coming in. Apparently, it was going to land in the street out in front. It was black and silver, with a giant gold CU painted on the belly.

Gage leveled that steady gaze of his on Collin. "Looks like Coach Everhart is dropping in to see how Willa's doing."

Collin reminded himself that he had to stay out of it. He needed to let Willa figure out what she wanted for herself.

But then, he couldn't do it. He could not just sit there.

He shot to his feet and headed for the door. Behind him, he thought he heard a low chuckle from Gage.

Willa was waiting on the sidewalk as the helicopter touched down. There were people all around her, folks she'd known all her life. They'd come running out of the library, the church and the town hall. Others had halted on the street. Everyone stared upward. It wasn't every day that a helicopter flew down and landed in the middle of town.

Leave it to Dane to make his arrival an event.

The chopper touched down. Dane jumped out before the blades stopped whirling, bending low to keep his handsome blond head out of danger. "Willa!" He ran toward her, rising to his full six feet six inches as he cleared the slowing blades.

Dread and misery and a healthy dose of embarrassment formed a leadlike ball in the pit of her stomach. She wrapped her arms around herself and waited grimly for him to reach her. Paige had given her the use of her house so she and Dane could be alone when she said the things she had to say.

"Willa!" The wonderful, rough deep voice came from behind her.

She stiffened, gasped, certain she couldn't have heard right. And then she whirled toward that voice, her heart in her throat.

Collin.

He was real. He was there. He reached out and put his warm, strong hands on her shoulders and she trembled with happiness just at his touch.

"Willa..." He stared at her with such frank longing in those beautiful dark eyes. She blinked at him, hardly daring to believe, and a ragged, hopeful sound escaped her. And he said, "Willa, damn it. I want you and I love you. Maybe I've always loved you, since way back when we were kids and I used spy on you playing with your Barbie dolls out in your dad's back pasture. Yeah, I know..." He tipped his head in the direction of the tall man behind her. "That other guy may be a better man. But there's no way he loves you like I do. And there's also no way I'm not trying again, no way I'm letting you go without pulling out all the stops." And then he dropped to his knees in front of her, the way he had last Friday. Only, somehow, nothing at all like last Friday. Because that had been all wrong.

And this, now, this moment? It was so very right.

He grabbed her hand and said fervently, "Stay, Willa. I'm asking. I'm begging. Stay here in Rust Creek Falls and be my wife."

People started clapping. Some shouted encouragements.

"You tell her, Collin!"

"Say it like you feel it!"

"Don't let her get away!"

There were whistles and catcalls.

Willa hardly heard them. For her, at that moment, there was only Collin, though he was looking kind of hazy through her happy tears. She confessed, "You really had me worried there."

"I know. I messed up. But I swear to you, right here on Main Street, in front of God, the library, that other guy—and way too many of our friends and neighbors—that when it comes to you and me, I won't mess up again."

She tugged on his hand. "Come here. Up here to me." And he swept to his feet once more. "I love you, Collin Traub," she told him. "I will always love you. And yes. Absolutely. You and me. From this day forward."

"Willa…" He grabbed her close and kissed her, a real kiss, deep and long and sweet. Everybody clapped all the harder.

When he lifted his head, she blinked up at him, dazed with joy. "Buster?"

"At Thelma's." He bent to kiss her again.

"Ahem," said the man behind her.

Willa pressed her hands to Collin's warm, hard chest. They shared a long, steady look, one of perfect understanding. And then, together, they turned to face Dane.

As it happened, Dane Everhart was not only a great guy, he was also a good sport. He said wryly, "Looks to me like I don't have a chance here."

Willa answered gently, "You're a good man, Dane. And I was wrong not to be straight with you from the first."

Dane gave a low chuckle. "Sometimes I'm a little pushy when it comes to going after what I want." He nodded at Collin. "You're a lucky man."

Collin pulled Willa closer to his side. "You're right. And I know it. I'm the luckiest man alive."

Dane held out his hand to Willa. She took it and they shook. "Be happy," he said.

"I will."

And then he turned and ran to the helicopter. The blades started whirling again.

Willa threw herself into Collin's waiting arms. They didn't see Dane go. They were too busy sharing another long, hot, perfect kiss, one that sealed their mutual commitment to their town, to each other and to the future they would build together with their own loving hands.

They were married three days later, on Saturday, July 27 with Pastor Alderson presiding.

It was a simple afternoon ceremony in the Community Church. The whole town attended and there was a big pot-luck afterward. Willa wore her mother's wedding dress. Paige stood up as her maid of honor and Collin asked his brother Sutter to come out from Seattle to be his best man.

If people whispered about how the maid of honor and the best man used to be together, they didn't whisper for long. Paige and Sutter conducted themselves with quiet dignity and the talk quickly died down.

It was one of those weddings where all the guests were smiling, a feel-good kind of day. Rust Creek Falls may have suffered through the flood of the century. But now the sun was shining and love ruled the day. Everyone could see that the bride and groom were meant for each other. Willa glowed with pure happiness.

And the former Traub bad boy had eyes only for his bride.

* * * * *

Danger, Donna Byrd, said a little voice in her head. *Danger!*

But she was in a rather reckless mood. "How interesting would you like to make this?"

He jerked his chin toward the board and, damn, it was sexy.

"If I hit the center," he said, "you will answer any question I ask."

"That's begging for trouble."

"I'll take it easy on you. Promise." He hit the bull's-eye with no problem.

"Okay. Have at it."

Her choice of words could've been better. Or maybe they were perfect, because a wicked gleam in his gaze told her that she'd hit her own bull's-eye in him.

Caleb sauntered over to the board, plucking out the darts, then leaning against the wall. In his faded blue jeans, tattered boots, long-sleeved white shirt and that hat, he seemed as though he should be out riding the range, not taking aim at her.

But when he did, his aim was true.

"What's the one thing I can do to persuade you to give me a chance, Donna Byrd?"

MADE IN TEXAS!

BY
CRYSTAL GREEN

MILLS & BOON

Crystal Green lives near Las Vegas, where she writes for the Mills & Boon® Cherish™ and Blaze® lines. She loves to read, over-analyze movies and TV programs, practice yoga and travel when she can. You can read more about her at www.crystal-green.com, where she has a blog and contests. Also, you can follow her on Twitter @CrystalGreenMe.

To Judy Duarte and Sheri WhiteFeather—
finally, our Byrds find life!

Chapter One

"Whoa there, Lady Bird, let me give you a hand with that."

As Donna Byrd heard the deep, drawling voice behind her, she kept on lifting the hand-carved rocking chair that she'd barely been able to liberate from the bed of one of the Flying B's pickups.

But just as she got the furniture under control, she looked over her shoulder to see who was calling her such a name as "Lady Bird," and her grip faltered.

Dimples.

That was what she saw first. Then the light blue eyes that pierced her with an unexpected shock. A shock that she hadn't felt for… Well, a long, long time.

A shock that she really didn't have time for with everything that was going down at the Flying B Ranch.

The owner of those dimples didn't seem to care about Donna's bottlenecked schedules or Byrd family scandals as he grabbed the wobbling rocking chair from her and deftly swung it on to one of his broad shoulders. Then he flashed that smile at her again, his cowboy hat now shading his face from the early July sun. "Where do you need me to put this…?"

"You can call me Donna Byrd," she said, correcting him before he could get too cute and call her Lady Bird again. She gestured toward the main house, with two separate wings spreading out from its core and a wraparound porch. It was the very definition of *Texas cattleman's domain* to her. "You can set the rocker in the living room, if you don't mind."

"I don't mind a bit."

He gave her a long look that covered her all the way from head to toe and sizzled along every inch of skin.

By the time his gaze burned a trail back up her body again, Donna's breath had completely stopped.

Even though she was trying to tell herself that she didn't know him from Adam, she vaguely remembered him. She'd seen him one time, a few months ago, back when her cousin Tammy had injured herself and this same ranch hand had been there to help her out.

He hadn't smiled at her this way, though… At least, Donna didn't think so. She'd been too focused on Tammy's injury to remember. Plus, there'd been a million other things distracting her, like turning the main house and surrounding cabins into a bed-and-breakfast business. She, her sister, Jenna and Tammy had inherited the property from a grandfather none of them had ever met before. Besides that, there were all the personal issues that she'd been trying to deal with.

Even if she had noticed this guy's dimples, she wouldn't have had time for more than a passing glance.

Now he winked at her and carried the rocker up the steps and through the front door she'd already opened. She took a moment, getting her first official good look at him, his worn Wranglers cupping his rear end, his white T-shirt clinging to the muscled lines of his back.

That shock she'd felt before returned with a blast of heat, and she chased it away by shutting the pickup's tailgate, the slam like a punch of reality.

She was thirty-one, too old and too wise to be ogling cowboys. Besides, after she, Jenna and Tammy finished up with all the logistics of the B and B, there would be a big marketing push for Donna to carry out—a task that she had embraced wholeheartedly, since she could accomplish it from New York, where she planned to rent a less costly apartment than she'd had before her grandfather's impending death had summoned all of the Byrd family to Texas. And when she got back to the city, she could return to real life—taking up where she'd left off after her online magazine, *Roxey,* had collapsed. She had ideas for a relaunch under a different title and premise in this new economy....

As she went into the main house, she tried not to think about how the stock market had taken a hit, and how her finances had made her magazine tank. Her wonderful life, her stylish apartment on Manhattan's Upper West Side and nights spent prowling all the new, hot restaurants nearby—it'd all fallen out from under her until Tex Byrd had called.

She silently thanked her grandfather for thinking of his grandkids during his last days. He'd at least been successful in introducing all of them to each other, even if his big hope of reuniting his estranged sons hadn't come true just yet.

In the living room, she found the cheeky ranch hand standing over the rocking chair, which he'd set near a stone fireplace. It was right where she'd been thinking of putting it.

"I appreciate your help," she said, thinking this would be the end of him and she could get back to work.

Yet, he wasn't leaving. No, he was running a hand over the mahogany wood of the high-backed Victorian rocker, making her wonder what it would feel like to have his long fingers mapping *her* with such slow deliberation.

"Where'd you find this beauty?" he asked with that lazy drawl.

She cleared her throat…and her head. "It was in the last abandoned cabin on the property."

"I hear that you and the other Byrd girls have turned all the rest of those cabins upside down and inside out," he said, looking up at her with a grin. "Then you fancied them up with gift baskets and flowers in vases, just like a hotel."

"We want people to be comfortable when they stay here."

God, those dimples. They made her angry for causing such a stir in her. Made her entire body tingle, too.

"It's true," she said, ready to go on her way now. "We Byrd girls have been very hard at work."

"I haven't been back on the Flying B for long, but I've noticed some of the changes you've made to the main house, too—the new swing on the porch outside, the flower garden and fountain you put out back for the guests."

He stood, but he kept a hand on the rocker, his thumb brushing over the carvings of ducks and swans that some man must've painstakingly etched for a woman who'd rocked his child to sleep years and years ago. A strange ache in the center of Donna's chest weighed her down for some reason.

But that was strange, because she'd never planned for children.

No time. Not her, the woman always on the go.

Yet that ache stayed in Donna as she ripped her gaze from the rocking chair and crossed her arms over her chest.

The ranch hand wasn't going anywhere. What—was he expecting a tip, like a doorman?

He sauntered across the room, his boots thudding on the Navajo rug until he got close enough to extend his hand to her.

"It's my turn to introduce myself," he said. "Caleb Granger."

Even his name sounded so very cowboy. Politely, she took his hand and shook it.

"Thank you for your help, Caleb," she said.

Most normal people would've let go of her by now, but not this guy. He kept a hold of her for an extra second—enough to send a pulse of pure need through her fingers and straight down to...

Well, to a location that twisted her around inside.

She let go of him and stepped aside, making it clear that the room's exit was all his.

"So what other gems did you dig up in those old cabins?" he asked, as if he had all the livelong day to charm her.

All right. Maybe it would be a good idea to go along with this. Donna knew full well that she came off as prickly to a lot of people, and she'd been trying to remedy that lately. Honestly, her remoteness was something she'd been aware of for a while now, ever since it had emerged after her parents had divorced and her mom had passed on from cancer when she was nine and Jenna was eight.

People left you. Donna had learned that early in life, and she'd only been readying herself for it to happen again and again.

"We've pulled out some good furniture from the cabins," she said, continuing the small talk. "Cherrywood end tables, a couple of handcrafted cedar chests, cute knickknacks that we've polished up and used to decorate all the guest rooms, even in the main house."

"You're using themes—like the Ace High Saloon Room and Fandango Room."

"We might as well capitalize on the Old West atmosphere of the area. Buckshot Hills has some colorful history to work with."

Donna didn't add that the Flying B had a lot of its own history that wouldn't make it into any room. When she, Jenna and Tammy had gone through what they'd started calling the "dream cabin," they had decided to make only mild improvements to it—especially with the so-called "magical" feather bed stored in there.

Too many weird vibes. Too *much* history for the Byrds.

Family legend had it that when someone slept on that bed, their dreams would come true. Donna hadn't believed a word until Tammy had experienced it firsthand, which had led to her engagement to "Doc" Mike Sanchez, who'd also had a dream. Then the same thing had happened to Jenna and her fiancé, J.D., bringing them together, too.

Yes, Donna was staying as far away from that mattress as possible, because Savannah Jeffries, the woman who'd started all the trouble between Donna's father, Sam, and his twin brother, William, had once slept on that bed, and Donna still wasn't sure what to make of the woman who'd caused all the warring in this family.

The silence between her and this Caleb guy had stretched on for too long, and for the first time, he seemed to be aware of her notorious standoffishness. It'd just taken him a little longer than others to realize it.

"Well then," he said, "if you need any help hauling around more rocking chairs, just give me a holler."

"Okay." Thank goodness, he was finally going to give her some peace.

He tipped his hat to her, and for a moment, she let herself be enthralled with those dimples.

Just one little second.

Then he left the living room, allowing Donna to catch her breath again, once she heard the front door close.

On a whim, she furtively glanced around the room, and since she was quite alone, she wandered over to the window. She peeked around the lace curtains to see Caleb Granger taking his sweet, slow time down the steps, one hand at his waist, his thumb hooked in a belt loop.

She watched until he rounded the corner of the house, no doubt heading toward his side of the ranch, leaving Donna to *her* side.

It took her a minute to recognize that her heart was throbbing—in her neck, in her chest....

And down lower.

But Caleb Granger? Was absolutely *not* her type.

So why was her body trying to tell her differently?

She liked men in pressed suits. Men with some city polish who figuratively got their hands dirty behind a desk, not literally in the stables. Men who smelled like cologne, not...

Saddle soap. Musk.

That was what Caleb Granger had smelled like, come to think of it. And, when Donna had initially come to the Flying B, she'd discovered that being too close to hay made her sneeze, and she'd stayed well away from it ever since, stocking up on allergy medicine and lingering near the main house and cabins instead of the stables.

There was no doubt in her mind that she would be allergic to cowboys like Caleb Granger, too, and that suited her just fine.

Donna was still gazing out the window when she heard a chuckle behind her. Two chuckles.

She looked over her shoulder, to where her cousin and sister stood near the living room entrance. Tammy's dark hair spilled over her shoulders, covering the spaghetti straps of her stylish flowered summer top—one result of a complete makeover for the former tomboy, who could still rope and wrangle with the best of the ranch hands. Jenna, who was the same shade of blond as Donna—although her sister's hair was longer and wavier—was just as pretty in a light blue blouse that brought out the color of her eyes, plus skinny jeans and fashionable yet practical boots.

"What's so funny?" Donna asked.

"You." Jenna leaned against the wall. "We saw you giving him the eye."

Tammy bit down on another laugh.

"Him?" Donna pointed toward the window. "That ranch worker?"

"His name's Caleb Granger," Jenna said.

"Don't I know it." Donna shook her head and walked away from the window, as if to show that she hadn't been interested for even a hot moment. "He made it a major point to introduce himself."

"I think he has a thing for you, Donna." Jenna again.

"He does not."

Tammy spoke up. "The first time he laid eyes on you, he was smitten. And I know the meaning of smitten, since I felt the same way when I met Mike."

A flutter winged around Donna's chest, and she rolled her eyes, thinking that would stop it.

It didn't.

"As if you'd know what Caleb was doing the first time he saw me, Tammy," Donna said. "He was there when you fell and ate it in the dream cabin that day, and you were no doubt hurting too much to dwell on what he was thinking about me. He just didn't leave an impression on *me* because all I cared about was getting you some medical help."

Tammy and Jenna laughed again, and Donna inwardly cringed. They had to be thinking about how clueless she was sometimes, how mired she tended to get in the bigger picture, whether it was Tammy's injury or all the projects they had going on the Flying B. But that's how it had always been with her, because work shut everything else out.

Divorce, death… Work was far more comfortable. And so were goals, like having her own successful magazine and a bright-lights-big-city life again.

Of course, goals could change. Before she'd come to the ranch, she'd never thought about forging a better relationship with the sister she'd been so distanced from her whole life, seeing as Jenna didn't seem to have much in common with Donna when they were young and their dad had raised them to be single-minded women who went after what they wanted, no matter the cost. She'd never thought about getting close to the cousins she'd never known, either.

But losing Grandpa Tex just when he'd come into her life had shown Donna, once again, that you had to tread lightly with others, that getting close was still a chancy proposition that she was just now dipping her toes into.

Not too deeply, though.

Never too deeply.

After Tammy and Jenna had laughed it up quite thoroughly, Tammy said, "I hear that most girls do remember Caleb. *Really* well."

Jenna added, "*I* hear there're more than a few of them, too."

"Who knows how many there've been since he's been off the Flying B?" Tammy gave Donna a sly glance. "He took a leave of absence for some family matters—something about helping his father and aunt move to Buckshot Hills and get settled."

"J.D. took his job in the stables for a while," Jenna said.

At least Donna had been paying enough attention to know that Jenna had met J.D. when he'd been wandering the Flying B Road to the ranch. He had lost his memory, and Jenna had helped nurse him back to health along with Doc, until J.D. had regained his senses.

Jenna was waggling her eyebrows. "But now Caleb's back—and this time it looks like Donna actually had time to notice."

Tammy cracked up again as Donna sighed in exasperation. Maybe she *had* noticed, but it didn't matter. Not when she had a million things to do today.

And definitely not when she wasn't planning to stay around the Flying B for much longer, anyway.

AFTER LEAVING THE main house, it hadn't taken Caleb long to hitch a ride at the barn with old Hugh in his Dodge.

They rambled along on the dirt road leading out to the east boundary of the ranch, where they were going to mend fences today. Before they'd hopped into the truck, Hugh, the foreman, had introduced Caleb to J.D., the man who'd taken Caleb's place during his leave of absence.

"He's been a real find," Hugh said now, "but we missed you, boy. Nothing's been the same without you around."

"Same here, boss."

Caleb rested his bare forearm on the windowsill as the truck grumbled along, passing the fields that yawned under a sky that reminded him of Donna Byrd's eyes. He'd been thinking about her since the day he'd met her. Or *not* met her, to be more exact. She'd been a little... *distracted* might be a good word, but, then again, it'd been a trying day for the Byrds after Tammy's tumble and fall, then her visit to the doctor. So how could he blame Donna for being preoccupied?

Still, Caleb was used to making more of an impression on women, and Donna's cool attitude puzzled him. It also lit a fire in him that he'd never felt before, because good times had always come so easy.

And that was something Donna Byrd was obviously not. Easy.

She was sophisticated, dignified and more beautiful than anyone he'd ever set eyes on. There was something else about her, though, that got to Caleb. A depth. A sort of sadness that he'd caught a few months ago as well as today, and she only seemed to show it when she thought no one was looking, covering it up before a person could be sure.

Yet that was another challenge about Donna Byrd—seeing if he could make that hint of darkness go away.

And, Lord knew, Caleb knew about a little darkness.

"I missed the Flying B more than you know," Caleb said.

"You didn't exactly take a vacation."

"Right." Caleb turned to Hugh. "Have you ever spent any amount of time off the ranch? You never seem to take a break from it."

"No reason to." The old man pursed his lips. "I grew up here, just like you, and this is where I prefer to be above anywhere else."

"Then you'd have the same reaction to the suburbs as I did. Buckshot Hills is still country, but some of it's developing. I moved my dad and Aunt Rosemary into a new place—Yellow Rose Estates, they call it."

"Sounds uppity."

"It's modest. A bunch of tract houses that all look the same. But it's safe and close enough for me to visit when I need to."

They hit a rut in the road, and the truck creaked on its springs.

"How is the old man doing?" Hugh asked.

Caleb shrugged, and that was enough of an answer. Some days with his dad's worsening dementia were good, some weren't so much. Mostly they weren't, though, and Caleb had endured a lot of those days this past month or so, as he'd finalized the purchase of a new home for Aunt Rosemary and his dad and moved them from her former house near Dallas.

He could just see his aunt now, as they set up his dad's room with his sleep apnea equipment and the walker he refused to use as much as he should.

"We're so grateful for everything you're doing, Caleb." Rosemary had seemed so tiny, sitting on the bed in a pair of sweats, her hair gray and thinner than it had ever been. But she had smiled as she talked, her cheeks soft and rosy, as she'd glanced around her new home.

Ten years older than Dad, Rosemary had always been a maternal figure for him since they'd lost their parents early on, sticking with each other through thick and thin. She'd insisted on taking care of him now, too, especially since Dad's dander rose whenever Caleb was around.

Yup, Caleb knew that Aunt Rosemary was grateful. Not so much Dad, though.

"It's the least I can do," he'd said to her.

They hadn't talked about how he and his dad hadn't ever been good buddies or how he had always refused any of Caleb's help, even back when he'd been in his right mind. An only child, Caleb had been too much of a "party boy," in Dad's estimation; although, as Caleb had matured, he'd always lived up to every vow he'd made and every responsibility he'd had. But that had happened only after Mom had died, shortly after Caleb had graduated from the local high school and he'd left home, finding work at the Flying B, where he'd pretty much been raised the rest of the way to adulthood by Tex Byrd and the ranch hands.

It seemed as if Hugh had sensed the direction of Caleb's thoughts.

"You know you've got family here, Caleb. You always have and you always will. You were like Tex's own son."

Tex. Even the sound of his name made Caleb's chest hurt.

"Hey," Hugh said. "I know what you're thinkin', and it isn't right."

"What?"

"That you weren't around when Tex passed on. It wasn't your fault that he lied to you about just how sick the doc said he was when he told you to go on and see to your own dad's needs. He would've been fit to be tied if you'd stayed with him and refused to see to your father."

That much was true. Tex had been adamant about Caleb making up with Dad, no doubt because the family rift with the Byrds had gone on for so long and Tex regretted that he'd missed out on being a part of his own children's—and grandchildren's—lives.

The last thing Caleb had wanted was for Tex to be disappointed in him, so he'd gone. But he hadn't made it back to the Flying B in time—he'd only been here for the funeral, staying in the background before seeing to the last of Dad and Aunt Rosemary's new home—and that dogged him.

Grieving for Tex alone. Wishing he could've done something to keep him around for much, much longer.

Even with the note Tex had left him, telling him how proud he was of Caleb and how he hadn't wanted Caleb to see him wasting away in his final days, there was still that raw sense of loss and failure.

Hugh gave him another sidelong look, and Caleb decided to move on.

"The Flying B's a different place without him, isn't it?"

"It's a kind of different that Tex would've approved of. When he gave the girls the east side of the property, with the ranch and its buildings, and the Byrd boys the land that wasn't being used, he stipulated that they use their inheritance money to develop both sides after he passed away."

"I like what they're doing."

"I hear you like even more than that."

Caleb grinned. "It's no secret I get along with women."

Hugh's chuckle was a rasp. "The snooty Byrd isn't the one I would've chosen for you."

"Donna Byrd isn't snooty. She's just a fish out of water."

"And you'll reel her in. Is that right?"

"Why not? It's about time I settled down."

He'd come to that conclusion after seeing Donna for the first time. It'd been an instant, overwhelming attraction, even if it would be a challenge to hook her.

Hugh shook his head, and it rankled Caleb. Maybe the older ranch hand thought Donna was out of Caleb's league, or that a ladies' man like him would never settle down for anyone, even a Byrd. Or maybe Hugh was even thinking that Donna might be way too much trouble for him in the long run and he shouldn't pin his hopes on anything with her.

But Caleb couldn't blame his friend for any of that. No one, not even Hugh, knew how much of a father figure Tex had become to Caleb after he'd taken him in— even more than his own dad. Tex had sorely missed his own sons, and somehow, Caleb had filled a void, sitting down with him on the main house's old creaky porch swing after a long day, smoking cigars, talking for hours and drinking the good bourbon and wine Tex used to collect. The old man had never told Caleb the details about what had torn apart his relationship with his sons Sam and William—and what had made them dislike each other so intensely that it'd caused a tear that made their relationship ragged even today. But Caleb had heard rumors around the ranch, anyway, about how Savannah Jeffries had been dating one twin, William, during college. She'd come home with him one summer, after he'd suffered a broken leg in a car accident, and during his convalescence, she'd supposedly fallen for Sam, Donna's father.

Nope, no one knew just how much Tex had meant to Caleb.

Hugh sighed gruffly as he pulled the truck off the road, toward the fences that required their labors.

He turned off the engine. "Maybe you think that there's some kind of love bug going around since the Byrd kids have come back, Caleb, but from what I hear, Donna's probably immune to it. She's a cool one."

"I've melted my share," Caleb said.

"So you have." Hugh grabbed Caleb's shirtsleeve before he could open the door. "Just keep in mind that she's got a lot going on."

Although the older man didn't explain further, Caleb knew that Hugh only meant to protect him, and he gave the man a gentle, fond shove.

"Don't worry about me, boss." He exited the truck, his boots hitting the dirt.

He was as grounded as ever, with his feet back on familiar territory.

And he was just as determined to show Donna Byrd that he was more than merely a heart-struck cowboy.

Chapter Two

At the first peek of dawn, Donna was up and about because, no matter how long she'd been in Texas, she was still on New York time—an hour ahead of the dear Old West.

After doing a quick check of her email—nothing new or exciting there—she tucked her iPad into the crook of her arm, then went to the kitchen to grab one of the luscious chocolate chip muffins Barbara the cook had already made. After downing that, then a mug of Earl Grey tea, she scooted out the back door before a real breakfast could be served buffet style in the dining room.

A million things to do, Donna thought as she made her way to the nearest renovated cabin. And the first item on her list was to double—no, *quadruple*—check this particular room's condition.

It had cute embroidered curtains and valances, rustic Southwestern furniture, faux-Remington sculptures and "hotel amenities," as Caleb Granger might've called the fancy bathroom vanity basket that included everything from soaps and shampoos to more private items, like toothbrushes and even condoms for the younger, hip crowd they were targeting for business. But, at the sight of that last item, a flurry of sensation attacked Donna, and she frowned, turning away from the bathroom sink and its basket.

Putting Caleb Granger and condoms in the same train of thought brought back those tingles she'd been trying to ignore ever since she'd officially met him yesterday.

Yet she left all of that behind as she focused—and focused *hard*, to tell the truth—on switching a rugged cowboy sculpture on one oak end table with a second horse sculpture on a highboy chest by the door.

Afterward, she stood back to assess the look of the room again.

Not bad. Not bad at all. The Flying B and B would impress anyone, even the college friend she'd invited for the weekend. Theo Blackwood worked at *Western Horizons* travel magazine, and Donna hoped he would be swayed enough by the ranch to do a layout during their grand opening in a little less than a couple of months.

After brushing some dust off the rough cowboy sculpture, Donna couldn't find anything else to nitpick. It all really was tip-top. That's how everything *needed* to be. That's how life had always been for her, and someday soon, it would be that way again. All she needed to do was create a smashing success of this B and B, and she would be on her way out of Hoop-De-Do, Texas, and back to the glamour and rush-rush of the big city.

She sat on the bed, the foam mattress and beige duvet as comfortable as sin, then fired up her iPad. The screen saver still featured the swirly, creamy logo she'd commissioned for *Roxey* magazine, but instead of feeling sorrow at its demise, Donna only wanted to live up to its failed promise.

But first, there were personal matters to attend to. One of her To-Do's today was an activity she managed *every* day—tapping the name Savannah Jeffries into an internet search engine. She was hoping that this time of all times she would discover something new that their P.I., Roland Walker, hadn't found out about the woman who'd torn this family apart.

Yet all that popped up on the screen were the same old results and links Donna always got, so she checked her email for the second time this morning.

But there was no word from their P.I., either, even though Donna contacted him religiously.

She blew out a breath. She didn't like being ruled by anything—another person, life's circumstances…even a growing obsession like this one. And just why *did* Savannah have a hold on her? Maybe it was because Donna had taken such stock in whatever her father, Sam, had taught her throughout life—at least, before he'd fallen from grace in Donna's and Jenna's eyes.

Know your opponents, he would say from behind his corporate desk whenever he brought her and Jenna to work. *Don't ever let them surprise you.*

But was Savannah the enemy? Or was it her dad, who had betrayed Uncle William and stolen his own brother's girlfriend that one summer when they'd all been on the Flying B?

She kept remembering something else her dad had taught her and Jenna. *Go after what you want at any cost, girls…*

His voice faded from Donna, and she tried to believe it didn't matter. Ever since the news about Savannah had come out, she'd been avoiding Dad. It'd been easy, too, since he was off with Uncle William again, this time in Hill Country, hunting and trying to iron everything out with his twin.

She was still attempting to figure out how she could talk to the stranger that Dad had become. They'd never been ultraclose, but she'd worshipped him as a daughter; she'd at least *thought* she'd known who he was, and it wasn't a man who would work his brother over.

Chasing all the alienating numbness away, Donna fully immersed herself in her computer, mostly with news of the publishing world. She liked the isolation of the cabin since it allowed her to get a lot of work done without interruption.

Then she heard something outside the door.

Boot steps on the small porch.

A knock.

Finally, the whisper of the door as it opened to let in a stream of morning sunlight.

"Anyone home?" asked a voice that had become all too familiar to Donna, since she couldn't seem to forget what it had sounded like yesterday when it had scratched down her skin, infiltrating her every vibrating cell.

Caleb Granger.

She sat up straight on the bed. "I'm in here."

Dumbest announcement ever, but what else could she do? Pretend she was invisible, just so he would go away?

When he pushed open the door, her heart started to beat with such an all-consuming volume that she could barely hear herself breathing.

Or maybe, just like yesterday, she'd stopped breathing

altogether at the sight of Caleb Granger in those boots, Wranglers and T-shirt.

And when he doffed his cowboy hat in her presence to reveal shaggy dark blond hair, then smiled with those lethal dimples, she wasn't sure she would ever breathe again.

THE MERE SIGHT of the early light flirting with Donna Byrd's shoulder-length blond hair and her skin, which she somehow kept smooth and creamy out here in the elements, was enough to send Caleb's pulse into a kicking frenzy.

She was something to behold, sitting on a bed wearing a sleeveless white halter top that was kind to every curve of her body. Her creased dark blue shorts clung to her lush hips, and even her Keds somehow came off as classy. She was certainly a far cry from when he'd seen her that first day, months ago, in suede boots and an expensive outfit that had marked her as anything but a country girl.

She seemed to realize that she was sitting on a bed, and she stood, brushing off her shorts with one hand while the other put one of those computer pad things that everyone in the suburbs had seemed so enthralled with down on the mattress. He noticed a fancy logo on the screen saver and recalled some gossip about a defunct magazine she'd run back in the city.

Drive and gumption. That's what this woman had, and hard times hadn't seemed to dampen her ambition at all, based on what she was doing with the B and B.

"Can I do something for you?" she asked.

He wasn't going to touch that innuendo-rife question

with a ten-foot stick. "I saw you headed in here earlier, and I thought I'd say a good morning."

For the first time in Caleb's life, a woman was looking at him as if she couldn't understand why in the world he would've gone out of his way for something so unimportant.

Was Hugh right when he'd told Caleb yesterday that Donna Byrd wasn't winnable? Or was she so far into her own business that she had no idea that Caleb was even interested?

Well, he didn't know just what to think of either option, but it didn't stop him from making himself at home and leaning against the door frame.

"I suppose I had another reason for stopping in," he said, flashing his smile at her again, pulling out the big guns.

She wrinkled her brow, as if he were a creature who'd wandered out from the woods, a previously unidentified species that absolutely perplexed her.

"Your reason being…?" she asked.

"Simple hospitality."

She laughed. "I've gotten plenty of that, Mr. Granger. Everyone on the Flying B has been more than cordial."

"And I'll extend that trend by asking you to call me Caleb. There's no need for 'misters' around here."

"Caleb it is, then."

Now she was looking at him expectantly. But that—and the compelling depth of her blue eyes—only made him forge on.

He'd never turned down a challenge before, and now wouldn't be the first time.

"Word has it that you're putting on some sort of movie night this weekend," he said.

"Oh. Right. Yes, we're attaching a screen to the side of the barn and setting up a picnic area in front of it for the staff, just like we'll be doing for our guests when we open the B and B. Barbara is planning a country menu, so you could call this a dry run for the real thing."

"A *country* menu? You mean basic Texas staples, like barbecue baby back ribs and steaks, hot biscuits and corn?"

"That's exactly what I meant." She stuffed her hands into her pockets. "We've got a special guest coming to the Flying B this weekend, so that's another reason for the show. He's a journalist friend of mine, and we're hoping he'll write an article for a B and B marketing push."

All Caleb heard was "friend" and "he."

"A friend, huh?" he asked carelessly.

"Yes, a…" She narrowed her eyes at him. "Never mind."

"No, go on, Lady Bird. I'm just curious."

"First off, my name's not Lady Bird."

Caleb smiled. "Okay, Donna Byrd." He liked the ring of that better, anyway. The way it flowed made her sound exotic, which she was to him; it made her sound as if she was a hothouse breed. But even if she wasn't so *hothouse* on the surface, Caleb would bet there was a soft, melting center to her, and he was going to find it.

She didn't seem amused by the adjustment to the nickname. "You were about to tell me why you were here?"

Yeah, that. "As I said—movie night. There's a lot of excitement in the air. Everyone's talking about how the ranch hasn't seen much in the way of celebration since Tex passed on."

He hadn't meant to change tone after saying Tex's name. Quieter. Reflecting a grief that still lingered.

When Donna removed her hands from her pockets and slightly tilted her head, as if in sympathy, he stood away from the door frame.

He hadn't come here to be a downer.

"I heard that you were close to Tex," she said softly. "I barely got to know him, but…"

She pressed her lips together, as if banning herself from saying anything else.

Yet he'd seen that sorrow in her gaze, and as much as she was attempting to cover it now, it wasn't working.

She cleared her throat. "I'm sorry for your loss."

"And yours," Caleb said.

She paused, then casually walked to the other side of the bed, straightening the thick quiltlike thing on top of it, but her actions didn't fool him for a moment. She was putting a barrier between them, just as she did with everyone else.

Good try.

"As far as movie night goes," he said, getting back on the subject, "I was only wondering what your plans were for it."

Donna stopped her fussing with the bed and watched him again, obviously trying to sort out his true meaning.

Caleb put on the charm once more. "I thought I'd bring some wine and—"

"Are you inviting me to my own function?"

"In a manner of speaking, yes, I am." He shrugged. "You'll have to take a break sometime that night."

Astonishment. Was that what he was seeing on her now?

He'd take it, because that meant he was getting a rise

out of her, and if there was nothing about her that was interested in *him,* she wouldn't have bothered with any kind of reaction.

"You've got some chutzpah," she finally said.

"What I've also got is great taste in wine."

"Do you really."

"Sure. Tex and I used to sit on his porch swing and talk about everything while we drank from his spirits collection. He was a wine guy, you know."

Donna had her arms crossed over her chest now. She seemed to do that around Caleb frequently.

"I saw his cellar," she said. "It *is* extensive."

"He had vintages shipped from all over—Napa Valley, Bordeaux, Chile, the Rioja region of Spain."

She surveyed him, seemingly taking a second look at the cowboy loitering near the doorway, and hope sprang in Caleb's chest.

Was she seeing beyond the Stetson and boots?

When she went back to straightening the pillows on the bed, he wasn't so sure.

"Thanks for the offer for movie night," she said, "but I'm afraid I won't have a second to rest."

Caleb let her excuse go. If she didn't come around this weekend, he would find another time to be alone with Donna Byrd.

Before he went, he took one last opportunity to be complimentary, glancing around the room. "As I said yesterday, you've done a real good job with the ranch so far. You should be proud."

She actually beamed, and it made him think that all the trouble she'd been dealing to him had been worth it.

"That's nice of you to say," she said.

"It's just the truth."

She sat on the bed, as if forgetting he was in the room and she had been using the mattress as an obstacle only a short time before.

Beds.

Donna Byrd.

Stop it, Caleb.

She said, "I've been going over the cabins again and again, looking for faults. It's good to hear that we've been successful."

"There's one place that you left out of your makeover, though. Savannah's old cabin."

The name hovered, as if circling them.

But if he was going to get to know Donna Byrd, Savannah was bound to come up sometime or another.

"It's a cabin that's just as good as any of the others," he said.

"No. That antique bed has been stored in there for a while, and… Well, we modernized the kitchen, but moving anything else around in there seems like bad luck or something."

This was unexpected. Was she superstitious?

Maybe she would believe in fate just as much as he did—that his destiny was tied to hers….

"You know all about that bed," she said. "Don't pretend you're oblivious."

"Tex told me a thing or two about it." *But not everything, I suppose.*

"I know that my great-grandmother first brought that bed to the ranch. This sounds like such a cliché, but she was supposed to have the gift of second sight, and she would dream of the future when she slept on that feather mattress." She hesitated, then said, "I know other people who've had…experiences…in the bed, too."

"You?"

It was dangerous to ask such a forthcoming question about beds. About Donna Byrd.

But she didn't shoot him one of those *what-are-you-all-about?* looks this time. She only laughed a little.

"No, I haven't been on the bed. But I do wonder if Savannah ever had dreams there since she stayed in that cabin."

"You think you'll have the chance to ask her?"

Now he knew he'd gone too far, because she stiffened.

Was she thinking that Byrd business was Byrd business, and he had no part of it?

Before he could decide, she gave him a curious look. "You haven't been around the ranch in a while, right?"

Aha, she'd noticed. The news did him good. "Right."

"There's a lot that's been happening with Savannah Jeffries. Nobody caught you up on all of it?"

"I'm afraid not."

Donna sighed. "Tammy found a grocery receipt while she was snooping around Savannah's cabin. You remember that day."

The day Tammy had injured herself in the cabin and he'd first seen Donna. He'd never forget.

"A receipt?" he asked.

"It was from the time Savannah spent on the ranch, and there was a pregnancy test on it."

Caleb froze. "Are you saying there might be another Byrd running around out there?"

"There could be."

He was getting better and better at recognizing Donna's body language. She was already shutting him out with her cool voice. But damned if he'd let her do that. He had an investment in this family, too, an interest in seeing that Tex's love for this land and his family was never tarnished.

But Caleb would have plenty of time for trying to make Donna come around, and he moseyed toward the door. "You'll want to be deciding on your favorite vintage, Donna Byrd. I'll have it ready when you are."

He received one of her miffed expressions in return, putting them back to where they'd been when he'd first entered the cabin. And just before it seemed that she was about to follow it up with a tart remark, the sound of a cell phone—a businesslike digital ring—interrupted them.

She stood, reaching into her pocket to answer as Caleb smiled at her in parting.

As he exited, he glanced back, just one more time, and when he found that Donna Byrd was watching him while answering her phone, he went on his way, his smile growing even wider.

HOURS LATER, DONNA was in her room in the main wing of the big house, sitting in the bay window and rubbing her temples to chase away a headache as she waited to go downstairs to share the news from the call she'd received earlier.

She was still reeling from what their investigator, Roland Walker, had told her, and, surprisingly, the only thing that was keeping her from stressing out entirely was the thought of Caleb and his promises of wine.

How strange was it that Caleb seemed to be her only bright spot during the day? She wouldn't have predicted that in a thousand years because he was a distraction. A man with a killer smile who only messed up her head and took her offtrack.

But every time he would cross her thoughts—and he seemed to be doing that quite a bit—she would find herself fighting a smile.

Her—the remote Byrd. The prickly one who had never found the kind of love Tammy and Doc or Jenna and J.D. had, and the one who probably never would, based on her record of dating, then deciding her time was better spent on whatever project she had on the front burner.

Speaking of which…

Her alarm clock read 5:00 p.m., and she inhaled, standing, then leaving her bedroom. When she got to the living room, everyone was waiting: Jenna, who sat in the new rocking chair by the fireplace; Tammy, who perched on a leather sofa in between her brothers, Aidan and Nathan, both dwarfing her with their size.

"What's so all-fire important that you pulled me out of my cabin?" Nathan, the younger brother, asked lightly. He and Aidan hadn't just been staying in their own cabins on the property, they had been making improvements bit by bit, practicing their home contracting business skills on the Flying B's structures.

Donna tried to smile at Nathan's high spirits. At least her cousin's jocular sense of humor was intact…for now.

Aidan, the serious one, merely waited for Donna to start.

"I got some good news today from Roland Walker." Donna had learned from Dad that you always started out positive if you were about to lower the boom on someone. "But it's also news you'll want to brace yourselves for."

Jenna sat forward in the rocking chair. "Roland found out that Savannah did have a child?"

Donna nodded, letting them all take that in.

On the sofa, Tammy bit her lip, suppressing a smile. She'd been the most curious out of all of them when it came to Savannah. Jenna just sat back in her chair, thoughtful, but Aidan was running a hand through his black hair, cursing under his breath, exchanging a look with an equally darkened Nathan.

"It's a boy," Donna said, still not knowing exactly how she felt about all of this, herself, now that matters had gone so far. "His name is James Bowie Jeffries."

Aidan let loose with that curse, following up with, "Are you kidding me? That woman had the gall to name him—"

"In the same way our dads were named?" Nathan interrupted, his mood definitely blacker.

"William Travis Byrd," Aidan said. "Sam Houston Byrd. Now James Bowie Jeffries. All named after Texas heroes."

"Except James Bowie isn't a Byrd," Nathan said, all traces of humor gone now.

Tammy said, "*I* have to admire Savannah."

"For what?" both brothers asked.

"For owning what she did." Tammy's black hair swung over her shoulders as she looked at one brother, then the other. "I wonder if she told James who the father was or if she raised him to be a Byrd."

"What *is* a Byrd?" Aidan asked. "None of us even knew that until we met Tex, and based on what we gleaned from the little our dads have told us, Tex didn't want any part of Savannah. So how would *she* know the definition?"

Nathan folded his bulky arms over an equally wide chest. "Tex threw her off this ranch after he found Sam and her together then everyone went their separate ways."

The last thing Donna wanted was for this to disintegrate into a Sam versus William match. All of them were getting along way too well for that to happen.

"The bottom line is," she said, "we're going to have to make a decision. It doesn't have to be tonight, but Roland said he can track James down if we want to meet him."

The boys chuffed.

Jenna rose from the rocking chair. "He's our brother... or cousin. Any way you put it, James is one of us."

Aidan stopped laughing. "That's another thing. I'd like to know just why it is he *needs* to be tracked down. Roland found Savannah already. Why isn't James easier to find?"

Donna automatically walked toward her sister, whom she had supported during the family's first vote, when they had debated whether to hire a P.I. to investigate Savannah in the first place. She'd had mixed feelings about locating Savannah then, too, but she had wanted to turn over a new leaf and support Jenna and her desire to find Savannah more than anything else.

"Roland told me," Donna said, "that James and Savannah are estranged."

"Seems like she has somewhat of a pattern," Aidan muttered.

Tammy elbowed him in the ribs and he gritted his jaw. "Why're they estranged?" she asked.

Donna shook her head. "Roland doesn't have that information right now, but we could ask him to find out."

Now Nathan was on his feet. "This is how I see it—we've already had any curiosity about Savannah appeased." He shot a look to Tammy, making sure everyone knew that she had been working overtime to assuage his feelings about *that* family decision. "But do we really want to take this further?"

Aidan stood, too, and although Nathan was a big man, his older brother was even larger. "Right now, we don't know who fathered James. I'm fine with keeping it that way."

"Why?" Tammy asked from her seat on the sofa.

"Because knowing the answer is going to put a real wedge between all of us," Aidan said. "Can you imagine trying to work together on the Flying B after we know the truth? Tex didn't bequeath his properties to us in order to tear us apart—he wanted us to stay together."

Nathan raised a finger. "We haven't even talked about what kind of canyon this is going to put between our dads. They're off traipsing around the wilderness right now on some male twin bonding ritual that I hope will finally do the trick and bring them together again, and here we are, debating about ruining that. They both have egos, and…"

Donna had gone pricklier than ever. "You mean my dad has the ego, don't you?"

Jenna came closer to her as the boys, and even Tammy, got an *I'm-not-saying-another-word-about-that* look on their faces.

Donna sighed. "It's true that our dads have mended a lot of old wounds lately. But part of me wonders if putting this information in a proverbial closet will do more damage than ever."

Then again, no one was talking about how James might feel about a decision that was really his.

"I agree about ignoring the truth," Tammy said. "We should just lay everything to rest *now*. It could be that the revelation of whose son James really is will heal us altogether since *not* knowing would eat away at us and make things much worse."

Silence bit the room until Jenna took a breath, then spoke.

"We should get in touch with our dads to see what they think."

When Donna glanced at Jenna, she knew that her sister would take it upon herself to contact their father since she had already reconciled with him. Donna sent her a smile of thanks, even while she ached to talk to him, too.

But how, after everything he'd done to let her down?

Tammy fetched a phone from a holster on her jeans. "I'm calling Dad now. I talked to him last night, so I'll bet they're within service range."

"We really want to ruin their idyllic nature walk?" Nathan asked.

Tammy moved her thumb over her smart phone screen. "I don't see that there's a choice. They can hash this out together in the boonies."

"*My* vote's still a big no about having our P.I. find the kid," Aidan said.

Nathan chuffed. "That 'kid' is just a little bit older than Donna."

This seemed to bug him, too, since it was obvious that his uncle Sam had gone straight into the arms of another woman—Donna and Jenna's mom—after his affair with Savannah. Honestly, Donna didn't like the thought of this, either, because it made it seem as if love was cheap to Dad. She'd never known that about him. Never even expected that he could be so loose with his affections, and it made her feel protective for Mom, even if she'd been gone a long time.

"All the same," Nathan added, "I vote no on this situation, too."

"It's a yes for me," Jenna said, "and I'm guessing Tammy, as well."

As Tammy nodded, she glanced at Donna, and no one had to tell her that she just might be the tiebreaker, depending on what their dads said.

Jenna jerked her chin toward the room's exit, and it was apparent that she wanted a private word with Donna.

As they left the room, Jenna addressed Tammy. "Can you give us a few minutes before you call Uncle William? I'd like to reach Dad at the same time, if possible."

"Sure."

And, while they exited, Tammy launched into every argument she could probably think of to sway her brothers.

After a little walking down the hall, Jenna pulled Donna into the dining room, the dark wood and stag horns above the long table looking more imposing than usual.

Jenna shut the double doors behind her. "You don't seem convinced, Donna."

Was it that obvious? "I'm sorry. But the ramifications of *this* decision could be…"

"A real challenge? We're up to it."

For the first time in Donna's life, she actually felt as if she was close enough to her sister so that she could confide in her. The realization tightened her throat, and she had a hard time getting the words out.

"It's just that we were about to mend all of our own fences because of our dads, and then Tammy found that clue about Savannah's baby. We were doing so well for a while."

"You're still mad at Dad for being with Savannah, aren't you? He didn't try to fall in love with her, Donna."

"He didn't try to stop having sex with his brother's girlfriend, either." Harsh. But this wasn't the man Donna had grown up idolizing.

She calmed down. "I just remember how he used to tell us to go after everything we wanted, Jen. It looks like he really practiced what he preached, and the fall-out isn't pretty."

Jenna laid a hand on Donna's arm. She was getting used to the contact. Donna's *friends* didn't even show this kind of sympathy, but since coming to the Flying B, Donna had begun to wonder if she'd actually had friends or just people she went out with after work at night to blow off steam.

"After I finally talked to Dad about this," Jenna said, "I found out that he was inconsolable when Savannah left the ranch and disappeared afterward. He got hurt in this, too, and I only came to understand that after I fell in love myself."

Was she saying that Donna didn't have a chance in hell of understanding since she had no one?

An image of dimples flashed into her mind. Pale blue eyes sparkling with humor and lightness.

Caleb.

She shook him off. "Yeah, Dad was so inconsolable that he married Mom on the rebound. No wonder they split up."

"Donna, you really should talk to him. We can call, right now."

Her stomach turned with nerves. "No. I don't want to say to him what I have to say over the phone."

"Then when will you do it?"

"Soon." She walked to the doors, paused. "Thanks for taking care of this, though. It means a lot."

Jenna merely nodded as Donna opened the doors, closing them behind her, yet hardly shutting out her sister's voice as she said, "Hey, Dad, it's Jenna."

As Donna walked away, her footsteps echoed off the walls, the sound mocking the dull thud of every isolated heartbeat.

Chapter Three

Chow time at the ranch employee cabins was never a dull affair.

The next night, while Caleb sat next to Hugh at a long dinner table outside the mess hall, the usual end-of-the-day cowboy talk swarmed around them, just as thick as the smoke coming off the barbecue. On the other side of Caleb, a young ranch hand named Manny plopped down on the bench, immediately pushing back his hat to reveal a patch of curly brown hair before chomping into his corn bread.

"Did y'all hear about the hot times in the main house last night?" he asked with his mouth full, nodding his head toward the Byrds' domain.

Caleb, who'd already pushed away his emptied tin plate, leaned his elbows on the table while holding a beer bottle between two fingers. Donna was in that house, and he was all ears.

Hugh was nursing a ceramic mug of coffee. "There've been more than a few hot times since the Byrd kids came home to roost."

"But last night was a real doozy." Manny dipped his bread into his chili bowl. "Maria and I have both been working, so she told me about it only an hour ago when she took a break."

Caleb glanced at Hugh, who cocked his bushy eyebrow in response. Manny was dating a housemaid, so she must've been dusting or some-such last night while the Byrds conducted business.

"How much of a doozy was it?" Caleb asked, turning back to Manny.

"On a scale of calm to loud, it was at about a bellow. Maria said that the little Byrds were going at it like they were on the *Maury* show, including a lot of who's-the-daddy talk."

Caleb recalled what Donna had told him about Savannah's pregnancy test. "Is there a long-lost kid?"

"Yup, their P.I. located him," Manny said. "And it really chapped some of their hides that Savannah named him in the style of Tex's boys. James Bowie Jeffries is what he's called."

Next to Caleb, Hugh made a grumbling sound, seeming to be just as offended as some of the Byrds apparently were.

Then Hugh said, "Did Maria have her ear to the door or something?"

"Very funny, old-timer." Manny polished off the last of his chili, standing to get seconds, like he always did. "No matter how Maria heard it, she didn't like the news. That family is coming apart at the seams now that Tex is gone, and she doesn't know how long we might have jobs here."

Caleb put down his beer. "That's a load of bull, Manny, and you know it."

"Do I? Caleb, we don't know these Byrd kids from seven holes in the ground. I like them well enough, but what if they end up dismantling the Flying B? What if Tex was all that was keeping the ranch together?"

Something seemed to crack in Caleb, breaking him in a thousand directions inside. This was his home— the only one he'd ever felt comfortable in after his mom had passed on.

Manny had gone back to the food station, leaving Hugh and Caleb alone.

The foreman chucked the rest of his coffee on the ground.

"Before Tex died," Caleb said, "he told me that, under the conditions of his will, the ranch couldn't be dismantled. The grandkids have to spend their inheritance on bettering it, so Manny's worrying for nothing."

"It's not the ranch I'm thinking about." Hugh ran a hand over his grizzled face. "You can't have more than one person inheriting something and expect them to all agree on every decision."

"So you're worried about the family itself. Boss, you've sure become pessimistic about things lately."

"And why shouldn't I be? It might be time to retire, live off my savings, fish all day. Who needs all this nonsense?"

Hugh's words were flippant, but Caleb knew better. Like him, the foreman loved this place, as well as the ragtag family of ranch hands that Tex had put together.

Gathering his plate, Caleb prepared to go.

"Where're you off to?" Hugh asked.

"Where do you think?"

"Aw, no." Hugh shook his finger at Caleb. "You're not going to the house like I think you are."

"I am. There's no way I'm going to see a rift destroy Tex's family."

"So what're you gonna do—help Donna Byrd carry in another rocking chair and chide her about family business at the same time? That's no way to get into her good graces, son."

"This has nothing to do with that. She and the others need to know that we—the staff—have a stake in seeing the family at peace, too."

"You're overstepping, Caleb."

Was he?

Would Tex have told him that, too?

The last time Caleb had seen him, lying in bed, looking like half the hale-and-hearty man he'd always been, Tex had told Caleb that he would be leaving him a bit of money. Not a whole lot, but enough to tell him that he valued him.

"Money doesn't show everything that's in a person's heart, though," Tex had said.

"Of course it doesn't."

He had closed his eyes, so weary. "If I could buy goodwill from my sons and their children, I would. I'd do anything for them to realize that they could have something wonderful out here on the Flying B together. At least you've always known what you've got on this ranch, Caleb."

"That's right, Tex."

The money hadn't been the point, though. In fact, Caleb had never expected to be treated like Tex's blood,

and he'd been blown away that the man had even given
him some seed money for his own future. Naturally,
he'd spent it well, on the new house he'd purchased for
his dad and aunt, but it was too bad money couldn't buy
a positive word from his father during one of his more
lucid times, either.

Now, Caleb began to walk away from the table, saying over his shoulder, "Tex would've wanted me to interfere, all right. The Byrds need to know that their
decisions affect more than just the few of them."

He left Hugh sitting on the bench while he scraped off
his plate into a receptacle and then headed for the main
house, where the dim lights buttered the back windows
in the falling dusk.

And where Donna Byrd was about to get an earful.

NEEDING PRIVACY, DONNA had come outside to the wraparound porch, where she sat on the new cottage-style
swing she and the girls had chosen for the renovation.

Just do this, she thought, looking at the cell phone in
her hand. *Go. Now. Dial!*

But she couldn't, even if Dad and Uncle William had
finally checked in this morning with their own votes
after one heck of a long night of waiting.

They both wanted to find James. And they were both
evidently done with their Hill Country trip, on their way
back to their respective homes in Houston and Uncle
William's ranch. Even the most clueless person in the
world could infer that there'd been a setback with the
brothers because of last night's news, but Donna and the
rest of her relatives had promised each other that they
would do everything within their power to make things
right between them again.

Yet there was *this* to deal with, as well. And, since Donna had been riding their P.I.'s tail this whole time about Savannah and a possible child, she was the one who'd volunteered to give him the go ahead on tracking down James.

Still, the phone was incredibly heavy in her hand, almost as if it was something that could drag her down until she wouldn't ever be able to get back up.

Was she going to let one phone call beat her, though?

She dialed without another thought, listening to one ring. Two.

Then, an answer.

"Walker Investigations," said the P.I.'s rusty-nail voice.

"Hi, Roland, it's Donna Byrd."

"Miss Byrd—I haven't heard from you for a whole day. I thought you might've dropped off the face of the planet."

Hilarious. "We were only waiting for our dads to weigh in on Savannah and James."

"And?"

She closed her eyes, opened them. "We'd like you to go forward on finding out more about James and setting up a possible meeting."

"Consider it done." She could hear Roland tapping on a keyboard. "What about Savannah?"

"Right…Savannah."

Donna bit her lip before giving a real answer. Last night, the Byrd children had discussed James's mom, too, after they had called their dads and then met in the living room again. That's when Donna had told them what she'd left out during their first gathering—news about Savannah Jeffries that just hadn't seemed as important as the more urgent revelation of James; facts such as how Savannah was a very successful interior designer with her own business and how she was going by her late husband's last name and how it seemed that she had gotten married long after James Bowie Jeffries had come of legal age, hence the reason he used his mom's maiden name.

So *much* information. And so much conflict, because after Donna had filled in the family, they'd been just as divided as ever—this time about including Savannah in a reunion.

Donna sighed. No turning back now. "If you could go ahead and contact Savannah, we want to invite her to meet us, as well."

It would be a smash-up family reunion, emphasis on the *smash-up*.

After she took care of particulars with Roland, then hung up, she stayed on the swing.

Dammit, she only wished she had zero interest in Savannah. But she had voted yes both times last night, and part of the reason was because the idea of the woman just wouldn't leave Donna alone. She was everything Donna had ever looked for in her role models—obviously ambitious, based on her business skills. Donna also liked that she knew how to decorate a room—a hobby that she, herself, had recently turned into somewhat of a vocation with the B and B.

Most of all, though, Donna respected that, from what she knew, Savannah had raised James by herself.

An independent woman in every way, she thought. And even though she hadn't planned on ever having a family herself...

Well, there was an empty place in Donna that actually perked up at the thought, now that she finally *did* have a family she was starting to feel closer and closer to.

But really? Her? The überprofessional Donna Byrd? A mom?

It would've been laughable if there wasn't a string of yearning tying her up because of the lingering notion.

The wind stirred and, from the side of the porch, she could hear some chimes tinkling. The sound reminded her of a soothing song that a baby mobile might make above a crib. Someday.

Maybe.

The porch swing was creaking back and forth in a lazy rhythm when Donna saw someone coming around the side of the house.

And guess who?

But instead of groaning with exasperation, her heart gave a jaunty flip.

Oddly, though, Caleb Granger's grin wasn't as dimply as usual. And she could've used one of his sexy grins right about now.

She spoke first, just as he began to mount the porch steps, coming into the light from the caged lantern near the door.

"Are you here to say a good evening to me?"

He stopped near the top, his hands planted on his hips. "I heard some talk, so I thought I'd come over to let you confirm or deny the rumors."

Whatever kind of peaceful bubble she'd just created for herself busted like a balloon.

"Rumors?" she asked tightly.

"About the new Byrd. About all the arguing you and your family were doing about him."

"Maybe the next time we Byrds have a conversation," she said, "we can broadcast it to the entire ranch. Do you know anything about installing closed-circuit television?"

He ignored her sarcasm. "Just listen to me on this. For years, this ranch has been what you might call 'harmonious.' Tex made sure everyone was happy, inside and outside the main house. He even went the extra mile at the end of his life to guarantee that his family made amends with each other, and it's a damned shame that all his hard work seems to be for naught."

Donna couldn't say a word. Not *one*. Anger was roiling in her...and maybe even something else. She'd never had a man presume to talk to her like this. She'd never stood for someone to so boldly nose into her business.

But...*damn* whatever it was weaving around all that anger in her. It was something that had her utterly confused, and she struck out in an effort to erase it.

"Is your lecture over now?" she asked. "Because I'm already bored."

"Bored?"

He narrowed his gaze, and she did the same right back at him.

"Yes," she said. "Bored. You know why? Because I have a hundred other issues all poking at me from every side, and yours don't even begin to compete with them."

He took a moment, looking down at the porch, as if to compose himself. Then he let out a curt laugh.

She didn't know what to make of that.

"Believe it or not," he said, "I'm only looking out for Tex's interests. Do you know what it would've done to him if he'd heard y'all arguing?"

"There's more going on than even Tex knew."

Caleb locked gazes with her, reading her, and she

stiffened. But she also melted ever so slightly, deep in her core, where she never melted.

He cared. She could see that. But she didn't want his care, didn't want anyone to meddle because she and Jenna and their cousins would have this under control soon.

She rested her hands flat on the swing, leaning forward. "I told you before—I know how close you were to Tex, but that doesn't mean—"

"Sometimes I wonder if you Byrds have any idea what Tex gave to you, what he did for you."

Donna felt her face go pale, and she knew that *he* knew he was wrong.

He gentled his tone. "What I'm trying to ask you to do is to stop battling with each other and appreciate what you have. That's all he would've wanted."

He said it with such longing that her heart bumped against her ribs.

But her anger had been fully roused, and her voice was torn when she answered.

"I know what I have now, believe me, because I didn't have much of it before."

Before now, her life had been defined by a father who was all business, plus a mom who hadn't been alive for years and whom Donna had missed so much that she had told herself to never put her heart out there again, where it could be stomped all over.

When Caleb took a step onto the porch, one booted foot still on the stair behind him, Donna didn't move. Was he coming up here to get his point across even more emphatically?

But he didn't advance. Instead, he slipped his thumbs into his belt loops, a sheepish look on his face.

"Sorry for laying into you like that," he said. "I didn't realize how seriously you were taking this."

"As seriously as you do, evidently." *Breathe, just breathe.*

But when he came all the way up onto the porch, breathing wasn't easy. Plus, he was making her skin do funny things, raising goose bumps and causing her fine hairs to stand on end.

If he noticed the evidence on her bare arms, he didn't say anything.

"Promise me you'll let me know if you need help with any of this mess," he said.

"I've got it covered."

Brother, did *he* have a lot to learn about her.

His voice lowered. "I'm being serious. Just give a yell if you need me for anything."

She wasn't sure they were talking about family business anymore.

"Thanks, but no thanks." She rose from the swing, and it creaked, as if in protest.

As she passed him on her way to the door, she smelled that saddle soap on his skin, and it filled her head, making her dizzy.

A chuckle stopped her in her tracks, and she glanced over her shoulder to find him shaking his head.

"What?" she asked.

"You're what we call a 'firebrand' out here."

"I guess that just means if you insist on getting in my business anymore, you're going to get burned."

He laughed, and the dimples made a grand appearance, tweaking her heart with sparks that showered down until they settled in her belly.

But just as quickly, she shoved the ridiculous feelings aside.

Not her type. Never would be. And just as soon as she got back to the city, it'd be much easier to remember that fact.

As if he had sensed the direction of her thoughts, he gave her another one of those sultry up-and-down looks, sweeping her skin with flame.

When he got to her eyes, his gaze snagged hers with an electric jolt.

"Thought about that wine yet, Donna Byrd?"

She rolled her eyes, opening the front door and going through it, hearing his laughter while she leaned back against the wood.

And, damn it all if she couldn't help the smile that wouldn't leave her alone afterward.

THE WEEKEND WAS ushered in with a blast of July heat, and even after the sun started to dive down to the horizon, it was sweaty business.

But the misters and fans that had been planted around the yard near the side of the barn helped, as Caleb spread a blanket over the grass and put down an ice-filled bucket that held a bottle of rosé.

The other night, when he had confronted Donna about the Byrd-fight rumors, he'd left on a better note than the one he'd come to her on. And tonight, Donna Byrd was going to have that wine with him so they could completely make up...whether she knew it or not.

Manny and Maria were just coming from the buffet line, where the cook was dishing out the food to the staff and their children.

"Lookee here," Manny said, one hand holding a plate

loaded with barbecue and all the trimmings, the other hand holding Maria's. "Someone's getting romantic with themselves."

Caleb reached into the bucket for a piece of ice and flicked it at his coworker. Maria laughed until Manny offered Caleb a rascally smile and pulled her away to their lawn chairs, which were closer to the makeshift screen that Donna had hung from the side of the barn.

Even though other female staff members cruised by Caleb, grinning at him, maybe even expecting him to revert to form and do some flirting, he wasn't swayed. He patiently went back to waiting for Donna to appear and, when she finally did, his hormones went into overdrive, growling like a roadster before a race.

White summery sundress, strappy sandals, blond hair twisted and pinned so that her neck was bare…Donna Byrd slayed him and, as usual, he couldn't take his eyes off her.

Except when he saw the man she was with.

It was as if Caleb's engine sputtered. Her "friend from college" who was supposed to be here to write an article did indeed carry an expensive camera with him, aiming it around the area. And if this pricey accessory wasn't enough, he had an East Coast crustiness about him, dressed in brand-spanking-new jeans and a short-sleeved plaid shirt that marked him as a dude. He even had yacht-boy hair, light blond and flipped up in front, as if it was gelled to within an inch of its life.

When Caleb saw him and Donna across the lawn, laughing together at some private joke, he wondered if he should've read more into the moment when she'd told him about this "friend."

Of course a knockout like her would have "friends."

But a niggle of doubt still hounded Caleb, although he did have the feeling that tonight really might not be the time for getting Donna to leave her buddy and sit down to drink some wine with him.

He glanced at the bottle and at the glasses. Hell, why let a good vintage go to waste?

He reached into the bucket to pull out the wine just as Tina Crandall, the elderly housekeeper who stood out in a crowd with her silver-streaked black hair, strolled by.

Everyone knew Tina enjoyed a splash of spirits every now and then, so he whistled, and when she turned around, he lifted up a glass to her.

Her gaze sparkled. "You devil. What do you have here?"

"A Domaine Tempier rosé." He'd driven to the suburbs during the week after a full day of work to visit his aunt and his father. It'd gone as it usually did, with Dad loudly complaining about dinner, and the highlight of Caleb's night had been dropping by a store farther over in Houston to buy this bottle.

Tina gingerly sat on the blanket, spreading her flowered skirt around her ample hips. "That sounds like a fancy label, Caleb. I think Tex would've loved it."

"Then let's drink to him."

He poured a glass for her, then himself. They toasted and drank to Tex.

After they took that first sip, he kept his eye on Donna as she and the yacht boy passed close to the barn. When she seemed to hold back a sneeze, he recalled hearing that she occasionally took allergy medicine whenever she absolutely had to spend time near any hay.

Hell, she was taking one for the team tonight.

Tina drank some more, being ladylike and discreet

about it, but Caleb didn't have much taste for the wine tonight. All he could do was percolate as Donna and her friend walked around the area, still laughing and touching each other's arms.

Full darkness—and movie time—arrived, and Donna Byrd and Gilligan went to some reserved lawn chairs. But, first, the guy took flash pictures of people enjoying their food while waiting for the film.

When Donna strolled by Caleb's blanket by herself, her gaze met his. He toasted her with his nearly full glass, then reached over to refill Tina's.

"Looks like you brought the wine, after all," Donna Byrd said casually. A nearby mister blew a strand of hair out of her upswept 'do, and the tendril caressed her neck.

Caleb's fingers itched to do the same. "If I had an extra glass, I'd pour some for you, but I gather you're busy."

Tina obviously had a buzz on, and she grabbed the neck of the bottle, pouring even more into her glass. "You're missing some good stuff, Donna."

She smiled at the housekeeper, but just as she was about to turn her attention to Caleb, her friend meandered over with his camera, snapping a picture of Caleb and Tina on the blanket.

Caleb pulled down the brim of his hat, discouraging any more of that nonsense.

Donna linked arms with Jimmy Olsen. "Theo, this is Tina, who runs the household. And this is Caleb, one of the hands here."

Theo bent down to shake Tina's hand, then Caleb's. "You both run a good operation. Donna and the girls have got a real gem on their hands with this B and B idea."

When he straightened back up and wrapped an arm around Donna's shoulder, Caleb just about rocketed off the blanket.

But he kept his hat on. Literally. And he offered a vague smile to the dude.

Donna linked arms with her boy pal, and for a bright second, Caleb wondered if she was being deft, avoiding what had obviously been an attempt to cuddle.

"Have fun," she said to Caleb and Tina, then strolled away with her guest.

Caleb kept watching them from under his hat, especially when Donna sneaked a glance back at him.

But what did that mean? And what was with the arm linking?

He was still wondering that when the movie flashed onto the screen, much to the delight of the crowd, who applauded and hooted as the title of *The Man from Snowy River* appeared.

And when Caleb saw Donna seating Theo in a chair of honor right in the center of things, then excuse herself, he couldn't hold his questions any longer.

He leaned over to Tina, who'd turned the empty wine bottle upside down in the bucket. "I'll be back."

"Take your time," she said with a happy lilt as she watched the screen.

He followed Donna to the back of the house, where the new bucking bronco fountain splashed playfully.

And where she sprawled in a cushioned chair, her white skirt hanging down like angel's wings.

His heart caught in his chest as he stood there, taking her in, his body going warm.

Tired Donna. Beautiful Donna.

Maybe this was just lust, but Caleb wasn't so sure

about that. There was something chemical between them he couldn't explain and, more than anything, he wanted to see why he always found himself coming to her when most women came to him.

He sat on a wood bench nearby, taking care to make enough noise so that he didn't scare her, and when she glanced over, she put her palm to her chest, as if to keep her heart from leaping out of it.

It was like the moment he'd initially laid eyes on her all over again—attraction at first sight.

And maybe something more?

Chapter Four

Why wouldn't Donna's heart calm down around Caleb Granger?

She'd never been this flustered by any man before—not when one sent her a drink during happy hour in a dimly lit bar, not when one locked gazes with her in Central Park on the weekends, when she would lounge on a blanket and bask in the summer sun with a good book.

Was it dark enough to hide the blush that she suspected had consumed her?

Right. *A blush*. That had to be another first for her. But, then again, why not? She'd been sitting here by the fountain, thinking about Caleb, and he'd suddenly appeared like a tempting devil that never gave her a moment of peace.

It would help if he didn't look so mouthwatering as he sat on that bench, an angle of light from the nearby patio revealing the sparkle in his pale blue eyes and the dimpled barely there grin. Not even that ever-present cowboy hat could hide his charms.

"What are you doing here?" she asked.

"I live on this ranch, remember?"

"You know that's not what I mean." It seemed she was always getting her wires crossed with him. This time, all he'd done was show up where she was, and it was enough to... Well, *fluster* her. "I meant to ask why you're not watching the movie with everyone else."

"I'm not so much the movie sort." He shrugged, sitting back on the bench, propping his booted ankle on his knee and nudging back the brim of his hat with his knuckles. "I don't see the use in watching someone else's fictional life go by when I've got a perfectly good and real one myself."

A curious little bug inside of her wanted to ask what he did do for entertainment. Read books? Go on a computer? But that would mean she was interested.

And she wasn't.

"I'm afraid a movie is all the amusement that's being offered tonight," she said. "Unless you came here to stare at this fountain, too."

"That's as perfect an excuse as any." He looked at the bronze bronco sculpture covered by running water. "It's peaceful. But I'm sure that's why you came over here. To get some peace."

"It has been a long day."

She leaned her head back on the wicker chair's cushion, and a breath escaped her. She didn't intend to give so much away with that sigh, though.

"More family stuff?" he asked, his tone a surprisingly serene distraction for her. It didn't hold the judgmental edge she'd detected in him the other night, when he'd confronted her on the main house's porch about how the Byrds were handling ranch business.

She found herself talking. "The family's just on pins and needles waiting for a call from our P.I."

"Did he approach Savannah or James about meeting with you?"

"Yes, but he hasn't gotten word from either of them so far." She paused. "It certainly wasn't an easy decision to ask him to go forward with this."

"Meeting either one of them will change everyone's lives. I can imagine it wasn't easy."

He lapsed into silence, and it gave way to the trickle of water from the fountain and the sounds of the summer Texas night—crickets and a hundred other things a city girl like her couldn't identify yet.

It was nice that he seemed to sympathize with her family's problems, but now would be a good time to stop revealing her emotions to him. Truthfully, there was a lot more bothering Donna than Savannah and James. She'd also gotten an email from her financial advisor this morning, letting her know that her portfolio was in sadder shape than the last time she'd checked in with him.

But wasn't that news just the sprinkles on top of the crumbling cupcake of her life?

Caleb shifted in his seat, and that strange tingly sensation Donna felt whenever she was around him traced the lining of her stomach again.

"You left your 'friend' all alone to watch the movie," he said.

She sneaked a sideways glance at him. He was trying to look casual after asking the question. That almost made her smile.

"Is that why you plopped down on that bench?" she

asked, amusement coloring her tone. "So you could quiz me about Theo?"

He shrugged again, oh so carelessly.

Was the cowboy jealous?

She recalled how he had watched her walk away with Theo as she led her guest to his movie seat. Caleb had been wearing a burning look that had flipped her tummy inside out, making her all too aware that she shouldn't have been glancing back at him in the first place.

Had she *wanted* to see if he was curious about Theo?

Caleb tipped back his hat even more, and she caught the side-slant grin on his face now. "This Theo fellow is sure your type."

"What do you mean, my type?"

"It looks like he walked straight off of the Queen of England's polo field with those perfect pants and that hair of his."

Now Donna did laugh. "His hair does have a glamorous life of its own."

"That's not what I'm trying to get at, Donna."

She could tell he'd become serious because he hadn't added the playful "Byrd" to her name. Also, he had leaned forward, planting both boots on the ground and his forearms on his thighs.

She wasn't going to ask what he was getting at. No, she would end this civil conversation and then go back to check on Theo and the movie. That way, she wouldn't encourage Caleb any more than he'd obviously been encouraged by that glance she'd given him while walking away with Theo.

Dammit, why hadn't she been able to keep herself from checking out his reaction to her leaving?

"I told you," she said. "Theo's a friend. We met at

NYU. He even married one of my sorority sisters and they've been going on eight years together."

At the word *married,* Caleb's grin had reappeared.

It goaded Donna. "He isn't the only man I know from New York. And the others are of the single variety."

"How many of those *do* you know?"

Now was the time to make sure he realized that he had no chance with her. "Enough to keep me occupied."

He chuckled, and she crossed one leg over the other, leaning away from him.

"Well, Donna Byrd," he said, "you seem to have a real good life to get back to after you take care of this B and B here in Texas. I hear you'll be able to market the place from a distance."

See—he was getting her drift. "It's an ideal situation."

"So you're looking forward to getting back to all the traffic and crowds."

"Believe it or not, all of that is just as natural to me as everything on this ranch is to you."

"From what I hear, your sister's not the same as you are. She's taken to the Flying B like a swan to water."

"It sounds like you're asking in a roundabout way why she turned out one way and I turned out another."

He cocked an eyebrow, keeping his gaze on her, causing another stunningly pleasant shiver to travel her skin.

Donna didn't see the harm in briefly talking about Jenna. "She grew up with a fascination about country life because of a deep curiosity she had about Grandpa and his side of the family, since Dad never talked about either of them."

"He didn't?"

"No." Donna smoothed her skirt over a leg. "You know the story, though—how Savannah came between

my dad and my uncle William and how the situation estranged them from Grandpa. As I said, Jenna wondered
about Grandpa, but so did I, even though I never said
much about it or acted on it. Dad discouraged any interest, and I worshipped the ground he walked on, so I
listened to him when he said that there was a big world
out there to explore and I shouldn't bother myself about
his side of the family."

Once again, he'd gotten her to talk more than she'd
meant to. How did Caleb Granger manage to do that?

And why did it feel okay to finally be releasing some
of the weight that had been perching on her for months
now?

He sat still, and she could tell that he wasn't happy
about how Sam had turned his back on Tex. She didn't
reveal that, in the end, she wasn't so happy about it, either.

So much time wasted. So much opportunity squan-
dered.

She decided to go on…just a little bit more. Then she
would leave.

"Jenna was different from me in a lot of ways," she
said, "and she decided to embrace the Byrds' roots, with
or without knowing Grandpa. It was almost as if she was
born to be here."

Donna stopped herself before adding, *And I wasn't*.

As the fountain splashed, she wondered if it was so
easy to go on about this because Caleb had been close to
Tex. Was she looking for someone who knew Grandpa
well to forgive her for not seeking out this ranch and
her family?

Guilt found its way to her again as she thought of how
Grandpa's gaze had lit up the first time they'd met, and

how she wished, too late, that she'd gotten a lifetime full of those looks over the years, even though she would rather hide that wish than tell anyone about it.

"So that's why you forged a path to the city," Caleb finally said. "Because of your dad's influence."

"I would say he was instrumental in that."

She glanced back toward where the movie was playing. In the near distance, she could hear the sound track's music.

But Caleb wasn't done with her. "I also heard that you got some kind of internship, then a job at a magazine after college. One of those sophisticated ladies' publications."

He'd said it almost in a kidding way, as if emphasizing that she was one of those ladies.

"You've done some homework on us new Byrds," she said.

"Word gets around." He paused, then said, "A few years ago, you had an idea for a start-up publication, and you had your own magazine for a while."

Donna pressed her lips together, her chin tilting up a little.

"That takes some guts, Donna Byrd," Caleb said softly. "Bringing something big into the world like that."

The genuine admiration in his voice made her hesitate. When she saw how he was looking at her—straightforward, direct—it stirred her up, heated her to the very core.

He slowly got to his feet and, once again, something in Donna's chest was sparked to electric life, leaving a heated friction to trail down her body.

"I know," he said in that same low tone, "that you have new opportunities nowadays. You're going to turn this B and B into a rousing success, and you think you'll run back to the city after that. You think you're going to get your old life going again."

"I *think* I will?" she asked, and her voice didn't come out as strongly as she would've liked.

He took a couple of steps toward her, his boots thudding on the cement.

Every sound was like a contradiction to all her plans. What he wasn't saying outright was that she had a career here, if she wanted it. She had the family she'd never had before, right in front of her for the taking.

And she had other opportunities, as well….

Caleb took another few steps, until he was standing in front of her chair. She still couldn't move.

"If I were a betting man," he said, "I'd put money on the notion that you won't be going anywhere after this, Donna Byrd."

"After…what?"

"After you give everything on the Flying B a chance," he said, his voice so sensual that it glided over her skin like water sluicing down the smooth contours of the fountain.

He took his damned time bending down, bracing his hands on either arm of her chair and, oh, God, he smelled so good—saddle soap and only enough hint of hay to make her think she might not be allergic to this ranch after all.

Her head swam, making her thoughts race by in a whir of sensation. Adrenaline zipped through her, a shot to the heart.

Was he going to kiss her? This cowboy who had no place in her life?

As he bent lower, she closed her eyes, her lips buzzing with anticipation.

But, beneath her eyelids, everything she'd ever wanted rushed by: bright neon lights zigging and zagging, laughter and the sound of clinking glasses from crowded rooms, her favorite fountain in Central Park, splashing....

The sound of her memories melded with the present, and she heard another fountain instead —this one, here in Texas.

She opened her eyes, holding her breath while she slipped under one of his arms and came to a stand by the side of her chair. Her heartbeat was throttling her now.

He glanced over his shoulder at her, his eyebrow raised. But it seemed like he was more amused than surprised.

"You move fast," he said.

"I think the same could be said for you."

Another chuckle from him.

Even if her body was responding with a runaway pulse that kept her breathless, this wasn't what she needed. Him. Just another piece of trouble to add to all the crazy emotions that were attacking her day by day with Savannah and James and the insanity of her entire life. There were men back in New York who would be far more suited for her—men who fit into the existence she was made for.

She flailed for something to say. "I like movies."

Articulate? Hardly. But it made Caleb straighten up ever so slowly from her former seat, anyway.

"So you do," he said.

"What I mean is that you don't like them. I do. And that's just one glaring difference between us."

"Ah." He adjusted his hat, then negligently rested his hands on his jeaned hips. "You're talking me out of wanting to kiss you."

Good—once again he'd caught on. "I'm also used to men who are a little more subtle, by the way."

"Fellows in fancy suits and ties and slicked-back hair? I wouldn't call them subtle, just well-disguised."

"What do you mean by that?"

"A man's a man. But some of us don't hide behind fancy words or twenty-dollar cocktails that we buy in the hopes of winning a woman over."

She crossed her arms over her chest, yet it was only because of the goose bumps that had risen over her arms, prickling her skin. Good goose bumps that seeped through her, arousing her when that should've been the last thing happening.

"I think there's another way to describe the kind of men I usually associate with," Donna said. "It's called *couth.* Instead of stealing kisses, those men ask a woman out on a date, get to know her over a nice dinner."

"I'll bet I already know more about you than any of your couth men ever did."

"Doubtful."

Yet, even as she said it, she realized that he might be right. She'd never gotten serious with any of those dates in the city—not emotionally, anyway. There'd just never been time.

Or, if she was honest with herself, she'd never been as interested in a man as she had been in seeing to the success of her magazine.

But here, on the Flying B, she was another Donna, wasn't she? And Caleb had gotten a glimpse of her.

And he *still* wanted to kiss her....

When he finally spoke, he had become serious again. "I don't know if *couth* describes me, but it seems you're working under some wrong impressions, at any rate."

"Like what?"

"Like mistaking why I might want to be around you. Did it ever occur to you that I'm trying to figure out just what it is about you that impressed me in the first place?"

She waited for it—the inevitable glance at her chest, her curves. And, somehow, she was already disappointed that Caleb wouldn't be much different from the rest of the men she'd gone out with.

But his gaze was still on her face. "I've seen a lot of pretty girls, but there's something about you that sets you apart."

"You could tell that just by looking at me one time?"

"Could be." He smiled. "Could be that I could tell right off that you didn't take guff from anyone, and that appealed to me. I've never met a woman who keeps me on my toes like you do. And there's a lot more to you, too, Donna. A lot that you don't seem to want anyone to see."

She tried not to show how much he'd just stunned her with his all-too-keen observation.

But he'd obviously said what he'd come here to say, even if he hadn't gotten a kiss out of it. He tipped his hat to her, then walked away without any more explanation.

She watched him go, unable to tear her gaze away.

Unable to figure out just why *he* got to *her* more than any man ever had before.

CALEB HAD SPENT the night staring at the ceiling of his cabin, trying to puzzle out the enigma that was Donna Byrd.

And trying to answer that ever-elusive question of just *why* he couldn't get her off his mind.

He'd never believed in fairy dust and magic of the heart, but he did believe in the chemistry one person had with another—and he knew he had something like that with Donna. He really hadn't been stringing her along when he'd said that she kept him on his toes. No woman had ever challenged him like that before—and it pleased him that Donna, who came from a world with art museums and theater to keep her stimulated, seemed to be on her toes with him, too.

During the past year, Caleb had gotten an earful, listening to his dad telling him how useless he was, thanks to the dementia as well as the knowledge that his dad had probably felt like that for years but kept it to himself when Mom was alive. So half of Caleb had started to believe he was simple and would never amount to much. Of course, Tex's belief in him had changed some of that, but there'd still been a lingering suspicion that his dad was right.

Yet how could he keep up with a bright, sophisticated woman like Donna if any of that were true? He might not like movies and he might not wear ironed yuppie shirts and trust-fund hair like Theo, but Caleb instinctively knew that he affected her in a way that she wasn't used to when it came to men.

When he'd nearly kissed her, he'd seen her get all hot and bothered. He'd also seen some kind of vulnerability in her that he'd noticed before, as if, below her surface, she was far more than the superficial cosmopolitan woman who'd found herself stuck in the country.

Chemistry, he'd thought, before finally getting to

sleep. It was only part of what he suspected there could be with Donna....

By morning, he knew what his next step should be with her.

After a day mainly spent bathing and grooming horses, he headed straight for his cabin to clean himself up, then went to the main house's kitchen and sweet-talked Barbara out of a few ingredients from the pantry, as well as some of the fresh-baked bread and apple pie she'd made for dinner. Then he went to the place everyone called "the dream cabin," since it would suit his purposes just fine for the night.

Back in the day, Tex had used all the cabins around the property to entertain guests at the big parties he'd thrown—but that had been before Savannah had come around. After she'd broken up the family, the cabins had been abandoned until the Byrd women had revived them for their B and B. They'd decorated this particular building with a sheepskin throw over the brown quilted bed—the so-called magic mattress that had given the cabin its "dream" nickname. The room also had birchwood accents, lending the feel of a cozy retreat.

In the small kitchen, he prepared a salad, seasoned mushrooms and two rib-eye steaks, and as they sizzled in a skillet, he grabbed the clothing bag he'd draped over a chair and pulled out the nicest suit he had. After turning off the stove, tossing his cowboy hat on the bed and then getting dressed, he knotted a tie at his throat, picked up his phone and texted Donna's cell number, which he'd finagled from Barbara, too.

Something's cooking in the dream cabin. You might want to check it out.

He could've predicted Donna's response.

Who is this?

He answered with a lone question mark, then put his phone away.

If there was one more thing he would've guessed about Donna, it was that she wouldn't ignore such a message, especially about the dream cabin, which had been so integral to the story of Savannah and the Byrds.

During the time he estimated it might take Donna to get down here, he was able to spread a cloth over the small table in the tiny kitchen, light a candle, scoop the food onto plates, plus pour two glasses of Cabernet Sauvignon that he'd already decanted. Tex had once given him a dozen bottles of red from his cellar, and Caleb had been keeping them for a night like this.

When Donna arrived, she opened the door, then stood stock-still while Caleb tried not to let his heart get the better of him. She was wearing a filmy, flowery sundress with elegant, flat, strappy sandals, and her light hair was up, revealing the neck that he'd fantasized about kissing time and again.

"What's going on with you now?" she asked while eyeing the candle on the table, the wine, the food.

His suit.

"I'm taking you out to dinner tonight. Or maybe I should say that I'm bringing dinner to you, since I highly doubt you would've gone to any restaurants with me."

Her mouth shaped into yet another question—*"What?"*—but it never quite came out, because he interrupted her by holding up a hand.

"Don't tell me you don't like wine. I made some steaks, too."

"It's just that I don't remember making a date with you, Caleb."

"You didn't."

"Especially not in the dream cabin."

"I knew that if you got a text inviting you to my own place, you wouldn't go near it. This cabin is neutral ground."

"Then —"

He didn't allow her the chance to squirm out of this. "Last night, you said I was different from the men you usually meet. I don't think that's the case. You need subtle? Well, I can provide the suit, some cocktails and then dinner, just like anyone else."

She was shaking her head, but she didn't look as pissed at him as he expected she might be.

"I don't know what to say."

"A 'yes' would suffice. You don't even have to change clothes. You're already dressed for an evening out."

Okay, she didn't look pissed at all, just confused now. Once again, he thought she might be wondering if he was an alien from planet Loco.

Then she broke into a clearly reluctant smile. "You did go through some trouble."

"I wanted to show you that—"

"I was wrong about you. That's abundantly clear by now." She sighed. "And you're going to keep on trying to prove your point until I give in, aren't you?"

She was wrong about *that*. "No, I won't. If you want to go, then you should. But I would like you to sit down here to see that there's more to us in Buckshot Hills than meets the eye."

He could detect the battle in her gaze—should she sit down or shouldn't she?—and it heartened him a little.

Then she put the kibosh on that. "I don't know. I was planning on having Barbara fix me a plate for my room because I've got a lot of work to do."

"Is your magazine friend Theo still here?"

"No. He spent the day with Tammy and Jenna showing him the outdoor activities we'll have on the ranch, but he left this afternoon."

"Then there's always work that'll be waiting, Donna."

This seemed to make her think twice, and he saw that vulnerability—or was it loneliness?—in her gaze that he'd seen before.

"I'm tempted to say yes," she said softly, "just so you can see that a night out with me wouldn't be what you expected."

"Then prove *your* point to *me*."

She met his gaze square-on, obviously making a decision.

Lifting a finger, she said, "This is the only time this is going to happen."

"Good enough."

While she slowly made her way toward the table, as if he was going to pounce on her and she needed to be on her guard, she surveyed him in his suit. His body rushed with a flood of heat, because it was an appreciative look, whether she'd meant it to be or not.

He went to pull her chair out for her, and she sat. Then he set a filled wineglass in front of her.

"I didn't realize that you can cook," she said.

"There're times when the skill comes in handy." He'd done a lot of cooking during his leave of absence from the ranch, when he'd gotten Aunt Rosemary and Dad settled into their new home. Rosemary had needed the break.

He didn't want to think about that, though—not with Donna so near, her lemon-drop perfume tickling his senses.

"Is it too old-fashioned for a man to cook?" he asked, taking his own seat. "Or is it a sign of the kind of modern man you think I'm not?"

She ignored his question as she sipped her wine. "Mmm. This is good."

He toasted her with his glass and, as if she were giving him a well-earned point, she did the same, then drank more.

After she put her glass down, she took up her fork. "I think it's only fair that I be clear about things, Caleb. Very clear."

He waited her out.

"You seem to believe that I'm looking for something that I'm not looking for."

"Like a constant man in your life?"

"Yes, something like that."

Well, maybe he was hoping for that.

And, by the end of the night, he was going to do everything within his power to change her mind about being a single city girl.

Chapter Five

So far, this "date" or whatever it was with Caleb Granger wasn't quite the disaster Donna had thought it would be.

Then again, what had she been expecting? For them to be at a loss for something to talk about? For the date to be so awkward that the sky would fall down on them?

Neither seemed to be happening…

So far.

He was breaking off a piece of sourdough bread from a loaf in a basket. "Since we're in the process of being clear with each other, I'd like to add something to the conversation we were having last night. You asked me why I was drawn to you and you didn't seem satisfied with the answer I gave you."

Straightforward as always.

He buttered the bread. "It's no secret that, when you Byrds first came to the ranch, stories circulated about your family. And those stories piqued my interest. Especially about you."

"What did they all say? That I was stuck-up? That I could destroy anyone with a withering glance?" She laughed. "*I* heard you're a ladies' man who likes a good chase, but I'm surprised that even the most experienced Casanova would want to go through the trouble of dealing with an ice queen."

He gave her a slanted grin, and for a moment, with him dressed up in his suit and with his dark blond hair tamed, her heart fluttered.

Then he said, "They did say you were a blonde bombshell, but that's not what interested me the most."

"Really."

"All right," he said. "I was curious about whether you lived up to the descriptions. And you do."

Blush.

She had to learn how not to do that around him.

"But," he said, "as I mentioned before, I liked the idea of how damned independent you were. Some men admire a woman who knows herself and doesn't necessarily need anyone else."

Did she know what she was about?

She brushed the question aside and played with a mushroom on her plate with her fork. "Just as I thought—you like the idea of a chase. It sounds like you created a bit of a fantasy about me."

"Maybe I did. And maybe part of your appeal was in the idea of what it might be like for me to eventually be a part of the Byrd family, too...."

She sat there, stunned, as he stopped abruptly.

Had he just admitted that he wasn't merely trying to

date her—he'd had much bigger fantasies in mind that had to do with marrying into her family?

As the shock wore off, she realized that he looked unsettled, as if he regretted what he'd said. But more to the point, she wondered if his tone had been a bit wistful, too.

Had his fantasy involved officially being like a son to Tex, if her grandfather had lived longer?

"Well," she said, easing the tension. "So much for fantasies. You've probably intuited that I'm not the marrying type."

His gaze was stalwart, solid, as it met hers again, whipping her into a silent frenzy before she got hold of herself.

"As usual," he said, "that came out the wrong way. I didn't mean for you to think that I was attracted to you because of your family ties. It was just something that'd crossed my mind long after I saw you."

She wasn't going to give him hell for this. She actually believed him. "I understand how you might still want to feel close to Tex through the Byrds, and why dating one of his granddaughters seems like a good idea."

He laid down his fork, and the candlelight flitted over his tanned skin, reflecting a lone flame in his pale blue eyes. "I can't say enough how much Tex and the rest of the people on this ranch meant to me."

What was Caleb's family like that he felt as if he had more of one here?

Donna didn't want to ask questions. She didn't want to get that deep.

"You don't have to explain this to me," she said.

"I should, after putting my foot in my mouth like

that." He shrugged. "See, I don't have what you'd call a perfect relationship with my own dad."

"You took a leave of absence to be with him, right? At least, that's what I heard."

He nodded. "My parents never had any other children, so I'm really the only one besides my aunt Rosemary who can take care of Dad. He's got dementia, and Rosemary tries her best, but it's a lot to ask of her. Even before he needed care, though, we weren't the closest."

Maybe it was the dormant journalist in her, but she ended up asking, "What about your mom?"

"She had an accident in the house one day, using a ladder to clean a high bookshelf, falling. It was just after I graduated high school and left home."

Maybe Donna did have a few things in common with Caleb, after all. "I'm sorry to hear that. My mom died when I was nine. I know what it's like to grow up without her around."

"It's like half of you disappears, and there's no way to replace that part of you, isn't it?"

Donna nodded, not wanting to say anything else, because Mom's cancer had meant that she and Jenna had needed to go live with Dad. Their parents had been divorced by that time, and she and Jenna normally saw him only on the weekends. He'd had a very different philosophy of child-rearing than their mother, raising Donna and Jenna to organize their lives as they would a business. And why not, when the most successful thing Dad had ever been was a businessman?

Even though Donna hadn't been as close to her mom as she should've been—another regret—she'd never felt so numb as she had after her death. That's when she'd

realized that emotional distance—her dad's practice—
was the easiest way to go about living.

"How's your dad doing?" Donna asked.

"These days, he barely even recognizes me. And
when he does, he lets me know how happy he is to have
Aunt Rosemary taking care of him instead of his 'irresponsible kid.'" He laughed a little. "At least, back when
I was younger, he didn't outright tell me how much he
disliked me."

Donna frowned. "It stinks that you have to go through
that."

"It is what it is."

"Besides, you don't sound all that irresponsible to
me. Maybe a little…impulsive…but—"

"I had my days of hell-raising, believe me. I wrecked
two trucks because I had a foot of lead, and I can't even
count how many times I ended up in the principal's office. Dad was never amused, and that's the kid he re-
members most times."

Something was chipping away at Donna's chest, as
if trying to get inside, but she picked up her glass and
drank. The wine slid down her throat, warm and soothing, chasing away everything that was trying to get to her.

Caleb had moved on, though. He grinned as he said,
"You know—if my dad could see me setting my sights
on one woman like I've done with you, he might look
at me a different way on his lucid days."

He was back to teasing her, maybe because the conversation had gotten a bit heavy.

She said, "How many ways can I tell you that I'm
the last person you should even think of settling down
with?"

"You can say it until you're blue in the face, but it's

not going to change the fact that I'm ready for another phase of my life."

"I'm not your next phase."

He grinned that dimpled grin, leaving a response up in the air.

Blowing out a breath, Donna decided that she needed some food in her stomach. But before she dug into her steak, she said, "I'm going to say this once and for all—I'm not ever going to settle down."

"Whatever you say, Donna."

As they ate, he didn't press the subject, and she felt herself relaxing little by little, even at the end of the evening, when he walked her out of the cabin to the porch.

"Thanks," she said, meaning it. This had been a great night. "You're a good host."

He left it at that, hovering over her, making her wonder if he was going to try to kiss her again.

Before he did, she started to walk. Fast.

"I'll take you back to the house," he said.

"I can make it on my own. Thanks, though."

As she made her way down the path from the cabin, she told herself not to look back, just as she'd done last night at the movie screening.

Don't encourage him.

Don't...

She did, stealing a glance over her shoulder. Then, in an effort to cover herself, she raised her hand in one last good-night to the handsome cowboy who'd put together such a beautiful candlelit night.

Just for her.

CALEB SLEPT LONGER than usual since it was his day off, then took coffee at his leisure on the porch.

Last night's dinner had been a success as far as he was concerned. Donna hadn't looked at him as if he were a mutant from a parallel dimension—not even once—and she'd even opened up to him a little.

Or, at least, as much as a self-admitted ice queen might allow herself to do at this point.

He was slowly winning her over. He was sure of it.

The one moment he regretted was when he'd mentioned the fanciful—and somewhat screwy—notion of marrying into the Byrd family. He'd sure needed to ease his way out of that slip of the tongue. The last thing he wanted was for Donna to think that he'd wallowed around the ranch for years, dreaming of snagging a Byrd granddaughter just so he could officially be a part of their family. True, the idea was a nice one, but it didn't define him—or his attraction-at-first-sight to Donna.

There were just some things that were meant to be, he thought, and Donna Byrd was one of them.

After the coffee and a simple oatmeal breakfast, he took his truck off ranch, driving toward the Yellow Rose Estates, where Aunt Rosemary and Dad had taken up residence. He'd promised he would visit them once a week, and he hoped today would continue being the good day it'd started out to be…especially when it came to Dad.

When he pulled into the sunflower-lined driveway, he immediately spotted Aunt Rosemary on the porch, sitting in the swing. She was wearing white capris and sandals, along with a loose pink blouse that hid how skinny she'd been getting lately.

She saw him and stood up stiffly, as if her joints were tight. The overhead fan blew the sparse gray hair that was caught back in the plastic barrette she always wore.

Caleb waved, grabbing the bag of groceries he'd stopped to buy at the corner market, then getting out of the truck.

"How's your day going?" he asked as he came up the walkway that wound over the manicured lawn. Sprinklers were spraying water over the grass, huffing under the early-morning sun.

Rosemary smiled, but it was a polite, fixed one. "Today's not the best."

Caleb's heart sank. His visits always started with a "How's your day" and Aunt Rosemary's first reaction always set the tone.

He came up the steps, then enveloped her in a one-armed hug. She opened the door for him, leading him into an air-conditioned living room filled with knick-knacks she had collected from auction barns as well as the floral-patterned sofa and chairs Caleb had recently purchased for the house. The scent of potpourri rode over something medicinal that Caleb couldn't identify.

He found his dad in a recliner in front of the wide-screen TV, watching a baseball game. He wore gray slacks and an old white T-shirt with a dark stain over one side of his chest. His silver hair was wiry and stood straight up, as if he hadn't combed it yet.

"Hey, Dad," Caleb said. "Brought you some of those blueberry muffins you like."

"Shut up. I'm watching the game."

Yup, not a good day. No wonder Rosemary had been outside.

Caleb had learned this past year not to engage with his dad at times like this, so he continued into the kitchen. Rosemary followed him there.

"Caleb," she whispered in apology as she began unpacking the groceries, "yesterday he was fine. He was even telling me stories about some of those shows he watches. Ice truckers or some sort of thing. But this morning…"

Her voice faded while, in the family room, the volume of the TV rose. Sometimes any kind of noise—even the sound of refrigerators closing or bags rustling in the kitchen—could distract Dad from what he was concentrating on. He wanted to hear the game, not them.

"Don't worry, Rose." Caleb kissed her on the forehead and started walking with her toward the hallway, where they could talk without the din of the TV. "You doing okay?"

"We had a rough morning. He wanted to wear that darn shirt with the gravy stains that I've tried to throw away, but he always pitches a fit about it when he sees it's missing."

She clenched her hands by her sides, and Caleb could tell that there'd probably been some ugly words said. But she was as patient as a saint, and she'd promised herself that she would take care of her little brother through thick and thin years ago. He'd vowed the same, after their parents had died when they were younger.

"Choose your battles, right?" Caleb said, although it was occasionally impossible to do when Dad was on a roll and he said things that a person shouldn't have to endure. "Why don't you go somewhere fun today? See some friends, visit that tearoom you like."

Rosemary gave him a look—the "I don't think it's a good idea to leave you two alone" glance.

"I can deal with anything." Back when the dementia had first set in and Dad had refused to live with Caleb, he had done all the research he could about the malady—

and about keeping an eye on the primary caretaker, too. It was important that Aunt Rosemary get out of the house more than occasionally.

He scooted her toward her bedroom. "We'll have dinner together tonight when you get back, okay?"

She grabbed his hand. She had a strong grip, even though her skin was starting to look like worn, thin parchment.

"You're a good son," she said. "He's lucky to have you."

She kissed him on the cheek and went into her bedroom.

After she'd gotten her purse then gone, Caleb went back to the kitchen, eventually taking off his cowboy hat and hanging it on a rack by the back door. Then he fixed a snack for Dad—a muffin and iced tea—and brought it out to him on a tray.

He set it on a coffee table, near where Dad was propping his slippered feet.

Handing Dad the tea glass, he waited for the man to acknowledge him.

When he did, there was a muddled anger in his eyes, and Caleb felt an invisible punch to his gut.

"Your mom told you to get a damned haircut," Dad said. "You gonna defy her again?"

"I'll get it done."

"Useless idiot."

Caleb clenched his jaw and made sure his father had a grip on his tea. Then he sat on the nearby sofa. It was hard to even look at the once-vital man who had lost his power and his faculties. Knowing that it could happen to anyone scared the crap out of Caleb.

Even worse was the pent-up rage that roiled in him.

When most sons grew up, they had the chance to become closer to their fathers. But that opportunity had been taken away from Caleb.

More than ever, he had no idea who this man was from day to day.

As the baseball game loudly played on, Dad's eyes closed, and he drifted off to sleep. Caleb rescued the tea glass from the armrest where his father was loosely gripping it, then sat down again.

Maybe things would be different when Dad woke up. Maybe he would be lucid enough today to say something polite to Caleb; it'd happened a couple of times before.

Then again, maybe things wouldn't be different at all.

But if Tex were still here, he would've urged Caleb to keep on trying, no matter what. He would've reminded Caleb that the price of letting your family go without a fight was much too high.

As his father began to snore, Caleb liberated the TV remote and lowered the volume. There was still a chance that this would turn out to be a good day for Dad.

And a good day was all Caleb was asking for.

DONNA WOULD NEVER admit to it, but since her dinner with Caleb, she'd been keeping her eye out for him.

And it wasn't because she was planning to sprint off in the other direction at the sight of him, either. Yesterday, which she'd known was his day off, she'd actually realized that she was hoping she would run into him by the fountain again, or maybe get another cocky text message telling her to check out the dream cabin.

But neither one had happened.

She told herself that was fine, though, because she was ever so busy with the same old stuff. Tracking her investments, keeping tabs on the state of the magazine industry, marketing the B and B and putting the finishing touches on the property, still checking in with their P.I. about Savannah and James to no avail....

Definitely busy.

Yet some kind of strange compulsion was making her yearn a bit for Caleb Granger, and it was confusing and very, very wrong. Hormones had been the downfall of so many—just look at her dad, Uncle William and Savannah for proof. But now, after she started to head toward some walking trails that she intended to design signage for, it was as if everything she'd learned about being independent and smart went by the wayside as she finally spotted Caleb's truck by the main house.

She slowed down without thinking, then watched how Caleb got out of his faded red vehicle to unload the last of the furniture that had been stored in a shed. As he grabbed an oak lamp stand that she had polished, bringing it up the steps of the main house, the muscles in his arms bulged, and she held her breath.

Muscles made by hard backbreaking work, she thought. Not the kind you got in a gym.

She was already halfway back to the house when she realized that she was traveling in the opposite direction than she'd first intended.

Caleb saw her as he came back out of the front door, and she braced herself for the dimples, for the overwhelming charm that had started to get the best of her.

But all she received from him was a tip of his hat.

"Morning, Donna," he said, then continued down the stairs toward his truck.

"Morning."

Would there be some banter now? Some teasing about how she had tracked *him* down this time?

Nope. He merely grabbed a small walnut magazine shelf and took it up the stairs.

Okay. She got it. Now that she'd had dinner with him, he was playing hard to get, challenging her to make the next move.

Well, good luck with that.

As he exited the house again, she noticed something about him. Even as he grinned at her, he seemed…distracted. He was still friendly, but he just wasn't the same Caleb.

Had something happened between their dinner and today?

"Caleb?" she asked as he walked past her.

His steps slowed, and he turned around.

"Is there…" Something going on?

He seemed to know what she was getting at, and he shrugged—his usual careless go-to gesture.

"It's just…" she said. "You seem preoccupied."

There. She'd left the door open for him to say one of his patently direct comments. *I'm already tired of you. The chase is over. Bored now.*

She could take anything he had to dish out.

It seemed as if he was about to say something, but then her damned phone rang.

One side of her wanted to check the number since she was waiting on so many calls. The other side wanted to hear what Caleb had to say, for whatever reason.

The side that told herself that caring was a bad idea finally glanced at the phone screen.

Unidentified number.

In the time it took for her to do that, Caleb was already on his way back to the truck. "I'll catch you later, Donna. They're waiting for me in the stables."

Was he playing hard to get?

As Caleb started his truck's engine, Donna realized that whoever had been trying to call her had gone to voice mail. She waited for them to leave a message while walking in the direction of the trails again, just to make it seem that she was as busy as Caleb, in case he was watching her in his rearview mirror.

When a blip of sound let her know that the caller had finished their message, she accessed it, telling herself not to look at Caleb as he drove off to wherever ladies' men went when they were done with a woman.

She came to a scuffing halt when she heard a female voice, traced with a dignified Texas drawl.

"Hi, Donna. I think you've been expecting my call."

An awkward pause—one just long enough so that Donna could hear her heart pounding in her ears.

"This is Savannah Carson. Or Savannah Jeffries. You would know that name better, I think."

Oh, God. This was happening.

Really happening.

The message continued. "Your P.I. contacted me a few times and…I've been trying to figure out how I was going to respond. I have to start off by saying that I'm not terribly surprised that I'm hearing from the Byrds. It's just been a long time since I…since I knew your father and uncle. I realized that somebody would get curious someday, but that doesn't mean I was prepared for this."

Another hesitation, and Donna crossed one arm over her chest, the other still holding the phone. Her pulse was drilling at her.

"Your P.I. explained everything—even that you all are aware of James. He's always known that I raised him as a single mom by choice, and he knows that his father has always been out of the picture. That he's in the world somewhere. But James doesn't know the entire story. It's not something I've ever been willing to share, and that's probably the reason..."

Savannah cut herself off. Had she almost said something about why she and her son were supposedly estranged?

"As I was saying," she said, her voice thick, "James is an adult, and I realized that I do owe it to him to tell him what I've learned from your investigator about your interest in us. I'm not sure how he'll respond to the possibility of meeting your family, though. And you should know that I'm not going to reveal to anyone who James's father is. There's been too much trouble about that already, and as long as you accept those terms, I'll go along with this."

As she paused again, Donna wondered, *What does she mean by "this"?* What was Savannah willing to go along with? Introducing herself to the family? Coming over for a fun-filled dinner with the Byrds with James in tow?

The woman ended by leaving her phone number, and Donna absently saved the message.

She wasn't sure how long she stood in the grass, with the roar of a Flying B truck in the distance and with the song of some birds blithely warbling nearby. But, eventually, she walked toward the dream cabin, dialing both Jenna and Tammy on the way so they could meet her in a place where there was no chance of anyone overhearing.

They'd been checking out the riding trails, so they

arrived at the cabin within fifteen minutes, tying their horses to a post at the side of the building and joining Donna on the porch, where the scent of honeysuckle massaged the air.

Donna played Savannah's message for them on speakerphone. When it was over, both Jenna and Tammy leaned back against the wall.

"Hot damn," Tammy said.

Jenna, who, like Tammy, was dressed in riding gear, asked, "So she's going to meet with us?"

"I'm not clear on that," Donna said. "I'll have to call her back to see. Not that I'm looking forward to it."

"We'll need to tell Aidan and Nathan about this," Jenna said.

"We can do that after we're done here. I just wanted to hear what you two thought first."

Tammy slid a hand to the back of her neck, under her dark ponytail. "What do you think James is going to say?"

"No use speculating," Donna said shortly. But then she thought better of it. Most of her life, she'd followed in her dad's footsteps, businesslike to the point of abruptness sometimes. Putting people at a distance.

But Tammy and Jenna deserved more.

They had to realize that she was just getting used to girl talk, because they both smiled patiently at her, waiting for her to go on.

"Sorry to be curt with you," she said. "This hasn't been the best week ever."

"Because of Savannah?" Tammy asked.

"Not just that." Donna told them about her financial advisor's email, too, but she skipped over Caleb's brush-off today.

That was something that shouldn't be affecting her at all.

Tammy came over to Donna, affectionately resting a hand on her shoulder. "Why're you worried about money when you already have a place to call home?"

Jenna flanked her other side. "You've got everything right here."

They meant well, and Donna tentatively reached out, touching her cousin's hand, then smiling at her sister. A warmth gathered around her heart, baking it.

Family, she thought. She really did have it.

She had almost everything except…

That emptiness that she often felt inside her seemed to expand, but she ignored it. She didn't even know what it was, not even when the image of Caleb's face flashed before her.

Jenna tilted her head. "You know what you need?"

A head examination? A winning ticket for the lottery?

Tammy was already grinning. "I know what you're going to say, Jen—half the staff is going for a night out, so we should go, too. After we talk to my brothers, we'll dance our cares away before we call Savannah in the morning. I have to say that Mike also needs to cut loose. He's been busier than usual this week, what, with all that flu going around Buckshot Hills."

Jenna linked arms with Donna. "I can hear Lone Star Lucy's calling us now."

Donna had never been to a honky-tonk in her life, but suddenly, a good time sounded like just the ticket.

"Why not?" she said, pausing, then drawing the women who'd become her best friends into a group hug.

A honky-tonk just might be as wonderful as the newest dance club or trendiest wine bar. She *would* dance her cares away there and maybe even meet someone who would temporarily take her mind off her problems.

Someone who wasn't named Caleb.

Chapter Six

"Caleb," Hugh, the foreman, said at the end of the day as they sat at one of the staff's mess tables. "You really need a night out."

Caleb had been clearing his plate, and he looked down at the grizzled Hugh, who was just sitting there analyzing him like some kind of lifestyle coach, or whatever they called them.

He knew that Hugh had only addressed the subject now that they were the last ones to clear out tonight, seeing as a bunch of the other staff had planned to go to Lone Star Lucy's. It was Buckets of Beer night, and Caleb hadn't been to the honky-tonk since he'd gotten back from his leave of absence.

Hugh stood up with his plate, too. "You've looked about as blue as blue can be today, so I think a good time is in order. I could see that your dad did a number on you the minute you showed up to work this morning."

"I should be used to it by now."

"So what happened with him?"

"The usual." They walked alongside each other to the dish tubs, then deposited their tableware. "There're times I wonder whether it's the dementia that makes Dad say the things he does or if it's just because that's how he really feels about me and nothing's stopping him from telling me now."

"Don't let that stuff hound you. Forget about every bit of it. That's what honky-tonks are for."

The old man nudged his arm before he went his own way, to his cabin, where he never bothered with young men's nights out anymore himself.

But Caleb thought his friend might be right about letting loose with the rest of the staff....

As he walked to his cabin, he caught sight of the main house in the distance, and he wondered what Donna was doing tonight.

One thing was for sure—a woman like her wouldn't be at Lone Star Lucy's. And if ever she did happen to wander through the bar's doors, he doubted very highly that she would want to have a beer with him—not after he'd been so deep in his own problems this morning while trying to figure out just what he could do to make matters with his dad better.

He relived the moment when he'd seen her. Donna, with her blond hair and swerves and forever-long legs showcased by her sundress. But he'd been so distracted that he hadn't done the usual flirting, and it seemed that she'd taken his mood as a slight to her.

He hadn't even had the opportunity to tell her differently, because of his tight schedule and her ringing cell phone. Hell—she probably hadn't even thought about him once she'd gone about her business.

Turning away from the house, he went into his cabin. Maybe a night at Lucy's would make him forget about his ridiculous fascination with her. And maybe not.

As he spruced himself up, he kept thinking what she might make of the new cologne Aunt Rosemary had bought for him as a thank-you or the silver belt buckle he never got around to wearing.

So much for forgetting about Donna.

He decided against the cologne and the buckle, then hopped in his truck, zooming down the Flying B Road, his tires kicking up dust as he followed a few other vehicles that the staff were riding in.

It didn't take long to get to Lucy's, and once Caleb was inside the low-lit main room with its cramped tables and sawdust-covered floors, he ordered one beer, then settled in a chair next to Manny and his girlfriend, Maria.

"Small Town Saturday Night" was playing while Manny's cowboy hat rode his dark hair, his arm slung around Maria's shoulders.

"The man is *back!*" he said.

He clinked bottles with Caleb and they drank.

"So who's it gonna be tonight?" asked Manny.

Maria rolled her big brown eyes at the boy talk. "This is where I powder my nose. Excuse me, you two."

After Manny watched her go, he leaned his elbows on the scarred table and nodded toward the bar. "That cute redheaded vet is right over there, sneaking peeks at you. As I remember, she looked ready and willing to give you a thorough exam the last time we were here."

Caleb couldn't be less interested. He felt restless, as

if he didn't belong in places like this anymore. "I'm just here to kick back, Manny."

"Say it ain't so. Do you know how many good moves I've cribbed from you? Don't leave your student hanging."

"You've got Maria now, remember?"

"Who said I wasn't going to try everything I learn on her?"

Manny laughed and drank some more. Caleb couldn't help joining in with a chuckle, feeling a little more like himself as the songs changed from swinging numbers to two-stepping ballads.

Soon, Manny and Maria were on the floor, swaying to a Sugarland song, leaving Caleb to his own devices.

And that's when he looked up to see a stunning sight.

Donna Byrd, with her light hair shimmering around her shoulders, coming through the honky-tonk's door with her sister and cousin and their fiancés.

Caleb nearly did a double take, but after he gathered himself, he merely put his beer bottle on the table before he dropped it.

Donna. Here?

She sure as hell looked like a fish out of water, not necessarily because of the way she was dressed, but just because of the way she surveyed everything, as if each rustic chair and kitschy cowboy decoration on the walls might jump up and give her country cooties at any second.

Except for all that, she nearly blended in, wearing brand-spanking-new jeans and boots, plus a flirty cowgirl blouse that clung to every curve. But she was still straight from the city.

A fast Clay Walker song came on, and Caleb's heart

beat in time to the rhythm—skittering, banging, creating tightness in his belly.

A longing that built up the steam inside of him when all he'd meant to do tonight was work some of it off.

As Jenna and Tammy led Donna to a table in a corner, their fiancés, J.D. and Mike, went to the bar.

It was as if the room had gotten far more colorful and interesting with Donna in it, the music louder, the world less dull. It was like the first time Caleb had seen her all over again—chemistry and desire, wrapped into a searing bundle.

But there was something else, too, and once again Caleb wasn't sure what to name it. All he could do was want and need.

Manny had returned from the dance floor, leaving Maria across the room to chat with some of her friends near a stage where bands sometimes played. Unfortunately, Manny had seen where Caleb had been looking.

"Forget the redhead at the bar," he said. "Look who's here now."

Caleb shot him a don't-say-another-word glance, and Manny held up his hands.

"Sor-ry. It's no secret you have a thing for Donna Byrd, you know. Why don't you just go up to her and ask her to dance?" Then Manny chuckled. "Listen to me, giving the master tips."

Yeah, listen to him. Wasn't it strange that Caleb didn't know what to do with her?

Wasn't this a first?

Out of the corner of his eye, he saw Donna get up from her table and weave her way through a bunch of appreciative cowboys, over to the bar.

Before he could tell himself to stop watching her, he was standing, grabbing his half-full beer bottle.

"That's the man!" Manny said.

Caleb didn't react except to say, "I just need to fill the well, Manny. You want anything?"

"Yeah—a good view of what's about to happen."

Caleb narrowed his gaze at him before he left. So what if Manny was onto him? Wasn't everybody?

Wasn't Donna?

With each step he took toward her, his confidence grew. Everything his dad had said yesterday over dinner—about Caleb having as much value as a one-legged dog, about how much trouble he'd always caused him and Mom—seemed to dissipate as Caleb got closer to Donna.

Like Hugh said, he *could* forget.

She was at the end of the bar, where Doc Sanchez and J.D. were laughing with her. Caleb guessed it had something to do with the pink drink in the martini glass that she'd ordered in this land of beer and tequila.

J.D., whom Caleb had been working with in the stables lately, noticed him first.

"Caleb," he said, nodding in greeting.

Doc Mike smiled and raised one of the beer bottles from the bucket they'd purchased in a hello, too.

Donna slowly turned her gaze toward Caleb, her lips parted. In surprise?

But did he see a hint of a smile there before she corrected herself and went back to being blasé as she sipped her cocktail?

From their table, Jenna called to the men, and with knowing looks, they left Donna alone.

Just as Caleb thought she was about to follow them back to her group, he moved closer to her. "Wait a sec."

She lifted a cool eyebrow.

Great. It was obvious that his distance today on the ranch had pushed her back to square one, erasing any progress he'd made with that dream cabin dinner.

He didn't know if he should apologize or what, so he started out with a compliment. "You look real nice, Donna."

"These are my urban cowgirl clothes," she said. Then, as if she wanted to prove that she didn't give a crap about what he thought, she tossed back half her drink.

He chuckled. "What's in that glass?"

"It's called a Ruby. Grapefruit juice and vodka. In New York, there'd be sugared grapefruit slices as a garnish and maybe some sugar around the rim of the glass."

"We're not that fancy here."

"No kidding." She took another healthy swig.

If he hadn't known it before, he knew it now—she was definitely wielding some attitude.

"Listen," he said. "I didn't mean to be remote today when you said hi."

"You were? I didn't notice."

"Good."

She was so full of bull. It tickled him that she was pretending his attentions didn't matter. Mostly, the tickle got him in his chest, where, again, there was something more than lust happening with Donna. Something he hoped she *would* notice.

She finished off the drink, holding up a finger to the bartender to request a second.

"Another rough day?" he asked.

"Probably as tough as the one *you* were having earlier." She bit her lip, as if she was trying too late to hold back the words.

"Donna, I visited my dad yesterday. That's why I wasn't exactly Mr. Sunshine this morning."

As she pushed her finished cocktail away, she seemed sorry that she'd been giving him guff. "The visit didn't go well, I take it."

"Not so much."

She shifted her gaze to him and sighed. "Sorry for being difficult. Sorry for…I don't know. I think I'm sorry for everything lately."

Caleb didn't want her to be sorry.

Right then and there, he guaranteed that he would do anything he could to take away all the sorry from her.

THE LAST THING Donna wanted to be tonight was a bummer, so after the bartender brought another drink, she motioned with her glass toward the back of the bar, where she'd seen pool tables.

"Care to join me in some game therapy?" she asked Caleb. It was as good as she could do for an olive branch.

He stepped back from the bar, indicating that she should lead the way.

As she passed him, she caught a whiff of his scent— a smell that belonged only to him. A smell that came to her at night sometimes, whether she wanted it to or not.

The Ruby cocktail had given her a lift, so when they got to the back room, with some empty pool tables on one side and dartboards on the other, she put her drink down on a tall table. She went to a board and pulled out the darts.

"Are you safe to drink and dart?" Caleb asked with a grin.

"I'm fit as a fiddle." It was true. And she was also pretty relaxed, at that.

She proved it by moving into position away from the board and throwing a dart. She hit the nineteen point zone below the bull's-eye.

"Yee-haw," she said teasingly, then stepped aside for him to take a turn. "I strike first blood."

When Caleb took the dart from her, his index finger brushed hers. She didn't think he'd done it purposely, but even if he had, she wouldn't have felt a more powerful reaction.

A rumble deep inside.

A stirring that rocked her.

She realized that she'd held her breath, and as she forced herself to utilize oxygen like a normal person, she did her best not to look at him, to make eye contact and allow him to see what he'd done to her.

"What're you waiting for?" she asked instead, her tone challenging.

He shrugged, threw the dart, effortlessly hitting for twenty in the same kind of narrowed zone as she had, but for a point higher.

"Anything you can do," he said, grinning.

I can do better. She took his place, aiming with one eye shut, then nailing the green strip just outside the bull's-eye this time.

He waggled his eyebrows, his dimples at full force. "We could go on like this all night, or we could make this interesting."

Danger, Donna Byrd, said a little voice in her head. *Danger!*

But she was in a rather reckless mood. A Ruby-cocktail mood. She was tired of being beaten down by circumstances that she barely had control over. She was exhausted by attempting to stay even with the treadmill of problems that kept speeding under her.

"How interesting would you like to make this?" she asked.

He jerked his chin toward the board and, damn, it was sexy. Manly. The gesture tumbled her belly and tied it into knots of desire.

"If I hit the center," he said, "you will answer any question I ask."

"That's begging for trouble."

"I'll take it easy on you. Promise."

This time, when she crossed her arms over her chest, it wasn't a protective gesture. She was being just as cocky as he was.

"It's going to be fun to see you humbled," she said.

Wrong. Because he hit the bull's-eye with no problem. Damn.

She spread her arms wide. "Okay. Have at it."

Her choice of words could've been better. Or maybe they were perfect, because a wicked gleam in his gaze told her that she'd hit her own bull's-eye in him.

Hah.

Caleb sauntered over to the board, plucking out the darts, then leaning against the wall. In his faded blue jeans, tattered boots, long-sleeved white shirt and that hat, he seemed like he should be out riding the range, not taking aim at her.

But when he did, his aim was true.

"What's the one thing I can do to persuade you to give me a chance, Donna Byrd?"

The directness of the question made the air snag in her lungs.

She'd only had one drink, and she was capable of holding a lot more liquor, but what she'd consumed had loosened her up enough so that she didn't mind answering.

Not this time.

"If I had the answer," she said, "I'd…"

"You'd tell me?"

Yes. Yes, she would, because tonight she'd informed Jenna and Tammy that she was going to dance and let go and have some fun. Maybe she would even do it with Caleb Granger because of that dinner they'd had together—an event that had broken some of the ice between them. Maybe she would do it because he'd so confidently bellied up to the bar and snapped her out of the funk that'd been caused by Savannah's phone message today.

Now, Donna took the biggest step she'd ever taken with a man—and it was in Caleb's direction.

As he saw her coming, that familiar heat took over his gaze.

But then, still in a teasing mood, she merely held out her hand for the darts.

He gave them over. "You're impossible."

"I try my best to be."

But she honored their bet, anyway, giving him a chance with her. Letting him in, just a little.

"You know why I came to this Lucy's place tonight?" she asked.

He seemed to know that she was giving him an opening. "Why?" he asked gently.

His voice. Why did it dismantle her?

"We got that call from Savannah today," she said.

He raised an eyebrow. "That's a good reason to need a drink."

"Tell me about it. She left a message, and I played it for Jenna and Tammy first. Then we had a chat with Nathan and Aidan before we came here, but we're going to wait until tomorrow to try to reach her."

"What did she say?"

"We think she really does want to meet us, even though she didn't come right out and say it. But she isn't sure how her son is going to react to everything."

"Understandably."

"She didn't sound happy about finally having to come clean with James about her past."

"She never told him?"

"It seems so." She shook her head. "After Tex asked her to leave the Flying B when he caught her and Dad together, she filed an incomplete at school, and neither Uncle William or Dad ever heard from her again. Neither of them tracked her down, either. There were hurt feelings all around, and I'm sure she didn't want James growing up knowing that there was a lot of pain involved with him."

Caleb furrowed his brow. "You sound pretty sympathetic to her."

"Maybe I am." Donna wasn't sure, but hearing Savannah's voice had made the woman more real than ever. "It's just…" *You can say it to him, Donna.* "It's just that I'm still so angry at Dad about this."

Even now, the anger was simmering in her. And, here, she'd thought that she'd put a lid on it for the time being.

She started to stick the darts back into the board, probably with more force than necessary. "Jenna made her peace with Dad, but I haven't yet. I used to think that man was the ultimate when I was growing up. I pushed back my anger about the divorce and what it did to my mom and tried to tell myself that he was my father, for heaven's sake, and he had to know much more about life than I did, so any decision he made had to be a decent one. But then we heard about Savannah…"

Caleb hadn't said a word. He just let her talk, then trail off, and she liked that about him. She'd never known many people who really knew how to listen like this.

She went on. "He's not the man I grew up admiring. He betrayed his own brother with a woman. Who does that?"

"I don't know."

"Jenna told me that he had his reasons, and even though she doesn't approve of what went down, she's forgiven him. I don't think I can."

"Maybe it'll just take some time."

"Maybe it'll never happen."

Caleb went quiet, and in the background, the country music played on, almost distant and blocked off by the walls of the dart room.

Finally, he spoke. "We never really know who they are."

His words didn't sink in at first. Perhaps Donna didn't want them to. But when they did, there was a profound ache that twisted in her.

He said, "We grow up thinking we know our parents, but then there comes a point when that changes. My situation's a little different than yours because my dad's literally someone I don't know on most days. But you had a rude awakening with yours. You never saw it coming."

She swallowed back the swelling in her throat. "He

is like an entirely different person now that this secret is out. And it's a hard thing to face."

At this moment, she'd never felt closer to anyone, even if she and Caleb were standing in a dim corner of a honky-tonk by a dartboard. Even if he was from a totally different world.

In spite of all her misgivings, she reached out with her free hand, touching a button on his shirt. But just as if it were made of fire, she let go.

What was she doing?

Her body knew, though, and it sizzled with the want of him…or of someone who understood her just as much as he did. And his body must've been doing the same thing, because as she was drawing back her hand, he clamped his fingers around her wrist.

"Don't," he said.

"What?" There was a clump of scratches in her throat that made her voice ragged.

"Don't draw back into that ice queen shell, Donna."

God, how she wanted to. It was safe in that shell. It was easy.

But as his fingers branded her, sending a trail of flame through her veins and then every other inch of her, she knew that the ice was melting.

Him, touching her. It felt so good, flaring her hormones so that every dark part of her lit up.

Donna finally raised her gaze, meeting his own. It was filled with such a fierce passion that she realized that she knew exactly what she needed tonight more than anything else.

She wanted them both to feel good, and she had no doubt that Caleb would know exactly how to accomplish that.

FIFTEEN MINUTES LATER, Caleb was still trying to wrap his mind around what had gone down with Donna inside Lone Star Lucy's.

One minute, they were playing darts. The next, Donna was making good on their bet and answering a question he'd never thought she would touch with a ten-foot pole.

And the next, her fingers had been on his shirt button, reaching out in a tentative gesture that had given him shattering pause.

She was *touching* him.

She was reaching out in a way he suspected that Donna didn't often do, if ever.

Even if his reputation might deny it, he would never take advantage of a raw moment for any woman. Caleb liked to play, but not if the board was tilted and he had an unfair advantage.

So he'd asked Donna if she needed to leave. She'd said yes, then said goodbye to her sister and cousin before getting into Caleb's truck.

And here they were, driving with her window down, the wind tangling her hair as she leaned back and closed her eyes. It wasn't until they reached the Flying B Road that she rolled up her window and looked at him straight on.

"Has anyone ever told you that you have a way about you, Caleb?"

He wasn't sure what the hell that meant. "A bad way?"

She laughed. "A good one. Believe it or not, I feel better than I did earlier tonight. It felt nice to spill my guts to someone who has another perspective."

He steered into the ranch, slowing down as they approached the main house.

As he came to a stop, she didn't make a move to get out.

"We're here," he said, as if she couldn't tell.

"It's still early. Don't you think it's still early?"

He gave her a curious glance. "Do you want to go *back* to Lucy's or something?" He wouldn't put it beyond her to change her mind.

"No. How about we drive around?"

All right, then. Without questioning her, he took off. When they were well on the road that traveled past the cabins, Donna pointed toward the east. "You can drop me off at the dream cabin."

"What?"

"I'm too hyped up on Ruby cocktails to go back to my room. But I have an idea. I'm going to lie down on that mattress. Why didn't I think of this before? I could have some sort of dream about how my family should handle everything with Savannah."

Maybe she *was* a lightweight who'd gotten drunk off of a little alcohol. "You know those stories about dreams coming true on that bed are just a heap of bull."

"No, they're not. Tammy had a so-called magical dream about Doc Mike on that bed that came true and vice versa. J.D. and Jenna, too."

"Are you sure you're not drunk?"

"Positive. You should see how many Rubys I've thrown down the hatch back in New York. Tonight was child's play."

Who was he to argue? He drove to the dream cabin, letting the engine idle.

Even then, Donna didn't get out. She merely unbuckled her seat belt.

"I guess I should wish you sweet dreams," he said.

She seemed at a loss as she toyed with the bottom of her blouse. But when she slipped him a look that he'd seen a hundred times from other women, he understood.

A "soft" look was what he would've called it.

Before he knew it, she'd slid closer to him, pushing back his hat and planting her other hand in his hair.

"Since the dart game," she said, "I've been waiting for you to kiss me."

Now it made sense, her touching his shirt button at the bar. It'd been Donna's way of starting things off between them.

But he'd thought it might take longer for her to come around. That it'd be a little more romantic. Was she reacting to all the stress she'd been under? Had tonight been her breaking point?

She tightened her hand in his hair, but he'd imagined a kiss like he'd never had with any other woman, not something fueled by whatever was egging her on.

"Donna," he whispered, stopping her.

Her gaze started to go cool as she released his hair.

"Donna," he said even more softly, cutting the engine, then easing his hand behind her neck, taking a moment to look into her eyes and to see the bewilderment there.

And the pure need.

Then, with all the time in the world, he kissed her right—his lips gently pressing against hers, fitting so perfectly as he tilted his head and rested his other hand under her jaw.

As he sipped at her, he rubbed his thumb against her neck, a slow cadence, promising so much more than the rushed encounter she'd been suggesting.

She moaned against his mouth, giving in, grabbing at his shirt as she went boneless against him. He tightened his grip on her, bringing her against him a little harder—but not too hard.

Just enough so he could deepen the kiss, opening his lips a bit more, demanding and asking all at the same time.

She answered by pulling him toward her and leaning back so that her spine was flush against the seat, her light hair spilling over the vinyl.

"Caleb," she whispered.

The sound of his name coming from Donna Byrd was like sparks coming into contact with oil.

And, suddenly, Caleb wasn't sure how he could hold back anymore with the woman he was crazy about.

Chapter Seven

Just one time with him, Donna thought as a bolt of desire split her straight down to the piercing ache between her legs.

She needed Caleb tonight, and there didn't have to be more to this than anything physical. After all, she was going to be leaving this ranch as soon as the B and B opened and she could run the marketing program from miles away.

Their differences wouldn't matter if he kept on kissing her like this, his lips nestled just under her ear and sending brutal shivers through her, making her lift her hips against his. They were just two people who wanted the same thing.

Each other.

Desire seared her from the inside out as he dragged his lips to the center of her neck. She knocked his hat all the way off, and it hit the floorboards as she threaded her fingers through his shaggy blond hair.

"You do know how to kiss," she said on a thin breath.

He ran his mouth up to her jaw, skimming over it, his body pressing the wind out of her as he lay half on top of her. His muscled length felt so good, a fit that allowed her to wiggle her hips and encourage him.

She felt his excitement through his jeans, and that urged her to reach a hand between them, grasping for the buttons on his fly.

That emptiness she'd been feeling for a while now... she needed to fill it, and this was how she would accomplish that mission. It was the only solution she knew.

"Whoa, Donna," he said, rising up just enough to look down at her. "Not so fast."

His eyes were so blue. "You're usually faster than I am."

"Not tonight."

He leaned on his forearms, slowing everything down except for her wild heartbeat. And when he gazed at her, using his fingertips to coax her hair back from her face as if all he wanted to do was memorize her, something scary and silly rotated in her belly, flipping it and sending another zing of passion to the juncture of her thighs.

"What do you mean you're not fast tonight?" she asked.

"I mean that this isn't going to be wham-bam-and-thank-you-ma'am."

He eased his mouth to her temple, kissing her there. She closed her eyes, her pulse suspending.

"What I mean," he said, leisurely kissing her lower, near the tip of her mouth, "is that we're going to take our sweet time together."

Another twist of need got her where it counted, making her want him all the more, especially when he kissed her full on the mouth again.

His lips were softer than she ever could've anticipated and, for a second, taking things slow seemed the best idea in the world.

Slow kisses, slow fingers unbuttoning her blouse, slow anticipation as he parted the material.

Her chest heaved, her breasts pushing against the lace of her bra. The moonlight coming through the windshield showed his expression of sheer, ragged appetite as he ran a gaze over her.

When Caleb tenderly slid his hands under her back and returned to kissing her, long and sultry and adoring enough to rip her apart, she made a tiny sound of delight under his mouth. She hadn't expected another kiss, just groping.

Just wham-bam, because that's all she'd ever really had before.

Languidly, he drew on her mouth, then used his tongue to prolong the kiss, to taste her, to explore so much of her that she couldn't stop herself from arching against him, making him moan.

The primal sound put her back in a safe mental place, because it reassured her that he also wanted what she'd come here for—they wouldn't need emotions, just action. She'd known just what she was doing when she'd asked him to bring her to the dream cabin. It wasn't as if she could suggest that he come to her room in the main house, and she didn't love the idea of the other ranch hands catching them sneaking into his place.

When he kissed down her chin, her neck, then to the

tops of her breasts, she pressed her hand against the back of his head, enticing him to go on.

"Front clasp," she whispered. She was talking about her bra.

He reached up, and with no fumbling at all, undid it.

As her breasts were freed, she felt the night air on them, felt his lips as he covered every inch, using his hands to shape her, too.

She reached over her head, grasping for the door. She needed to hold on to something because his mouth was taking her for a ride—he was sucking at her now, his fingers pleasuring her other nipple until both of her tips stood at stiff peaks.

So sensitive there. So...

She hauled in a breath, sharp and surprised, as he used his tongue to work her into an even more demanding frenzy.

"Come on," she said, nearly pulling at his hair again. "Almost—"

As a crashing bang shot through her, she bucked, the sensation reverberating through every cell with violent echoes. She thought she heard herself cry out, but she wasn't sure—not as Caleb gnawed his way down her stomach, toward her belly.

Just as she became a squirming mess again, he slowed down even more, then halted altogether.

"What is it?" she asked.

"I just realized," he said against her skin, looking up at her with that devilish gaze and that dimpled smile. "We've got a feather bed waiting for us."

She'd intended to get there at some point—but the sooner the better now.

He whisked her into his arms, and before she knew

it, he'd barged out the truck door and was carrying her up the porch steps.

When they entered the cabin's door, it was with another crash. Immediately, she pushed herself out of his arms until she was standing, pulling at his shirt, leading him across the floor of the one-room cabin with his lips against hers, kissing feverishly.

They bumped into a chair, banged into a table. She didn't know where the hell they were going—she just hoped they somehow made it to the bed before they both exploded.

When he lifted her up, onto the table—in the kitchen area?—she forgot the bed altogether.

He was already stripping off his shirt, and she did the same with hers, tossing that and her bra to the floor, then taking care of her boots and socks, too. She tore at the fly of her jeans.

But his hand halted her.

"Let me," he said.

Her chest was rising and falling as she gave him all the control he'd asked for, as she leaned back and braced her hands on the table's surface.

He rested his palms on her thighs as she pulsed with ravenous hunger. Then, with deliberate care, he brought his hands upward, until one of them reached the middle of her legs.

As he rubbed her there, she almost fell backward onto the table, but he made sure she didn't by bringing his other arm around her back, holding her up.

"Is my technique modern enough for you?" he asked, grit in his tone.

"You'll..." She gathered her breath. "You'll have to give me more of a demonstration."

He laughed, low and sexy, traveling his fingers to her zipper. As he undid it, the sound filled the room, eating its way through her, too.

He coasted his fingers into her open fly, into her panties, spreading her legs wider.

"Does that help you reach a conclusion?" he asked.

"It will."

Donna could feel him watching her face, and something told her to make him wait for a so-called conclusion, to put him through as much as he was putting her through before she rewarded him with a climactic reaction.

"Even so," she said, barely getting the words out, "you're making great progress."

He stroked her thoroughly with his fingers, up and down, his thumb circling her most private spot just before he slipped inside of her.

She couldn't take anymore, and she lost all strength, falling into his arm, which had been supporting her this entire time.

With a guttural sound that told her he'd almost reached a breaking point himself, he scooped her into his arms again, then laid her down on the feather bed.

It was soft against her back as they sank into it, as he guided the jeans from her body, then her panties, leaving her fully exposed to him in the moonlight coming through the nearest window.

More exposed than she wanted to admit, because her heart felt tight in her chest, as if it didn't know which way to go now.

He left the bed, and she heard him doffing his jeans and the rest of his clothes, then returning to her.

As he came body to body with her again, she bit her

lip. His flesh against hers. When had it ever felt this wonderful?

Why was it feeling this wonderful when all it should be was a casual encounter?

He'd put on a condom, and the tip of him nudged her, teasing her.

She realized she'd never needed anything more in her life than what she needed now—him inside of her. Caleb Granger, the man she'd thought was wrong in every way.

When he entered her, she held her breath. He traveled deep, but she took him all in, moving with him, holding one of his hands as they churned, hips to hips, her to him.

She imagined water, her favorite fountain in Central Park, then the one outside of the Byrds' main house. The rhythm started slow, lazy, but then began to rush through her, flooding her with feeling, gathering into a wall of emotion that threatened to crash down on her.

But even though Donna would've run away from sensations like this before tonight, she felt herself opening to this man, waiting for the crescendo she could feel building inside of her, and of him.

And when it finally pummeled her, it got her with a crushing smash, once, twice—

As she stiffened at the third incredible assault, she let out all the breath she had, coming down from her high, her legs wrapped around him so tightly that they were pretty much one person. He had climaxed before her and had his mouth pressed to her neck, his lips formed into the silent shape of her name.

As their breathing evened out, she didn't let go of him.

Not yet.

CALEB MOVED HIS lips to Donna's in the aftermath—a sweaty, no-holds-barred, postorgasm kiss—and, after they drew away from each other and looked into each other's gazes, he half expected her to tell him this was it.

Impressive, she might say, suddenly cool, then hopping out of bed to hurriedly get back into her clothes. *Glad we made it to the bed, at least.*

But she wasn't going anywhere, instead curling into his chest.

He reveled in the intimacy, cradling her as she pulled him even closer with one of her legs, which was wrapped over his hip. He was still inside of her.

Near silence reigned—the still of a country night, the thud of his heartbeat slowing down from all the excitement. He drew circles on her lower back. He loved feeling the swell of her rear end just below his fingers, loved how curvy she was.

Loved…

Just about everything about her?

Or was this still an attraction at first sight?

"That was…" she started to say.

"How about we don't talk just yet." He didn't want to know what she was going to say to work her way out of bed and through the door.

"I want to tell you that I'm glad you kept pursuing me, Caleb. Tonight was worth it."

He laughed softly into her hair. The sweet lemony scent of it filled him.

They lay there like that for a bit, quiet and satisfied, but he knew he'd have to move soon, clean up, then come back to bed where she would hopefully be waiting.

Yet, when she slipped her hand between them and touched his belly, trailing a finger along the line of hair that brushed down to his groin, he wondered if he knew anything about where this was going at all.

"What're you doing, Donna?" he asked.

In answer, she lifted her face to kiss him, and it wasn't long until he was getting revved up again.

What was he—seventeen?

Without doing much thinking—yup, just like the seventeen-year-old he used to be—he told her to wait. Then he discarded the rubber, barely even looking at it because he just wanted to be back in bed again.

They made out like starved kids on homecoming night, exploring more of each other's bodies, laughing, clinging, coming to completion until they were both exhausted.

This time, as he held her, he closed his eyes.

"Men," Donna said, laughing. "Who's the weaker species—the women who can stay awake after some exertion or the guys who don't have an ounce of gas left?"

"No debating," he said, his voice already fading.

"Okay."

From the pressure on the mattress, he could tell that she was shifting her weight, and he opened one eye to see her leaning on an elbow, propping herself up to look at him. They'd gotten under the sheets somehow, but he could see the swell of her breasts above them.

He smiled, closing his eyes again.

"So how many girlfriends have you had?" she asked.

Oh, brother. "Don't know."

"Yes, you do. You just don't want to tell me."

"Not as many as you think."

"That's okay. A gentleman never tells, right? And that means I don't have to talk about my past, either."

He felt the tip of her finger running down his nose. It

gladdened his heart and gave him a tingle, and he forced open one eye again to gauge her.

But then the reality of what she'd said hit him: She didn't want to tell him about ex-boyfriends because that's what people did with each other only if they planned on having more than a one-night stand.

Donna must've read the look on his face, because her voice lowered to a more tender tone than he'd ever heard from her.

An afterglow voice.

"You've got that expression, Caleb, like you're expecting something from me."

He really didn't want to talk about this now, and he put his hand on her hip, hoping she would understand what he was saying without him having to say it. Hoping that they could save this conversation for later.

She leaned over, kissing his forehead, then whispered against his skin.

"I meant what I said about your giving me a great night."

But he was already going to sleep, thinking that there'd be time enough in the future to persuade her that there was much more to come for them.

After all, hadn't she already been persuaded this far?

HE LOOKED SO sweet when he slept, Donna thought as she watched the moonlight comb over Caleb. It was only now, when he couldn't see her that she felt free to think such things, to look at him as much as she wanted and to smile as she did it.

Her skin—and everything under it—was still singing. And, once again, that danger signal lit through her, telling her to watch it—that there was a possibility that she might get addicted to him.

That she might never want to leave the Flying B.

But she was sure that, once morning came, she'd be back to normal, wanting the same things she'd always wanted, never deviating, always focusing like a laser on success and security.

And Caleb wasn't secure. No one was.

Donna had always depended on herself and it'd worked out pretty well so far.

She lay down, closing her eyes and listening to the cadence of his breathing, realizing that she was matching it with her own. She tried not to acknowledge that lonely gaping spot already reopening in her, because she was merely emotional right now. Swept away by hormones.

It would pass. She'd never felt this much before, but she was sure it would go away.

Soon she was floating toward sleep, her mind cartwheeling with vivid memories of tonight—Lone Star Lucy's, kissing in Caleb's truck, the feel of his hands and mouth all over her.

Plus even more than that.

She was only faintly aware of the new images, though—strange ones that wove in and out of reality: An open blue sky above her, stretching forever in all directions. The scent of grass, the feel of a blanket beneath her back.

She had one hand tucked under her head, and she was wearing a loose flannel dress with long sleeves and cowboy boots. A country dress. Around her, birds sang and, in the near distance, she could hear...

Laughter?

Lots of it. And she was one of the people laughing,

but it was to herself, because she had her other hand cupped over her belly and—

Donna woke up with a start. A trickle of sweat was winding its way between her bare breasts, the sheet dipping to her waist as she pressed her hand to her stomach.

Had she been dreaming that her tummy was curved, as if she were...

Pregnant?

It all came back to her now—the nightmare, the course of events that had gotten her here, in a feather bed where so many others had had dreams that came true.

Most of all, though, she realized that Caleb Granger was lying stomach-down next to her, the emerging sunlight streaming through the window, making his skin golden as it stretched over the muscles of his back and arms.

For a stray, happy moment, her heart reached out to him, remembering last night. But it wasn't her heart that'd been touched by him, right? He'd done a good job with the rest of her.

He was never going to get to her heart.

As she tried to make sense of everything, panic set in. That dream...

A baby?

No way. Because how would one of those fit into her life?

How would the father of that baby fit?

Right, there was just no way. There was no future.

Attempting to be as silent as a ninja, she slipped out from under the sheets. One of her feet hit the floor, and she was just about to touch down with the other when she heard Caleb moving.

Dammit.

She took a peek over her shoulder, but he had merely stretched out an arm, as if he'd wanted to feel her body next to his.

Okay. She could get out of here before he woke up. She'd already heavily hinted for him not to expect anything beyond one night, so was there really any reason to say goodbye before she left?

Yup, because after she slipped out of bed all the way and was putting on her jeans, she saw him sleepily running his hand over the indentation where she'd been.

Then he opened his eyes.

Donna almost folded her arms over her naked breasts, then thought better of it, quickly jerking her bra off the floor and shrugging into it.

Caleb got one of those arrogant grins on his face and leaned his head on his palm. "Don't tell me—you turn back into a pumpkin at the crack of dawn."

"You need to start work soon, don't you?"

She snatched her blouse off the floor, her pulse going a mile a minute as she pulled the material over her, fumbling with the buttons until she made herself slow down.

"Funny," he said. "It's almost as if you were trying to sneak out of here before I woke up."

Damn, she couldn't take her eyes off his chest and the corrugated abs that disappeared beneath the sheet. She managed to deprive herself, though.

"I thought I'd let you sleep a little longer," she said. "No use bothering you."

"Donna."

All right—there wasn't an excuse in the world that would get her out of this.

She would button the rest of her blouse later. "Caleb.

This wasn't meant to be something that was going to last a lifetime. I thought you knew that."

"You've been clear about a lot of things, but somehow, a lot of your convictions disappeared last night. Why wouldn't you change your mind about other matters, too?"

"I was caught up in a moment."

"And you could have a lot more of those moments with me."

Good heavens. He just never gave up. Unfortunately, she'd given him good reason not to.

Her shoulders sank a bit. She didn't want to be cruel, but she didn't want to raise his hopes for the long run, either. She'd never promised anything but one night.

"No matter how good the sex was," she said, "this isn't going to happen again."

"Pardon me for saying so, but your body language speaks volumes more than what comes out of your mouth."

She frowned at him as he sat up in bed, not seeming to care that the sheet bunched just below his belly. It was a move that shouted his confidence about her giving in to more than she'd ever bargained for.

"Last night," she said, "was an aberration. I was emotional and, hence, willing."

He nodded, as if he was merely hearing her out until she came to her senses.

"I mean it," she said. "Good sex isn't enough to keep me on the Flying B forever."

"It was more than good sex, and you know it."

Her mouth hung open with a retort that never came. That's because she suspected he might be right.

But he couldn't be. She hadn't fallen for him as he'd

supposedly done for her already. Plus, the Flying B wasn't who she was or what she was meant to do.

She decided to try a different tack with him. "Even if I wanted to stay here, I've got way too much going on to have some kind of relationship with you."

"You mean distractions like Savannah, James, all that."

Caleb lay back and tucked a hand behind his head, just as she'd been doing in that dream. It was unnerving.

"The thing is, Donna," he said lethargically, "you seem to like it when I understand your troubles. Admit it—I'm probably the only man who's ever really gotten you."

He was making way too many good points.

"I'll admit you're a great listener," she said. "And I feel much better now, after last night."

"Sexual healing, huh?"

He had the grin of a man who recognized a desperate woman's justifications, and it was frightening her to death. Because what could you say to a guy like that?

How could you convince him that he was wrong?

She didn't even take the time to put on her socks and boots, because she had to get out of here before he worked his wiles on her again, making her think it was a good idea to give in to every heated whim that had started to attack her at the sight of his skin.

What had she been thinking, giving him an inch when she knew he'd take a mile?

"I've got to go," she said, her hand on the doorknob.

"See you soon."

She huffed out an exasperated sigh, but once she'd exited and gone down the steps, her libido began to take up where Caleb's arguments had left off.

You'll see him again, all right.
And you'll like it.

She began walking away, bare feet and all, before her confused heart could chime in, too.

Chapter Eight

Caleb realized something important after Donna left and he cleaned up the dream cabin, then drove back to his own place to get ready for the day's work.

Donna, who'd always moved so fast in the city, really *did* need a slow touch when it came to matters of the heart.

But if she and he had gone a little too quickly last night, he certainly didn't regret it. Nope, he firmly believed that what he needed to do now was persuade her that it wasn't just sex that she wanted.

He wouldn't even let it bother him that she had taken off like a shot as soon as dawn had hit the sky.

Actually, that did bug him a little. She'd been jumpy as hell, as if... Had she dreamed in that feather bed last night, just like in all the family legends?

Nah. He didn't want to jump to conclusions. After all, Caleb himself had slept like a rock, so he still didn't believe all those magical tales. He didn't need any supposedly charmed mattress to give him dreams when he already knew what they were: to make Donna Byrd see that he was the one for her.

And he stuck to that theory as he arrived at the stables, where Hugh asked Caleb to deviate in his regular schedule for the time being. The foreman left J.D. with the horses—a job that had belonged to Caleb for about fifteen years now—and had Caleb work only on the cattle side of the operation today, just as he'd done back when he'd been new on the ranch.

No horses. No setting his own schedule.

Hugh didn't explain his reasons while he performed maintenance on ditches and pipes with the hands until lunch, and Caleb didn't ask.

At the midday meal, he ran into J.D. in line for the pork chops, potatoes and grilled vegetables.

Caleb greeted Jenna's fiancé, then said, "If I didn't know better, I'd say Hugh's giving my old job to you. I was always the horse guy around here."

"I heard you grew up doing a little of everything on this ranch. You started out with the cattle, right?"

"Until Tex asked me to personally maintain his stables. I know we've added to them lately, but…"

J.D. smiled. "You don't think that Hugh's getting ready to retire soon and he's gearing up to groom you as the foreman?"

It'd occurred to Caleb, but he didn't want that to happen sooner rather than later. "Hugh's got a lot of good years left in him."

"Who knows?" As they sat at a bench, J.D. nudged back his hat, revealing some of his short, dark hair. "Change is in the air here, and not just with Hugh. There also seems to be a lot of pheromones floating around the Flying B lately and throwing a lot of curves to the personnel."

From the teasing glint in his brown eyes, he was referring to last night and how Caleb had driven Donna home from Lone Star Lucy's.

Caleb sat down, too. "I think I should be pretending that I have no idea what you're talking about."

"Is that what Donna wants? Secrecy?"

Caleb grinned. "Donna who?"

They laughed.

"You can pretend all you want, Caleb, but there isn't a person here who doesn't know better."

They dug into their food. J.D. wasn't kidding—everyone probably knew that he'd driven Donna home last night. What happened afterward was up to anyone's imagination, but Caleb was a realistic man.

And he wasn't into hiding how he felt about this woman.

Labor ended at dusk. Since he was used to hard work in the stables, anyway, Caleb had a quick dinner in his kitchen then got ready to go out. But this time he didn't put on a fancy suit or slick back his hair, and he wasn't preparing to make his way to a honky-tonk.

He was going to be his very own kind of subtle with Donna tonight.

By the time he drove up to the main house, night had fully embraced the sky. He parked under the window he knew belonged to Donna's room. The light was on, so he gambled that she was in there, working.

Taking out his phone, he sent her a text.

Take a look outside, Donna Byrd.

While he waited, he removed his hat and held it in his hands. His pulse was skittering, just like some kid was throwing stones over the surface of a pond.

Was he really ready for this—a relationship with Donna?

As he stood there, he realized that she really hadn't just been something different that had caught his eye and his fancy. He had sincerely lost his heart to her on day one.

It didn't take but a minute for the window to open and for Donna to lean out. She was wearing a simple yellow sleeveless blouse, her blond hair tied back.

Were her eyes shining as she looked down at him?

"Caleb…" she said with a warning tone.

Maybe not. "Sorry for resorting to a text message, but I chose that instead of tossing pebbles at your window. It's a more modern way of communicating, you see."

"I thought I told you—"

"That I should stop by tonight to give you a break from work?"

As he flashed his best smile, she rolled her eyes, but she didn't shut the window on him. Surely *that* was a good sign.

"Take a break, Donna," he said. "There's some country culture I want you to partake of before you go back to your hors d'oeuvres in the city."

She lowered her head as she leaned on the windowsill, and he knew that he was breaking her down, minute by minute, night by night.

"Donna," he said softly. "I'm not here with the hopes that tonight's going to end up like last night. Consider my intentions pure."

"Pure baloney," she muttered with her face still lowered, but it was loud enough for him to catch it.

He laughed. "Have you ever had a fried Oreo?"

She peered up. One thing Caleb knew was that women and sugar went well together. He was hoping the same would hold true in Donna's case, and it would serve as an excuse for her to come out with him tonight, even for a short time.

"They've got them at the high school," he said. "The PTA is putting on their usual summer festival to raise money. One of the booths has deep-fried everything, and the Glee Club moms make homemade vanilla ice cream to go with the Oreos. They say it's a Buckshot Hills tradition."

She finally stood, then sat on the windowsill. The sheer curtains flirted with her bare arm.

"Couldn't you just bring me back a few?" she asked.

"They're no good if they're not fresh. At least, that's my expert opinion."

"I don't think fresh is a big selling point with a so-called 'food' that's preserved to within an inch of its life." She slid a glance to him.

She needed just a tiny nudge more. "It's only a fifteen-minute drive," he said.

"It's not the travel time that's making me hesitate."

There it was. Caleb wasn't going to get anywhere with her until they faced the fallout from last night.

"Just come down here, Donna," he said, his tone determined. "Oreos or not, we've got a thing or two to straighten out."

She paused, shrugged, then shut the window.

Shoving his hat back onto his head, he meandered

over to the passenger side of his truck, hoping she'd just climb inside for a ride without giving him much grief.

Sure enough, she came out of the back of the main house, looking so gorgeous in that yellow shirt, a short jean skirt and sandals, that he couldn't take his gaze off her.

But he managed, just so she would see that he was serious about a talk.

She went for the door handle, then got into the truck before he could hold the door open for her. His blood surged at the citrus scent of her.

"Let's go get some of those heart attacks waiting to happen," she said, looking out of the windshield, as cool as ever.

But she had a flush on her cheeks, as if she was recalling last night.

In an optimistic mood, he went to his side of the truck, starting up the engine, well on his way to where he ultimately intended to go with Donna.

DONNA HAD NEVER known that she could be just as impulsive as Caleb was.

If anyone had asked her what she would be doing tonight, she wouldn't have answered, "Oh, I'll be on a joyride with the guy I burned rubber away from this morning. And I'll have no earthly idea why I said yes to taking off with him when I knew better."

She kept telling herself that they really did need to talk this out. If anything, it wasn't a bad idea to stay friendly with Caleb, because who needed drama between them when there was enough of that going around, anyway?

But clearly, the fact that he'd shown up at her window

tonight like a thickheaded Romeo told her that nothing she'd said this morning had sunk into that noggin of his.

So why had her heart given a bunny leap when she'd seen his cell phone text? And why had she rushed to the window like a misguided Juliet before she'd gotten ahold of herself and calmly opened it?

Because she'd been thinking about him the entire day, she thought. Because she *was* addicted, just as she'd feared she would be. Addicted to the memory of bodies rubbing against each other. Addicted to an overwhelming rush she'd never experienced before.

Yes, it was a good idea to talk to him and put a stop to his nonsense once and for all, and an Oreo run was as good a time to do it as any.

They were on the Flying B Road going away from the ranch when he asked, "What's got you holed up in that room tonight?"

"Wild guess." She protected her emotions, because it was family talk that had gotten her into the position—or, rather, the *positions*—she'd found herself in last night with him.

"You returned Savannah's call?" he asked.

"You've got it." In her peripheral vision, she saw how he casually rested his hand on the steering wheel and mildly slumped in his seat—sexy and careless. She blew out a breath. "Everyone in the family got together this morning and made the call together. Savannah wasn't available, so we left a message. I'll admit, though, that I was just waiting around in my room tonight, doing busywork and hoping she'd call back."

"What if she still does?"

"I've got my phone with me. But it could take days

for her to get back to us, just like before, when our P.I. contacted her."

Caleb smelled so good, damn him. Donna got as close to the door as she could, but it was still as if he were on her skin, sending shivers over it, caressing it.

"It could be," he said, "that Savannah's trying to talk James into the answer most of the Byrds want to hear."

"What—that he'll meet with us? I have to say that there's a cowardly side of me that wouldn't mind if he avoided us for the rest of his life. But the other side of me has gotten too curious about him and Savannah, and I don't know if I'll ever be able to let it go if they don't materialize."

And…here she was again, talking to Caleb as if he were her best friend in the world.

It was as if it'd happened so quickly that she hadn't seen it coming, but it'd started to feel as natural as…

As water flowing, carrying itself from one place to another.

Why not truly be Caleb's friend? Wouldn't that be good enough, now that they'd gotten the chemical attraction out of their systems?

"Uncle William and Dad are coming back to the Flying B this weekend," she said. "You probably heard that I planned a party to make the staff officially at home for the B and B, even though we aren't having our grand opening for about a month and a half. Dad said they'd be there for it."

"Is it time for you to hash things out with Sam?"

Hearing him say it out loud made her stomach bunch up. "I won't be able to avoid him, as much as I'd like to."

Caleb got quiet as they turned onto a road that led toward town, ghostly white fences whooshing by.

Finally, he said, "If you have the chance to make things right, Donna, take it. You never know when it'll be too late."

He was talking about *his* dad, and she felt petty. Because he was right.

"Are there ever times when you believe your father is thinking clearly?" she asked. "When his mind is strong enough so that you can have the same kind of conversation with him that I need to have with my dad?"

"There're moments. Few and far between. But I can't catch all of them because when I'm around him, he usually gets worse. And that's bad for Aunt Rosemary."

"God, Caleb."

"It is what it is." But she could tell that it still disturbed him.

They didn't say much else until they reached the high school, which consisted of a large brick building that stood across a parking lot from a matching structure— the combined grade and middle school.

After they parked, he went around to her side and opened her door, standing aside to let her pass. He was giving her room tonight, and she almost missed the more persistent Caleb.

Almost.

The festival was in a field at the back of the high school, where there was a simple sign that read, Fairgrounds. A small Ferris wheel lit up the night, and there was a Tilt-a-Whirl, Scrambler and Round Up completing the ride selections. Basically, there were booths featuring student-run midway games, snacks, homemade goodies like jams and quilts, plus campus clubs that were getting a head start on the school year.

The unmistakable aroma of deep-fried fat snaked to

her as they passed a bunch of kids out on a summer's night. It was too late for families, it seemed, and some of the booths were even beginning to close up shop.

"Is this the place to be in Buckshot Hills right now?" she asked.

"For the few nights that the PTA puts this festival on."

"What does everyone do when there's not a festival?"

"Mostly, the families hang out at their homes during the summer. Kids still play on their neighborhood streets and come in when the lights turn on. The teenagers cruise by the bowling alley and sometimes go to the movies and the local hamburger joint."

Donna would've screamed with boredom if she'd grown up here, but there was something very homey about the knowledge that there was still a place where kids would rather run around outside with their friends instead of staying inside to play video games.

They came to the deep-fried booth, where a whipthin woman in a Glee Club apron was managing orders while a few more took care of the cooking—blending the batter, dipping the cookies into it, then sinking the Oreos into pots of oil.

The apron woman gave two already-prepared plates to Donna and Caleb when it was their turn in line. The cookies were sprinkled with powdered sugar, and there was a mound of vanilla ice cream on the side.

They walked toward a picnic bench away from everyone else. In the background, rock and roll played from the Ferris wheel.

"Well," she said, sitting down. "Thanks for killing me slowly."

"Enjoy." He grinned, then dipped his Oreo in the

ice cream and took a big bite, leaving powdered sugar around his mouth.

Really? Did she *have* to sit here and die to wipe that sugar off him?

Or, worse yet, to kiss it off?

She concentrated on her own snack, using the napkin efficiently so she wouldn't give him any powdered-sugar ideas.

He gestured toward the Tilt-A-Whirl. "Fair warning—I just saw a couple of ranch hands who work with our cattle over there. We could leave if—"

"I'm not embarrassed to be seen with you." She put her cookie down. She was already full, even after a couple of bites. "I merely don't want anyone to get the wrong impression about us."

"People aren't blind, Donna."

"I know. I wasn't exactly discreet last night." She'd never had an undercover affair in her life, so why did she feel as if she couldn't flaunt Caleb here and now?

Was there something she wanted to keep intimate? Something that *mattered* with him?

She shook off the very idea. "In a couple months, you're going to laugh about your romantic ideas or this... whatever it is you have for me. It's all going to wear off by then and you'll have moved on."

"How do you know that?"

His gaze was that steady light blue that always swayed her.

"We discussed this," she said, her voice hoarse. She cleared her throat. "You've been working off of a fantasy. Last night was just an extension of it, because I was in that cabin for one thing, and I think you were in it for another."

He pushed away his empty plate, and what he said next jarred her more than anything he'd ever said before.

"I'm fully aware I created a fantasy at first, but now it's the real thing, Donna. And I'm not going to give up on something I know is so right."

She knew her eyes had never been so wide, her gaze never so confused, and she didn't want him to see that in her.

So she cooled, just as she always did. "I'm only trying to save you the trouble."

And she meant it, as she got up from the bench and walked back to the truck.

She'd failed at her magazine business and failed in her finances. He didn't need to be included in that list.

EVEN THE NEXT DAY, Caleb's confession rang through Donna.

And that was why she finally called her first ever silly girl talk meeting off the ranch at the Longbranch Diner.

She, Tammy and Jenna were in a corner booth, under one of the faux antique rifles that decorated the log-jammed, rustic interior.

"*What* did he say to you?" Jenna asked from across the booth, sitting next to Tammy.

Both women were as wide-eyed as Donna had been after his confession.

"He said what he's feeling is 'the real thing.'" Donna shook her head. "Luckily, he didn't push the subject on the ride home or when he dropped me off, but I know he's still got this mistaken impression about…well, whatever he thinks he's feeling for me."

Tammy and Jenna traded glances. Then her sister said, "It's love, you doofus!"

Donna sank down a bit in her seat. "That's not what he meant." He couldn't have.

Tammy disagreed. "And here I thought *I* was the innocent one in this group. You act like you've never had a man tell you he loves you, Donna."

This was the very definition of mortifying. But Donna was beyond lying to them. She genuinely needed some advice.

"I...haven't had anyone say that to me before."

Both women gaped.

"Oh, don't give me those looks like, 'Isn't that so sad? Poor Donna.' Because I was never looking for love. I'm still not."

Jenna stirred the straw in her cherry cola as if she was attempting to bring the conversation down a notch. "Love sure came to you, though."

Donna stared at her untouched salad. Time to get real.

"So here I am," she said softly. "Someone who has no idea what to do with deep feelings. And there he is—a well-known good-time guy who's the same way."

"Wait." Tammy had just piled lettuce onto her Buffalo Bill burger. "How do you know that Caleb has no idea what love is like?"

Donna glanced around the near-empty diner. It was off-hours, so only a few customers ate in their booths on the other side of the room. Caleb's name had seemed to echo, though.

But maybe she was just hearing his name all around her, bouncing off every wall...including the ones around her heart.

Jenna spoke. "You're making excuses, saying he doesn't know what love is when you don't know if that's true or not."

Tammy added, "He loves his family enough to take care of them. And Caleb loved Tex."

"Not the same kind of love," Donna said, finally spearing some of her salad.

Jenna rolled her eyes. "Excuses, excuses."

"That may be so, but does that mean there's any kind of future for me with Caleb Granger?"

She shoved a bite of salad into her mouth, not tasting any of it, because there was one word she'd said that stood out from the others.

The future. *Her in a field, on a blanket, her hand on her rounding belly...*

She had a hard time swallowing, and one of those furious blushes consumed her, but this one was exponentially worse than any she'd dealt with before as she remembered the mattress dream.

Had fate already dictated her future? Because that had definitely been the case with both Tammy and Jenna.

But there was absolutely no way she'd ever be pregnant. They'd used a condom, and Donna was not going to sleep with Caleb again.

Donna caught Jenna and Tammy looking at each other once more.

Then Jenna said, "Did you just freak out a little on us, sis? You mentioned one little word—*future*—and you started blushing and nearly choking on your food as if you've *seen* your future. Is that because you two spent the night on the feather bed?"

Tammy set down her burger.

Wonderful. Now she had this to deal with, too. "Who told you two about me and Caleb and the dream cabin?"

Jenna spoke up. "First of all, you two left Lone Star Lucy's together, then J.D. went into work earlier than

usual and he saw Caleb's truck at the dream cabin. I just
want to hear it from you."

"Okay. We did make a stop there."

Tammy asked, "And what exactly happened?"

Jenna poked her with an elbow. "Nosy pants. Only
sisters should dig that far into someone's business." She
turned to Donna. "And what exactly happened?"

Really. These two should've taken their act on the
road. "You guys have fiancés. Surely I don't need to go
into the details."

Donna thought that the women might've done a se-
cretive low-five beneath the table.

"Why're you two so ecstatic about it?" Donna asked.
The memory of that mattress dream was pulling at her,
now that they were talking about it. She'd tried to dis-
miss it yesterday, but here it was again.

"Because you can be happy," Jenna said. "Remember
that list I made naming off the qualities that my perfect
man should have?"

"Who can forget?"

"Well," Jenna said, looking rather satisfied, "it turns
out that all my plans on that list were for nothing. I didn't
see J.D. coming, but here we are."

She flashed her diamond engagement ring, and
Donna couldn't help smiling.

Still, she wasn't going down easy. "You always were
more adaptable than I was."

"Not by much."

Tammy broke in. "Can we please get back to what
happened in that cabin? And I'm not talking about the
nitty-gritty. You slept on that mattress, so did you have
any dreams like we did?"

"I don't remember."

Jenna wadded up her napkin and threw it at Donna.
It hit her in the forehead.

"Hey," Donna said. "I have no dreams to report."

As Jenna and Tammy frowned in disappointment,
Donna told herself not to feel bad about lying to them.
Why even relate something that was never ever going
to come true, anyway?

Donna Byrd with a baby.

Inconceivable. Even if she sometimes felt that empty
space inside of her pulsing.

They finished up their meal, then drove back to the
ranch. Jenna and Tammy sang to the radio like teeny-
boppers, making Donna smile. Someday, when she was
back in the city, she would invite these two to stay with
her, and they'd have a real girls' night out on the town.

Tammy pulled her pickup in front of the main house,
where there were two familiar cars parked in front of
the porch.

One was a classic Trans Am, the other a white, stylish Cadillac.

It seemed as if the air went still. Jenna even rested
her hand on Donna's shoulder in solidarity.

"Do you think," she said, "Uncle William and Dad
are even in the same room right now?"

"Why wouldn't they be?" Donna asked. "They've
been working on getting along."

"But the news about James," Tammy said. "It made
things kind of tense again, set them back a little."

Donna barely heard the girls, because Caleb's voice
was dominating her head. *If you have the chance to make
things right, Donna, take it. You never know when it'll
be too late...*

As usual, he was right, because she couldn't stand

the notion of avoiding her dad, or even sitting across the dinner table from him with neither one of them recognizing the elephant in the room.

All the issues between them.

Donna was the first out of Tammy's pickup, and she went straight for the door.

She found Uncle William, Aidan and Nathan sitting in the living room drinking bourbon, relaxing and chatting.

After saying hi, then giving her gray-haired uncle a welcoming hug, she asked, "Do you know where my dad is?"

William took a drink of his liquor, not revealing a thing about the status between the twin brothers. But Nathan gestured toward the exit with his cut crystal glass.

"Try the kitchen. He went straight for it, saying he wanted to fill his stomach before he joined us for a drink."

Or maybe, Donna thought, Dad still wasn't on perfect terms with his brother, thanks to the James discovery.

She passed Jenna and Tammy in the entryway and gently took her sister's arm, pulling her down the hallway.

"What's going on?" Jenna asked.

"You'll probably want to see Dad before I say my piece."

When Jenna began to utter something, Donna interrupted. "I'm getting this over with once and for all, Jenna. I can't stand another second of it."

At the kitchen door, she didn't hesitate—she pushed it open to find their father at the nook table, huddled over a plate with a ham sandwich that'd barely been eaten.

His eyes, which had always been such a bright blue,

were faded to the color of jeans that'd been carelessly left in the sun, but he was as handsome and imposing as ever with that graying brown hair and exercise-honed physique.

Jenna went over to say her hellos, then with a good-luck glance at Donna, who was lingering by the window, she sent one more smile over to Dad and left the room.

The air just hung there, heavy and loaded, until Dad gestured to the seat across from him.

"I expect you're here to give me an earful like Jenna once did."

She was trying so hard not to give in to all the anger, and she straightened her spine, going to the chair and sitting.

*If you have the chance to make things right...*said Caleb's voice again.

Donna pushed that anger aside, finally facing the father who'd so bitterly disappointed her.

Chapter Nine

Sam spoke first as he grabbed the napkin from his lap and put it on the table. "I readied myself for this. I've been getting it from all sides lately."

Donna's temper flared. She didn't want to hear excuses.

But then she thought of Caleb again.

"I'm not here to point out blame," she said. "And I'm not going to ask you to rehash everything you told Jenna about what happened with Savannah all those years ago. She's told me everything."

"I figured she would." A slight smile got to him, even though his gaze was still faded. "You two have become closer."

"Yes. That's one positive angle in of all this." And there'd been Tex. There was another, too, but she wasn't going to tell him about Caleb. He hadn't earned it.

Then again, why would she announce anything about Caleb to her father when there was nothing major there?

He started up again. "I should have paid more attention to you and Jenna when you were growing up. It's only now, after I've spent time with William again, that I see what we all lost over the years with family. Brothers and sisters should never have a distance between them. Tex came to that realization, too."

"Jenna and I weren't estranged, like you and Uncle William. We were just…"

"Seemingly indifferent."

"No, that was me. Jenna knew how to express emotions as well as she could in our house."

Sam shook his head. "That was definitely my fault. I had my head in my business so far that I didn't see how your mom's sickness affected you both. I didn't see how our divorce made you, especially, pull into a shelter that you rarely came out of, except to design your little girl magazines and decorate those shoe boxes like they were tiny rooms in a house."

"Dioramas." Her chest tightened. "That's what they were called."

When he smiled, it was almost as if Donna was back in the days when his approval meant everything to her. That hurt more than anything.

"Yes," he said. "You'd buy scrap material from the store and use it for wallpaper and bedspreads. And you used to make paper people out of tissue. They lived in those rooms."

"I remember." She'd always been goal-oriented, even when she was in grade school.

"And look at you now—still decorating those rooms,

but on a much larger scale. Still putting together magazines, too."

She used to hope for moments like this, but they had come so much harder from him. She would carry those dioramas and magazines into his home office after her parents had divorced and she and Jenna would visit him on the weekends. He would reluctantly pull himself away from whatever report he was going over, then look at her efforts, making suggestions here and there that she would implement immediately.

Approval had been her idea of love. Of course, Mom had given affection more freely—she'd fawned over each of her daughter's creations. Donna had valued that, too, although she'd been in such a shell from the divorce that she hadn't known how to handle the hugs Mom tried to give her, the kisses.

And when Mom had gone, Donna had regretted the way she'd treated her so much that she'd fallen even further into that shell.

Donna risked a glance at her father. He was watching her with such melancholy that she almost forgot all her frustration with him then and there.

"You really blew it, didn't you?" she asked softly. "And I'm not just talking about with Savannah, William and Grandpa."

"You're talking about your mom." There were faint red circles under his eyes that Donna had just noticed. "As I told Jenna, when I met your mom, it was on the tail of my relationship with Savannah. I was a mess, but your mom was drawn to a brokenhearted bad boy. She was never able to change me from that to a good husband, though."

"She thought she could? That's why she married you so quickly after your breakup with Savannah?"

"Yes. But doesn't every woman in love think that they're the only one who can fix what's broken in a man?"

Donna almost told him no—she was a perfect example of the opposite. But there were definitely men out there who thought they knew how to mend a woman they'd fallen for.

Caleb, for one.

Some of the heaviness rolled off her, just at the thought of him.

She saw her dad measuring her with his gaze, but she didn't want him to see that what he'd said had struck her in a meaningful way.

"So here we are," she said, sitting back in her chair.

He nodded. "Here we are."

Was this enough to repair their relationship? She didn't think so. There were still so many questions to be asked and solved.

"What're you going to do if Savannah ever calls back and says she and James are paying us a visit?" she asked.

Sam ran a hand through his hair. "I know that after Tammy found the grocery receipt with the pregnancy test on it in Savannah's cabin, I told your sister I hoped that Savannah didn't get pregnant. I wouldn't be able to look at the child if he was William's—a child would be a reminder of how Savannah and my brother had been together and how he'd felt about her."

"And you told Jenna that you were such a crummy parent to us that you didn't want to be one a third time to a possible child." Donna's tone darkened. "You know that you don't have a choice now, and I swear to God, if you shirk this duty as James' uncle or his father, I'm never going to forgive you."

It was as if she'd reached inside of him to pull his heart out.

The daughter he loved, leaving him just as he and William had left Tex.

She hadn't realized the parallel until now, and she wanted to take it back.

But he saved her from doing that. "I've had time to think," he said. "William gave me a lot of perspective on this last trip. And when you kids called us with the definite news about James…"

Please don't disappoint me, she thought. *I don't know what I'll do if you put this final nail in me.*

He sighed. "I can't get James off my mind. But no matter how much I think about him, it's impossible to predict how I'd feel about knowing who he belongs to, one way or another."

"It sounds to me like James is the type of person who feels as if he doesn't belong to any kind of father. I suspect he's the one holding up Savannah's phone call." Donna frowned. "But you're going to welcome him into the family, no matter what. Just tell me that much, Dad."

Again, he got that decimated look that said he'd never wanted to hurt Donna or Jenna. That he was full of remorse, and he just wasn't sure how to go about reaching a reckoning with himself.

At that moment, Donna realized that her father needed her, just as much as Caleb's needed him. Maybe Mr. Granger wasn't capable of admitting it, but Sam was doing so as he reached across the table to her.

She didn't have it in her to turn him away, ice queen or not.

Touching her fingers to the top of his hand, she said, "How will it feel to see Savannah again?"

A haunted cloud passed over his gaze before he averted it toward the window, and Donna's heart softened even more.

Did he still love Savannah?

She grasped his hand all the way, and as he turned his gaze to her, she saw that it'd gotten a little brighter at her willingness to make things right between them.

THE WEEKEND ARRIVED, bringing with it a partial day off for Caleb.

It'd been a long couple of days, because, although Donna and he had texted a few times about trivial things—how the visit with her dad was going, how her plans for the staff party today were shaping up—he hadn't seen her around.

He'd vowed to back off, because at this point, if this relationship was meant to be, she would come to him.

Right?

But she'd better do it soon, he thought, as he drove his truck toward Dad and Aunt Rosemary's house, because the first thing this morning, Hugh had pulled him aside and told him that he was going on an extended trip than included an out-of-state agricultural business conference and then several visits to state-of-the-art ranches.

And Caleb would be leaving tomorrow morning.

"I got you registered at the last minute, and I just received confirmation," Hugh had said. "Sorry for the late notice."

"Isn't this something you'd rather go to?" Caleb had asked, thinking of how long this would keep him away from Donna.

"Don't worry—your girl will still be here when you get back. And absence might make her heart grow fonder. Besides, Tex always meant for you to take my place, and I'd like you to be up on all the latest business when that happens."

A sense of pride had bolstered Caleb, but then again, what *about* Donna? He would be gone for a few weeks altogether with both the conference and the ranch trips and he wondered what she'd say when he told her about that.

Would she be relieved that she'd finally gotten rid of him?

He was still mulling it over late that afternoon when he arrived at Dad and Aunt Rosemary's, where they were already waiting for him to pick them up for the Flying B's party.

Or, at least, Rosemary was waiting.

She was outside the open garage, where his father's old green Dodge Aspen was stored. Her thin arms were crossed over her chest, her long polka-dot skirt blowing in the slight wind.

Caleb could already see it was another not-so-good day.

He parked his truck to the side of the driveway, got out, then greeted Rosemary.

She canted her head toward the car in the garage, and he could make out in the shadows that Dad was sitting in the driver's seat.

"He's all ready to go," she said.

"Does he think he's driving?"

"That's what he's demanding."

She didn't have to add that she'd had no idea what

she'd been in for when she'd volunteered to look after Dad. But what caretaker did know?

It's not his fault, Caleb kept thinking. *He's only still trying his best to feel as if he's in control.*

A ball of wariness shaped itself into Caleb's gut. What would it be like to lose yourself like this?

All he knew was that life was too short, and maybe that's why he'd gone after Donna full force after he'd decided so strongly that she was the one for him. Maybe Dad and Tex had shown him that you didn't have all the time in the world.

Caleb girded himself and sauntered over to the driver's side of the car.

"Hi, Dad."

When he glanced at Caleb, it was obvious that he'd shined himself up for the party. His gray hair was combed back, nice and neat, and he was wearing a spiffy Western shirt and black jeans and boots, no stains in sight.

The excited gleam in his eyes surprised Caleb. He'd expected meanness, not this.

"I'm ready," Dad said. "Got the keys with you?"

Caleb glanced at Rosemary, who'd come to his side. She wore a smile now, as if she was just as happy to see Dad in this sudden good mood as Caleb was.

Had Caleb put that smile on his face?

His heart expanded, then went back to its normal size when he started thinking about how to sustain Dad's levity.

"Here's the thing, Dad," Caleb said. "The Aspen needs some repairs. How about we take my truck today?"

"I can repair this baby. What needs to be done?" Dad

frowned, as if racking his brain for memories of what might've been ailing his treasured car.

Caleb felt terrible for lying to him, but as it was, Rosemary had to hide the keys so Dad wouldn't be a menace on the road.

"I'll tell you what needs to be done after we get back," Caleb said, opening the door, treading lightly. "See, there's a barbecue where we're expected. Ribs galore."

"Oh." That got Dad out of the car. "Kathy doesn't like to be late to functions. Better get a move on."

Kathy had been Caleb's mom, and the reminder that Dad wasn't quite in the present again was just another smackdown.

One good moment, one step back. But Caleb wouldn't have traded today's good moment for anything.

After they were all in Caleb's truck, Dad in the middle and Rosemary by the door, the ride to the Flying B was pleasant enough. Dad talked about the "functions" he and Mom had gone to back in the day, and Caleb only prayed that he wouldn't ask just where Kathy was right now.

Thank God he didn't. And after they arrived in front of the main house of the ranch, with a banner saying, "Welcome to the Flying B and B!" stretched over the porch, Dad wandered straight over to the line of picnic benches that moaned under a buffet of Texas food. Staff members—including the ranch hands who'd taken a meal break from running the cattle operation to the housemaids to the cowboys and cowgirls who'd be facilitating the outdoor activities for the B and B—mingled. The sweet-smoky scent of barbecue tickled the air, along with the sound check that a local band was doing on a stage that had been set up.

Aunt Rosemary touched Caleb's arm, smiling at him, then she followed Dad to the refreshments.

It was nice to see her having a good day, too.

As he was watching after them, he felt someone come to his side. The goose bumps up and down his arm told him who it was.

"Donna," he said.

Just one look at her made it an even better day.

She was wearing a dark pink sundress that looked like it'd been culled out of a '50s catalog. But the old-fashioned style suited her, hugging her curves, making her upswept hairdo seem chic and down-home at the same time.

His blood pumped, as if filling him with all that color she brought with her, just by being in the same place he was.

"Is that your father and aunt?" she asked.

"It is."

"I'm glad he was well enough to be here."

"I'll introduce you as soon as he's done loading up on the goodies."

He looked into those blue-sky eyes of hers. "You've been busier than usual this week."

"I was getting this party in shape. And if you're asking me for an update on Savannah and James, I don't have one. I've been debating whether to call her again or just take this as a sign that she's not ever going to contact us and neither is James." She threw her hands up in the air. "What can I do but enjoy today, right? What do you guys say in Texas? Yippee ki-yay?"

"We don't really say that."

"But it sounds so fun."

Donna was actually...chipper. "Have you had one of those Ruby cocktails or something?"

She laughed, and as it faded, he could tell she had something else on her mind.

"I wanted to thank you for something, Caleb."

He stopped joking around.

She said, "I mentioned in a text that I had a talk with my dad. I didn't tell you that we're on firmer ground now. Everything's not perfect, but we're communicating. It's a start."

"I'm glad to hear that."

"It's a credit to you that it happened. I kept hearing your words of wisdom, and they calmed me down when I needed it the most."

Had she just admitted that he...mattered to her? Even in some small way?

Across the yard, he saw Dad and Aunt Rosemary taking a seat in padded lounge chairs. His dad's plate was piled with a mound of meat with a cupcake on top while Rosemary's looked like a patch of garden.

"Come on," Caleb said. "I want you to meet my family."

Donna's smile was tentative, as if she wondered what exactly that meant, meeting the family. To him, it meant he was introducing them to his future. But Donna didn't have to know that right now.

He brought her over, then ushered her into an available chair next to Dad while still standing himself.

"This is Donna," he said. "She put this shindig together and is one of the Byrds who's running the B and B."

While Rosemary flashed a brilliant smile at Donna, then a more subtle, curious one at Caleb, Dad finished chewing on some ribs, still as happy as could be.

"Hi, Donna."

It didn't matter that Dad had a searching look in his eyes that told Caleb he had no idea who the Byrds were and probably never would, even if Donna was introduced fifty times over. All that mattered was that Donna and he began chatting about food, laughing about the Red Velvet cupcake that he'd balanced on top of his ribs.

All the while, Rosemary kept giving Caleb the eye, and he shrugged.

Tell you later.

When it became hot enough for the misters to spray the crowd in front of the music stage, where the band was ready to strike it up, Donna had to excuse herself.

"Here's where the logistics come in," she said as Caleb escorted her away from his family. "Gotta keep this shindig running smoothly."

"See you in a while," he said. "And I mean that in a few ways."

"Like…how?"

He would just mention the business conference. If she cared, she cared. If she didn't…

He put it out there. "In the morning, I'm off to an ag business conference for about a week, then an extended tour of some high-tech ranches across the state, just to keep up with the times. I'll be gone for a few weeks."

She blinked. "A few weeks."

Bull's-eye. She didn't even have time to cover up the dismay he'd seen in her gaze and heard in her voice.

"It's not forever, Donna."

"No, but…" This time, she did recover. "I'm sure the staff will miss you."

"I'm sure they will."

He tried not to smile as she walked away, toward the stage.

He spent the rest of the afternoon making sure Rosemary and Dad were comfortable, but he knew the good times wouldn't last forever. It was clear Dad was tired a couple hours in, and Caleb asked Rosemary if they were set to go back home.

"Definitely," she said. "I think he'll even fall asleep in the truck."

He certainly did, snoring, overriding the radio that Caleb had turned on before giving up and snapping it off, much to Rosemary's amusement.

When they got to their place, Caleb took care of getting Dad to bed.

That was when they hit the big glitch in their day.

As Caleb was easing Dad down onto his mattress, the old man awoke with a start, then reared away from Caleb and onto the bed, obviously not recognizing him.

"It's all right," Caleb said, holding up his hands. "It's Caleb. Your son."

Before Dad fell back asleep, he gave Caleb a nasty look, no doubt because he was thinking those terrible thoughts about him.

But he did float off right away, and Caleb met Aunt Rosemary in the kitchen, where she offered him some lemonade.

"No, thanks." He wasn't going to mention what'd just happened with Dad. It was par for the course. "I'll be getting back to the ranch."

"Back to Donna," Rosemary said, a glint in her eyes.

Caleb kissed her on the cheek and prepared to bail. "That's a conversation for another time."

"I look forward to it, because from the way you were

looking at her, I get the feeling she's more than one of your…"

"Distractions?"

"That's a fine way of putting it. And she looked at you the same way you did her."

The ground seemed to shake under his feet. He didn't even have the grace to play it cool. "She did?"

"Oh." Aunt Rosemary came to pat him on the face. "It's finally happened, hasn't it?"

Caleb smiled as she hugged him.

Falling head over heels had finally happened to him, but how long would it take for it to happen to Donna?

AS DUSK ENVELOPED the ranch and the music from the country band played on, Donna sat away from most of the crowd, on the main house's porch, surveying the party from a chair.

Everyone seemed to be having the time of their lives, swinging to a song by a singer she'd recently come to know as Toby Keith. Tammy and Mike were out there, and so were Jenna and J.D. Dad and Uncle William were even sharing a beer by the barn. They were obviously having another of their heart-to-hearts.

It stank not having someone she could dance with or talk to. She already missed not having Caleb around.

But, just as if she'd conjured him out of thin air, he ambled from around the corner of the house, probably from where he'd parked his truck.

She couldn't stop the smile that overwhelmed her, but she sure did calm it down as she stood from the chair. "Your dad and aunt are back home, safe and sound?"

"Dad's in a food coma, but he left happy, that's for sure."

"It was good to meet him and Rosemary today."

"They thought the same with you."

The Toby Keith song ended, easing into something like a Texas waltz.

She licked her lips, her pulse kicking her. Why did she all of a sudden feel shy around Caleb? Because she'd never been introduced to a man's family as she'd been introduced to his? Because, from the time she'd met him until now, something had definitely changed and she couldn't deny it any longer?

Today, she'd seen a quality in him that she'd never gotten to witness before—the way he looked at his dad, protective and caring and concerned. The way he treated his aunt Rosemary as if she were a lady and he appreciated every moment she took in taking care of the family.

Caleb was the real deal, she thought. And he was standing right here next to her, reaching out a hand.

"At Lone Star Lucy's," he said, "you never did get on the dance floor."

Was he asking her to do so now? In front of everyone?

But why was that such a big thing when the whole ranch was gossiping about them, anyway? And how was a dance somehow more intimate than what they'd done on that feather bed?

A flash of her mattress dream rattled her again, but she ignored it, just as she did his outstretched hand.

"This isn't my kind of music," she said. Lame.

"It's easy to dance to." Without waiting, he took her hand in his, resting the other one on her hip. "You just sway, Donna. That's all."

In spite of herself, she'd come to place her fingers on his arm. She felt skin and muscle underneath his shirt. Felt *him*.

Her heartbeat took off like a fearful creature, seeking cover.

"I've never been any good at this," she said.

"Dancing?" His voice was low, like a caress skimming her.

"No. I've never been good at relating."

"You mean relationships."

"Both."

He laughed. "You've already warned me."

She was going to lay it all out in a last-ditch attempt to get him to understand that she wasn't cut out for him, for this, no matter what she was starting to feel.

"First," she said, "there was my parents' divorce. That's never a good thing for a kid to go through. Then, my mom's death. I learned early that I was the only one who'd always be there for myself."

Caleb pulled her a little closer as they swayed, and she absently adjusted her hand higher up his arm.

"I always had this vague feeling that Dad never talked about Grandpa because something had gone terribly wrong," she said. "Dad had this black-sheep vibe, and it's something I sort of adopted. That's why I've never had any serious relationships, Caleb."

"There's a time for everything," he said.

"How can you be so cavalier about what I just told you? Haven't I given you enough to frighten you off?"

He smiled down at her. "You've given me enough to make life interesting."

"I don't think you need a more interesting life."

"Not in the way you're talking about." He squeezed her tighter. "I want to live, Donna. Tex wanted that for me, too, and every time I see my dad, I get that much more determined to start the rest of my life as soon as I can."

"You should do it with a nice girl."

"You are a nice one. You just don't know it yet."

He'd told her that they never really knew who their parents were—but did that go for them, too? Because she really did feel different around Caleb.

She was trying so hard to love the person her dad had become these days, so why was it impossible that Caleb could love the woman *he'd* come to know in her, even if she didn't think of herself that way?

Without analyzing a second more, she threw caution to the wind, stood on her tiptoes and pressed her lips to Caleb's.

They stopped dancing, but the waltz in her head kept on playing, swirling, sweeping down through her. She pulled him close, not wanting him to go to that conference and ranch tour that would take him away for a few weeks.

Not wanting him to go anywhere.

But then, as she pulled away and looked into his gaze, she saw the hope she'd just planted in him, and it killed her.

She'd been impulsive, and even though she shouldn't be giving anyone hope, she wanted some of it for herself so badly.

But he seemed to read on her face that she was caught between emotions that she couldn't quite grasp, and he let her go.

He tipped his hat to her, just like the gentlemen he'd never seemed to be, but was.

"It'll only be a few weeks, Donna," he said. "I'll be back before you know it, so no shenanigans, you hear?"

Then he walked off the porch, leaving her wanting even more from him.

And she suspected that's what he'd been hoping for all along.

Chapter Ten

Three weeks seemed like forever to Donna. They felt more like three aeons, even though she'd been tied up with visits from travel agents and magazine writers who would hopefully be recommending the Flying B and B after it opened in a little over a few weeks.

They already had the first month booked, thanks to her college friend Theo's published magazine article, but it was still a stressful time.

At first, that was why Donna thought she missed her period. Because of the stress.

And it wasn't until she started to think about the pregnancy dream she'd had in the cabin again that she wondered, even doubtfully, if there might be something else going on.

So she turned to the only person she felt comfortable in telling her worries to these days, asking Jenna to meet her in her room.

When her sister knocked on the door, Donna opened it right away and ushered her inside. Jenna's blond hair was in a braid down her back, and in her dark blue Western shirt and jeans, she looked as if she had always belonged here, on a ranch. But Donna, herself, must've appeared as nervous as a stray cat who'd blundered into a dog pound, because Jenna immediately asked, "My, God, what's wrong? Did Savannah call?"

"No."

Savannah had actually left one message for them, saying that she was still talking things out with James and she would be in touch again either way. Donna had almost called the woman back, but she didn't want to harass her.

Give them time, she kept thinking. Even so, the Byrds were beginning to accept that they might have run into a dead end.

And maybe it was for the best if Savannah and James wanted nothing to do with them.

"What's wrong then?" Jenna asked.

Donna went to her dresser, pulling out a bag with the name of the town's drugstore spelled out over the white paper.

Then she took out what was inside the bag.

When Jenna saw the boxed pregnancy test, she was speechless.

"I never miss my period," Donna said. "Not until lately."

Her fearful tone apparently put Jenna into action, and she came over to touch Donna's arm.

"You're scared, aren't you."

"A little bit." But there was more to it than that. A

wad of nerves actually was spinning in the center of her, but there was excitement, too.

Donna hadn't expected that.

A baby, she kept thinking. *And me, as a mother.*

But even with her doubts, something fluttery in her kept awakening.

Could she be a mom?

Donna knit her brows. The empty place inside of her that she'd felt before hadn't existed for the past couple of days. Warmth had taken its place, like a soft bundle nestling at the core of her.

Unexpected, all right. Yet it felt like the most natural thing in the world right now.

"I never knew I wanted a baby," she said to Jenna.

Her sister hugged her until reality invaded Donna again.

"I don't know if the timing is where I would've wanted it to be," she said. "My investments are shrinking by the day, and that's not an optimal situation for raising a child. And then there's the matter of who the father is…"

"Caleb."

Just hearing his name sent a pang through her. She'd missed his laugh, his smile, his easy way of making her feel as if she could slow down for once and see a different part of herself with him.

But, as Donna glanced at the test in her hand, more doubt shaded her. Just because she and Caleb might be having a child, that didn't make everything okay. It didn't make all their issues magically dissolve.

"I've had good times with him," Donna said. "But this is a curveball. We used a condom, Jen. So how did this happen?"

"It must've leaked."

"I couldn't tell."

Jenna held Donna's hand. "Don't think I'm selfish, but I would love to be an aunt. And you'd be a great mother, even if you might not think so."

"Would I?"

Jenna pulled back and peered into Donna's eyes. "You think you're such a tough cookie, but you've got a core of butter."

"I do not." Donna laughed a bit, but she was on the edge of tears, too.

She was about to get news that might change her life...and Caleb's.

A baby, she kept thinking, but this time, she couldn't stop a genuine smile. True, it wavered, but there it was. And, for the first time ever in her rush-around life, she took the time to imagine what it could feel like to hold someone who thought she was the entire world, someone she would give her life for.

Powdery smells, a nursery, a quiet night in a rocker, singing lullabies to her son or daughter...

Yes, Donna thought. This was what she had been missing. Someone to share every day with.

Then a jarring thought intruded. *But I got pregnant during a one-night stand. Does that mean I'll have to live the rest of my life with Caleb, even if I* know *a relationship won't work in the long run?*

It was a terrible thought. But it was also a practical one. Yet what was she going to do—run away and never tell Caleb about their child?

The warmth around her heart seemed to burn her, as if trying to tell her something she just wasn't understanding.

Jenna obviously sensed Donna's conflict. "You're still scared."

Her sister was the only one who would ever fully get what Donna was about to say.

"You remember how it felt when Mom and Dad divorced?"

"Like the world was ending."

"Jenna, what if I'm about to set this child up for the same devastation we had to go through?"

Jenna frowned. "Are you already planning to get a divorce from Caleb or something?"

What *was* she saying?

She gripped the pregnancy test in one hand. "I'm only being careful. Trying to think things through, here. You, more than anyone, know how Dad rushed into marriage with Mom. This thing I have with Caleb… It's not even as serious as Dad and Mom supposedly got with one another before they said 'I do.'"

Donna realized she was almost crushing the box. Still, more irrational thoughts swamped her.

If I am pregnant, should I tell Caleb? Or should I think of the child so he or she can be saved from what's sure to be a dysfunctional relationship for his or her parents?

A relationship that would mimic the thwarted marriage that had thrown Donna and Jenna into a tailspin for years…

Then another unreasonable notion barged into Donna's head. *Wasn't that what Savannah did with James? She ran away and kept the baby a secret?*

The comparison definitely didn't cheer Donna up. The only thing that was going to either improve the situation or not was taking that test.

She pointed toward the bathroom. "If I go in there, will you stick around until I come out?"

"You bet I will."

Jenna squeezed her hand, and Donna headed for privacy, closing the door.

As she removed the stick from the packaging, it seemed as if time had warped into a speed that was both slow *and* fast, clouding her head. Somehow she managed to take that test.

Then all she could do was wait, and she did so by opening the bathroom door and sitting on the bed with Jenna. The digital alarm clock on the dresser flashed the seconds.

"Thank you for being here, Jen," she said. In the past, it would've been a hard thing for Donna to say. Not anymore.

Jenna smiled, her eyes shiny as she put her arm around Donna. "Of course I'm here. And whatever the outcome, I won't tell anyone."

"Thanks for that, too."

The few minutes that were required for the test had passed, but Donna wasn't moving.

"Are you ready to look?" Jenna asked.

Was she ready?

The image of a blue-eyed, dimpled child nuzzled up to Donna again, the warmth in her chest nearly overtaking her now.

She really did want to be ready, more than she had ever thought possible.

But would Caleb turn tail and flee if her test was positive? Maybe the impulsive part of him would consume him, just like the ladies' man he'd been rumored to be, and she could go her own way…with their child.

Donna went into the bathroom, where she'd set the stick in the sink. Jenna was right behind her.

Before Donna peered at it, she did something she hadn't done in a long, long time.

If it's a yes, God, please have me be the best mom ever.

She took a huge breath as she checked the marker.

When she saw the smiley face on it, she turned around, heading right into Jenna's waiting arms. As she cried into her sister's hair, she barely got out the words.

"It's a yes," she said.

Jenna started crying, too, yet Donna realized that, like her own sobbing, these were tears of surprising happiness.

I'm going to have a child, she thought once more. But, then again, so was Caleb.

A DAY LATER, when Caleb returned to the Flying B, he wasted no time in going to the main house, where dusk hovered over the roof like a display of orange, pink and blue feathers.

He'd been aching for Donna for three damned weeks, during every workshop at that conference and during every visit he had paid during the tour of the ranches that were ahead of the mainstream agricultural curve.

It'd been three weeks of torture, but he'd refrained from calling or even texting her.

Give her room, he kept thinking. This separation would show him what their future really was.

Half nervous and half elated, he pulled his truck to a skid near the back patio, then got out, straightening his hat and walking right up to the kitchen door, where he knew Barbara would be cleaning up from her dinner prep.

After entering the house, Caleb was caught off guard by the sight of Tammy, who occasionally liked to use the top-of-the-line kitchen to bake goodies for the ranch staff, just as she was doing now with batches of fudge brownies that rested on wire racks and lent the room a sweet aroma.

She wiped at her cheek, leaving a flour mark that matched the ones on her red frilled apron. "You're home!"

Then she came over to give him a friendly punch on the arm, just before cleaning her hands on the apron. Her cute and perky smile remained, though.

"I can get Donna for you," she said.

"That'd be great, Tammy."

She started out of the kitchen, but then hesitated. "You know she's going to act as if she didn't miss you for a second, but I know better. She's been wandering around looking like she lost her dog. Or...you. Or..." She tucked a long dark lock behind her ear and smiled. "Just let me go get her."

"Thanks." Caleb stayed by the door, taking off his hat and smoothing back his hair.

The last time he'd felt like this, he'd been taking Kelly Tartleton to the prom and standing in her family room with her corsage. Luckily, by the end of the night, the nerves had worn off, just as quickly as Kelly's fancy dress.

But memories of prom smoked away when Donna arrived, garbed in one of her sundresses. She was like a breath of the fresh Flying B air he'd missed—fragrant and bringing with it just a touch of humidity.

And she was alone, bless Tammy.

The girl had been right about Donna's standoff-ishness, though—she was waiting on one side of the kitchen, him on the other, although Caleb was pretty sure that she was telling herself not to look too excited.

Unfortunately for her, her bright gaze betrayed her. Those blue eyes were shining, even if she was resting her hand on her stomach in a posture he'd never caught her in before.

Was it because her stomach was somersaulting, just as his was?

A beat passed, and he wondered if she was about to throw herself into his arms.

But then she smiled, almost shyly, and it captured his heart. Still, there was something else about her...

"You're back," she said.

"It had to happen sometime."

"How was the trip?"

"Long." He took a step toward her. "Too long."

It was as if she was searching for something to say that would keep him on the other side of the room. Would he have to start all over again with winning her over?

Hell, he was sucker enough to do it.

"Your family?" she asked. "Have you seen them yet?"

He wanted to say he had come here first because he couldn't stay away another minute. But, dammit, he'd realized long ago that Donna needed slow.

She couldn't be pushed.

"I'll be going to Dad and Aunt Rosemary's tonight," he said. "She's expecting me, at least."

"You could've gone to see them first."

It was as if she had thrown a wall between them,

and he exhaled a long breath. Then he said, "Maybe I should have."

He hadn't meant that. It'd just been frustration speaking.

Donna had her hand over her stomach again, as if shielding herself. She sat in a chair at a small table.

Cursing under his breath, Caleb said, "As I mentioned, I wanted to be here first."

She gestured to a chair, and when he sat, her gaze was serious in a way he'd never seen before—puzzled, as if she was putting together a thousand pieces in her mind and he wasn't fitting anywhere.

"If you could talk to your dad and he understood every word," she asked, "what would you say to him, Caleb?"

Odd question. Then again, this was Donna. She would be coming around to some kind of point, probably about her own dad. Maybe they'd had it out today and that was the reason for her distance.

"I don't know what I'd say to him." Caleb laid a hand on top of his hat as it rested in his lap. "I suppose I'd ask Dad if he ever changed his mind about me from when I was a kid until now. And, if I got brave, I might ask if he meant to be so remote with me when I was growing up. If he disliked me for some reason besides the trouble I gave him."

"What do you think of the way your dad raised you?"

What was this? Twenty disquieting questions?

"I'd do things a little different than him," he said. "I'd take the time to see what it was my son or daughter was doing every day and involve myself, even just a little. But I wouldn't interfere or hover. Not unless they wanted me to. And I wouldn't think I was acting strong by being emotionally distant."

She sat back in her chair, that weird look still on her face. She was picking at the edge of the table, too, as if she were fretful.

"With my dad," he said, "strength was always a big thing, and I think he'd be decimated to realize that he's lost it now with his dementia. I would be the same, though. It scares me to think that anyone could become a shadow of what they used to be."

It seemed as if she wanted to ask him more questions, but she was holding back.

Yet when she glanced at him again, he saw something else in her eyes—a longing.

Was she dying to touch him as much as he was her?

"Donna," he said, "aren't you the one who kissed me goodbye before I left, or was I imagining that?"

"You weren't."

"Have things changed so much while I've been gone?"

She blanched, then stood very slowly.

"I guess they have," he said.

"Caleb, I just need to figure a few things out…."

Patience, he thought. He'd told himself he could wait. But for how long?

He stood, too, putting on his hat. "I'm not a man who rushes, Donna. You know that. But I don't linger around forever, either."

Her gaze went shadowy, as if he'd played right into every one of her Donna-Byrd neuroses about her parents' divorce and her mother's death and being abandoned.

"Thanks for seeing me first, Caleb," she said, averting her face so he couldn't read her at all.

As she left the kitchen, she sent him one last look over

her shoulder, and it was almost enough to take him to his knees with its yearning.

But then it was gone, just as she was.

MAYBE FRUSTRATION WAS a ranch hand's best friend, because it sure kept Caleb's mind off Donna the next day as he worked his fingers to the bone in the cattle fields, maintaining those pipes and ditches from sunup to sundown.

He hardly even talked to anyone he was so busy... until he found Hugh sitting on the porch after dinner, just as Caleb was walking toward his cabin in the fallen night.

"You're doing a real fine job," Hugh said from a pine rocker, smoking a pipeful of cherry tobacco under the lantern by the door.

"Are you sure about that?" Caleb said, thinking of Donna, as always.

Hugh laughed. "I'm just telling you that you're gonna be a good foreman. It's always been clear that the fellows like you, they look up to you and they see that you'll work every corner of this ranch without complaint. Plus, you're now the most technology-savvy cowboy we've got, after that conference and ranch tour. I expect you'll be putting the stuff you learned into practice."

J.D. had been right about Hugh's intentions after all. "I expect so."

Puffing away on that pipe, Hugh gestured for Caleb to join him, just as if it were his own cabin he was lollygagging at. Nevertheless, Caleb climbed the steps of his porch, then leaned back against the railing, smelling the tobacco and summer grass around them.

Hugh inspected him with a squinty gaze.

"What?" Caleb asked.

"I told you that Miss Donna Byrd was going to give you headaches." *Now* Hugh was talking about her. "She's skittish, ain't she?"

"There's actually got to be another word for Donna's kind of skittish. She goes beyond it."

Hugh peered into the distance. "I'll tell you what— if I'd been shy and unassuming with my Minnie, we would've never gotten anywhere. She wasn't as stubborn and high-falutin' as Donna, but she gave me a run for my money. I suppose I can't fault you for your persistence."

Minnie had been Hugh's wife for about four decades. She'd passed on five years ago, and Hugh had never looked at another woman since.

Caleb rested his hands on his hips. "I'll bet Minnie wasn't half as ornery as Donna."

"Oh, you'd be wrong about that. Minnie made me jump through hoops like a show horse, and it wasn't until she realized that I was sincere that she gave me what I'd been hoping for. I knew there was no other woman for me. Isn't that how you feel about Donna?"

Caleb grinned. "Yeah, it is."

"Then even if I once had reservations, there's nothing I'd like to see more than you getting your heart's desire, no matter how skittish Donna gets. From what I've seen and heard, you've made more headway with her than I ever expected. Don't waste that kind of progress, Caleb. Do our mankind proud."

"If you came here to cheer me up after a long day, you're doing a good job."

The sound of a vehicle growled in the near distance, and Hugh took the pipe out of his mouth while standing from the rocker. Then he nodded toward the road that passed by the cabins.

There was a ranch-issued Dodge truck coming at them, and when Donna Byrd cut the engine and got out, Caleb could've been knocked over with a twig.

As Hugh passed by, he wagged his pipe at Caleb and loudly whispered, "Speak of the she-devil."

Then he winked and tapped out the tobacco to the ground before deserting the porch.

He tipped his hat to Donna while heading for his cabin, and she watched him go, then nudged at the ground with the toe of her sandal. She looked up at Caleb, contrition in her gaze.

"Looks like I caught you on your way in for the night."

He gestured toward the porch but she shook her head. "I don't have a great reason to stop by. I just…did."

When she tugged at the front of her sundress, as if there was something about it that wasn't fitting—even though it did—he frowned.

"I expect you're going to say what you have to say to me sometime tonight, Donna."

Now she met his gaze straight-on, just as if she was ready to finally come to terms with him.

LAST NIGHT, WHEN Caleb had stopped by to see Donna, she hadn't quite been prepared for him.

Then again, she was fairly certain she would never be—not with the news she knew she should be telling him, but couldn't. For privacy's sake, she had even gone out of the county to a doctor's appointment, avoiding Tammy's fiancé, Mike. The other doctor had confirmed the pregnancy.

So what excuse did she have now?

Nonetheless, excuses kept coming up: she should really give Caleb some time to get back into his routine before turning his life upside down. Also, Caleb was probably too busy with his dad to give his full attention to her, anyway.

But when she had asked him about being a father last night, she'd done it to test him. And the answers he'd given her were touching.

They were also right.

Tonight, she'd wanted only more reassuring answers from him, because this was the most momentous thing that had ever happened to her, and she'd sat in bed since she'd taken that pregnancy test, cupping her tummy just as she had in her mattress dream, although she wasn't as round as she'd been in that particular image. Not yet.

Was Caleb father material?

Or would all his attraction-at-first-sight games end, making him run away now that matters had become very real?

"I just came here to ask you something," she said. "And please don't take this as anything more than a question, Caleb."

"I won't."

Okay. So far, so good.

"If there *were* a future between us—and I'm not saying there is—but if there were…how would it work out?"

Hope lit his gaze, but he didn't revert to the charming smile he'd always used on her. This was a sincere look that gripped her heart and soul.

"There're options," he said, leaning against the porch pole. "It looks like they want to make me foreman of the Flying B."

"So you'd want to stay here."

"Not necessarily. I'm not just a country boy, Donna. If you wanted me in the city, I'd damned well go to the city and find something to do there. God knows what, but I've always been pretty fast at learning."

She could feel the tears starting to gather in her eyes. This man *had* to be too good to be true. Surely the rug was about to be pulled out from under her at any minute, just as it'd been with her parents and her finances and the magazine.

"But," he said, "I would ask that we didn't go too far to a city. I'd want to stay near my dad and Rosemary."

Of course he would. "You'd compromise that much?"

"I'd change however I needed to change for you, Donna."

She focused on the ground, her vision wet and blurry. She longed to rest her hands on her belly, just as she had caught herself doing so many times lately, the gesture so comfortable.

Did you hear that? she thought to their baby. *He'll already do anything for you.*

And she would, too.

When Donna looked up at Caleb again, he seemed as if all he wanted to do was come down off his porch to embrace her, to end all her worries with one all-consuming hug. Her heart sang.

"Caleb," she managed to say. "I'd never want you to change."

He straightened up from the pole, as if she'd said words that had altered his world. That had made his dreams come true.

Should she tell him?

Caution—deep-seated, hard-to-shake—got her tongue.

Just as she was wondering what should come next—
God, why couldn't she just bring herself to *tell* him?—
she heard a sound in her dress pocket.

Her phone.

At first she didn't do anything, but then Caleb
laughed, as if thinking, *Isn't that always the way with
us?* Then he motioned toward the sound, telling her to
just answer it.

When she glanced at the screen, she saw Savannah's
number.

Chapter Eleven

That night, the living room of the main house was silent as the Byrds, minus William and Sam, waited on their chairs, poised for the sound of a car to drive up out front.

Donna sat between Tammy and Jenna on the leather sofa. They were fairly composed in comparison to Nathan, whose dark hair was ruffled from running his fingers through it a thousand times. He was standing by the stone fireplace, opening and closing a lighter he occasionally used to smoke cigars outside.

Click, clack—

Aidan lingered next to him, and he stared a hole through his younger brother.

"Stop that."

Nathan stilled himself, but only for a minute. Then he was back to it.

Click, clack—

"Stop it!" said Donna, Tammy, Jenna and Aidan at the same time.

If the sound hadn't been mocking the stilted rhythm of Donna's heartbeat, she wouldn't have minded so much, but her nerves were fried after talking with Caleb and then having to leave him so abruptly after her phone had rung.

"You should answer it," he'd said when she'd revealed who was on the other end of the line.

She'd told herself that there would be another opportunity for a conversation with him, so she'd picked up Savannah's call....

A wash of illumination swept over the room as a car's headlights beamed through the front window, and Donna came to attention.

Tammy stood and straightened the pretty dress she'd put on. "That's gotta be them."

Donna and Jenna got up from the sofa, too. When Savannah had told Donna on the phone that she and James were in town tonight, staying at Buckshot Hills's only motel and asking if they could meet, there hadn't been much time to prepare anything like hors d'oeuvres or even their nerves.

The doorbell rang, and Tammy rushed to the foyer to get it. Donna felt detached from reality, as if she were watching things happen through a lens.

Surreal, she thought. And it got even more so after Donna heard the door opening, voices, then the door shutting.

The next moment, Tammy was leading a woman with straight, chin-edged light blond hair into the room. Her eyes were a deep brown, her face flushed, her figure tiny and trim in the blue lacy blouse, white pants and wedge sandals she was wearing. She appeared at least a decade younger than what Donna knew her age to be.

The notorious Savannah, Donna thought as the woman looked them all over, smiling politely, although tensely.

But the man who followed her into the living room was the person who really drew every gaze.

James Bowie Jeffries was tall and lanky, yet muscled, in his khaki pants, untucked white shirt and Doc Martens boots. He had a mixture of William's and Sam's hair—a thatch of brown highlighted by the sun—and bright blue Byrd eyes.

The spitting image of *both* Uncle William and Dad.

And he was only about a year older than Donna, living proof that Dad had loved someone else before he had supposedly loved Mom. Donna's emotions got even more muddied than usual, although she was trying very hard to be open-minded.

As Tammy came back to the sofa, everyone greeted the new arrivals.

Donna sat again, then said, "Thank you so much for coming."

Nathan, the natural host, motioned to a couple of cherrywood upholstered seats by the fireplace.

Savannah took one of them. "I apologize for not calling earlier than I did."

Her voice was sweet, like honey-laced milk, and Donna could imagine why two young men might've found it appealing, especially with the girl-next-door face that went with it.

She added, "While we drove to Buckshot Hills, I wasn't sure if we'd be turning the car around at some point, and I didn't want to disappoint you if that happened."

She didn't have to explain that their trip had been touch-and-go, filled with doubts about what they were doing. That's probably why Savannah had asked to come over right away tonight—before she or James changed their minds.

James had stayed standing this entire time, and it was telling that he'd distanced himself from Savannah's chair. "What my mom isn't saying is that I've been difficult."

Jenna spoke. "That's understandable."

Leaning against the opposite end of the fireplace from anyone else, James went quiet, merely surveying everyone in the room. He had the air of a man who'd come here only because it was something that needed to get done—and the sooner it was done, the better.

Savannah seemed willing to make up for him. "We're happy we made it."

A fraught moment passed before Donna introduced herself, then went around the room, naming each name.

"Donna," Savannah said, tilting her head and smiling at her. "I'm sorry about all the phone tag we were playing. James was at his home in New Orleans, knee-deep in a project. He becomes a hermit when he's got a deadline."

Donna doubted that was the reason for the holdup, but she would've been just as cautious as James.

Nathan clearly saw an opening for some small talk to lighten the moment. "What do you do for a living, James?"

Savannah answered for him, maybe because she knew

her son wasn't up to trivial chatter. "He's made a quiet fortune with software and computer apps."

James wore an edgy smile. "God knows where I got an aptitude for technology."

His pointed comment about not knowing who his father was sliced down the middle of the room.

This man was hurting, Donna thought. More than any of them, and she couldn't blame him.

She got angry, too—at Sam again, and at Savannah. James could be her brother or at least her cousin. She wanted to know everything about him, but it didn't look like that was going to happen with the way things were going.

Savannah tried to cover the awkwardness by smiling again. Dammit, she was likable, unassuming, but still with a steel magnolia sense about her. It was so hard for Donna to despise her because of what she'd inadvertently done to her parents' marriage and to James.

He seemed restless. "Where're the others?"

He meant William and Sam, and everyone in the room knew it, based on the way they all shifted.

Aidan spoke up. "My dad and uncle will be here shortly."

Donna added, "They wanted us to get to know you first. I hope you don't mind."

"I don't," Savannah said. "It was probably a good idea, seeing as things might get heated."

She sent a glance to James. After Aidan's answer, he had fixed his gaze on the room's entrance, as if he was waiting to face down the two men.

Savannah let out an exasperated sound. "Well, there's not much point in beating around the bush, is there? You kids have questions. Just as many as we do about you, I imagine."

James pulled his gaze from the entrance and wandered over to the front window, leaning against the wall, staring outside. His mouth was firm, as if he were barring himself from everything.

Savannah rested her hands in her lap. "I'm going to tear the bandage from the wound and start things off. Your P.I. might've told you the basics about me, but he couldn't fill in why I did what I did…why I made the decisions I made. I came here to set the record straight, among other matters. I promised James I would."

She glanced at her son, who'd closed his eyes, then opened them again, his gaze still trained out the window.

She waited a moment, as if hoping James would look her way, but he didn't.

Then, with reserved dignity, Savannah started.

"I didn't have a good family life when I was younger. But I had ambition—a hunger to make something of myself and get out of my foster home. I made it all the way to college on scholarship, and I was on track for a much better life."

Donna looked at Jenna. Savannah sounded a lot like them—focused, driven.

Savannah went on. "I always had my nose in my books, until the day William asked me out. Handsome, Prince Charming William. He had everything—good grades, a good family. I respected him and loved being around him. We had a deep affection for each other, and when he started hinting that he wanted me to meet his dad, well…my dream machine took off. It all sounded perfect to me."

"Then," James said, "William had that car accident."

His tone wasn't sarcastic, as Donna had anticipated it might be. It was almost as if listening to his mom handling this with such grace had made him want to support her, even a little.

She gave him a loving, yet somewhat injured glance, then nodded. "William was banged up, with a broken leg being the worst of it all. But school was nearly out for the summer, and I told him I would drive him back to the Flying B and stay with him to nurse him back to health. I didn't tell William that I had nowhere else to go that summer, but I meant what I said. I wanted to be with him. And I wanted to meet the family."

This time, Donna supplied what came next. "My dad was back here for summer vacation, too."

James's gaze connected with hers, and she sent him a sympathetic smile. *I get it—the anger, the isolation. You're not alone.*

She wasn't sure what he was thinking, because he canted back his head and rested it against the wall, listening.

"I'm going to be absolutely truthful," Savannah said, "and I hope I don't hurt any feelings more than they've been hurt. But I owe everyone honesty."

Tammy had been on the edge of the sofa the whole time. "Don't worry about us. Go on."

From across the room, Aidan and Nathan didn't look as sure as their sister. They had their thick arms crossed over their chests.

"When I met Sam…" Savannah said, a faraway look in her eyes now. "How can I say it except, *'Bam'*? It was more powerful than anything I'd ever felt before. And he felt it, too."

Tammy's posture wilted, as if she was feeling sorry for her dad. Nathan's and Aidan's jaws tightened.

"The summer went on," Savannah said, "and Sam and I were more and more drawn to each other. William couldn't get around much with his broken leg, so Sam took to entertaining me. That's where Tex comes in. It was pretty obvious that he favored William over Sam, and there were some competitive issues between the brothers, but Tex seemed happy that they'd been getting along during the summer. I think he was even optimistic that they were going to forge a new kind of relationship."

So much for that, Donna thought, dreading what was coming next. She put her arm around Tammy, who leaned into her.

"Tex had put me up in one of the cabins," Savannah said.

The dream cabin, Donna thought.

"I think," Savannah added with a slight smile, "he didn't want any funny business going on with me sneaking into William's room in the main house. But that backfired, because, one night after dinner, when I was returning to my cabin, I met Sam along the way. One thing led to another, and…"

She stopped there, appearing remorseful, but also a little wistful. "Sam told me he loved me, and I'd fallen for him, as well. I never wanted to hurt William, and since he was still under the weather, we decided to wait until he got better to tell him about us. I thought about leaving the ranch, too, but again, there was nowhere for me to go. And, truthfully, I couldn't tear myself away from Sam. We just had to find the best way to let William down easy."

By this time, Aidan had walked away from his spot

at the fireplace, clearly having a hard time hearing this. Nathan and Tammy didn't move.

It was Jenna who spoke next. "Dad felt guilty about being with you. He told me."

Savannah smiled gently. "And he told me that he'd never been so in love with anyone before. He didn't think he ever would be again."

Donna thought about how Dad still seemed to have feelings for Savannah, even now. He hadn't lied to Donna about that—only to the wife he'd married on the rebound.

Aidan finally asked a question, his voice wire-tight. "Not long afterward, you and my uncle were caught red-handed."

"Yes," Savannah said. "We were. Tex saw Sam leaving my cabin late one night. He gave Sam hell, and their fight was so ugly that Sam took off in his truck."

Jenna said, "I'm positive he meant to come back, after he cooled off."

"He didn't have the chance," Savannah said. "Tex knocked at my cabin door, then called me every name I deserved—a trollop, a whore. And I couldn't disagree. I was more ashamed than I'd ever been in my life, so I didn't wait for Sam. I talked one of the hands into giving me a ride into town. I left, just as I should've done at the beginning of the summer, when I first saw Sam. Then, about a day later, I heard from a friend that William and Tex and Sam had all gone their separate ways, so I cut ties with Texas A&M and everyone else and decided I would do everything I could to erase myself from the Byrds' lives. Maybe then they could find their ways back to each other, without me standing in between them."

A stinging laugh came from James's corner of the

room. "Because you knew there was an even bigger reason they would all fight with each other."

Savannah looked at him again, her eyes shining with tears. "James is referring to the fact that I was pregnant."

The grocery receipt, Donna thought. It was all coming full circle.

"Still," Savannah said, "I decided that no matter who the father was, I was blessed, even though I was still never going back to this ranch."

Donna brushed her hand over her belly. Blessed was right. She felt for Savannah, saw herself in her in a lot of ways.

But the more Savannah spoke, the more Donna began to believe in the rightness of telling Caleb about their child as soon as possible. Just look at what Savannah's secrets had done to this family.

Savannah said, "I came upon a small town in West Texas where I could disappear, fell into a reception job with a woman who decorated homes, and she took me under her wing. Then I had James, and I couldn't have lived a fuller life. My mentor left her business to me—she didn't have any sons or daughters—and then I met a man who married me later in life, after James had gone to college. Years later, after my husband passed away, I got a call from a private investigator, telling me that the Byrd family was looking for me."

"And looking for your son," Donna said, not wanting James to be excluded. "We wanted to get to know him, too."

He glanced at the group, and Donna could see that he was still struggling with his bottled emotions. A man who'd grown up without siblings, a man who'd been a boy without a father.

He had a lot to get used to...if he didn't turn them away.

Tammy asked, "Why didn't you ever contact my dad or Uncle Sam after years had gone by and things had cooled off?"

"There was no way I was going to cause more of a rift than I already had, and I knew this kind of news would stir up old trouble." Savannah's steel was showing now. "And I told Donna already that I'm content to never talk about who the father is. It's up to James to ask, and no one else."

"And I'm not going to," James said.

All of them started to talk, but before there could be any argument, James moved away from the window, silencing everyone.

"I didn't come here to cause a family implosion," he said. "And even if Mom and I have been over a rough road lately, I'm with her on this. From what your P.I. said, it sounds like this family is finally on the mend, and I'll be damned if I'm responsible for messing it up again. No man should be asked to live with that stain on him."

A new voice echoed through the room. "It wouldn't be a stain, James."

Donna whipped around to find both her father and Uncle William at the entrance, where they'd obviously been listening. William's gaze was on Savannah, as if he were seeing a ghost. So was Sam's, but Donna had to look away from him, because it was as if his entire soul was drawn to Savannah.

As if she'd torn it out when she'd left.

Savannah, herself, was wearing a poker face as she gripped her armrests.

God, Donna wanted to leave the room, leave them all alone to work this out. Uncle William looked conflicted about Savannah, and maybe even James, whom he now watched as if he was seeing a second spirit, one who resembled both him and his brother. Tammy had once told Donna that Uncle William, a widower and very much settled in his bachelorhood, wasn't sure how to react to the news of a possible love child, and here was proof.

But Dad… As he turned his gaze to James, he paled, fisting his hands by his sides.

James merely stood ramrod straight again by the window, his expression more embattled than ever.

Jenna was pulling at Donna's hand. *Time for privacy. Time to let William, Savannah, James and Dad talk this out.*

As everyone but the main players headed from the room, toward the patio, Jenna held on to Donna's hand, keeping her back from the group as the rest of them went outside.

"That was something," Jenna said.

Her voice was shaking, and Donna hugged her close.

Jenna whispered, "You think Dad'll be okay?"

"I think," Donna said, as they pulled away from each other, "we need to be his daughters more than ever, after the debris clears."

And as she thought of James inside that living room, a casualty of secrets, she put a hand to her belly, knowing that she needed to go to Caleb tonight.

CALEB HAD BEEN bound and determined not to fall asleep.

He knew tonight was make-or-break on a lot of levels—with the Byrds, and with him and Donna.

If she needed him at all, it would be after the emotional fallout that was sure to come with Savannah's visit. So he'd showered, put on a pair of sweats and a

T-shirt, then planted himself on a lounger in front of a show about cops in the bayou.

But the long day got to him, and he floated off, dreaming of blond hair, blue eyes and that kiss Donna had initiated before he'd left the ranch a few weeks ago.

A rapping at his door yanked him out of his light slumber, and he clicked off the TV, combing the hair back from his face with his fingers. When he opened the door, he found Donna standing in the lantern light.

"I know it's late," she said.

"It's never too late." He opened the door all the way, his pulse on fire, warming him.

She'd come back, just as if she did need him.

Once inside, she surveyed his cabin with its rodeo paintings and plaid curtains. He realized that this was the first time she'd been inside his home.

When she sat in a chair, he thought she was finally right where she belonged—with him. But when her body seemed to lose everything that had been keeping her together and she buried her face in her hands, Caleb wasn't so sure.

He went to her, bending to a knee, putting a hand on her back. "Want to talk about it?"

"They're gone now."

"Savannah and James."

"Yes. When they left, they said goodbye to us, and Tammy had the presence of mind to invite them to dinner tomorrow."

"So it went well?"

Donna raised her face from her hands, her gaze so tired that he ached to gather her into his arms and tell her everything would turn out fine.

"There were no nuclear explosions," Donna said. "At

least, not before Uncle William and Dad came into the room. But after Savannah and James left, Dad told Jenna and me that their private conversation started off badly. James is carrying a grudge, and he really let Dad have it. He doesn't blame William for anything, though."

"Didn't both of them sleep with her?"

Donna nodded, then told him the entire story Savannah had related. Caleb had known some of it, and he could see why James would've seen Sam as the bad guy.

"James had already let his mom know how he feels about her part in it," Donna said, rubbing her temples. "So it was Dad's turn tonight."

"James got it out of his system. That's a good thing."

"I'm not sure. He's carrying a lot around with him. It's obvious from the way he cuts himself off from everyone. He could be my brother, but I'm not certain he's the type of man you can ever know."

Caleb stroked her hair back from her face. "That's what I would've said about you, once upon a time."

Her eyes went teary.

"Hey, now," he said. "I wasn't being cruel."

"I know you weren't."

After a moment, she told him the rest of it. Then added, "I think the problems are only beginning. When all of us left Savannah and James alone with our dads, we met in the backyard. We started to debate about whether we should try to persuade James to ask for a paternity test."

"It's no one's place to do that."

"I agree. But the arguments aren't going to end there. From the way our dads were carrying themselves at the end of the night, it looked like there was a wall between them again. They were always naturally competitive, and actually seeing James might've given new life to that."

"It was a charged night, Donna. Things'll calm down."

"But, already, it's as if it's Byrd against Byrd again."

All Caleb could do was keep stroking her hair.

He knew in his heart that, even though he'd never had a long-term girlfriend or a wife, this was how it should be between two people: supporting each other. Honest in everything. Helping each other through thick and thin.

She slid her hand into his, and there was a new fear in her eyes. He wasn't sure why.

"Tonight," she said, her voice wavering, "I found out from Savannah that she left the ranch and never contacted Dad or William again because she didn't want to force them into a decision that might throw their lives into chaos. But look at what her silence did." She shook her head. "Look at what keeping secrets *does*."

As she searched his gaze with her own, he got a bad feeling in the pit of his stomach.

She took a shaky breath. "I might be too emotional right now, but I saw how Savannah's decisions hurt James, and I…"

When she touched her belly, Caleb let go of her hand. Instinctual, a moment of suspicious shock.

What was she saying?

"Caleb," she said through tears now. "I'm going to have a baby."

It was as if a giant hammer had come down from the roof, swinging into him and knocking him over. The news reverberated through him, his thoughts ringing.

Hadn't they used a condom?

Had there been a leak?

He thought of how he hadn't really checked it after they'd made love, because Donna had been touching him, gearing him up for another go and his mind hadn't been in smart mode.

"A...baby?" he asked dumbly.

But an instant after he uttered it, he was already smiling. He couldn't imagine what he would want more than a child who had Donna's eyes and her brains and...well, her everything.

He'd spent a lifetime sowing his wild oats, but he was ready now.

He was so happy, it took him a second or two to recognize the shadows in Donna's gaze, and with a falling sensation, he knew intuitively that they weren't there because she was having a baby.

They were there because she was having a baby with *him*.

Suddenly, every excuse she had used to put him off swatted at him: she was a city girl and he was a country boy. She went to fancy restaurants and he wore suits from the depths of his closet and served skillet steaks.

She still thought she was too good for him and she was trapped by a pregnancy.

His chest seemed to crack open. Here was the truth—one that was on naked display in front of him.

"You're never going to change your mind about me, are you?" he asked.

Now her tears clouded his view of her eyes, and he wasn't sure if he'd seen those shadows or not.

"I already have changed my mind, Caleb."

She got out of the chair and, as he took a step away from her rather than toward her this time, she paused.

"Caleb?"

He held up a hand, numb. The truth did that to a person, made them numb. It also gave them time to allow pain in.

Could you be more useless? his dad had once said to him, not long ago. And then there'd been the recent, *Useless idiot.*

Donna thought the same about him, didn't she? He was pretty sure he'd seen it in her very gaze tonight.

"I've been pursuing you for over a month, all the time believing in fate," he said. "I didn't even need to have any dream on that mattress to tell me what I wanted out of life."

When she got a guilty look on her face, his heart split even more.

"*Did* you have a dream?"

She hung her head, nodding, but then she looked up again. "I was in a field, laughing, touching my stomach. It was a good dream, Caleb, but I wasn't sure how I felt about you, so I didn't say anything."

"Because you're never going to be sure." He cut out a laugh. "I should've seen it long before now. Maybe I'm as idiotic as my dad says."

"*Don't* say that." She was pointing at him, her tone furious. "I know you don't believe that."

Did he? He wasn't sure, especially now. When the woman you thought you loved had those kind of thoughts about you, you couldn't be sure about anything.

"You couldn't hide what you really feel just now, as you told me about the baby," Caleb said. "That one moment—that flash into your soul—I could see it in your eyes, Donna. You don't want me to be the father."

She was moving toward him again, but he put up his hand once more.

"I wasn't sure at first," she said thickly. "I won't lie to you about that, but—"

He turned on his heel, unable to hear anymore. On his way to the door, he grabbed his keys from an unused ashtray, then went for his boots, pulling them on.

"I would never force you into living with a man you can't respect, Donna. We'll work something out with our baby, but I won't live the rest of my life knowing that, deep inside, you think you just settled for me. That you had no choice in being with me because we shared one night together and it didn't mean a damned thing to you in the end."

"But it did."

He blocked her out as he pulled open the door, but she put her hand against it, closing it.

His voice didn't sound like his own. "Don't even pretend anymore."

"I'm not pretending."

He almost stayed...and he would've if she had said what he needed most to hear.

That she had fallen for him, too.

The optimist inside him whispered, *She's coming around to it. Just give her a little more time.*

But he'd already waited too long, and look what it'd gotten him—a destroyed heart.

"Unfortunately," he said, "I don't believe you'll ever change enough to stop pretending with me."

Cleary crushed, she backed away, and he told himself to go forward, out the door, don't look back.

And he didn't look back—not even after he started his truck's engine and drove away, unsure of where to go.

Or what he'd just done.

Chapter Twelve

"Donna?"

It was the next day, and Donna had just needed to get away, licking yet one more set of wounds.

So when she heard Jenna's voice outside the dream cabin door, she didn't answer. Anguish kept pummeling her as she lay on the dream mattress, the ceiling as blank as she felt. She'd come here to see if she would dream of the future once more, but there'd been nothing, only the sound of her heart murmuring his name again and again.

Caleb. She'd never known that she could miss anyone so much, even though he was still on the same ranch, a few minutes away. But it felt like a million miles. Worse yet, the distance seemed too far to ever cross, no matter how long she walked; it would keep stretching and stretching, rolling beneath her like the treadmill it felt as if she'd been on for months now.

"Donna," Jenna said again, "please open the door for me and Tammy. You're starting to worry us."

She closed her eyes, hugging her arms over her belly. There was one good thing that had come out of this at least. Her baby. All day, she'd been thinking of names, but then she would get sidetracked yet again.

What would Caleb think of *Emma?* Or *Kyle?* Or...

The sound of the lock being tampered with brought Donna out of the bed, and she went to the door, opening it.

Both Jenna and Tammy were waiting, Jenna holding a key. Their eyes were wide with concern.

"What's wrong?" Jenna asked.

A year ago, the city girl in Donna would've laughed, shrugged and moved on from a bad night.

But not the woman who'd gone through an ego-breaking financial crisis and now this ultimate heart-ache.

Grief finally overtook her, and she bit her lip to keep herself from crying. Not that it did any good, because the tears came anyway.

Tammy and Jenna came to the rescue, entering the cabin to embrace her.

That just made the tears come harder. "Caleb..." she said, barely getting his name out.

Jenna guided her farther into the room, to the bed. They sat down while Tammy closed the door.

"What about Caleb?" Jenna asked.

"I told him about the baby."

Tammy leaned back against the door, her eyes even wider now. Donna had almost forgotten that she'd told only Jenna about the pregnancy.

And Caleb.

Her crying began anew as Jenna comforted her. She cried every tear she'd held back all these years and, eventually, she was too tired to continue.

As Jenna brushed the water off Donna's face, she softly said, "We all need a good cry every once in a while, especially after... What *did* happen with Caleb after you told him about the baby?"

"He looked happy." Donna swiped at her face. Damned stray tears.

"Happy is good, isn't it?"

Donna shook her head. "It didn't last long, because he saw the look I must've had on my face. All my doubts were there, and he saw them. It was the last straw for him, I think. He said we would work something out with the baby because he'd been wasting his time with me."

"He said that?" Tammy asked.

"Basically." When Donna sniffed, Jenna got up to fetch her a tissue. "I crossed a line, and I don't know if he'll let me back over it. I didn't mean for it to turn out this way...."

The room was quiet for a second, but then Tammy said, "Hugh will swear that Caleb's a stand-up guy, Donna. Same with the rest of the hands. He won't let you down."

"No, you should've seen him," Donna said. "He was crushed, and I'm pretty sure it was because my doubts validated everything he's heard from his dad."

"Like what?" Jenna asked.

"That he's useless, without value. His dad says things like that because of his dementia, but they're far from true." A wobble of emotion threatened to take her down again. "Caleb told me that I hadn't changed enough for him to believe that I want him. That hurt a lot."

Jenna sat next to her on the bed again. "If you could see how you've changed from then until now, you might not recognize yourself. Do you realize how far you've come since we moved to this ranch and since you started seeing Caleb?"

An answer stuck in Donna's throat. Yes, she *thought* she'd noticed a change in herself. That's why Caleb's words last night had wounded her so thoroughly.

I don't believe you'll ever change enough to stop pretending with me.

"Do you think," she asked in a raw voice, "Caleb will ever believe that I want to be with him? That I..."

Fell in love with him?

As Donna gathered herself, she knew this was true. Love had happened somewhere along the line. Maybe not at first sight, but it had come slowly, as he had patiently courted her.

But did she have any shot of convincing Caleb of how she felt?

And how could she do it?

Jenna and Tammy were still waiting for Donna to complete her last sentence.

She sat straighter on the bed. "I fell in love with him. I really did."

Both women smiled, as if Donna had taken forever to come to a conclusion that had been obvious from the get-go.

Jenna took Donna by the hand, helping her off the bed. "Come to the house with us. Savannah and James aren't here yet for dinner, but they should be soon."

Tammy said, "After they leave, we can talk more about Caleb. Plan a little."

"Get him right back where you should be with him," Jenna said.

Donna felt better already. Then, with one last hug, they all went out the door, walking to the main house. Once there, Donna went to her room to freshen up.

By the time she got downstairs, her mind was exploding with questions.

How should she go forward with Caleb? How should she even approach him? And would he give her the opportunity to spill her heart out to him, the right way this time?

She went out back so she could collect her thoughts before dinner, sitting in a chair by the splashing fountain. Every play of water reminded her of the night Caleb had come out here to try to kiss her.

She rested her hand on her tummy, rubbing it. *We're going to figure this out. Don't worry.*

Then she heard footsteps, and she sat up, her heart thudding.

But it wasn't Caleb who stood nearby—it was James, who had wandered outside with a cocktail glass in hand, watching Donna as if he hadn't expected to find anyone else out here. Under the surrendering sun, his blond-brown hair looked burnished, his lean form shadowed by the bucking bronco fountain sculpture.

"Sorry," he said. "I didn't mean to impose. I thought I'd find myself alone."

He looked so much like Uncle William and Sam— her father—right now, especially her father, and in more than just the superficial blue-eyed way. James and Dad were both carrying the same frustrated tautness and the same haunting darkness in their gazes.

The resemblance kicked something into motion inside Donna, and she started talking, just as honestly as she should've been talking to Caleb or her sister or Dad or anyone else, all along.

"We really don't know each other, James," she said. "And I firmly believe that any decisions you make about this family or discovering the identity of your father are none of my business, but I'm going to say this, anyway."

He seemed to gird himself, yet she was too far gone to stop.

"I'm a lot like Savannah. I had a secret, too, and what I mean by that is… Well, I'm having a baby—the same secret she carried. And I mishandled the way the father discovered the news, just like your mom did."

James's spine had gone stiff, as it'd been last night when they'd first met. "You don't need to tell me any of this, Donna."

"Yes, I do, because if I can do anything to put *my* new family together as well as *our* new family, there shouldn't be anything that stops us."

James assessed her with those Byrd-blue eyes. Was he going to tell her to go to hell? That this definitely wasn't her business?

But then his gaze strayed to her belly, which she was touching again.

"A baby, huh?" he said.

She nodded.

"Congratulations." He furrowed his brow. "I guess that's going to make me either an uncle or…"

Donna smiled, too. "Wouldn't you like to know for certain what you'll be to this child? I mean, either way I hope you'll be an important part of his or her life, but wouldn't it be nice to know if I'm carrying your niece or nephew?"

"Or a second cousin." James smiled for the first time she could recall. "I'd like to be an uncle someday, though. I don't ever plan on having kids, but I'd be a great uncle. One of those cool ones who plays with computers too much and sneaks the kids treats."

"I'd like that, too. Very much."

Just as she wondered if James was about to decide that he wanted a paternity test, he paused. She had no idea what might've been going on in his head, but then again, he didn't give her a lot of time to analyze, because he toasted her with his drink, then sauntered back toward the house.

Nonetheless, Donna's heart warmed as she glanced off into the distance, in the direction Caleb's cabin was located.

As the sun set, the space between her and that cabin felt shorter than it ever had, and she scooted to the edge of her seat.

It was time to cover the distance that separated them.

CALEB SHOULDN'T HAVE taken the day off, but he'd done it, anyway.

He felt like crap for what he'd said to Donna last night, and he wished that he could be with her now as the sun dipped below the horizon. He wished that he could put his head to her stomach, getting close to their child.

And he wished that he hadn't said a lot of things that just weren't true.

First, he shouldn't have told Donna that she would never change from who she'd been, because that had only come out in a defensive way. But he also shouldn't have said that he might be just as idiotic as his dad told him he was.

Sure, he'd thought that the sentiment had been written all over Donna's face when she'd told him about the baby, but was it the truth?

The more he thought about it, the more he believed her when she'd told him he was wrong. Still, the little boy in him who'd heard "useless idiot" from his dad couldn't help but to put stock in those words.

Maybe Caleb had taken the day off and come here to tell Dad that he was wrong, and he could be *very* useful, as a son...and as a father and husband. Or maybe Caleb needed to convince himself more than anyone.

Dad had been napping when Caleb arrived, and that, plus Caleb's presence, had allowed Aunt Rosemary to leave the house to go to the tearoom in town. He hadn't mentioned anything about Donna or the baby to her. He even hid his troubles under the smile he always reserved for Rosemary, who didn't need any more discord introduced into her life.

After she'd left, Caleb had sat down in front of the TV, not really seeing what was on it.

A couple of hours must've passed, because Dad eventually meandered out of his room. Caleb looked for signs in his dad about what kind of day it would be.

Dad was quiet, so it was hard to tell. Caleb got him a snack—a bran muffin and orange juice—then took to the couch as Dad channel surfed.

When he settled on a woman's fashion show, Caleb knew something was up, and he turned to his father.

He was watching him. Shock jolted Caleb, because it was the first time in a long time that he could see his dad in those eyes. They seemed clear. Lucid.

Or was he wrong?

"What's got you down?" Dad asked.

Emotion crumpled up in Caleb's throat, but he swallowed it away. "Nothing. I'm doing fine."

Dad just kept looking at him, and Caleb didn't know what to say or think.

Finally, Dad rested his head against the back of his chair, closing his eyes. "A solid man is a man who's always around for a loved one."

And he went silent, breathing evenly.

At his dad's cryptic comment, the jagged ball in Caleb's throat returned. Had Dad been insinuating that he *wasn't* a solid man because Dad didn't remember everything Caleb had done for him and he didn't know how often he'd been around? Or had he known that this was his son he'd been addressing? Had he even been referring to how Caleb had bought this house for his family and was taking care of them now?

Had his dad been thanking him in the best way a distant man could?

As Caleb turned to the TV again, a smile captured him through and through.

He would never be able to be one hundred percent sure, but he was damned well going to take this as a good day.

Rosemary returned before Dad woke up, and Caleb went back to the ranch, a certain weight lifted from his chest.

There was a bigger one that remained, though, and he wanted to stand beneath Donna's window as the day melted away, wanted to send her one of those flippant text messages and bring her to the sill so she could lean over it to talk to him.

But had he turned her off for good last night? Would

she, a modern city woman, say good riddance and leave the ranch with their baby, daring him to challenge her?

Caleb remembered the decimated expression on her face, and he just wasn't sure.

After driving up the road to the ranch, he passed by the main house, every muscle telling him to turn into the driveway. But every doubtful cell inside of him was also warning him to wait, to think carefully about what he should say to Donna.

He would formulate a plan of attack. That was the way to do it. And tonight, he'd...

What?

How should he go about this?

When he drove up to his cabin, his plan of attack crumbled before it even started because right there on his porch sat Donna.

All his anguish fell to the wayside, and he'd barely cut the engine before he got out of the truck, taking a couple steps toward her as she rose from her chair, coming toward him, too.

Without a word, they closed the distance between them, step by step, finally meeting in the middle.

His pulse beat in his ears as he read her expression.

Did he dare hope he saw what he thought he saw?

She embraced him, just as he scooped her up into his arms and held her to him, intending never to let go.

"I WAS SO WRONG," she said, the words rushing out of her while Caleb held her up against his body.

She'd knocked off his cowboy hat in her fervor, but it wasn't because she was trying to get them to a bed this time. It was because all she wanted to do was be next to him, body and soul.

"And I shouldn't have left you last night," he said, cupping the back of her head until her cheek was pressed against his.

Then, in a burst of elation, she kissed him, hardly able to believe that he was willing to forgive her.

He hadn't let her down after all.

As he still held her, she pushed his hair back from his face, looking into his eyes.

Those forever blue eyes.

"I meant it when I said I believe in you, Caleb. And that I've changed."

"I know you have. But I was stinging from pride last night. I was wrong about so many things."

"But you're not wrong for me. I love you, Caleb." Her voice was breaking. "I love you so much that I couldn't eat or sleep without you. It's you I want—not the city, and definitely not raising our child alone."

"You won't have to. I'm here, Donna. I'm never going to be anywhere else."

They kissed again and, unlike before, this wasn't about pistoning heartbeats or torn-off clothing or the pursuit of satiation. This was about them, together.

A family of three now.

He carried her up the porch steps and into his cabin, kicking the door closed behind him, sitting her gently down on his bed. He got to his knees, then leaned his head against her belly, just as if he'd been wishing to do this the whole day.

"You won't be able to feel him or her kick for a while," Donna whispered, stroking Caleb's hair.

"It doesn't matter. I know someone's in there."

Someone who had brought two of the most unlikely

people together, Donna thought. The youngest match-maker in history.

It seemed enough for them to hold each other like this, but soon, she reclined on the bed, and he kept his head against her as she played with his hair.

When he kissed her stomach, she automatically rocked against him, because just one kiss from him did that to her.

What would a lifetime of them do?

She threaded her fingers through his hair as he kept nuzzling her belly. A pounding cadence began to throb between her legs.

"I should be having dinner with Savannah and James," she whispered.

"I think they'll understand why you'll be late." He lifted her blouse, pressing his lips to her bare stomach while working at the buttons on his shirt.

She wiggled, biting her lip, then saying, "They're going to be our family now. I'm not going to rest until they both see that we're not letting them go."

"That's my Donna," he said as he pushed her blouse up higher. "Relentless."

And she was powerless, too, as he kissed her some more. She always had been that way with him, even if she'd fought what was between them tooth and nail.

After helping him take off her blouse, she pushed the material off the bed, and he slid up her body.

The sensation of his skin against her breasts sent her reeling—a whispering tumble of water that was turning into a growling rush, moment by moment.

"Will you help me to stay away from the hay on this ranch?" she asked as he got ready to kiss her. "It makes me sneeze."

"So you really do want to stay."

"You're here. My family's here."

He smiled, flashing those dimples. "I'll do anything I need to do for you. Anything else?"

"Can I redecorate this cabin?"

"You can even do that, Donna Byrd."

He explored her mouth with his, parting her lips with his tongue, slowly engaging her in rhythmic pleasure. Meanwhile, Donna reached between them to undo her bra.

"I want to feel you," she said against his mouth. "All of you. It seems like it's been forever."

"Hasn't it been?"

She laughed as he unzipped her jeans, then took off the rest of her clothing, leaving her bared to him.

As he watched, she coasted her fingers over her tummy, wondering when the baby would start to show. With all her heart, she knew Caleb's eyes would fill with even more adoration when he saw her belly grow, that he would love this child as much as she already did.

He was on his knees on the floor again, but now he took her by the hips, pulling her toward him.

A restless sigh escaped Donna, and he grinned that cocky grin she'd longed to see, then worked her legs over his shoulders.

When his mouth kissed her most private place, she let out a cry. And as he loved her, slowly, tenderly, she moved her hips with him, liquid pressure building inside of her.

Simmering.

Bubbling.

Boiling until she couldn't hold back any longer and she called his name, desperate and delirious.

As she came to her peak, he was with her all the way, making her crash, moan, say his name again and again.

Then he undressed, too, going to the bed, pulling her on top of him.

He was already hard, and she straddled his hips, taking him in, then churning on top of him.

My baby's father, she thought, watching his face, his pleasure, as he climbed to the same steaming place she had already been.

When he climaxed, he gripped her hips, and she laid herself against his length, skin to skin.

Future husband to future wife.

Donna was so swept away that she couldn't hold back, and she whispered in his ear.

"Marry me, Caleb."

He chuckled, utterly breathless. "Marry *me.*"

They laughed, and it felt good to do it together, their bodies still against each other.

He touched her belly, and they both quieted.

"I don't want to wait, Donna," he said. "You'd better marry me before the year's out."

She snuggled her face into his neck and smiled, knowing she'd found exactly where she belonged.

"There's nothing I want more, cowboy."

Epilogue

Four Months Later

Laughter from the crowd at the Flying B and B guest barbecue dinner filled the air from a distance as Donna lay on a blanket, blocked from the party by a few old oak trees.

She looked up at the perfect November blue sky, tucking a hand under her head. Birds warbled from a nearby oak as she laughed along with everyone else.

The B and B's opening months had been more successful than any Byrd could've dreamed, but that wasn't all. Over at the barbecue, the entire family was in attendance because Aidan and Nathan had announced that they had finally gotten a geological survey going on the west side of the ranch, where their undeveloped property given to them by Tex had been waiting.

There was a lot to celebrate, and the Byrds tended

to throw a party for just about everything these days—Tammy and Mike's wedding, then Jenna and J.D.'s. Soon there would even be a baby shower for Donna and Caleb's child.

She used her thumb to play with the diamond ring on her finger, her other hand resting on her rounding belly. A loose flannel country dress draped her, barely showing how she had just started to pop.

All I wish, she thought to her baby, *is that you could've met your great-grandpa.*

She sighed, closing her eyes and picturing Tex holding his great-grandchild in his arms.

But when she heard footsteps moving through the grass nearby, she glanced toward the sound.

It was Savannah, and she was smiling down at Donna.

"Mind if I join you?" she asked.

"Please do."

The sun shone on her chin-length blond hair. In the sunlight, there were faint wisps of silver visible—not that this made Savannah look any older.

Donna had uncovered some old pictures at Dad's house a couple months ago, and she and Jenna had painstakingly gone through every one that showed their mom, who was doing things like cradling the two of them as they said cheese to the camera in their little-girl dresses.

Donna hadn't realized it at first, but there was something about Savannah that reminded her of Mom. Was it the light hair? The kind eyes?

But that wasn't the only realization for Donna. Had Mom reminded Dad of Savannah? Was that why he'd married her?

Any way about it, Savannah had become a part of their lives. She had accepted monthly invitations to stay at the B and B, and James had even visited a time or two himself, hunkering down in one of the cabins to work on his projects. He was still bullheadedly maintaining that he didn't want to know the identity of his father, but some of the Byrds had their fingers crossed.

Savannah turned her face to the sun. "It's good to get away from the crowd for a few minutes."

Donna didn't ask if Savannah needed a break because of Uncle William and Dad. They'd all been on tentative ground since she'd come into their lives and, while William still didn't show his emotional hand around an equally neutral Savannah, Dad sure did. His heart was in his eyes every time he looked at her.

But that's the way the Byrds were, Donna thought. A walking, talking drama that would probably never end, even if they'd come pretty far.

As Donna kept surveying Savannah, the birds sang, the laughter still sounding in the near distance, her hand lingering on the curve of her tummy.

Savannah caught Donna watching her, and she laughed. "What is it?"

Should she ask?

Oh, why not.

"I've been meaning to broach a particular topic with you. The cabin you stayed in so long ago…?"

"I heard that you all call it the dream cabin now."

Donna propped herself up on her elbows. "Then you've heard the stories about the bed."

"I did."

"Did *you* ever have a dream on the mattress?"

Savannah pressed her lips together, and Donna was sure she would never tell. But when the woman glanced at her, Donna saw the same haunted shade in her gaze as she always saw in her father's.

"I did have a dream," she said. "I remember swinging in a swing that hung from one of these old oaks on the property. There were two men in front of me, and even though their backs were turned, I knew who they were."

Donna could make an educated guess on her end. Uncle William and her father, Sam.

"I swung higher and higher," Savannah said. "Then, I couldn't hold on anymore. I went flying through the air, and I was so afraid of crashing to the dirt. But I was exhilarated, too."

"Did you hit the ground and wake up?"

"No." Savannah knit her brows. "One of those men turned around and caught me."

"Who?"

A mysterious smile appeared as she stood, brushing off her crisp tan pants.

"I'll see you at the barbecue, Donna."

As Savannah left, Donna lay back down, watching the sky. Was that mattress an excuse for everyone's psyche to work itself out? Or was it really magic?

More importantly, which man had caught Savannah, and did that mean anything for the future?

She closed her eyes. Maybe they would find out in time, but for now, she listened to those birds, the laughter. And when she felt Caleb's presence, she didn't look over at him.

She knew it was him. She always would.

He settled down next to her on the blanket as she smiled.

"Ready to eat yet?" he asked.

"Soon."

This time, she varied her mattress dream, taking *his* hand and putting it on her belly.

When he kissed her, a memory of the dream she'd had on the night she'd first been with Caleb swirled in Donna's mind. But now it turned into something new: an image of her, Caleb and their child on this same blanket, sitting beneath the sun on the Flying B and laughing with each other.

A dream that was *definitely* in their future.

* * * * *

A sneaky peek at next month…

ROMANCE TO MELT THE HEART EVERY TIME

My wish list for next month's titles…

In stores from 19th July 2013:

❑ How to Melt a Frozen Heart – Cara Colter

& A Weaver Vow – Allison Leigh

❑ The Cattleman's Ready-Made Family – Michelle Douglas

& Rancher to the Rescue – Jennifer Faye

In stores from 2nd August 2013:

❑ The Maverick's Summer Love – Christyne Butler

& His Long-Lost Family – Brenda Harlen

❑ A Cowboy To Come Home To – Donna Alward

& The Doctor's Dating Bargain – Teresa Southwick

Available at WHSmith, Tesco, Asda, Eason, Amazon and Apple

Just can't wait?

Visit us Online

You can buy our books online a month before they hit the shops! **www.millsandboon.co.uk**

0713/23

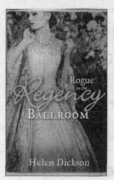

Where will *you* read this summer?

#TeamSun

Join your team this summer.

www.millsandboon.co.uk/sunvshade